ANNA
JACOBS

A Time for Renewal

Rivenshaw: Book Two

HODDER

First published in Great Britain in 2015 by Hodder & Stoughton

An Hachette UK company

First published in paperback in 2016

1

A CIP catalogue record for this title is available from the British Library

ISBN 978 1 444 78774 0

Typeset in Plantin Light by Palimpsest Book Production Limited,
Falkirk, Stirlingshire

Printed and bound by Clays Ltd, St Ives plc

Hodder & Stoughton policy is to use papers that are natural,
renewable and recyclable products and made from wood grown
in sustainable forests. The logging and manufacturing processes
are expected to conform to the environmental regulations
of the country of origin.

Hodder & Stoughton Ltd
Carmelite House
50 Victoria Embankment
London EC4Y 0DZ

www.hodder.co.uk

PART ONE
July 1945

I

Early July

Victor Travers left his little daughter at home in the maid's charge and enjoyed a brisk walk to the village school, a mile away from their home. Like many other ex-servicemen, he was eager to vote in the General Election that was being held now the war in Europe had ended.

For the first time since his wife's death, a few days after he'd been demobbed, Victor felt a sense of peace. Poor Susan had been failing for months, had been a mere shadow of the woman he'd married. He hadn't realised she was so close to the end, because he'd been involved in some hush-hush work and hadn't been able to get leave.

His mother-in-law ought to have told him, though, and she hadn't. The Army would have allowed him compassionate leave in such circumstances. He was still upset about it all.

Tomorrow he'd start arranging his move to the north where he was going to be a partner in a new building company. He was looking forward to that, but most of all, to having his daughter to himself and getting to know her better. What a delightful child Betty was!

He was surprised at how few people were voting. He saw no one he knew from Helstead, but got talking to a couple of young soldiers from a nearby hamlet. They were still in uniform, so obviously not yet demobbed.

What they said confirmed his own feeling that Churchill

and his party were due for a few surprises. However, the results wouldn't be announced for another three weeks, to allow the votes of service personnel overseas to be counted.

When he got home, he found his mother-in-law's car outside the house, which surprised him. Since her daughter's death, Mrs Galton hadn't visited them, but had expected him to take Betty to her.

Inside, he stopped in shock when he saw her at the turn in the stairs, her hat awry, trying to drag his seven-year-old daughter down. Betty was hanging back, holding on to the banisters with both hands, sobbing and protesting loudly.

When she caught sight of him, Mrs Galton looked flustered, but she didn't let go of his daughter.

'What on earth are you doing?' he demanded.

Betty tried in vain to tug her right hand from her grandmother's grasp. But Mrs Galton still kept tight hold.

That did it! He strode up the stairs. 'Let go of my child this minute!'

'Don't you dare touch me!' she shouted and to his astonishment, she tried to stand between him and his daughter. But Betty managed to jerk away suddenly and flung herself at him. 'Daddy! Daddy! Don't let her take me away from you.'

He held her close as he repeated his question, 'What are you doing here, Mrs Galton?'

His mother-in-law hesitated, looking as if she didn't know what to do or say next.

It was Betty who answered his question. 'She said you wanted me to go and live with her now Mother's dead. She told Jane to pack all my clothes. Don't let her take me away, Daddy! I want to live in Lancashire with you, not stay here with her.'

'Of course you're coming with me, darling.'

She clung to him even more tightly and a hot little tear fell on his hand.

He looked up to the top of the stairs, where Mrs Galton's personal maid was standing with a suitcase in her hand, looking nervous. 'If that suitcase contains my daughter's clothes, Jane, and you take them out of this house, I'll have you charged with theft, because that's what it'll be.'

The maid's mouth opened in shock and she dropped the suitcase as if it were red hot. Taking a quick step to one side, she looked to her mistress for guidance.

He turned back to the older woman and gestured towards the front door. 'Don't let me keep you, Mrs Galton. I'm sure you have a busy social schedule.'

His mother-in-law let out one of her angry huffs of sound. 'I tried to do this quietly, for the child's sake, Victor but, if I have to, I'll go to the court for custody of my granddaughter, make no mistake about it. And I shall win. I'm sure this is what my poor dear daughter would wish. She told me so.'

'Nonsense. I was with Susan at the end and she told me she trusted me to look after our child.'

'You're lying. But I'll make sure Betty comes to live with me, whatever it takes.'

'I think you'll find the law is on my side there, since I'm her father.'

People only had to look at the two of them to see that. Betty had his dark, straight hair and olive complexion, not her mother's fair hair and pale skin. But the child's features were shaped like her mother's and he thought she too would be a beauty one day.

Mrs Galton glared at him. 'You've been away from home for most of the last few years. You don't even know that child.'

'Like many other men, I've been fighting for my country. I think the courts will take that into account.'

'They'll also take into account the fact that a seven-year-old girl needs a woman to raise her. You've let Betty run wild in the short time you've been back and see the result: she came down with a severe head cold when you and that silly young maid of yours started looking after her. A man simply can't fill a mother's role. He has a job to do, money to earn.'

'My job will never come before my daughter, and it won't have to, thank goodness, because I have a private income. I'll find a woman to help where necessary, but make no mistake about it, I'm bringing Betty up – and in the way I choose.'

In the few weeks he'd been back, they'd already had several serious disagreements about what that way should be.

'A maid is not the same as a grandmother. And your income is very small. My husband left me financially comfortable and I can give that child everything she needs. You still have your way to make in the world, unless you're intending to live like the hoi polloi.'

'I have my business life carefully planned, and it'll be a successful one, I'm sure.'

'My lawyer thinks you're about to make a highly risky investment – and using the proceeds from selling this house, too. How dare you sell it?'

'I believe I own it. It was your wedding present to us, after all.'

'We bought it so that Susan could continue to live near us in Helstead. Now my poor daughter is dead and you have no right to take my only grandchild away to the other end of the country, to a nasty industrial town.'

'Rivenshaw is a small town on the edge of the moors, with very little industry, actually. I'm told it's a pretty place.' He found it an effort to be polite to this arrogant woman. The more he'd got to know his in-laws, the more he'd disliked them. Cecil Galton was dead now, but Amelia was still running the village as though she were its queen. If the war hadn't taken him away from Susan, Victor would not have stayed in Hertfordshire this long.

He suspected her parents had threatened her when he was called up and made her afraid of moving away from them, but he couldn't prove that. And what did such details matter now that she was dead? He contented himself with repeating what he'd said several times already, 'You'll find that I'm perfectly capable of earning a living and looking after my child. Your lawyer knows nothing about the building industry.'

He kept his arm round Betty's shoulders and her whisper was all he needed to validate his choice.

'I want to be with you, Daddy.'

'And I want you with me, my little love.' He glared at the sour-faced woman still standing nearby. Her views of the world were as old-fashioned as her clothes. The recent war hardly seemed to have dented the shield of arrogance she held between herself and those she deemed her inferiors.

He could understand her distress at the death of her only child, but he didn't think she or her late husband had loved their daughter for her own sake, any more than they'd loved their granddaughter. They'd simply considered the two of them possessions. No wonder Susan had insisted on running away to get married, her one major defiance of them. She knew they'd have stopped her.

That Betty was now seen as a replacement for the frail, compliant daughter they'd lost showed how little Amelia understood the child. His Betty would never be meek. She had a mind and opinions of her own already and he liked to see that. He wanted a freer and happy childhood for her, one not dominated by the great god Money.

The silence had gone on for too long, so he went past his unwelcome visitor to open the front door, with Betty still clinging to his hand. 'I think you should leave now, Mrs Galton, and please don't come back without an invitation.'

Her face turned a dull shade of red and she glared at him. For a moment he thought she was going to refuse, then she marched down the bottom few stairs and out of the house, her heels drumming their way across the tiled hall floor.

Since she hadn't given any instructions to her maid, he looked up and jerked his head to indicate that Jane should follow her mistress out.

She slowed down as she passed him and whispered, 'If you want to keep her, you should get Betty away today, Mr Travers. They knew you were away voting, so thought this would be the easiest way to do it. But Mrs Galton has her lawyer waiting to step in within the hour if this fails.'

She continued down to the hall and out of the front door without waiting for an answer, leaving him staring after her in shock, unable to believe his own ears.

He realised Betty was crying, so sat down on the bottom stair and pulled her into his arms, cuddling her close and pushing his handkerchief into her hand. 'Sorry, love. I won't leave you on your own again. What happened to Edna? She was supposed to be looking after you.'

'Grandmother sacked her. She told her to leave the house and never come back again.'

'How could she do that? She doesn't employ Edna.'

'When Edna said she wasn't leaving me, Grandmother said if she didn't, her family would be turned out of their house in the village.' Betty wrinkled her brow. 'I don't think that was fair, do you?'

'No, darling, it wasn't.'

'I like Edna. She's fun. But Grandmother tells her off for letting me play outside and shouts at her a lot.'

'You can play outside all you want when we get to Rivenshaw, my darling.'

'And you won't get me a strict governess?'

'Heavens, no. I'd be terrified of one myself.'

Betty giggled and cuddled even closer, still clutching the damp handkerchief. 'Mother always said you weren't frightened of anything. She said I was to stay with you. She said it lots of times.'

The child seemed to need cuddling, so Victor didn't move, but he began thinking furiously. They'd meant to leave the village two weeks ago, but Betty had had a bad cold. Since his wife had been an invalid for years, he hadn't wanted to take any risk with his daughter's health, so hadn't protested when Mrs Galton called in her own doctor, rather than the man in the village. Victor had followed the man's instructions to the letter, of course he had.

'How do you feel now, Betty? Is your cold completely better?'

'It's been better for ages. I don't know why the doctor said I had to stay in bed so long.'

He closed his eyes for a moment, angry with himself for being fooled like that. He'd not expected a doctor to lie to a father about his child's health. That woman must have been making plans all the time, no doubt with her lawyer. Fitkin spent a lot of time with her since her husband's death, handling all her business affairs.

Well, his mother-in-law was in for a few shocks when the young men and women who'd served in the forces or other service groups like the Land Army were demobbed. He didn't think men who'd faced death would kow-tow to Amelia Galton, as their parents had. Nor would young women who'd lived and worked independently want to go into service at the Hall and bob curtsies to that old harridan. Those days were past.

In the end he decided to take the maid's warning seriously. The situation might not be that desperate, but he'd seen Fitkin driving up to the Hall in his big black Wolseley as he was walking back. He wasn't risking losing his daughter. 'I'll tell you what, my little love. We'll leave for Rivenshaw earlier than planned.'

'Why can't we leave straight away? It won't be dark for ages.'

'Your grandmother's lawyer might try to stop us if they see us leaving.'

'She always knows what we do, anyway. Mr Fitkin's been paying the Peeby brothers to keep watch on the house ever since you came home and brought me back here to live.'

'What? How did you find that out?'

'I heard Grandmother talking to him about it and every time I look out of my bedroom window, I see Brian or his brother in the street opposite. Brian's there now. I can show him to you.'

'Do that.'

She led the way up to the nursery and pointed out a shabby youth standing on the street corner opposite their gates. He didn't seem to be doing anything except watching the house.

As they stood there, a man went up to Peeby and said something. The youth straightened up and nodded vigorously.

Victor spoke his thoughts aloud. 'I wonder who that man is?'

'His name's Barham and he works for Mr Fitkin. He collects Grandma's rents in the village and from her houses in Watford too. Everyone in the village is afraid of him.'

'Are you sure?'

'Yes.' Betty stared down at her shoes. 'Is it wrong to eavesdrop, Daddy? Mother always said it was. Only I can't help hearing things sometimes, and anyway I get bored just sitting still or reading the books Grandma chooses for me. They're so silly and old-fashioned, all about children dying or going to church. So I listen to what she's saying, even when she's in the next room.'

'You have excellent hearing.'

'Grandma always speaks loudly. I heard one of the maids say she must be going deaf.'

He'd noticed that too. 'I don't think it's wrong to eavesdrop when people are trying to trick you.'

How dare his in-laws treat him like this? During his years in the Army, Victor had had a lot of experience in keeping his feelings under control and he managed that now, because he didn't want to alarm the child. But Mrs Galton had chosen the wrong man to tangle with, by hell she had.

'How about you and I turn this into a little adventure, Betty? We'll creep out of the house by the back way once it's dark and catch the last train to London. No one will be able to see us go. What do you think of that?'

'Grandmother will be very angry.'

'Yes. But we won't be here, so she won't be able to shout at us.'

She shivered. 'I think we should go right away, not wait. I heard her say to Jane that her lawyer will get people here to take me away by force if necessary.'

He was horrified. Was Mrs Galton really prepared to go to those lengths? Sadly, yes. She always had to have her own way, whatever it took. She had men like Barham and the young fellow waiting outside already. He couldn't fight off the two of them.

'No one will see us leaving if we go through the back garden next door, Daddy. There's a gap in our hedge. I play with the boy who lives there sometimes, though I'm not supposed to. That's how we get through to each other.'

'Can you show me?'

She took him to one of the back bedrooms and pointed it out.

He glanced at his watch. If they got away quickly, they might take Mrs Galton's people by surprise, and be in time to catch the next local train into Watford Junction. From there they could go on to Lancashire, which was on the same line. He used to know all the train times, but things had changed during the war, so they'd just have to take their chance. 'You're a clever girl. That's exactly what we'll do.'

He'd been intending to use his own back gate, but who knew whether that too was being watched? He glanced out of the window again. The rear alley curved round, so they might be able to stay out of sight of a watcher if they left through the garden next door.

Was he being paranoid? He didn't think so. He'd seen Mrs Galton do a few unethical things in the past few years, and he hadn't even been in the village most of the time. And even her maid had warned him to leave.

He stood up. 'I'll pack my bag. Wasn't it kind of your grandmother to have your things packed for us? Come on, princess. We're going to have an adventure.' He held out his hand, and with another of her delicious little-girl giggles, she took it.

2

Betty sat on the bed watching him hurl his clothes into a suitcase. Victor didn't intend to let her out of his sight for a minute.

Mrs Galton and that Fitkin fellow would find that he too could plot and plan. He wasn't going to try to hide where he was once he got to Rivenshaw, would hate to live like that. He had allies there who would help him keep his daughter safe, men he'd fought with in the war, men he trusted to watch his back. And he too could find a lawyer.

No one was going to take Betty from him. She had quickly become the joy of his life. Her mother had been ill for so long that Susan had seemed to fade into the background, like a beautiful picture he didn't dare touch. But Betty was a vivid, loving little creature.

As he finished packing, Victor glanced out of his front bedroom window.

Mrs Galton's motor car had just drawn up further down the street. The man who'd spoken to the youth keeping watch got out of it and went into the village policeman's house. She wasn't in the car, but Fitkin was and he stayed there, not caring whether Victor could see him, staring disdainfully round.

Dear heaven, they were starting to take action already! Well, they'd have to catch him first.

He heard Betty gasp as she too saw them, so he pulled her to him for a quick hug.

'They're coming to get me, Daddy.'

'Well, they're not going to succeed. Come on, my darling! We'll leave the back way.'

He knew Mrs Galton had a key to the front door of the house, so took the time to shoot the bolts on the inside of it. Then he took the key out of the back door and locked it behind him from the outside, dropping the key in his pocket.

That might slow them down a little.

He followed his daughter through the gap in the hedge and found the neighbour's gardener standing a few yards away, a spade in his hand, looking at them in astonishment.

'You haven't seen us.' Victor held out a pound note.

For a moment all hung in the balance, then the man snatched the generous bribe and ran off into the walled vegetable garden, shutting its gate quietly behind him.

Carrying two suitcases, with Betty staying by his side, Victor went to the back gate and checked that the lane was clear. When he heard footsteps, he closed the high wooden gate again, crouched behind it and put his finger to his lips.

He watched through a gap in the hedge as the village policeman ran past. But the man didn't even look their way. His footsteps stopped at their house, though.

Victor opened the gate and checked. The policeman was round the curve and couldn't see them. He bent down to whisper, 'We have to hurry. We'll go along the lane and take the back way to the station. Keep quiet.' He started off again, walking on the grassy verge, his daughter trotting along behind him.

They were in luck and caught the two o'clock train to Watford just as it was about to leave the village. He shoved the suitcases up in the rack and sat on the seat, panting and grinning at Betty. 'Our adventure has started, princess.'

'They'll come after us. I know they will, Daddy.'

He hated to see such anxiety on a child's face. 'By that time, we'll be with my friends from the Army. And we'll have our own lawyer, too.'

But Betty's expression remained anxious. A child of seven shouldn't look like that. Damn the Galton woman!

At Watford Junction he checked train times and, to his dismay, found that no train to Lancashire was stopping there until the evening, and that would be a very slow one. He didn't dare wait around, felt he was in danger every minute until he was out of reach of Mrs Galton and her lawyer. The best solution was to go to London and then take an express train to the north, even though that meant they'd be backtracking.

There was a train leaving for London in a quarter of an hour. And half an hour after their arrival in the capital, an express train would be leaving for Manchester. From there, they would just be in time to catch the last local train to Rivenshaw. He sighed and bought the tickets.

This would mean a long day's travelling for a small child, and several changes of train, but it was necessary. He explained what they were doing and why.

Betty nodded her head. 'I'll be all right, Daddy. Mother always said I was strong and healthy, like you, not like her.'

Her voice wobbled as she said that, because she'd been very close to her mother, so he gave her another hug. He loved cuddling her, had been deprived of too much of her short life by the war.

His poor wife had had rheumatic fever when she was a child, and it had affected her heart. He hadn't realised how badly when they married, but after Betty's birth the doctor had told him Susan must never have another child and must lead as peaceful a life as possible.

When the train left, he felt relief flood through him.

'We're safe now, aren't we Daddy?'

'Yes, princess.' For the time being, anyway.

In London he tried to phone his friend Mayne to ask him to meet them at the station in Rivenshaw, but only got through to Mayne's father, who was notorious for his absent-mindedness about practical matters. Well, if things went awry, he'd just have to turn up at Mayne's house and knock him up.

He was quite sure his friend would welcome them. The two of them had been part of a small team working on a very hush-hush project for the last year of the war. Differences in rank had ceased to matter, and a strong bond had been formed between team members.

Betty fell asleep for a couple of hours on the way to Manchester. She didn't complain when she woke, stiff and thirsty, half an hour before they were due to arrive. Luckily he'd been able to buy something to eat in London, and a bottle of lemonade, because there was no restaurant car. Wartime conditions still prevailed on most trains.

It was late in the evening by the time they arrived and Betty was white with exhaustion. But the last train to Rivenshaw hadn't yet left.

'We're doing really well,' he said encouragingly. 'Can you manage to travel a bit further, my love?'

'Yes, Daddy. I don't want them to catch us.'

There it was again, that anxiety in her voice and face. It hurt him to see that.

Victor accepted a porter's help with the two suitcases, and carried Betty and the rag doll she took everywhere, except to her grandmother's house. She said the doll didn't like it there.

The porter was a chatty fellow and Victor encouraged it.

You never knew when a piece of information would come in useful.

'Didn't think we'd have any more first class passengers tonight, sir. Don't usually get many on the last train. They only ever put on two carriages for it. We've got five of you travelling in first class but the third class carriage is full, as usual. Standing room only now.'

Victor stopped as he noticed something about the train. 'What's wrong with the link between the two carriages?'

'This one's faulty so they don't never connect it. You'll have to stay in your carriage till you get there. It's because of the war, sir. It's an old train, brought out of retirement, I 'spect, like me. Oh, thank you, sir. Very generous of you.'

He insisted on lifting their two suitcases up on the rack, not without difficulty, saying, 'Everyone will have voted by now, won't they? I did myself before I started work. I daresay Mr Churchill will get back in again. What'd we have done without him during the war doesn't bear thinking of, eh? No, not many people will vote for them socialists.' He closed the door to the compartment as he left, still talking to himself.

Victor was pretty sure that most people who'd been in the forces wouldn't have voted for Churchill and the Conservatives. A lot of the ordinary soldiers felt the country needed something different now – a new start, fairer treatment for everyone. He'd voted Labour himself.

'Ugh!' Betty wrinkled her nose. 'It smells horrid in here, Daddy.'

'Someone's been smoking cigars, even though it's a non-smoking compartment. I'll let in some fresh air.' Victor used the leather strap to let down the window in the door and leaned out of it to watch the guard yell, 'Mind the doors!' and blow his whistle.

As the train jolted slightly, getting ready to move off, Victor saw a young woman run towards it from behind some trolleys full of milk churns. She was in some sort of uniform, carrying a kitbag and yelling, 'Someone open a door! Please!'

A porter began chasing after her, yelling to her to stop, but Victor saw the desperation in her face and on impulse, opened the door of his compartment. She put on a spurt and leaped into it just as the train started to gather speed.

The impact of her body knocked him to the floor and she fell on top of him.

The porter who'd been chasing her banged the door shut, yelling, 'Don't do that again, miss, or—!'

His last words were indistinguishable as the train rattled out of the station.

Ros closed her eyes in sheer relief that she'd caught the train. It had been touch and go, and she'd had to vault over the barrier of the adjoining platform because the ticket inspector had refused to let her on to this platform. But if she hadn't caught the last train, she'd have had to sleep on a park bench again.

She suddenly realised she was lying on top of the man who'd opened the door for her and he was trying to get up. Flushing in embarrassment, she scrambled to her feet. 'Sorry. Thanks for helping me.'

He stood up, brushing down his clothes. 'You looked desperate to catch this train.'

'I was.'

'I don't think I've ever seen a woman run as fast as that. You must be very strong.' He looked at her admiringly.

She gave a wry smile. 'Life in the Wrens keeps you active. And I never was a frail creature. I'm five foot ten tall, after all.' Nearly as tall as him, she thought, taller than most men, which could put them off asking her out.

As she brushed down her clothes, she stared round and

realised something. 'Oh, no! This is first class. Sorry. I'll leave at once. I'm only travelling third class.'

'You can't get into the other carriage while the train is moving. The link is broken, apparently, and they never connect it. You'll have to wait till the first stop to change and, actually, I don't mind you staying. You could pay the difference in fares. It won't cost much for such a short journey. The porter said the third-class carriage was standing room only.'

He had such a kind face, she blurted out the truth. 'I can't afford it.'

He looked at her thoughtfully. 'Then how about I pay the extra and you do me a favour in return? I could do with a woman to help me with Betty while we're on the train.'

Ros hesitated. 'If you mean going to the lavatory, you can stand outside the door while she goes in. I can't take your money for that.'

'I too need to use the facilities. I don't want to leave her on her own while I do that, not for a second. But I also need someone to help her tidy herself up. I'm not very good with girls' hair.'

The child had been watching them solemnly, her eyes going from one to the other, her hair in a mess and only half of it still in the two plaits she must have started the day with. She was a pretty little thing with her dark hair and brown eyes. Ros smiled at her automatically.

'Daddy and I are running away,' Betty announced.

Startled, Ros looked back at him, but his smile was rueful rather than guilty.

'My daughter can sometimes be too honest. We are indeed running away. My wife has died and her mother wants to take Betty away from me.'

'Can't she share her with you?'

'Galtons don't share things and they insist on doing

everything their way. I want to bring Betty up differently from how her mother was treated.'

'And I want to be with my daddy.'

Ros gave in to fate, which for once seemed to be treating her kindly. 'Oh well, in that case I'll say thank you and stay. This is much more comfortable than standing in a crowded corridor, even though it's not a long journey.'

He held out his hand. 'Victor Travers.'

She took it. 'Ros Dawson.' She held out her hand to the child afterwards. 'I'm pleased to meet you and your father, Betty.'

'Grown-ups don't usually shake hands with me.'

'I didn't want to leave you out.'

They shook hands and Ros saw the father smile, as if he liked her including his daughter in the greetings.

'Shall we sit down now?' Victor suggested.

'Yes, let's.' Ros sank on to the seat, relieved to be off her feet. She'd hitchhiked into Manchester today, wearing her Wrens greatcoat, which they'd let her keep because it was very worn. That had helped her get lifts, but once she'd got near the city centre, she'd taken a bus.

Only she'd got on the wrong bus and nearly missed the train. She felt exhausted for lack of sleep last night, but she'd saved herself some money by sleeping rough and hitchhiking. That was so important now she was no longer earning.

'Where are you going?' he asked.

'To a small town called Rivenshaw.'

'What a coincidence! We're going to Rivenshaw as well. Do you know it?'

'I grew up there, but I left four years ago when I joined the Wrens and I've only been back a couple of times. You don't have a northern accent, so you can't be from Lancashire.' And she'd have remembered if she'd seen him around the town. He was a good-looking fellow, over six foot tall, not film star handsome, but then who was in real life?

'We've never been to Rivenshaw before but we hope to settle there. I'm going to start up a business there with a friend: Mayne Esher. Have you ever met him?'

'His family own the big house; I'm from the back streets. I've seen him but I've never spoken to him.'

'Ah. Are you going to rejoin your family?'

Her face grew sad. 'For a time. My mother's ill, dying. They demobbed me early, on compassionate grounds, so that I can see her before it's too late. My stepfather's out of work, and anyway, he's had to look after her, so I've been sending them money to help out. That's why I'm a bit short.'

She only had her last week's pay and the remains of her savings – five pounds seven and sixpence in all. She had sent money to her stepfather bit by bit, because Cliff wasn't a good manager with money. She wasn't letting her mother die in pain, if it took her last penny to buy something to help her.

'I'm sorry about your mother,' Mr Travers said quietly.

She nodded, the lump in her throat stopping her speaking. For a time there was silence except for the sound of the train wheels rattling along the tracks. The rhythmic sound was very soothing and—

Ros woke with a start as the compartment door opened, embarrassed to realise she'd fallen asleep with her head on a complete stranger's shoulder.

'Tickets, please.'

Victor smiled at the ticket inspector. 'My friend nearly missed the train and didn't have time to change her ticket so that she could join us. I wonder if I could pay the difference between third and first class, so that she can stay with us?'

The man looked at her suspiciously. 'You could have changed carriages at the last stop, like I did.'

'Miss Dawson is helping me look after my daughter,' Victor said. 'There are some things a man can't do.'

The man studied the little girl, who was staring at him wide-eyed, and his expression softened. 'Yes, of course, sir.'

When he'd gone, Ros stretched and wriggled her shoulders. 'Thank you, Mr Travers. What time is it?'

'Nearly eleven o'clock. The train stopped for a while to let a troop train through, so I let you sleep. You'd think there was still a war on.'

'There is in the Far East,' she said. 'I've got a cousin out there. Well, I think I have. Mum didn't stay in touch with her family after she married Cliff.'

'That conflict will soon be over, I'm sure. The troop train was probably bringing men who'd been fighting in Europe back to the Dispersal Centre in Manchester to be demobbed. The government must have been planning the demob procedures for a while. They gave me a fistful of leaflets about how to adjust to my new life when they turned me loose again. I threw them away.'

Her voice grew softer. 'How can the authorities know what we're facing? The country's changed so much. Life will be different for everyone, I should think and no one can really predict how it'll be.'

He laughed. 'They gave me an ugly demob suit, too. I'll never, ever wear it – except perhaps for digging in the garden.'

She looked down at herself and up at her kitbag on the luggage rack, smiling. 'I haven't finished up with much, that's for sure. I shouldn't have kept these trousers, really, but, like my overcoat, they're nearly worn out, so they turned a blind eye to me keeping them. They gave me twenty clothing coupons in return for my uniform, but I haven't enough money to buy anything. And anyway, twenty coupons won't go far. Perhaps there'll be a clothing exchange in Rivenshaw, where I can get somebody's castoffs.'

'There probably will be. Those clothing exchanges have been invaluable.'

She studied him. 'I thought you had the look of someone who'd been in the Army. You can't mistake it. Look, I apologise for falling asleep on you. I spent last night on a park bench, but I didn't get much sleep.'

'A park bench! Are you that short of money?'

'I was trying to be economical. I'll have to try to find a job straight away once I get to Rivenshaw. My stepfather said the money I sent made a big difference to my mother, kept up her strength, so I was glad to do it. I was terrified she'd die before I saw her again. We were very close . . . once.'

Betty had been listening to them chatting, but now she started jigging about. 'We kept quiet while you were asleep, but now, could I go to the lavatory, please? And do you think you could help me with my hair, Miss Dawson? It's falling into my eyes and I want to look nice when we meet Daddy's friends.'

'Of course.' Ros stood up, looked at her kit bag and hesitated.

'I'll keep an eye on it,' Victor said. 'I'll swap it for my daughter when you get back.'

She smiled. 'All right.'

Ros found out a lot more about him while they were away, because Betty chatted non-stop the whole time they were in the jolting ablutions room, mostly about her father.

It made you think, it really did. Fancy people like them having to run away. Life didn't always run smoothly even if you were comfortably off financially. But he seemed a kind man and his daughter clearly adored him. Ros still remembered her own father, wished he hadn't died, wished her mother hadn't married again so hastily.

She was quite sure that once she got to Rivenshaw, her

life would be far from smooth. She had never got on with her stepfather – which was why she'd volunteered for the Wrens – but now she'd have to try to live with him, at least, until her mother died.

But if Cliff tried to mess about with her, as he'd tried before, he'd better watch out. Just let him lay one finger on her! She knew a few tricks now to defend herself and was much stronger physically than she had been, after all her training.

3

In Rivenshaw on July 5th, Mayne Esher voted early. He listened with amusement to the better-dressed voters, most of whom still believed Churchill would win the day. He had found time to glance at the *Manchester Guardian* the previous day and it had said, 'This is not the election that is going to shake Tory England'.

He begged to disagree. He didn't have any strong political affiliations himself, but he doubted Churchill and the Conservatives would be planning to build a new Britain, as most people wanted. They'd be more likely to try to recreate the old one. So this time he was prepared to give the Labour party a chance. Mr Attlee seemed a modest, reasonable man.

Before he was demobbed, Mayne had listened to the rank and file soldiers talking about what they wanted from a peacetime Britain. Their modest desires included family allowances, higher old age pensions, houses with bathrooms and a National Health Service, so that poorer people could obtain medical care as needed without worrying about cost.

Not a lot to ask for, in his opinion. After all, most people had given their all to fight this war. Now it was the turn of the government to do all it could to make their lives more comfortable.

Through the long years of war he'd been planning what to do afterwards, if he survived. That had given him something to look forward to. When he got home to the big old house, he had gone to speak to the building department at the local council, and the amount of paperwork needed to start his new building business had shocked him.

He'd considered working in the library, but didn't feel comfortable leaving important documents there. No, he had to find himself a smaller room to use as an office, then move all the building paperwork there.

That wasn't going to be easy. Esherwood, his family's minor stately home, had been requisitioned for use during the war as a convalescent hospital and had been badly damaged inside, presumably by the patients and their attendants. They'd removed some of the banisters – which had vanished completely – carved their initials in the 17th century panelling and knocked off pieces of the beautiful plasterwork from cornices and ceilings.

He was angry and he wasn't alone in that. He'd heard of similar or worse treatment of other requisitioned houses, a couple of which had been burned down because of careless smokers. Such information was only just starting to come to light.

At least the structure of Esherwood seemed to be basically sound still, even though no maintenance work had been done on it during the war years. One important task would be to check for problems like leaks in the roof or dry rot – the scourge of stately homes.

He'd managed to save some of the more valuable smaller furnishings by hiding them, but many pieces of beautiful old furniture were too big to hide, and some had simply vanished. Had they been stolen or burned for firewood? Since space in the two secret chambers was limited, he'd spent the whole of one leave at the beginning of the war carefully selecting which paintings, silver, china and small but beautiful pieces of furniture were the most valuable.

He'd hidden these, either in the rear cellar or in the secret room up in the attics, not even telling his father what he'd cached there. By then his father had moved to the Dower House to make room for the Army.

Anyway, his parents were careless with money and would have sold things, if not during the war then now. They'd sold a lot of the family jewellery, which was in his mother's care and ought to have been passed on to the next generation. His mother was very vague about what had happened to the money. Indeed, she'd grown vague about a lot of things.

She'd always dressed well, though, war or no war. There was no sign of 'Make Do And Mend' about her.

No use getting angry at them all over again. He had to put the past behind him and look to the future. His father had handed over the estate and that was all signed, sealed and delivered by the lawyer.

Given the rationing and shortages, not to mention the bureaucratic mazes at all levels, it was going to take longer than he'd expected even to get permission to renovate the house and turn it into flats. Luckily housing and rebuilding were government priorities, and men from the building trades were being demobbed early on condition they went into a building job. They'd be recalled to the forces if they left that job, though.

Thank goodness Mayne had a private income and some savings to live on, till he started to make a profit. He had managed his money very carefully during the war years, living on his officer's pay and saving as much as he could from that.

He walked across the spacious, two-storeyed entrance hall to the small room behind the library, just off the corridor that led to the kitchen and servants' area. Yes, this would make a good office. It didn't seem to have been used by the occupiers as anything but a dumping place for all sorts of items.

He moved things about and freed up a path to the small bay window. The polished oak window seat was piled high with cardboard boxes and miscellaneous bits and pieces. It was a good thing too. No one had been able to carve their initials in the window seat, where he'd sat so often as a child.

He'd been lonely, with no brothers and sisters, and parents who didn't spend much time with him when he was home from boarding school, so he'd ranged the house, making it his castle. No one knew Esherwood as well as he did.

He heard someone come in through the front door and went on instant alert, because there had been a succession of people trying to loot the big house since the Army vacated it. He'd had to hire two night watchmen.

He hurried out to the entrance hall. 'Oh, it's you, Dad! How nice to see you!'

Reginald Esher looked round, grimacing. 'When I come here, I'm always glad I've handed the estate over to you, Maynard, even though your mother is still angry with me for doing it. I wouldn't know where to start clearing this mess up. What's in all these boxes?'

'Who knows?'

The transfer had only happened a few days ago and Mayne had immediately moved the Esher family affairs to the new lawyer who'd just opened up a practice. That had upset Gilliot, their former lawyer. He'd taken over the practice when the family's long-time lawyers had died and retired respectively. Nasty fellow, Gilliot. Mayne couldn't stand him and certainly didn't trust him, after he'd tried to help the magistrate take Judith's children away from her.

'How's Melford working out as your lawyer?' his father asked unexpectedly.

'He gets things done far more quickly than Gilliot. He

doesn't use the recent war as an excuse for inefficiency.' And he wasn't anti-Semitic, like Gilliot, an attitude which upset Mayne, given that he'd just spent several years of his life fighting against the Nazis.

The photos of concentration camps like Belsen, which had been shown in the newsreels at cinemas and in newspapers since VE day in May, had shocked the nation to the core. It was one thing to know about the appalling treatment of innocent people, another thing altogether to see the results of it in the people like walking skeletons who'd been liberated.

Mayne shook away those sad thoughts. 'Did you come to find some of your other research books, Father? You know your own way to the cellar storage area.'

'No, it's not that. There was a phone call for you and, as I was ready to take a break, I picked the phone up. I thought I'd get some fresh air and give you the message. At least it's still a pleasant stroll from the Dower House up the drive. The call was from your friend Victor, who rang to say he was about to set off and hopes to reach Rivenshaw by the last train tonight. He wonders if you could meet him at the station and book him a hotel room somewhere.'

'Oh good. I've been expecting him for a while. I'm glad he's decided to invest in the new business. We worked closely together during the last year of the war and get on well. Was that all he said?'

Reginald frowned. 'He was in a hurry to catch a train, so couldn't stop to explain properly. He said something about escaping from his in-laws, which puzzled me. Oh, and he's got his daughter with him.'

'Ah. I can guess what it's about. Victor told me his wife's mother wanted to take his daughter away from him now Susan's dead, but are you sure he used the word escape? I mean, he's the father. Who else would bring up the child?'

'Oh, yes, I remember it clearly.' Reginald grinned. 'I'd just finished writing a chapter, so I didn't have my mind on other things.'

'Mum usually answers the phone.'

'That young woman had called to see her again and they were in the small sitting room with the door shut.'

Mayne stiffened. 'Caroline, you mean?'

'Yes. The two of them have been seeing a lot of one another lately. Your mother's talking of inviting her to stay with us, because her brother has told her she can't stay with him any longer and should move back to the house her husband left her in Scotland. But she hates it there. Your mother is very sympathetic, I suppose because she doesn't like living in the Dower House.'

'Oh, hell! More likely, Mother is still trying to make a match between me and Caroline. We should never have got engaged – chalk and cheese we were – and I've always been glad she dumped me for a richer man.' Mayne heard the edge to his voice, even though he was trying to make light of it.

'Well, your mother's wrong. I won't let Caroline stay with us, and so I told Dorothy. That young woman is not only stupid, but the way she flatters your mother disgusts me. A woman like her would never produce intelligent children. Though she didn't produce any at all for her late husband, so perhaps she can't have any.'

Mayne couldn't help smiling. Apart from his historical research, his father's other obsession was the education of intelligent boys and girls from the lower classes. Mayne's great-grandfather had set up the Esherwood Bequest, a trust that paid the fees of one poor boy and girl to the Rivenshaw Grammar School every year. Judith's eldest daughter had won it one year, which was how Mayne had first met her.

Reginald's twin obsessions made him a very unsatisfactory

husband for a woman like Mayne's mother, who despised book learning. The two of them lived quite separate lives most of the time.

Mayne definitely didn't want a marriage like theirs. 'It was Caroline who chose not to marry me, Father. I was stupid enough to be taken in by her pretty face and by the time she dumped me, for a much richer husband, I'd realised my mistake and was wondering how to get free. I'd never take her back again.'

His father gave him a sly grin. 'Why would you want Caroline when you've found a new woman?'

'Please don't say that to anyone, Dad! I've not started formally courting Judith yet. Miss Peters says we should let the scandal die down first.'

'She's a very wise old woman, so she's probably right. But your Judith is a good choice as a wife. She's produced three extremely intelligent children already and still looks very healthy, so I hope she'll produce a couple more for the Esher family.' He held up one hand. 'It's all right. I won't say anything. Now, I must get back to work.'

Mayne watched in amusement as his father broke off the conversation abruptly and hurried away. It was fortunate the phone call had come during a lull in his research.

If his mother had answered the phone, she'd not have bothered to pass on the message at all, she was so furious with Mayne for taking on the burden of restoring this house instead of selling it and letting her spend the money on a life of luxury. He was sorry for her. She was a very unhappy woman. But he wasn't giving in to her demands, or marrying to please her.

He returned to his office-to-be and stood looking out of the leaded window. He wished he could afford to restore Esherwood and live here himself, but he couldn't and that was that. Even if he sold every one of the family's treasures, it wouldn't solve the problem of an ongoing need for income.

No, the best he could hope for was to preserve the old house by converting it into flats. If he could sell them at a profit, that would give him a start as a builder, and perhaps he'd be able to keep one flat for himself and live there.

He prayed his father would live for the required seven years, now that he'd handed the estate over. If he didn't, they'd be hit with huge death duties and the remaining land would have to be sold.

It wasn't just his own life that mattered. He wanted to play his part in rebuilding the battered country. Many of the war-weary demobbed soldiers were desperate for somewhere to live. He couldn't think of any more worthwhile way of earning money than providing homes for them.

Judith came to join him and Mayne felt himself relax at the mere sight of her.

She smiled and moved to slip her arm through his, kissing his cheek. Then she gave a little puff of annoyance at herself and let go, trying to be businesslike. 'I've brought you the post, Mr Esher.'

'Now I draw the line at you calling me mister.'

'I have to call you that in public.'

'Why? The others won't be doing it.'

'Because I'm working as your assistant.'

'I'll extract a kiss from you in private for every time you "mister" me.'

She blushed rosily, as he pulled her close and gave her a lingering kiss, not just a peck on the cheek.

When he let her go, she said breathlessly, 'What if someone came in?'

'Kissing isn't a crime.'

'No, but the way some people are treating me, you'd think

being married to a bigamist was as much my fault as his, so if they see me kissing you, it'll make things worse.'

'More trouble?'

She nodded. 'When I was queuing up at the grocer's.'

'Who?'

'Mrs Purvis. She said some . . . hateful things.'

One of his mother's friends. 'Ignore her. She's famous for being nasty. You're just the latest target.'

She nodded, but he could see the pain in her eyes and guessed she was thinking about her children, who were also facing unkindness from some people.

He valued Judith as well as loved her. In only a couple of weeks she had proved to be an excellent assistant. Even when they were married, he couldn't see a woman of her intelligence being content to become a housewife again. Anyway, he wanted her to lead a happy and fulfilled life with him.

'Shall you want to stop working and stay at home once we're married?' he asked.

She hesitated.

'The truth, mind.'

'I love what I'm doing. It's the first time I've ever had a job that uses my brain.'

'And you're doing it brilliantly. I've only to worry about a detail and you come up with a solution.'

She flushed, trying in vain to hide her pleasure in that compliment. Her so-called husband had been a heavy drinker and it had always been a struggle to put food on the table, so she'd had to take any menial job she could find. It was she who had kept their three children fed most of the time.

Then, after she left Doug Crossley, there had been a hearing about custody of their children, at which it had been revealed that he was a bigamist, and Judith wasn't legally married to him at all.

That had shocked the whole town, shocked her too. She

and the children were now using her maiden name, Maskell, but the taint of Doug's crime lingered on.

Mayne had heard his mother gossiping with a friend only a day or two ago, saying nasty things about Judith as the two women strolled round the garden of the Dower House. His anger had boiled over and he'd gone across to confront them, asking point-blank how Judith could possibly have known about her husband's other wife.

The friend had become flustered and his mother had been furious with him afterwards for his lack of manners, but he'd continue to challenge such remarks every time he heard them.

He'd heard some people openly calling the three children bastards and had seen Ben come home from school a couple of times showing signs of having got into a fight.

No one said the word 'bastard' in front of Mayne. They attacked the children, the easiest targets, when they were out on their own.

If only his mother were not so against Judith, she could have helped scotch the gossip, but there was no hope of that.

'Mayne? Are you with me?'

'Sorry, darling, I was just thinking about us, wishing we could get married now.'

'We agreed to give the gossip time to die down before we do anything about us. And don't call me darling.'

'It slips out. Look, I'm only waiting another month to start courting you openly, whatever Miss Peters advises.'

'Oh. Well, we'll see.'

'I shall then court you in style, take you walking in the park on Sundays, buy you flowers.'

She sighed. 'I've never been courted like that. Doug was . . . very straightforward about it all. Now, let's talk about something more pleasant. I've got an idea to help the business get started.'

'What is it this time?'

'I think we should hold a grand auction of the furniture and other things the Army left behind, the ones we know we're never going to use. There are quite a lot of hospital bed frames and mattresses. We'll need some of them, and your friends may, too, but we could sell at least half of them. There are so many furniture shortages and I'm sure things will still be rationed for years, so people will be eager to buy them. They're second-hand; they won't need coupons.'

'Good idea.'

'And that'll not only bring in some money, it'll also clear more space in the house for when we start turning it into flats. I can't believe how wasteful the Army was, leaving so much stuff behind.'

'Wasteful in one sense but, in another, they knew they'd not need all that equipment again once the war was over. If they'd kept it, they'd have had to find somewhere to store it, then transport it there and set men to guarding it. It'd have cost them more than it was worth.'

'But they might need the beds for other convalescent homes if the war with Japan goes on for a long time. We've still only got peace in Europe, really.'

Mayne trusted Judith enough to say, 'I heard about some hush-hush experiments with a new weapon before I left the special unit in the Army. I don't know any details, and you mustn't mention this to anyone else, but if things turn out as the boffins working on it predict, we won't be long in ending the war in the Far East.'

'I hope whatever it is works out, then.'

'So do I. Everyone's had enough of war, and we've lost so many good people already.'

They both paid the instinctive tribute of a minute's silence to the fallen, then he went on, 'My father came to tell me that my friend Victor phoned. He and his daughter are arriving tonight by the last train from Manchester. I know we talked about getting rooms ready for them here, but we never actually did it. We'll have to leave sorting out this office for the moment. Perhaps you could help me, if you have nothing else urgent on, that is.'

'Of course I can help you.' Then she couldn't help adding, 'I love being able to choose what tasks I do next. I've always hated working inefficiently.'

They went upstairs, carefully keeping a distance between them, but oh, so conscious of one another still.

'I think the rooms in the east wing of the house would be more suitable since we need to do this quickly,' she said. 'I was thinking that the children and I should move either there or up to the next floor, because the bedrooms in the main house are rather damp.'

'Yes. Another thing on my list is to find out why.'

She led the way down the east wing, which had four doors along each side of the corridor. 'There are six bedrooms and two bathrooms, one of which had its bathroom suite stolen after the Army left.'

She gestured to the two end bedrooms. 'How about using these two? There's a bathroom next to them that just needs cleaning.'

'Let's look at it.' He opened the door and sighed. 'It's filthy. It'll take a lot of work to get it right.'

'If I abandon my other jobs, I can clean it and make the rooms habitable.'

'No. You're never doing the heavy cleaning again.'

She laughed at him. 'I've been doing heavy cleaning for years. There's a certain satisfaction in getting a dirty place clean.'

'Well, you're not doing it any more. Do you think Al's mother would come and help us? Your former neighbour seems a very capable woman. She only works for my mother one day a week now.'

'Mrs Needham might help us, or she'll know someone who will. If I could borrow your bicycle, it wouldn't take me long to nip down there and ask her.'

She shook her head slightly as she added, 'When the children and I cleared our old house out, last week, she came and helped us. I was ashamed of how shabby and broken our possessions were, but she knew people who'd be grateful for the things I'd have just thrown away. There's always someone worse off than yourself, isn't there? Mrs Needham helps a lot of people.'

'Go and do that as soon as we've finished here.' He led the way into the two end bedrooms again, grimacing at the mess that greeted them. 'I think we should ask Mrs Needham to come here daily for a while. There are so many rooms needing cleaning.'

'I can't believe how many there are. You say Esherwood is small for a stately home, but it still seems huge to me.'

Judith unlocked the big Nissen hut and got out the bicycle. The Army had erected the ugly hut in the garden, and it was another place full of things to clear out. You couldn't even get through to the back part till you moved mounds of boxes and furniture, so they had no idea what was there, but they could at least store the bicycle safely in the front.

After locking the door carefully, she let herself enjoy the short cycle ride down the drive and along the edge of the park to Lower Parklea. She waved to Miss Peters and a couple of other people she passed, but didn't stop to chat.

In her old street, she was delighted to find Mrs Needham in.

'You're just in time for a cup of tea, love.'

'I can't stay, I'm afraid. I've come to ask a favour of you.'

'Well, come inside, at least. Better bring that bicycle into the hall, too. We don't want someone stealing it. It won't hurt this old lino. I wish I could get new lino for the floor, but who knows how long it'll be before we can buy things they don't consider essential?'

In the familiar kitchen, Judith sat down and explained the situation.

'Well, I've been dying to see what the big house is like and what young Mr Esher is doing to it, so I'll do you two days a week. I can't afford more time than that, because I clean for Mrs Esher one day a week and I still have my own housework to get through. She's a hoity-toity madam, that one, but she pays well and I know how to manage her.'

Mrs Needham grinned. 'She daren't offend me, because she's too scared of me giving notice now her old maid's retired.'

After frowning for a moment or two, she said, 'Young Ellie Turner might do some work for you, if you need more help. Since she lost her husband, she's gone back to live with her parents. She's grown very quiet, poor thing. I know she's looking for a job, but they've given most of them to the men being demobbed. I can teach her how to clean for posh people. It's not as straightforward as you'd think.'

'What a good idea.'

'Pity Ellie never had a kid to remember her Peter by, but there you are. Life isn't always kind.'

'Could you ask her for me? You know the family better than I do.'

'Yes, of course. In fact, I'll do it now if she's at home, then I'll bring her up with me to see what needs doing today. That all right?'

'That's fine. I knew you'd be able to help us one way or the other.' She gave the older woman a quick hug. The Needhams had been good neighbours to her for many years. And now Al Needham was working for Mayne as a temporary night watchman, with the promise of a better job when Mayne's new company got off the ground.

As Judith was cycling back, someone yelled, 'Whore!' at her and for a moment she let the bike wobble. Then she lifted her chin and regained control of it as she cycled up the gentle slope along by Parson's Mead. Their local park had been dug up for allotments. 'Dig for Victory' the posters had ordered, but people were more concerned with digging to provide more food for themselves and their families, if you asked her.

She could feel herself growing tense as she got to the Dower House and unfortunately Mayne's mother was just opening the garden gate. As usual Mrs Esher gave her a dirty look.

Incidents like this and people yelling at her in the street, or looking at her as if she was at fault in her non-marriage to Doug, were beginning to worry her. What would people say when she and Mayne got married? She hated to think. Was it fair to burden him with her problems?

She doubted she could stop him fighting her battles, though. He was a very determined man when he got something in his sights. She liked that about him. If she tried to move away from Rivenshaw, to spare him a lifetime of defending her, he'd come after her, she was sure. Anyway, she didn't want to leave the town and she very much wanted to marry Mayne. She wasn't noble enough – or daft enough! – to give him up.

Damn Doug Crossley! He'd made a mess of her and her children's lives. Only . . . he'd given her those three wonderful youngsters. And now she'd met his family, she'd found out what nice people they were. Doug had been the black sheep and the rest of his family wanted to be friends with her and her children. Ben in particular got on like a house on fire with his half-brothers and grandfather.

She liked the Crossley family too. She even liked Doug's real wife, who had been nothing but friendly towards her.

Judith had to dismount to wheel the bicycle round the bollards and chain, and up the drive. They needed to do something about this barrier, and soon, because there would be a lot of coming and going once they started the building work. They were using the back entrance for vehicles at the moment, but it was up a deeply rutted track and she dreaded to think what it'd be like in the winter.

She was facing a lifetime of hard work here, but her days had never been so interesting. And she'd never felt as loved.

Mayne watched Judith come cycling up to the house, admiring her shapely legs as she got off the bike. She disappeared from sight for a moment as she locked the bike away in the Nissen hut, then strolled towards the house, stopping for a moment to hold her face up to the sun.

He'd chosen this room as his office, because it overlooked the rear of the house and would be good for supervising building activity. The back yard of the old house was a big space, about two hundred yards by one hundred. The ruined stables, various outhouses and former staff housing lay round its edges, with the ugly corrugated iron curves of the Nissen hut just visible behind them. It would be a busy place when they got going, with deliveries being made and tradesmen coming in and out.

He went to meet Judith in the kitchen. 'Everything all right? You look a bit upset.'

'I thought I was hiding that. It was only someone calling out at me.'

'What did they call?'

'It doesn't matter.'

He came to pull her into his arms. 'Tell me.'

'Whore.'

'I have to do something about that.'

'There's nothing you can do, Mayne love, and trying will only make it worse.'

'Just let anyone say it in front of me! Now, what about Al's mother?'

'Mrs Needham is coming to help us two days a week and she's asking Ellie Turner if she can come too. You know Peter Turner was killed last year?'

His face creased in pain. 'No. I'm so sorry to hear that. Those two were very much in love. I'm not as up to date as I'd like to be on who's been killed, because my mother doesn't keep track of the so-called lower classes. Poor Peter. He couldn't have been more than what . . . twenty-two?'

'Twenty-three when he died.' They stood for a moment in silence, then she moved away from him. 'Come on. Let's tackle those bedrooms and make some space for your friend and his daughter to sleep in.'

She led the way upstairs to the smaller of the two large bedrooms and stood, hands on hips, studying the chaos. 'Someone must have been using this one as an office, as well as a bedroom. Look, they've pushed all the furniture to that side any old how and used the dressing table as a desk.'

She went over to look at it, clicking her tongue in disapproval. 'Cigarette burns. Why couldn't they use an ashtray?' She opened the wardrobe door. 'Good heavens! It's got clothes in still.' She pulled out some shabby men's clothes. 'These might fit Jan. He's short of clothes. Is it all right if I give them to him?'

'Of course it is.' He pulled back the bedcovers, then sat on the mattress and bounced, grimacing. 'Look at these dirty sheets. And what a hard mattress this is! I can't remember anyone sleeping in these rooms when we lived here. Mother loves her social life, but there were never enough servants to run round after visitors who stayed, so she rarely invited anyone from further away. She used to blame that on Rivenshaw, but I blame it on her laziness.'

Judith pulled him up and dragged off the dirty sheets. 'The mattress is clean enough, so if we can find a feather overlay to put over it, it won't be too bad. Let's look in the room next door.'

This time when she tugged off the sheets, it revealed a lumpy old flock mattress with stained ticking. 'Ugh.'

Mayne looked at it in disgust. 'That won't do at all. I'll get Al to help me carry some of the hospital bed frames and mattresses up when he comes to keep watch tonight, and we can move these old beds into another room.'

Judith stared at him challengingly. 'You and I can bring them up now. We need to clear out the unnecessary furniture so that Mrs Needham can do the cleaning. Do you think I'm a weakling?'

'No. But lifting heavy furniture isn't women's work.'

'Poorer women have always done heavy lifting. How heavy do you think wet sheets are when you lift them in and out of the boiler? It's only upper class women who've been treated as weaklings. And the war has put a stop to that for a lot of them. Come on! Let's pull the rest of the covers off and get rid of this mattress. We'll toss the dirty linen over the banisters and collect it when we go downstairs. I'll check the sheets later to see if they're reusable and if they are, I'll send them to the laundry in town.'

He didn't allow himself to smile at the happiness on her face whenever she said the words 'send it to the laundry'. She'd once confided to him how much she hated doing the weekly washing. Well, he'd make sure she never had to do that again. He had far better uses for her time, because she was proving herself brilliant at sorting out practical business details.

Judith hummed as they started clearing out the rooms and the cheerful sound lifted his spirits. Now that she was free of her fear of Doug Crossley, she seemed to take pleasure in every aspect of her new life, and he was a lucky man to have won her love, whatever his mother said.

He and Judith would be married long before Christmas, if he had his way. To hell with what the gossips might say. They'd say it anyway, even if the two of them waited years to marry.

'Anybody there?' a woman's voice called from downstairs.

'That's Mrs Needham.' Judith hurried along the corridor to peer over the banisters into the entrance hall where two women were standing. 'We're up here. Come and join us.'

When she'd puffed her way up, Mrs Needham said, 'Remember Ellie Turner? She can work however many days you need her for and she'll do anything.'

A pale, thin young woman whom Judith recognised by sight nodded as she followed the older woman up the stairs.

Mrs Needham stared round each bedroom in turn. 'What a mess!'

'Isn't it? I'm so glad to see you. We've been tossing the dirty linen down into the hall and we're about to dump the unnecessary furniture from this room into one of the others.'

The older woman put down her shopping basket and rolled up her sleeves. 'Let's get started, then. Ellie, you go and see which of the other bedrooms in this wing is the worst and we'll shove everything except for the heavy wardrobes in there for the moment, then someone can clear it all out later. You can leave this to us now, Mr Esher.'

He winked at Judith and did as he was told.

'I shall enjoy this job,' Mrs Needham said with relish. 'Nice young fellow, isn't he? Not at all like his mother.'

Ellie didn't say much but she worked hard.

Judith thought the young woman looked very sad, but these days there were quite a few sad people, who'd lost family members. Only time would heal their pain.

4

Just before half past eleven that evening, Mayne drove to the station to meet the train, glad his old car had proved usable. It had sat in the shed for most of the war, but he'd found a mechanic to check it out. He'd even managed to get hold of some new tyres, on the grounds of transport being essential for a business about to build some much-needed dwellings.

As the time for the train's arrival passed, he strolled up and down the platform, wishing he'd brought his overcoat. You could never quite be sure of trains sticking to their schedules, though things were improving.

When the station master noticed him, he invited Mayne into the little office. 'You'll be more comfortable in here, Mr Esher. The train's been delayed. I don't know exactly when it'll arrive, but probably well after midnight. They're not usually more than an hour or two late these days, though. Not like it was during the war, eh? They could be a whole day late then.'

'That's very kind of you. I don't want to go home and risk missing my friend's arrival. He has nowhere to stay but with me and he'll have his young daughter with him, too. Besides, it'd use some of my precious petrol going to and fro. You have to make every teaspoonful of fuel count these days, don't you?'

'Waste not, want not. Why don't you sit down? I can make you a cup of tea, if you don't mind a chipped cup. They're all chipped now, and you can't get new ones, but the tea still tastes all right.'

'That's very kind of you. Have you heard from your son, Mr Kendrick? Graham was in the Army, if I remember correctly. When will he be getting demobbed?'

'Not for some time yet, I'm afraid. He's Class B, construction worker, and they've got him putting up new prefabs for the fellows coming back from the war till he can find a civilian job. His old employer died during the war, you see, so Graham can't get demobbed till he finds a new job, and it has to be in construction.'

'I'd heard about that.'

'Yes, but did you know he has to stay in any job he finds or he'll be taken back into the Army. The war might have ended, but the government hasn't stopped running our lives, has it?'

'They're still churning out rules and regulations by the score. What exactly does Graham do in peacetime?'

'He's a carpenter, sir. He likes doing the big stuff, putting up roof beams and that sort of thing.'

'Does he now? I'm going to be needing carpenters if what I want to do at Esherwood is allowed. You must give me your son's details. Perhaps I might be able to find him a job later on?'

'So the rumours are true? You are going to be building houses on the Esherwood land.'

'Not yet. I'm going to turn Esherwood into flats. Who can afford to run a stately home these days? Not me. Keep this to yourself, though, if you don't mind, Mr Kendrick.'

The station master winked. 'I will, except for telling my boy, if that's all right.'

'Do you think he'd be interested? If the authorities will

allow it, I can put him to work as soon as we've got the building plans approved by the town council.'

'Interested! I can tell you now, he'll jump at the chance, because he wants to be with his wife and children. We've got a lot of lads coming back from the war who'll be needing their own homes, instead of living with their parents and families.'

He gave Mayne a rueful smile. 'There were a lot of wartime weddings. My lad had one early on and the two of them came to live with us. We're very lucky in our daughter-in-law, she's a good lass, but we're a bit old for having little children underfoot, and that's the truth. And it'd not be good for them when he comes back to stay, having to share our spare bedroom with two little 'uns.'

'Perhaps he can let me know what I'll need to do to help him get demobbed?'

The older man nodded, looked thoughtful and added, 'I've got a cousin working for the council building department, so maybe you'd like me to have a word in his ear about not tying you up in too much red tape?'

'That's a very kind thought. I'd be grateful.'

'Leave it to me.' Mr Kendrick touched the side of his nose, in the usual gesture for keeping quiet about something. A minute later the station bell gave two harsh rings and he stood up. 'That'll be the train. Your friend will be here very soon, sir. Like I said, just after midnight.'

'I'll leave you to do your job, then. Thank you for the tea.'

Mayne smiled as he waited on the platform. Of such small encounters much good could come. He might have found himself a carpenter and if Graham was anything like his father, he'd be a hard worker.

He enjoyed talking to people and it didn't matter if they were what his mother called 'the lower classes'. As far as he was concerned, ordinary people were the backbone of

England and without them and their stoic endurance, the war couldn't have been won.

The war had taught him a lot, made him the man he was now. A better, less selfish fellow than before, he hoped.

His mother seemed to be expecting the world to return to what it had been like pre-war. He'd tried to tell her that could never happen, but she refused to believe it.

'Mr Churchill will sort it all out,' she kept saying.

She was in for a disappointment once the election results were counted, he was sure.

What a lot had happened today! He checked his wrist-watch. Five minutes past midnight. It was July 6th now, the day after polling day.

The train from Manchester pulled slowly into the station, as if it too was tired. People poured out of the third class carriage and vanished into the darkness, but things happened more slowly with the first class passengers.

An elderly man got out of a compartment, carrying only a small suitcase. He walked stiffly out of the station, leaning on a stick. A middle-aged couple got out and walked slowly along the platform, their expressions brightening when another woman ran to greet them. Hugs all round. Good to see.

A tall young woman got down from one of the central compartments and reached up to receive a sleeping child into her arms. She stood holding the little girl, rocking her slightly, as a man began dumping luggage on the platform.

It was a moment or two before Mayne realised that the man was Victor, because although there was no longer any need for a blackout, the station lighting wasn't good.

Indeed, some people still felt uncomfortable using bright lights at night after the years of blackout, then the months of 'dimout' as restrictions were eased slightly. A few small children, who had known nothing else but dark streets at night, seemed positively frightened of bright lighting out of doors.

He wondered who the young woman was. She must be strong to be holding a child that big so easily. Had Victor found a nanny for his daughter already?

There wasn't a porter on duty at this late hour and Mr Kendrick was busy with the final first-class passenger, an elderly lady, so Mayne found a trolley and wheeled it over to his friend. 'Need any help?'

Victor swung round, smiling, and the two men shook hands, clapping one another on the back.

'Good to see you again.' They both spoke at once then laughed.

'Everything all right?' Mayne asked. 'My father wasn't entirely clear about your message.'

'I'll tell you the details later. Let me introduce you to Ros, who's been helping me with Betty on the train. Ros Dawson, my very good friend Mayne Esher.'

Ros nodded, still holding the sleeping child. 'Pleased to meet you.'

'Let me take Betty now,' Victor said.

'It'd be more use you dealing with your luggage and finding a taxi. She's not heavy.'

'No need for a taxi,' Mayne said. 'I've got my old car working again.'

Victor sighed in relief. 'Oh, good. Would you mind dropping Ros off first? Her mother's ill and she's been given a compassionate discharge from the Wrens to look after her.'

'I'm happy to do that. Where do you live, Miss Dawson?'

'Sycamore Street.'

Mayne didn't say so, but that wasn't a very salubrious part of the town. It always seemed ironic that all the streets there had been named for trees, because there were no trees or gardens anywhere in those narrow streets and alleys.

'Thank you, Mr Esher.' Her voice was low and pleasant with a soft Lancashire accent.

Betty stirred as Ros laid her gently on the back seat of the car, but the little girl didn't wake up.

'She's exhausted, poor love,' Victor said softly. 'Yesterday was a long and difficult day. Thanks for meeting us.'

'What else are friends for?'

When they got to Sycamore Street, they naturally found all the narrow terraced houses dark.

Ros got out of the car. 'Strange. I thought they might have left a light by my mother's bedside, since she's ill. I'll just retrieve my kitbag, then I'll knock them up. Say goodbye to Betty for me.'

Victor got out too. 'I'd prefer to see you into the house safely at this hour of the night.'

'There's really no need.'

He waited as she hammered on the door. She had to hammer again before someone switched on a bedroom light and yelled what sounded like a curse. It seemed a long time before a man opened the front door. He was about fifty, balding and with several days' growth of beard on his chin. Before the war, he must have been plump, but now his flesh sagged.

When he saw Ros, he scowled. 'Oh, hell, it's you! Just what I need.'

'How's my mother?'

'Dead.'

Victor heard Ros gasp and saw the anguish on her face. 'Mum's dead? I wasn't in time?'

A woman came downstairs to join him, linking her arm in his. 'Your mam died last year. But thanks for continuing to send the money. Me and Cliff have found it very useful.' She laughed heartily.

Cliff tried to close the door, but Ros held it open. 'When exactly did Mum die?'

'Last autumn. I can't remember the date.' He shoved her out of the way suddenly and managed to slam the door in her face.

Victor had heard the conversation and his heart ached for his companion. From inside the shabby terraced house came the sound of two people laughing.

Ros gave a whimper of pain and swayed. He put an arm round her, afraid she was going to faint.

She clung to him. 'She's dead. My mother's dead. He's been taking my money all this time, sending me messages from her, saying I was helping to buy her delicacies. How could he do that?'

Suddenly she began weeping, great wracking sobs. Victor cradled her in his arms and Mayne got out of the car to see what was wrong.

Victor explained rapidly. 'I can't leave Ros here. She's got nowhere to go.'

'Bring her to Esherwood. We'll find her a bed if she doesn't mind roughing it.'

She let Victor guide her into the car, not sobbing now, but with tears still running down her cheeks. She slumped into the corner of the back seat, holding her arms across her chest.

Victor had seen men hold themselves that way when they were in great pain. But there was nothing he could do to lessen this woman's anguish. He took Ros's kitbag into the front seat with him.

As Mayne drove away, he said in a low voice, 'That sounds like fraud to me. Possibly even theft.'

'To me, too.'

'We'll speak to Sergeant Deemer. He'll tell us what to do.'

'We'll ask her what she wants to do first,' Victor corrected. 'She might find it easier not to make a fuss.'

'She was serving her country when this happened. That man needs bringing to account. I can't bear thieves, and to prey on someone who's in the armed forces is unconscionable.'

Victor glanced back at Ros, who didn't seem to be listening to them. Her cheeks were still wet. He felt so helpless. 'We'll see.'

When they got to the outer wall of Esherwood's extensive grounds, there were no longer any iron gates, because they'd been taken for salvage. They drove between the gate posts and bumped slowly up the deeply rutted rear drive, from which the big chain had been removed that very morning. As they stopped outside the back of the house, Jan moved out of the shadows to greet them.

Mayne got out of the car first. 'All quiet?'

'It is now. Someone tried to creep through the gardens earlier. You could hear them a mile off, so I told them I had a gun trained on them and would fire at the count of ten if they didn't get the hell out of the grounds. They fell once or twice as they ran. They won't be back.'

'Thanks. Good idea about the gun. We might get one and put blanks into it, maybe fire them off once or twice. If people think we're armed they'll be less likely to come looting. I'll ask Sergeant Deemer if it's OK to do that.'

By this time Victor had helped Ros out and reached into the car for his daughter, who didn't wake as he lifted her.

'Here. Give Betty to me,' Mayne said. 'You look after Ros. Jan could you bring in the luggage, please? My friends are exhausted.'

'Yes, of course.'

Mayne stopped in the kitchen to watch Victor guide the young woman inside.

Judith appeared in the inner doorway, staring at the child

and the weeping woman then turning to the man. 'You must be Victor.'

'Yes. Pleased to meet you. That's my daughter Betty and this is our friend, Ros, who's just heard that her mother is dead.'

'I'm sorry to hear that. Put the little girl down in the big armchair. That's it. How about a cup of hot, strong tea?' It was the universal welcome and comforter.

Ros looked round as Victor drew out a chair for her, seeming surprised to find herself indoors. She made a visible effort to pull herself together. 'I'm sorry. I was . . . so shocked. Where are we?'

'Esherwood,' Mayne said. 'The house is in a bit of a mess, I'm afraid, because it was used as a convalescent hospital during the war. If you don't mind sleeping surrounded by chaos, we can find you a bed.'

'That's very kind of you.' She looked at Victor. 'I feel stupid, to let myself be tricked like that. I . . . don't know what to do now.' Her voice broke on the last words.

'We all make mistakes. Get a good night's sleep, then you'll be able to think more clearly about the future.'

'We'll put you in a room with Betty, if that's all right?' Judith said. 'Only we haven't cleared the others out.'

'Yes. Anything. Thank you.' Ros looked at them uncertainly. 'You're all being very kind. Why? I mean, I don't know you, not really.' She looked round. 'I grew up in Rivenshaw, but I've never even been inside Esherwood before.'

It was Victor who answered, 'If we can't help one another in times of trouble, we're not worth calling human beings. We pulled together during the war, and we must pull together as we cope with peace.'

Judith came across with a cup of tea. 'Here you are, Ros. My children and I live here too. We're a bit short of sugar, but I can put one teaspoonful in, if you like.'

'Thanks, but I don't take sugar. I got out of the habit when it became rationed.' She cradled the cup in her hands, as if she found the warmth comforting.

'Jan and Victor, you'll have a cuppa too, won't you?' Judith turned to the other newcomer. 'How do you take it?'

'As it comes, no sugar.' But Victor's eyes were on Ros, who was hunched over her cup, staring blindly down at the hot liquid.

When they'd drunk their tea, Mayne stood up. 'Let's go and sort out a bed for Ros, Victor.' He turned to Judith and gestured towards Ros and the child. 'Can you stay with them?'

'Of course.'

Half an hour later Mayne and Victor had set up an Army bed and mattress for Ros in Betty's room and found some bedding. Victor carried up the child, Mayne the last of the luggage, and Ros followed in silence.

Mayne quickly explained the layout of the upstairs to her, showing her where the nearest bathroom was, then the two men went back down to the kitchen.

By that time Judith had washed the cups and was just about to go back to her own bed. 'Anything else I can do?'

'No, but thanks for your help.'

She moved towards the door. 'I'd like to punch that step-father of hers. What a dreadful way to treat someone.'

When she'd gone, Mayne got out a bottle of whisky he'd been saving. 'A nightcap?'

'Just a small one.'

They sipped the amber liquid and both sighed in pleasure. As Mayne put his glass down, he said, 'You always were prone to pick up lame ducks, my friend.'

'Well, lame duck or not, this encounter could be of mutual benefit to Ros and me. I need someone to look after Betty and she was wonderful with her on the train. Can she stay here with us for the time being if I give her a job looking after Betty and me? I'll pay for her keep, of course.'

'Make it a job as nanny/general factotum, helping as needed, and she'll be a welcome member of the team, I'm sure, with no need for payment. We're all mucking in with whatever needs doing, and what's the betting your daughter wants to join in too, once she gets used to us? Now their father's locked away and they're not frightened of being beaten, Judith's kids are blossoming. They love turning out the drawers and cupboards, though Kitty's not fond of spiders.'

'I'll ask Ros tomorrow if she wants the job.' Victor yawned suddenly and drained his glass. 'Sorry. It's been a long day.'

'Get up when you please. If you can't find anyone, just yell and someone will hear you. There will be food in the kitchen. We're working here, there and everywhere at the moment. One thing seems to lead to another.'

Victor turned at the door. 'Thanks for taking me on as a partner. You won't regret it.'

'I knew that or I'd not have asked you. I already know you're a good worker, and a good organiser, too. And you'll be the one who understands wood.'

'Wood carving was only my hobby.'

'And your father was a carpenter who taught his little son a lot about using wood for practical purposes.'

Victor shrugged and smiled. 'It's strange how Dad wanted me to do better than him and now, here I am, about to use what he taught me.'

'You'll be a godsend to us.'

'I hope so. When's Daniel coming?'

'Any day now. He didn't say exactly when. His marriage broke up, by the way.'

'We all guessed they weren't close. There will be quite a few couples who can't live together again, don't you think?

I've seen forecasts that the divorce rate will skyrocket as more people get demobbed.'

'There were a lot of hasty wartime marriages.'

'There were a lot of hasty love affairs too while men were away. An old friend of mine came home to find another man's child in his wife's arms.'

Mayne whistled softly. 'Is he going to divorce her?'

'She doesn't want to divorce, says it was a mad moment in wartime and he should forgive her. He's still thinking about it, but I expect he'll come round.' He yawned. 'Got to get to bed or I'll fall asleep with my head on the table.'

5

Mayne wished he and Judith were married, then he could have gone to bed and discussed his friend's arrival with Ros in tow. As it was, he had to wait until she and the children came down to breakfast, then chat to them all about other things for a while.

Eventually, after what seemed to him a long time, the children finished eating and went off to get ready to do the shopping for their mother.

Mayne smiled across the table at Judith. 'There's no sign of our guests yet, so let's have another cup of tea and a chat, my darling.'

'I'd like that.'

Mayne watched the children leave the house shortly afterwards to take some letters to the post. All three were so much happier now their father was locked away in prison and not able to thump them. Ben talked a lot about the twin half-brothers he had discovered, and about his paternal grandfather.

Mayne too liked the Crossley family, even Doug's real wife, Mary. There was something very direct and kind about Robert Crossley, and his twin grandsons obviously loved and respected him. They'd been kind to their half-brother and sisters – who were all suffering from the humiliation of finding out their parents hadn't been married – and wanted to get to know them.

Judith was making plans for the three children to travel into Manchester by train soon to pay their first visit to the family they'd not known about before. They could catch the early morning train, then he and Judith would meet them from the early evening train. She was nervous of letting them out of her sight, but was trying to hide that, so as not to spoil their enjoyment.

He admired Judith's fresh morning appearance. Her lack of make-up and shining hair appealed to him far more than Caroline's careful make-up. 'What do you think of the latest additions to our Esherwood inhabitants?'

'I like your friend Victor – as you said I would. From what you told me about Ros's stepfather cheating her, I feel she's had a raw deal so I'm happy to help her. I hope they can bring him to justice. I wonder if there's any of her money left?'

'I'll take her to see Sergeant Deemer and my lawyer later.'

Judith smiled. 'Leave that to Victor.'

Something in her tone made him stare at her. 'You think he's interested? But he's only just met her. And his wife died recently.'

'A wife who'd been ill for a long time and he was away for most of the past year. But have you seen the way he looks at Ros? I can't help noticing such things. Anyway, it's early days, just a possibility. We'll leave it to flower or not, as fate chooses.'

'Well, as long as she makes a complaint about what's happened. It's a shocking thing to do to anyone.'

'She loved her mother very much. I'd have been the same if it'd been my mother. I'd have happily given my last shilling to make her final days more comfortable.'

They heard the sound of footsteps on the servants' stairs and Mayne reluctantly let go of Judith's hand, turning to greet his friend with a smile. 'Did you sleep all right, Victor?'

'Like a very tired log, thank you.'

'Have you seen your daughter and Ros?'

'There was no sound from their room, so I thought it better to let them sleep on. I didn't like to go into the bedroom of a woman I hardly know.'

Judith stood up. 'I'll go and check on her later. Cup of tea? Breakfast?'

'Can you spare the food? I've brought our ration books, but we'll have to register when we find somewhere to live and—'

'You've found somewhere to live,' Mayne said. 'We've plenty of space, though it needs sorting out. And thank goodness the Army put in a full electrical system, so all floors are supplied with lighting and power sockets. The house was still old-fashioned before, with only electricity in the main rooms and kitchen. Not even in the bedrooms. The Army may have damaged the interior but they also added various amenities which I hope we can incorporate into our design, like extra bathrooms.'

'Well, I also know a fair bit about electricity, thanks to supervising a few projects at the camp where I used to work.'

'You know a fair bit about a lot of things.'

Victor shrugged. 'I like to work with my hands, and to learn. I'll pull my weight, I promise you.'

'I know.'

Judith produced some porridge with a small spoonful of honey to sweeten it and one of their precious raspberries sitting proudly in the middle.

'I haven't had a fresh raspberry for ages,' Victor said in delight. 'We didn't have any in our garden. I don't think anyone had made an effort to grow fresh vegetables. My wife's parents bought whatever they needed on the black market.'

'The kitchen garden here is starting to revive a little, now that men aren't tramping all over it,' Mayne said. 'Are you any good at gardening?'

'No. But I'm willing to learn if that's needed and the Army taught me to dig at least.'

Mayne pulled a wry face. 'Latrines.'

'Yes. And ditches for defensive purposes. You have no idea what us common soldiers went through.'

'You should have enrolled as an officer.'

'No. I couldn't have.'

'You're too soft-hearted.'

'Is that a bad fault?'

'Not at all.'

When Victor had finished, Judith cleared up quickly, then she and Mayne went back to work clearing out the office, while they waited for Ros and Betty to get up.

Ros woke with a start, not knowing for a moment where she was. The sun was shining through an uncurtained window, showing a large bedroom with furniture heaped up to one side. She jerked upright in the narrow bed. Where on earth was she?

When she saw a child asleep on a nearby bed, she felt reassured that she was safe, and suddenly remembered what had happened last night.

Her mother was dead.

As tears started to flow again, she tried to weep silently so as not to wake the child, scrubbing her face with the sheet and stifling her sobs. But she couldn't seem to stop weeping.

'What's wrong, Ros?'

She looked up to see Betty standing by her bed, looking worried. She patted it to encourage the child to sit down and somehow she at last managed to stop weeping. 'I found out last night while you were asleep that my mother had died and . . . he . . . no one had told me.'

A small hand patted hers. 'My mother died too. But she'd
been ill a long time and she told me she was dying. She said
I was to live with Daddy and that he loved me very much
– and he does. But I miss her a lot. We used to whisper our
secrets. I have no one to tell things to now.'

'You can talk to your father.'

'Grandma says men are always busy and we mustn't bother
them. My grandad only used to say hello and goodnight to
me. He never talked. Or listened. He didn't talk to Grandma
much, either. I didn't see her crying after he died, like you're
crying for your mother.'

'I'm sure your father will always make time to chat to
you.' Victor had even been kind to a complete stranger like
her. What a lovely man he was!

Another frown from the child, then, 'Didn't your mother
know she was dying? Didn't she tell you?'

'She only said she was ill. I haven't seen her for months
because I was serving in the Wrens. I was stationed in
Scotland, you see, and it was hard to get back.'

Betty patted her hand again, and the soft, warm touch of
the child was more comforting than anything else had been.
Ros twisted her hand to grasp Betty's.

'What should I call you? It isn't polite to call a grown-up
by her first name, but I don't remember your surname. And
are you Mrs or Miss?'

'My name's Ros Dawson. Just call me Ros.'

'All right. Where are we, Ros? I don't remember much
about last night.'

'We're in a big house called Esherwood, which belongs to
a friend of your father's. You were fast asleep when we arrived.
You didn't stir even when they lifted you in and out of the
car.'

The child wriggled suddenly. 'I think I'd better use the
bathroom. Where is it, please?'

'I'll show you. I'll use it after you and wash my face. I must look a right old mess.'

Betty studied her, head on one side. 'Your nose is a bit red and your eyes are swollen. I used to cry about Mother in bed, because Grandma said I wasn't allowed to cry. She didn't like me to laugh out loud, either, just smile politely.'

'Dear me. What's wrong with laughing?'

'She said it was common. But now Daddy's back, things will be better. He makes me laugh a lot. Can we go and find him after we've used the bathroom?'

'We should probably get dressed first. Let's see what you've got in your suitcase.'

When they were both ready, Betty slipped her hand into Ros's and it would be hard to say which of them was the more comforted by that.

That was how Victor saw them as he started up the stairs to check on them. They looked at ease with one another, like mother and daughter. He couldn't remember his mother-in-law ever holding Betty's hand, though Susan had. But not when her parents were around. She'd been frightened of them till the day she died, poor thing.

'There you are,' he said. 'You're a pair of sleeping beauties. Do you want something to eat?'

'Yes, please, Daddy. I'm famished.' Betty abandoned Ros's hand to run down the stairs and give her father a kiss, laughing when he lifted her up and swung her round.

By the time he'd put her down Ros had joined them.

'Is Ros going to stay here with us, Daddy?'

'I hope so.' He looked across at her. 'Perhaps we can talk about that after breakfast? If you're looking for a job, I have one going.'

Her smile banished the sadness from her face. She wasn't pretty but she looked healthy and strong, pleasant on the eye, not a hothouse flower but a worker.

'That'd be wonderful, Mr Travers. I've not got much money left now.'

'We could try to get some back for you from Cliff.'

'How can I prove I sent him money?'

'I heard him admit to that yesterday, and the woman he was with did too. But that might not be enough. It depends how you sent the money.'

'Postal orders.'

'Did you keep the stubs?'

'No. I threw them away when I was packing. Well, I think I did. In the end I stuffed what was left into my bag. I'll check when I unpack.'

'Perhaps the post office here will have a record of him cashing them.'

Her tone was bleak. 'Is it worth bothering? I was a trusting fool and I've paid a high price for that. I'll be a lot more careful about trusting people in future. Anyway, the thing that upsets me most isn't the money, but not having a chance to say goodbye to Mum.'

'I think it's worth bothering to report him to the police, Ros. The way he used a dead woman as an excuse for taking your money absolutely sickens me. I think you should try to get what you can back. And maybe he'll think twice before cheating someone else if the police are involved.'

She swallowed hard, but nodded. 'It sickens me, too. I don't know what my mother ever saw in him.'

'Maybe he was different with her.'

'Or maybe she couldn't face life on her own. She was very dependent on my father.' Ros looked round and changed the subject firmly. 'Anyway, we'll sort it all out. This house must have been beautiful before they damaged it.'

'I never saw it then. I only met Mayne in the Army and had never been here till yesterday.' He gestured towards the door at the rear of the battered hall. 'There's something to eat in the kitchen.'

'Your friend's very kind to take me in.'

'He is. But he's shrewd and a good organiser as well, so I think he'll do well in business. I enjoyed working with him in the Army and I'm looking forward to working with him again on a more equal footing.'

When Ros and Betty had finished eating, Victor turned to his daughter. 'Darling, would you like to go and play in the garden for a few minutes while I talk to Ros? Don't go out of sight of the house.' He held out a skipping rope. 'I found this. You might know what to do with it.'

'I'm not very good at skipping. Grandma said it was un-ladylike.'

'Grandma was wrong. And practice makes perfect.'

'You won't go away and leave me?'

'Of course not. You and I are both here to stay. I'll keep watch on you from the kitchen window.'

She looked at him solemnly. 'Grandma will send someone after us, you know. She gets angry when people don't do what she tells them and she does unkind things to them. I don't want to go back to her ever again.'

He and Ros shared a quick, startled glance at that, then he said firmly, 'I won't let her take you away from me. And I'm not afraid of her.'

'You should be. Even Grandfather used to do as she told him when her voice got all sharp and angry.'

'Well, I don't do as anyone tells me unless I agree with it. Anyway, she won't know where we are.' Then he remembered some correspondence from Mayne. He'd stuffed it into a drawer, but if someone had searched the house . . . No, surely even Mrs Galton wouldn't have done that?

Betty studied his face as if trying to work out whether he

meant it, so he kept his doubts to himself. He waved one hand towards the door and she went outside, unrolling the skipping rope from the wooden handles. From the way she tried it out, it was obvious to the two adults watching her that she hadn't had much chance to practise.

Victor's voice was harsh with anger. 'That child is going to learn to play like other children. And I'm not letting her grow up afraid all the time. Look how close to the house she's stayed.'

Ros came closer to the window. 'She seems hungry for attention.'

'Yes. And she's going to get it, too. That woman has a lot to answer for. I'd run away to Australia rather than let her take Betty away from me, even if a court decided in her favour.'

'Surely they won't do that?'

'I doubt it.' He stared out of the window again, his brow furrowed in thought.

Ros waited a moment or two then prompted, 'You said something about a job. What exactly as?'

'There's definitely a job going, but it's hard to give it a name. I was talking to Mayne and he says we should call it a "general factotum" rather than a housekeeper or nanny, because we can't be sure exactly what will need doing.'

He gestured around them. 'To put you in the picture, four of us are intending to start up a building business. We'll begin by transforming this house into flats and selling them, then perhaps build houses in the grounds. You know how short people are of places to live since the war.'

'Don't Mayne and his family want to live here? My mother always said there had been Eshers at the big house for over a hundred years.'

'He'd like to live here, of course he would, but he can't

afford it. All he can do is save the old house from being totally demolished and probably buy one of the flats.'

'Oh. I see. How sad for him.'

'Anyway, back to your job: obviously, I need a woman to look after Betty, but she'll be at school in the daytime for another week or two. As they didn't have too many evacuee children sent to Rivenshaw, because of it being fairly close to Manchester, Judith says they didn't need to hold morning school for locals and afternoon school for newcomers, to fit them all in.'

Ros sighed. 'There's a whole generation of children whose education has been disrupted. You wonder if they'll ever catch up. Anyway, tell me more about the job. It'll be the school holidays by the end of the month, so she'll need looking after all the time then.'

'It looks like several of us will be living here, because Mayne says we should muck in together, so there will be other people and children around and I doubt you'll have to be with Betty all the time. Apart from there being a shortage of houses to rent, this place is free and we're on the spot to get things started.'

'Well, I'm quite used to living in groups after my time in the forces, so that's fine by me.'

'Did you enjoy being in the Wrens?'

'I enjoyed some parts of the job, not all. And you? How was the Army?'

'The same. I started as an ordinary soldier because I refused to order men to their deaths. But somehow I got into the training side of things and they persuaded me to move up the ladder to sergeant. I was happy enough doing that. I felt I had a skill for preparing those lads for combat.' He grinned. 'And I found out I have a very loud voice when I need it. That came in useful.'

'They shouted at us too when we were training.'

'They were also building new accommodation at the training camp, and I found myself supervising that a lot of the time. I enjoy working with my hands. 'He smiled down at them. 'And then I got transferred to the same unit as Mayne. Hush-hush behind the scenes stuff. I enjoyed that most of all, because I felt truly useful in working to end the war.'

They both fell silent. Memories hit you in unexpected ways, Victor thought, picturing some of the lads he knew who had been killed; some of the things he'd done. Then he realised she was waiting for him to go on. 'Anyway, what it boils down to is a job where you'd have to do whatever was needed. We'll give you board and keep, and I'll pay you whatever you consider a decent wage on top of that.'

'Whatever *I* consider right?' she asked in surprise.

'Yes. You can discuss a suitable wage with Judith, who is Mayne's assistant. I want you to be happy with us.' He waited, watching Ros bite the corner of her mouth and frown. When she didn't speak, he asked, 'Well . . . will you consider it?'

'I'll take it, please. It sounds interesting and I hate being bored. When I woke this morning, my first thought was that I'd not impose on you and leave Rivenshaw as soon as I could. But I'd have changed my mind even without your offer. I want to see my mother's grave, put flowers on it from time to time.'

'And you'll need to chat to her,' he added softly. 'That can be a great comfort. I used to visit my parents' graves and hold long conversations with them. Not my wife's grave, though. Her mother insisted on burying her in the family mausoleum and the place gives me the shivers. I can't seem to reach her in there. Besides, I have Susan with me still in one sense.' He gestured outside. 'Betty.'

'She's a delightful child.'

'I think so. Thanks to the war, I don't know her as well as I'd like, but she talks to me, and I listen, so we're both making progress.'

'What are your business partners like? I was too upset to notice much about Mayne, last night, and I've never spoken to him before, just seen him around town.'

'He's a strong personality, can stand up to anyone, and has a brilliant memory. He's the best of us at organising things. He'll be the majority shareholder by a long way, because he's contributing the house and land, but I have enough money to buy a small share. Daniel O'Brien should be joining us soon. He's an architect. I was a lawyer, but my father was a carpenter, so I grew up around tools and working with wood.'

'What sort of a lawyer?'

'Not one who dealt with rich people, to my in-laws' disgust. I preferred to help poorer people who needed justice.'

'That sounds a very worthwhile thing to do.'

He grinned. 'And you know what? I made enough money to live comfortably if not richly, because several people who'd won their cases were grateful and paid the proper fees bit by bit. Then a couple of people who didn't have close relatives left me their life savings, after which my old uncle died and left me his house. It's in the south and I'll probably sell it, but it's been rented out all through the war.'

'You've done well.'

'I like to think so. And I've done it without being greedy.'

'How did you meet your wife?'

'She was helping at a charity I was interested in. If they'd known she'd fall in love with a man who didn't have the right background, my in-laws would have locked her in their cellar, but charity work was a good thing to do socially. It was all appearances with them.'

'Go on.'

'Susan insisted on us running away to get married by special licence as soon as she turned twenty-one. She was right to insist. If we hadn't done, and we'd had banns called for three Sundays in church, they'd have found a way to stop us. I'm sure they looked into making the marriage void, but by that time Betty was on the way, so they had to make the best of it. And we'd never have agreed to split up, either.'

Ros smiled sympathetically. 'But you and Susan were happy together?'

'It would have been impossible not to get on with her. She was a gentle soul, but with a delightful sense of the ridiculous when she was away from her parents. Everyone liked her . . . and felt sorry for her.'

He hadn't actually said they'd been happy together as a married couple, Ros noticed. Had he found his wife too weak? Or had her parents spoiled their relationship? Well, that wasn't her business. 'And the fourth man?'

'Francis's family used to own a garage on the outskirts of London, but it was destroyed in an air raid, and his parents were killed by the same bomb. Francis is brilliant with vehicles – well, with any sort of machinery. I don't know him as well as the others. It was Mayne he knew. What did you do in the Wrens?'

'I was a driver, drove a staff car as needed or delivered vehicles sometimes right across country. I enjoyed that.'

'You can drive? Now that will be very useful in a general factotum.'

He smiled at her, such an open, friendly smile that she felt a twitch of attraction. Which was wrong with a man so recently widowed, but he need never know how she felt. 'What about Judith? How does she fit in?'

He hesitated, but Ros would find it easier if she knew how things stood between Mayne and Judith.

She listened carefully to his explanation. 'How terrible for her! I'll tread carefully, I promise you.'

'I'm sure you will. What I want – what all four of us want – is to help make a better post-war world. And if that sounds idealistic, well, there you are.'

'It's not idealistic. There will be a lot of renewal of all sorts going on, won't there? Rebuilding sounds wonderful to me, Victor.'

'We don't want to build for rich people, but not for poor people either, because we have to sell the flats and later on, houses, to stay in business. And we want these flats to have every modern amenity, so that the housewives' lives will be easier, like they do in the prefabs that have been designed.'

He gestured round them, as if seeing the new flats not the damage and general shabbiness of the old house. 'Take kitchens as an example. A modern housewife's work needn't be as hard physically or take as long as her mother's did. You should hear Francis talk about the new electrical appliances they're making in America nowadays. I'm interested in the uses of electricity, too.'

He hardly paused for breath, his enthusiasm carrying him along. 'Labour-saving machines like electric washing machines will be used more and more, so that will affect house design. There will need to be a space for them in the kitchens. Refrigerators too. There will be proper electricity everywhere in the home. We don't want people having to plug gadgets like irons into light fittings, as they did when these things were first produced.'

Ros was fascinated by the information he was sharing. 'That sounds like a wonderful project. I promise I'll work very hard at anything you ask me to do. I don't mind getting my hands dirty – or keeping them clean, for that matter.'

She held them out. They weren't beautiful, too square for

that. They were strong hands, the nails cut short, no rings on them. They'd clearly worked hard, her hands had. He respected that.

'I'll have to think about the pay, though, Victor. I'd much rather you suggested some amount you think suitable.'

'We'll ask Mayne and Judith. They're both very practical.'

He held out one hand and she shook it, surprised at him making this gesture for sealing a bargain, a gesture unusual between a man and a woman.

He didn't let go immediately and a frisson ran through her as she looked down at their linked hands. He was staring down too, as if a similar reaction to her touch had taken him by surprise. His hand was warm and firm, and the fingers were long and surprisingly elegant for a man.

When he let go, he gave her a thoughtful look, and she wondered what he was thinking. She'd enjoyed her busy life in the Wrens, but though she was looking forward to building a new peacetime life, she was also a little apprehensive, especially after yesterday's discovery about her mother's death. Standing on your own feet was one thing; having no one to confide in, no one to touch, or turn to . . . well, it was not only lonely; it was frightening sometimes.

She changed the subject, trying to banish the sudden tension between them. It was too soon to have reactions like that towards a man she'd only met the day before. She'd never fallen in love, she didn't know why, and this wasn't the time to dip her toe in that water, and certainly not with an employer. 'Can we look round the rest of the house? If I'm going to stay here, I should know what it's like.'

He moved further away. 'Yes. I'll call Betty in. I'm sure she'll want to come with us. Oh! Just one other thing. Will you be all right continuing to share a bedroom with her? And I'd better warn you: since we need to clear out all the rooms before we start preparations for the modifications, we're all likely to be moving from one bedroom to another as we make progress round the house.'

Ros couldn't help laughing. 'I've been sharing rooms with three or more other women for most of the war, and moving about regularly. I'll be fine with one child in the same room. More than fine when that child is Betty. Having an indoor lavatory and bathroom just along the corridor will be a luxury to me. I shall appreciate that, too.'

He hesitated. 'All right. But later, I think you should go to the police station and report your stepfather for fraud.'

'I suppose so.'

'Would you like me to come with you?'

'Yes, please. If you have time.'

'I always have time to help my friends.'

And there she went again, feeling as if he really cared about her. She was being very foolish.

Betty came running the minute her father called her, the skipping rope trailing, so that she tripped and nearly fell.

'Careful!' Victor called.

She immediately looked guilty. 'Sorry Daddy, I didn't mean to run.'

'I'm not angry about you running. I didn't want you to fall and hurt yourself. As far as I'm concerned, children should run about, or else how will they grow up strong and healthy? I called you in because we're going to look round the rest of the house and I thought you might like to come with us.'

'Ooh, yes please!'

They watched her coil up the skipping rope round the wooden handles and set it neatly on a shelf, then she came and slipped her hand trustingly into her father's. She'd asked whether that was allowed when he first came home and he'd been shocked that she felt the need to ask. Once he'd assured her he enjoyed it, she did it whenever she could, though she hadn't done it, he'd noticed, when her grandmother was there.

They found Judith and Mayne still clearing out his office.

He waved them inside. 'We've found a pile of old family photographs. Look at the stiff, high collars the men were wearing.'

'And the corsets the women are crammed into,' Judith added. 'No one could have such a tiny waist naturally.'

Victor explained what they wanted to do and Mayne waved him on. 'Go anywhere you like. And if either of you gets an idea about the conversion, small or large, don't hesitate to share it. I have to go into town to the bank. Maybe after I get back, we can all gather in the kitchen and decide what jobs to tackle and in what order?'

'That'd be good, but Ros and I have to go to the police station first to report her stepfather's thefts. Have you heard from Daniel yet?'

'No. You know what he's like. He'll probably turn up without warning one day, full of excitement about some buildings he's been looking at.'

'What about Francis?'

'He's not been in touch since he went home. I'm a bit worried about him, actually. We can manage without him investing his money, but things will be rather tight and it'll slow the work down.'

'It's strange that he's not replied,' Victor said. 'He was very enthusiastic last time I saw him.'

'Oh, well, nothing we can do at the moment.'

6

Mayne's business at the bank was soon completed and he walked outside, pausing for a moment to raise his face to the mild warmth of the sun.

That was enough time for someone to move in front of him, barring his way.

Caroline!

This was the second time she'd accosted him in town. He stepped sideways but she was ready and moved so quickly she managed to stay in front of him. He resigned himself to an exchange of some sort, but he didn't intend it to be prolonged or pleasant. It seemed to be taking a lot to discourage her from pursuing him.

'What do you want?' he snapped, pleased to see her blink in shock at his tone.

'Just a chance to see you. Mayne dear, can't we become friends again? We used to mean so much to one another.'

'I'm not your "dear", and I have no interest in seeing you again, Caroline.'

'But we were so close once.'

'And never will be again. You dropped me for a richer man, remember?'

'Well, that was a mistake, as I soon realised. Surely we can—'

'Hasn't my mother told you I'm not free?'

Caroline lost control of her smile for a moment, then shrugged. 'Your mother mentioned that common female who's got her claws into you, yes. But she's sure your infatuation will soon fade when you see what people think now that the creature's past has been revealed. Your mother's telling everyone that.'

He stared at her, alarm bells ringing in his mind. Surely his own mother wouldn't attempt to blacken Judith's name in order to sabotage his relationship?

Caroline gave him a knowing smile. 'Poor Dorothy is worried about you.'

His mother cared nothing for his feelings, he was sure. Her only concern was the Eshers' social position and that tired old phrase: keeping up standards. 'I don't choose a wife to suit my mother.'

Caroline's smile slipped a little. 'You're an Esher. You owe something to your family. Surely you wouldn't marry someone who's been involved in a scandal like that! The woman's been living in sin.'

'No, she hasn't. As far as Judith knew, she was legally married. She's done nothing wrong and never would.'

The smile vanished completely. 'You *are* serious about her. Your voice softens when you say her name.'

'Very serious indeed,' he agreed.

'Well, you might like to think about your parents before you let her ruin their life. And it wouldn't look good for your business to be associated with the Crossley whore, either.'

He couldn't speak for shock at the viciousness of this last remark, and was tempted to slap Caroline's face for that crude and unnecessary insult. He waited till he'd calmed down a little before saying slowly and clearly, 'Nothing you and my mother say or do will make me change my mind about Judith. Even less will such a remark make me associate with you again, Caroline. You disgust me.'

She glared at him. 'Oh, I think you'll feel differently about it all when you see how the woman is ostracised. People of our class will make sure you regret it if you marry her, believe me. And that she regrets it too. Her and her bastard children.'

A voice from behind them said suddenly, 'That's a dangerous threat to make in public, missus.'

Mr Woollard stepped out from the doorway of the bank and joined them.

Mayne stiffened. Woollard was one of the richest men in town. He'd wanted to buy Esherwood at a knock-down price but Mayne's father had refused and transferred the estate to his son. What was Woollard up to now? Would he join Caroline in threatening the woman Mayne loved?'

He felt sick at the thought of what Judith might suffer. And he was terrified she might refuse to marry him because she didn't want to hurt him. She was already worrying about that, he knew. Only he wouldn't let her go, couldn't bear to lose her.

The older man looked sideways at him. 'Whatever else I've done in my life, I've never threatened innocent women and children, Esher, and I won't condone others doing it, either. So if this woman tries to start any rumours about Mrs Maskell, I'll be happy to support you and that lady by telling people what I overheard today.'

Mayne was astonished not only at the words, but at the sincerity ringing in the other man's voice.

Woollard turned back to Caroline. 'You'd be doing yourself a disservice crossing me in this town, missus. A greater disservice than you realise. Unlike this gentleman, I've come up the hard way, and I'd have no scruples whatsoever about dealing with you. And if I want something – or don't want it – I do whatever is necessary.'

For a few moments her eyes challenged his, then she gave

him one of the looks she employed to attract men. 'Oh, surely you wouldn't hurt me, Mr Woollard? After all, Mayne's mother and I are only trying to save him from making a very big mistake.'

'Don't bat your eyelashes at me, missus. It won't work. I know your type. Upper class whores. Fur coats and no knickers, my mother always used to say.'

Caroline gasped and took a quick step away from him, her voice throbbing with outrage. 'How dare you speak to me like that?'

'I speak as I find. If you start slandering an innocent woman, who's been badly treated through no fault of her own, I shall definitely speak out in her support. And if he takes my advice, Mr Esher will take you to court if you ever do it again. Slander is a serious crime. There are big fines or even imprisonment if someone is found guilty, I'm told.'

After gazing at him in shock, Caroline swung round and marched away, heels tapping loudly on the pavement, back rigid.

He called after her, 'Remember, I heard what you said, missus. From now on, I'll be watching what you do.'

When she'd turned the corner, he winked at Mayne. 'I think that's got her worried.'

Mayne was so stunned at Woollard's support he couldn't work out what to say or do next.

The older man scowled after Caroline. 'She's bad news, that one. I despise women like her. I meant what I said. She's a whore at heart, going after money, not caring who she hurts. My missus is worth a dozen of her, and she speaks well of that young woman you're interested in. Good judge of character, my missus. I always listen to her where women are concerned.'

'Well, I'm extremely grateful to you for stepping in today.' Though he wished it had been someone else who'd helped him. He didn't like to be obligated to a man who had done anything and everything to make money, even including acting as a fence for stolen goods.

Woollard waved one hand dismissively. 'That's all right. Now, have you got time for a bit of a chat about something else?'

Mayne's heart sank. His companion might have spiked Caroline's guns for the moment, because Ray Woollard was definitely not the sort of man to cross, everyone knew that. But what did he want to chat about? Better to find out. 'Yes. Of course I've got time.'

'We'll go to my office. I'm not stupid enough to discuss private matters in public.'

Feeling apprehensive, Mayne turned and walked down the street with him. He was sure Woollard would want some sort of favour in return for silencing Caroline. Only what?

And would any threats silence his mother's vitriol about Judith? He didn't think so. She was made of sterner stuff than his ex-fiancée. She'd been acting strangely for a while, though, refusing to pay attention to what his father wanted, seeming . . . Well, it was hard to put a finger on it. Distant and preoccupied was the best he could say to describe her recent behaviour.

Reginald Esher heard the front doorbell and sighed in irritation. His wife was lying down with one of her sick headaches, so he'd have to answer it. He brightened up at the thought that it might be the parcel he was expecting from the bookshop he patronised in Manchester, so hurried downstairs.

He sighed again as he opened the door. Caroline McNulty was standing there, looking flushed and angry.

'Is Mrs Esher in?'

'My wife's not well. She's lying down.'

'Oh. It's rather important that I see her.'

He stared at her, seeing the anger glittering in her eyes. He didn't like this young woman and she was up to something, he was sure. It might be worth finding out what exactly she wanted. If it involved his wife, it might involve him or his son as well. Dorothy was still angry at them both for not selling the big house.

'I was just about to have a cup of tea. You can come in and wait, if you like. My wife went to lie down half an hour ago. She'll either get up within an hour, headache better, or fall asleep and be seen no more till morning.' He watched Caroline frown and debate this.

'It really is important. I'd better come in.' She seemed to realise this wasn't a very polite way of accepting his offer of refreshment and gave him a brilliant smile which faded as quickly as it'd appeared.

She looked pretty when she smiled, he supposed, but the smile didn't reach her eyes. What had upset her so much? And why had that brought her to see his wife? If she and Dorothy were plotting something, he wanted to know. It was hard to talk to Dorothy these days because she spent a lot of time staring blankly into space.

He led the way into the kitchen and put the kettle on, then looked round for the tea-making things, not used to entertaining their visitors.

She watched him fumble in cupboards for a moment, then moved forward. 'Shall I make the tea? I've been here before, so I know where things are kept.'

'Yes, please. I'm not very good at that sort of thing.'

'But you're famous for your historical research, aren't you? That's much more important.'

Flattery, he thought. What does this dull-brained creature know about history or its value? He began to tell her about his research, amused to see her eyes glaze over with boredom.

When he'd finished his cup of tea, he heard someone stirring upstairs. Casually, he went to open the window. 'What a lovely day! Let's have some fresh air in the house.'

Footsteps crossed the upstairs landing. 'Ah. You're in luck. My wife's headache must have gone or she'd not be getting up.'

'Oh, good.'

The relief in the visitor's voice wasn't feigned, unlike her show of interest in what he'd been telling her.

He waited till Dorothy came down, intercepting her in the hall to tell her she had a guest. When he said who it was, she brightened, so he left her to it.

Upstairs in his study, he opened the window and listened. Yes. On such a fine, still day you could hear what was being said in the room below quite clearly.

He intended to find out what Dorothy was up to. He'd always enjoyed solving puzzles.

After a few paces, Woollard chuckled. 'I'd rather you didn't look as though you were being taken out to be hanged, Esher.'

Mayne couldn't help smiling. 'Is that what I look like?'

'Oh, yes. I promise you won't regret speaking to me today, though.'

He wasn't so sure about that but tried not to let his feelings show.

Woollard chuckled. 'You'd never make an actor, and don't try to bluff anyone at cards, either. You wouldn't succeed.'

'I've already found that out.'

'Luckily we're here now so you can stop pretending you're happy to be with me.' Woollard led the way inside. 'I've moved here recently.'

Mayne looked round. The office was situated in the old Cathmore house, just off the main square of Rivenshaw, but the outside had changed greatly since the days he visited the family to play with Tommy Cathmore, who had been killed in '41, poor fellow. What a long time ago those days seemed now. It had been a long, weary war.

Workmen were painting the outside of the window frames. How had Woollard got hold of the paint? Like everything else, it was strictly rationed and scarce.

Woollard's voice was surprisingly gentle. 'Was young Cathmore a friend of yours?'

'Yes.'

'His sister inherited this house, but she sold it to me and went to live down south. She's married with two children. The husband came home badly injured, so they're living near his family.'

'She's younger than me. How dreadful for her!'

Woollard looked genuinely sad. 'Yes. We lost a lot of good people during the war and their families are still suffering. One of my nephews bought it. He was serving as a pilot in the RAF. They didn't last long in that job.'

He fell silent for a moment then brightened. 'It doesn't do to brood, though. Another nephew arrived a week or two ago. At least Irwin got through the war OK. He only stayed with us a day or two because he wanted to visit the families of two friends. I offered him a place in my business and he's thinking about it.'

'He got demobbed quickly.'

'He saw some nasty stuff and has a lot of trouble sleeping. They said he'd get better more quickly out of the Army and, anyway, he was keeping everyone in the barracks awake with his nightmares. I hope they're right and he will get over it.'

Mayne was surprised at these confidences. Was this their local war profiteer speaking?

Woollard gave him a sudden urchin's grin. 'I do care about other things than money, Esher. Family is the most important one to me. The missus and I never had kids, unfortunately, but I keep an eye on my brothers and sisters and their offspring . . . whether they want me to or not. I'm out of black market dealing now, you know. Which doesn't stop me trying to drive the best bargain when I buy or sell something.'

He went across to the nearest door and poked his head inside. 'Could Mr Esher and I have a cup of tea, Miss Tamlin, please?'

'Yes, sir. And some of your favourite biscuits?'

'Of course.'

Woollard had, Mayne noticed, spoken in a friendly tone to his secretary, who had sounded to be teasing him in her reply. He'd have expected this man to bark out orders, which just went to show that you could never tell exactly how people would behave and react, something he usually tried to bear in mind. He found this more difficult with Woollard, though.

The office was large with a bay window. It had been the living room in the old days, Mayne remembered. Things hadn't changed as much inside the house, and this was still more like a living room than a place of business. He had some happy memories of taking tea here, or having a sing-song round the piano. Tommy had been a good pianist, able to play anything by ear.

'We'll sit in comfort, eh?' Woollard gestured to an armchair.

'You bought their furniture as well.'

'Yes. The lady didn't want it and you know how hard it is to get new furniture, even for me.' He adjusted a cushion behind his back, waited till his guest was seated, then said bluntly, 'I gather you're setting up a building company to convert Esherwood into flats.'

Damnation! Who else knew about the flats? Most people thought he was going to build houses on the spare land, and he was content to let them believe that. 'Yes, I am. But I'd be grateful if you'd keep any details of what I'm doing to yourself.'

'Of course I will. It's a good idea. Perfect time to get into that sort of business.'

'We think so.'

'I know you've got friends coming into the project with you. What I asked you to come here for was to say I'd like to join you as well. I have money to invest and you might find it useful to have a little extra in the kitty.'

Mayne stiffened. 'I don't wish to offend you, but I doubt you and I could work together. We have . . . well, different views about how to do things.'

'What I did when making my way in the world was very different from how I shall be doing things now the war is over. I don't need to work another day if I don't want to, but I'd go mad with nothing to do, so I'm not retiring. I'm just working less, and changing what I do.' He chuckled. 'Turning fully legal, you might say, though I'll deny I admitted that to you.'

'That still doesn't explain why you want to buy into our particular company.'

'Because I think you're clever enough to make a success of it and because it sounds an interesting project. Frankly, it'd also do me and the missus good socially to be associated with an Esher, but that's not the main reason. I like to keep this busy.' He tapped his forehead to indicate his brain.

Mayne opened his mouth to refuse, but Woollard held up one hand.

'I can add a lot to your business on the supply side, and I'd make a fair profit on supplying you with materials, even at prices you'll find lower than most others. I have some useful connections.'

Mayne decided to be equally blunt. 'You'd try to take over, if we allowed you in.'

'Nay, I don't have the sort of mind to design housing, though my wife might take an interest in the kitchens and that sort of thing. You won't believe what she's planning for our house now the war's over. No, my main skill is supplying what's needed and knowing what to pay for it and what to sell it for, which is why I did well in the black market.'

'You're being very frank about your past.'

'Only between the two of us and only inside this office. I'm a lot more careful with what I say in front of other people than that silly young madam who was threatening you.'

He held up one hand as Mayne opened his mouth. 'No need to give me an answer now. In fact, I'd rather you didn't even try, because you might say no. If you think about it, you'll probably see that you and your partners would be foolish to spurn an offer of friendship from a man with my connections.'

'An offer of friendship?'

Woollard shrugged. 'Well, I wouldn't be joining you as an enemy, now would I?'

The other man wasn't as indifferent to this aspect as he was pretending, Mayne guessed. His own mind was racing. If Woollard was telling the truth about how he wanted to be involved, he might indeed be a useful partner. But his past still stuck in Mayne's gullet. He tried to speak tactfully. 'I couldn't do anything as important as taking on a new investor without having a very good think about it. And of course, I'd have to consult my partners. We hadn't planned for anyone else, you see, just the four of us.'

Another pause, then he added, 'I'm putting up the house and land, and some of the capital, and I'm keeping an absolute majority share, whoever joins us.'

'Don't blame you.'

'You don't?'

'Eh, get it out of your head that I'm the enemy, lad.'

Mayne shook his head slightly, still surprised at this conversation. 'You should know that it's very important to me to do this right. I may not be able to keep Esherwood in the family, but I can still preserve the house itself.'

'I didn't realise how much you loved it till I tried to buy it, because the way your mother talks about it, it's nothing but a liability. I don't usually make mistakes that big.'

They looked at one another, each assessing the potential of a business relationship.

'I will think about what you've offered, Mr Woollard, and I'll go as far as to say that I'm not rejecting your offer out of hand because I can see your connections might be useful to us. But I'm not rushing into anything, either. Let's leave it at that for the moment.'

'Fair enough, lad.'

The secretary arrived with a tea tray, which included a lavish display of fancy biscuits, of the sort popular with moneyed people before the war. Mayne's mouth watered and he couldn't resist eating a couple. How long was it since he'd had luxury foods like these?

He tried to think of something else to talk about, but it was Woollard who led the conversation, asking him about his wartime experiences and proving to be an intelligent listener.

Strange how peace seemed to be turning everything upside down, Mayne thought as he walked away from the office.

Was he really thinking of working with Woollard?

Could he forget what the older man had done in the past? He shook his head as he thought about it. He wasn't sure, would have to talk to his partners.

7

After an early midday meal, everyone gathered in the library to discuss the best way of going through the contents of the house and preparing it for conversion into flats. Every cupboard in the place seemed crammed with objects: some sentimental junk, some valuable. And in addition to the possessions gathered by the family were piles of things, some unused, left by the Army. It was hard to know where to start.

Ros said she was happy to wait until later to report her stepfather to the police. Victor was surprised at how reluctant she was to do that, given how much the fellow had hurt and robbed her. He was determined to change her mind, but didn't know her well enough yet to know how best to do that.

They were surrounded by chaos, with boxes piled round the edges of most rooms, contents unknown, mounds of books here and there, tossed out of the family library, and odd items of furniture, antiques and new metal-framed stuff, mingled. Some of the antiques were probably valuable, except the pieces that had been damaged, both recently and in the distant past, and who knew with those?

Ros found some children's books heaped haphazardly in one corner and suggested that Betty sort them out, straighten the pages and put them on one of the remaining arrays of shelves, instead of the floor.

'Can you separate the ones for older and younger children, do you think?'

The little girl beamed at her. 'Yes. I like reading. I can tell which are which.'

Victor watched without comment, surprised at how easily Ros seemed to manage Betty and find activities that pleased the child. He'd seen the two of them chatting quietly, and his daughter had looked at ease. Ros would one day make a good mother for some lucky children, he was sure. Even Susan, much as she'd loved her little daughter, hadn't been this good with Betty.

He wondered why Ros had never married. She might not be pretty but she was reasonably attractive with a kind nature. He abandoned that line of speculation and turned to listen as Mayne starting the ball rolling.

'Judith has suggested we hold an auction of surplus items, which is a good idea, don't you think? We could start by selling some of the less valuable items. Extra money is always useful, and that will also clear space for when we start work on the building.'

He added one simple question that got them going, something Victor had seen him do before. 'So how do you think we should start?'

'Before we do anything, we shall have to form some idea of what we might need in the future,' Victor pointed out. 'It'd be terrible to get rid of things and then need them, especially with all the shortages.'

'You're right. But that's not going to be easy, so let's concentrate on the clearing out and, if in doubt, we'll set aside any items we think may come in useful.'

At first Ros seemed reluctant to speak, but when Victor saw her open her mouth, then hesitate and close it again, he nudged Mayne, who said, 'Ros, you look as if you've thought of something. Don't hesitate to comment. You are, after all, now on the payroll . . . even if we haven't decided how much to pay you yet.'

After the ripple of laughter died down, she said, 'Why don't we work through the house downwards so that goods and mess aren't moving through clean areas?'

'Good idea!' Mayne said and everyone murmured agreement.

Judith extended the suggestion. 'Mayne needs to go through the attics before we clear them, because he has family possessions up there. In the meantime, the third floor, where the nurseries once were, is the part of the house most untouched during the occupation by the Army. Once we've cleared that floor, we can all move up there and then clear the second floor, where we're sleeping now.'

There was silence, with everyone looking at Mayne.

'Brilliant. Straightforward and yet logical. Well done, Ros and Judith. I think, Victor, we have two clever women here.'

Mayne smiled at Judith as he said her name. If his love for her was obvious, he didn't care. They were among friends here and he already counted Ros an ally if not yet a friend. She was very different from Victor's wife, being tall and looking fit and strong, presumably after her years in the Wrens.

He was beginning to wonder if something might be brewing between the two of them. He hoped so. He could see that Victor found Ros very attractive. His friend hadn't really had a marriage for a long time. Susan had been an invalid and too timid to break away from her parents. That had come between them at times, he knew. He did hope Victor would find a proper marriage partner and the happiness that could bring.

Mayne didn't mention the family valuables stored in the two secret rooms – one of which was in the attic, one in the cellar. He needed to think what to do with those. He had no idea what the paintings were worth but some of them were exquisite, and there were all sorts of smaller items stored there, including family jewellery and silver.

He saw Judith looking at him and shook his head slightly to remind her to keep this information to herself. She knew about the secret room in the attic, because she and the children had hidden there from her violent so-called husband when a former magistrate, now retired thank goodness, was trying to force her and the children to go back to a life of being ill-treated by Doug Crossley.

'I think it'd help to have a quick walk round the third floor,' he said. 'I've only glanced at it briefly.'

Betty asked if she could stay in the library and Victor nodded permission.

It took longer than expected to look round the third floor and Judith suddenly realised her children were due home from school. 'I'd better go down and get a snack ready. That boy of mine is a stomach on wheels.'

Ros went down to the library at the same time to find Betty, but the child wasn't there. She checked the kitchen, but Judith hadn't seen her.

Suddenly Ros felt anxious and ran round the rest of the ground floor, calling Betty's name. There was no answer and that wasn't like Betty.

By that time, the men had heard her calling and come running down to join in the search.

'She'd not have left the house on her own,' Ros said. 'She's too afraid of her grandmother. She seems sure Mrs Galton will come after her.'

'Surely Mrs Galton can't have sent someone after us already?' Victor paused for a moment then answered his own question. 'I should have been more careful, not left Betty on her own. I'd not put anything past that woman.'

He looked towards the French window that led out into the garden. 'We shouldn't have left that open.'

'We'll search the grounds and—' Mayne was beginning when there was the sound of yelling and screaming from outside.

It sounded to be coming from the rear, so Victor ran out through the kitchen. The yells were coming from near the old stables, and now another voice joined them, a man's deep voice.

As they turned the corner, they saw Ben and Kitty struggling with a man who was holding Betty, while Gillian was in the grasp of a younger man who was keeping her from helping the others.

The two men were so busy fighting off the children they didn't see Victor and Mayne running towards them till they were only a few yards away.

Ros paused outside the kitchen door to look round for a weapon, but could only find a piece of crumbling wood lying in a corner. She picked that up and started running to help.

'Let go of my daughter, you!' Victor roared, recognising Barham, the man who worked for Mrs Galton. The younger man was the one who had been keeping watch on his former home.

'Daddy! Daddy!' Betty struggled even more wildly.

Victor reached Barham, but the man tried to hold Betty in front of him. Ben yanked his arm from the side and Kitty landed a kick on his shins. Roaring in pain, he let go of the child, but quickly took up a defensive position against Victor.

Mayne had targeted the other man, who waited until he got close to shove Gillian at him then turned to run away.

But Ros had joined them now and swung the piece of rotten wood at the would-be escaper's head. Most of it fell to pieces as it hit its target, but the core was solid enough to hurt him. Yelling in shock, he stumbled sideways and tripped.

Ros jumped on him and Judith followed suit, diving to hold his legs. This left the two men free to tackle Barham.

But he'd seen the women play an active part, and took everyone by surprise by shoving Ben aside and running away.

Victor hesitated. 'Let him go, Mayne. I know who he is.' He didn't want to leave his daughter unprotected.

Mayne went across to the two women, who were still struggling with the other man. 'Let him up.'

Before he was fully upright, Mayne grabbed his arm, twisting it behind his back, so that he couldn't escape. 'You can answer some questions for us!'

Ros and Judith were still standing on either side of the captive. The pain he experienced if he tried to move kept him still.

He looked terrified and younger than Victor had first thought.

'Into the kitchen, I think,' Mayne said. 'Ben, Betty's skipping rope is on a shelf near the kitchen door? Can you get it?'

'Yes.' He darted ahead of them, eager to help.

When the captive was tied to a chair, Mayne asked him what his name was.

He sat silent, a sullen look on his face.

'He's called John Peeby,' Betty said from the safety of her father's arms. 'And the other man's Mr Barham. He works for my grandmother. He collects rents and does other jobs, but I don't know what.'

'I can guess,' Victor said. 'Anything that's needed to bully people into doing as they're told.'

Mayne spoke sharply, 'What were you doing on my property, Peeby?'

Still their captive said nothing.

Mayne turned to Ben. 'I think you'd better fetch the police.'

'No, don't!' Peeby begged. 'Please don't.'

'Why not? You tried to kidnap a child and now you're refusing to answer questions. We have a little girl to protect, so we'll do whatever it takes.'

'I didn't want to do it, but I didn't dare refuse Mr Barham.'

'Didn't want to do what?'

Peeby hung his head. 'Kidnap her. Look, I've got family in the village.' He looked pleadingly at Victor. 'I'd help you if I could, Mr Travers, but if I say anything, Mum and Dad will be thrown out of their cottage. You know what Mrs Galton's like.'

'I think it'll have to be the police, then,' Mayne said. 'I'm sorry for you, Peeby, but we need to stop this.'

The young man slumped against the ropes, but didn't say anything else.

Mayne looked at his watch. 'Al and Jan should be here soon to keep watch. Once they arrive, I'll go and fetch Sergeant Deemer.'

'If he's not there, don't bring the constable,' Judith said quickly.

'No, Farrow is—' He broke off and glanced at Peeby, changing what he'd been going to say to, 'not as helpful. I know.'

Constable Farrow looked up as Mayne walked into the police station.

'I'd like to speak to Sergeant Deemer, please.'

'He's out. Can I help, Mr Esher?'

'No, I need your sergeant. Could I ask where he is? It's urgent.'

'He's out on police business.' Sounding reluctant, he added, 'He'll be back in a few minutes.'

'I'll wait, then.'

Ten minutes later the sergeant came in, whistling cheerfully. He stopped when he saw Mayne sitting on the hard wooden bench, arms folded, then looked questioningly at Farrow.

'Mr Esher wants to see you. I offered to help, but it was you he wanted.'

'It's something rather serious,' Mayne said.

'We'll go into my office, then. Farrow, I'm parched. How about a pot of tea? You'll join me, Mr Esher?'

Mayne hesitated. 'Perhaps refreshments could wait till after I've told you why I'm here?'

'Ah. Come straight in, then.' The sergeant led him behind the counter, closed the office door and gestured to a chair, before going to sit behind his desk.

Mayne opened his mouth to speak, then noticed a shadow showing under one side of the door. He put one finger to his lips and pointed it out to Deemer who glared at it and gestured to him to open the door.

Mayne stood up silently, took one quick step across to the door and yanked it open.

Farrow stumbled in.

'We will discuss this later and a report will be made on your record,' Deemer said. 'Now tell me why you were eavesdropping.'

Farrow edged from one foot to the other, looking uncomfortable, as well he might, Mayne thought.

'Or should I ask who is paying you to eavesdrop?' the sergeant guessed.

The younger man went pink and there was no mistaking the guilty expression on his face.

'It wouldn't be a certain lawyer, would it?'

The pink deepened to red and now there was a look of panic on Farrow's face.

'What was the reason Gilliot gave for doing it?' He waited but the constable said nothing.

'You're not leaving this room till you tell me.' Deemer thumped one clenched fist down on his desk and shouted, 'Why were you eavesdropping?'

'Patriotism.'

Both men gaped at him.

'How do you work that out?'

'You've already let a Jew stay in Rivenshaw. He'll bring others of his sort in and they'll take over the businesses in town.'

'Where the hell did you get that load of twaddle from?' Deemer snapped.

'Mr Gilliot said so. He said we had to protect our country. And he's a lawyer, so it isn't twaddle,' Farrow said obstinately.

'I'm presuming you're talking about Mr Borkowski. I think you'd better start reading the rules of your job again. And from now on, you should remember that you aren't answerable to Gilliot, but to me! If I catch you eavesdropping or spouting such nasty rubbish when you're on duty, I'll see you're cautioned about it officially – which can lead to dismissal.'

He took a deep breath and continued, still loudly and emphatically, 'You were told when you joined the police force that it's not for us to decide what is legal and what isn't. It's the politicians who make the laws, not you and not even a lawyer like Gilliot. Mr Borkowski has a legal right to stay in England and he is not to be harassed. Don't you ever forget that again. Now, go and clear out that back cupboard and think about whether you really want a nasty sod full of hatred to persuade you to do wrong and cost you your job.'

When a frightened-looking Farrow had left them alone, Deemer turned to Mayne. 'Sorry about that.'

'I agreed absolutely with what you told him.'

'Waste of time. He won't last.'

'He won't?'

'No. I can spot them a mile off, the ones who don't settle down to do a proper job. A few of the dull ones manage to learn enough to stay around, but most of them leave of their own accord. I can't have an officer who's anti-Semitic or anti-Catholic or anti-anything else.'

He let out an angry snort. 'My mother's family was Irish and I well remember the days when people used to put up signs for jobs saying "No Irish need apply". We British have just fought a long hard war for our freedom, and freedom is what the people of Rivenshaw are going to get as long as I have any say about it.'

After a couple of deep breaths, he asked in a calmer tone, 'Now, what's the trouble, Mr Esher?'

When Mayne had explained, the sergeant stayed perfectly still, brow creased in thought. 'We'll need to bring Farrow back and tell him about this as well. Then I'll come and question the fellow you've kindly caught for me.' He raised his voice. 'Farrow!'

Footsteps hurried towards them. 'Yes, Sergeant?'

'Listen to this.'

When he heard what had happened, Farrow gaped at Mayne, then turned back to his superior. 'What do we do about that, Sergeant? I've never had to deal with a kidnapping before.'

'We'll leave Miss Rollins here to answer any queries. She's been station clerk for long enough to know what to do. You and I will go to Esherwood to question the man they've caught. Then, if what Mr Esher has told us is true, we'll arrest the fellow, bring him back here and lock him up. After that, I'll inform my superiors of the situation and let them decide what to do with him.'

'Yes, Sergeant.' Farrow was looking enthusiastic again.

Sometimes, Mayne decided, young men were like bumbling puppies. He wondered why Farrow hadn't been in the forces. He didn't seem very bright, but he looked fit enough.

Deemer turned to Mayne. 'If I may suggest, it'd be good to spread the word about this to as many people in the town as you can. The more folk who're watching out for that child from now on, the better.'

'I suppose so. I'll speak to her father, ask if he wants to do that. And if so, perhaps you will do your bit about spreading the news, too?'

Mayne led the way into the kitchen at Esherwood and, as he'd expected, he found everyone gathered there.

Deemer was introduced to Victor and Ros, then Betty. 'How did that man catch you, love?'

'He came into the library through the French windows and I didn't see him till he put his hand over my mouth. He's very strong and held me so tightly I couldn't stop him carrying me outside.'

'That must have been frightening.'

'It was, but he stumbled and let go of me for a minute, so I screamed and bit him. Ben and his sisters heard me and came to help.'

'It's good to have friends.' He nodded to the other children. 'You did well.'

He turned his attention to the captive, who was tied to a chair in one corner. Deemer gave the young man a long, hard stare that made him wriggle uncomfortably. When he did speak, the sergeant's voice was much harsher. 'Constable?'

'Yessir.' Farrow stepped forward.

'Get your notebook out and write everything down.' He turned back to the captive. 'Now, fellow, what's your full name?'

'Brian John Peeby.'

After taking the man's address and details of employment, he asked, 'Who told you to come here?'

There was a moment's hesitation, then Peeby shook his head. 'I daren't tell you any more, Sergeant. I'm sorry but I'm feared for my family.'

'Then, young fellow, I shall have to arrest you and lock you up.'

Peeby's face wrinkled as if he was fighting tears. 'It's not fair. People who have money can do what they want. It's fellows like me what have to do as they're told or pay the price.'

'Not if you tell us what happened,' the sergeant said.

But Peeby still shook his head.

Deemer turned to Victor. 'I shall need a statement from you as well, sir. Might be better if me and my constable talk to you in private. If we could go into another room, I'm sure Mr Esher will keep an eye on Peeby for us.'

Victor looked at Mayne. 'All right to use the library?'

'Yes.'

'This way, Sergeant. Betty darling, will you be all right with Ros?'

'Yes. I've got Ben as well.'

It was apparent from the way she looked at the lad that she considered him the real hero of the piece.

'I need to use the lav,' Peeby announced once they'd gone.

'If it's urgent, we'll fetch the sergeant back to supervise that,' Mayne said. 'You're not being left alone for a minute, not even in the lavatory.'

'I can wait.'

He'd probably been intending to make a break for it. Mayne hid a smile. Not a clever young man, but one who was more frightened of Mrs Galton and Barham than of getting into trouble with the law. That was worrying. What might such people do next to get hold of that child?

Victor had been sure Mrs Galton would keep trying to get hold of her granddaughter. Only he'd believed she would do this through the courts. After all, she had a very attentive lawyer.

Victor gave his statement, then said, 'I wonder if I could have a quick word with you on another matter as well, if you have time, Sergeant? Miss Dawson, who is employed to look after my daughter, has been swindled out of some money. We were coming to see you and report this today. Will you still have time to attend to it as well?'

'Swindled by someone in Rivenshaw?'

'Yes. A man called Cliff Nodden.'

'Aaah. I shall have as much time as you like to look into that. He's a proper slippery customer, that one is. I've been wondering where he's been getting his money from the past few months, but he didn't seem to be thieving. He doesn't earn enough to spend freely on booze, and he's still paying his rent and buying food. Could you bring Miss Dawson down to the station after we've finished with Peeby, say in a couple of hours? I don't mind working late in a good cause.'

He turned to the constable. 'And I'm sure you won't mind staying late either, eh, Farrow?'

'No, sir. Happy to help, sir.'

As the two officers walked back to the police station with their captive, Sergeant Deemer thought hard about what he should do next. He went through the senior people he trusted in his mind and decided that, given the power and money of the people behind the kidnapping, Miss Peters' brother would be the best person to advise him.

'I'm going out,' he told the constable. 'No matter who turns up or what they say, do not release that man, and do not let him speak to anyone, even a lawyer. You understand? If you disobey my orders, I'll make sure you're sacked forthwith.'

Farrow shivered and nodded.

Deemer was feeling tired and wasn't as spry as he'd once been, having come out of retirement to take up his old job because of the war. He trudged along towards Parson's Mead, mentally cursing rich sods who thought they were above the law. He didn't even spare the time to glance across to his allotment in what had been a pretty little park before the war, but now contained row upon row of vegetables.

He explained his dilemma to Miss Peters. 'Do you think your brother might advise me? I could telephone him.'

She smiled. 'No need. My brother is coming to tea on his way back from Manchester. If you wait a few minutes, he'll be here and you can ask his advice in person.'

Deemer nodded, then remembered the weak young man keeping watch. 'I think I'd better get back and keep an eye on that prisoner. And Mr Travers will be coming to see me with the young lady. Could you ask your brother to call at the station? Do you think he'd mind? I know it's asking a lot, but I'm a bit out of my depth with moneyed folk being involved.'

'A little girl was nearly kidnapped. I'm sure my brother will be glad to help.'

Feeling thankful, Deemer walked quickly back into town.

8

To the sergeant's amazement, Mr Gilliot was waiting for him at the police station, looking angry.

'Ah, there you are!' he exclaimed as soon as he caught sight of Deemer. 'I'm here on behalf of my client, Mr . . . um . . .' He consulted a piece of paper. 'Mr Brian John Peeby.'

'He's a client of yours? But he doesn't even live in Rivenshaw.'

'What has that to do with it? His employer is worried about him and, um, got in touch with me. We, um, have a mutual acquaintance. I gather Peeby's a bit simple-minded and has probably mistaken what they asked him to do.'

'He didn't seem simple-minded to me, Mr Gilliot, just too frightened of his employer to speak. And there was no mistake about what he tried to do, none whatsoever. What's more, if it was a Mr Barham who got in touch with you on behalf of Peeby's employer, perhaps you could tell me where to find him. He was the one trying to carry away the child, not Peeby.'

It hadn't taken Barham long to find a lawyer who was hostile towards the local police. How had that happened so quickly? Was it accidental or deliberate that Barham had chosen this particular lawyer, not the other one, Mr Melford?

Gilliot gave Deemer a sneering look. 'Why are you wasting my time like this? I know nothing about this Barham fellow, certainly not where he is now. I only saw him for a few minutes. It's his employer who's hired me to ask for the release of a poor, misguided young man. You can't have charged Peeby already, surely?'

'I'm about to question him, but as I have several witnesses to what happened, I have no doubt we will be charging him and getting a successful conviction.'

'Who are they?' Gilliot took out a notebook.

'People of good standing in this community whose word I trust. I'm waiting for my own legal adviser to arrive, since kidnapping is a very serious offence.'

'Do you mean Melford? How did he get involved?'

'Let me get past, if you please, Mr Gilliot.'

He didn't move. 'I must reiterate: there has been no kidnapping.'

'You weren't there, sir, so you can't be aware of all the facts. We'll wait for my adviser to arrive before we do anything.'

'This is very irregular. I must insist on speaking to my client. Your constable seemed afraid to let me near him. I hope no one has been beating the poor fellow.'

Deemer could feel himself literally swelling with rage at this accusation. 'No one has ever been beaten while in my custody, nor ever will be.' He pushed past the lawyer and lifted the counter flap, going behind the reception desk and banging it down hard behind him. He felt better to have put a barrier between himself and a man he didn't trust to tell the truth, lawyer or not.

He scribbled a note on a piece of paper and beckoned Farrow into his office, saying in a low voice, 'Run round to Miss Peters' house as fast as you can and give her this. Do not show it to anyone else.' He escorted the young officer out into the street, then turned to find Gilliot blocking his path to the counter once again.

'Where are you sending that man?'

'On an errand.'

'I demand to know where.'

'It's a police matter, and shouting won't make me tell you things which are none of your business . . . sir.'

A silence, during which Gilliot breathed deeply and scowled at the sergeant. 'What about my client?'

'He's quite safe.'

It was over a quarter of an hour and two tirades by Gilliot later that a motor car drew up outside the police station.

Deemer prayed that this would be Judge Peters, and breathed a loud sigh of relief when that gentleman walked through the door.

The judge stood for a moment taking in the scene, but as Gilliot moved forward to accost him, he said in the quiet but penetrating tone for which he was famous, 'I need to speak to Sergeant Deemer first. Kindly wait your turn, Gilliot.'

'I wish to see my client. I have a right to do that.'

'He hasn't agreed to be your client yet,' Deemer said quickly.

Gilliot raised his voice. 'Because he hasn't been asked.'

Mr Peters smiled. 'Allow me through, if you please, Gilliot.'

The lawyer opened and shut his mouth, then stepped back.

Deemer led the way into his office. 'I'm grateful you've come, Judge Peters. I wasn't sure how to deal with this.'

'Tell me the whole story. Never mind Gilliot. He can wait.'

The judge listened intently, then sat thinking for a moment or two. 'I'll speak to Peeby myself. Participating in a kidnapping would lead to a serious charge.'

As they went back into the reception area, Gilliot bounced to his feet.

'I'm about to speak to Mr Peeby,' the judge said, 'and I'll

ask him whether he wants you to represent him. If so, Sergeant Deemer will fetch you in to join us.'

'But I must—'

'Allow me to know my own business, Gilliot.' The judge followed the sergeant back to the two small cells and they opened the door to the one where Peeby was sitting.

'On your feet!' Sergeant Deemer snapped. 'This is Judge Peters, who's come to speak to you, and there's a lawyer outside sent by Mrs Galton. His name is Gilliot. Do you wish him to represent you?'

Peeby turned white. 'She's sent a lawyer? No! I don't want to see him. I can't do this. I'm sorry if my mam loses her house, but I just can't!'

He burst into tears, looking so young Deemer patted him on the shoulder till he'd calmed down. 'Are you all right now, lad?'

Peeby drew a deep breath and looked at them pleadingly, 'If I tell you everything, will you keep me safe from Mrs Galton?'

'We'll do our best,' the judge said. 'Go and ask Gilliot to wait for me, Sergeant. I'll speak to him afterwards. Then come back with a pad and take notes.'

'We could question Mr Peeby in the hearing room, Judge.'

'Good idea. We'll all be more comfortable there.'

After questioning the young man and finding he knew almost nothing about what was going on, but was quite sure who had given Barham the order to kidnap the little girl, Judge Peters followed the sergeant back to his office, ignoring Gilliot, who jumped to his feet at the sight of them.

'I pity that young fellow, Sergeant,' Peters said in a low voice.

'Perhaps the authorities will be lenient with him.'

'I hope so. I shan't be able to hear the case, of course,

not after being involved, but I'll find him a lawyer who'll represent him pro bono. Now, could you bring Gilliot in here and leave me to speak to him?'

'Certainly, sir.'

Whatever the judge said to Gilliot didn't make the lawyer happy. He walked out of the police station with a scowl on his face, not saying a word.

Deemer said farewell to the judge and thanked him for his intervention, then sent Farrow off to make them all a cup of tea, including the prisoner.

He heard the constable muttering about not joining the police force to make cups of tea for criminals and smiled. Everyone had to start at the bottom, doing the menial jobs. But if that young man had his wits about him, he'd be observing what went on and learning from it, instead of complaining.

By the time they'd finished their tea, Mr Travers had arrived with Miss Dawson.

Deemer took them into his office, found out exactly what had been happening and asked Farrow to listen as he took a formal statement.

'Do you think you can retrieve any of Miss Dawson's money?' Victor asked.

'I'll do my best.' A yawn caught the sergeant out. 'Sorry sir, miss. Been a long day. Me and this young man will get on to it first thing tomorrow. If you'll just sign the hand-written statement, in case anything turns up, we'll have it typed up properly tomorrow.'

Outside the station, Victor offered his arm to Ros, but she smiled and shook her head.

'I prefer to stride out, if you don't mind. Let's walk back really briskly. I'm not used to sitting around so much.'

Their strides matched admirably and though they walked in silence, it was a companionable one.

Ros's cheeks were rosy by the time they started up the drive to the big house.

'That's better,' she said. 'I love a good brisk walk.'

'I must admit I too feel better for it. Oh, look!' He stopped and pointed to one side, and they watched a fox slink through the undergrowth followed by three young ones.

'They're pretty when they're young, aren't they?' she murmured.

'Yes.' But his eyes were on her and she knew it.

She blushed and started walking again.

He strode along, wishing he were free to live his life without all these crises, with his beloved daughter and maybe a second wife. He was a man who wanted a quiet home life, who relished the small joys of daily endeavour. And he rather thought Ros had similar tastes.

He hoped he wasn't misreading the situation.

As they got to the kitchen door, he said quietly, 'I've enjoyed your company.'

She nodded, but didn't echo his words, only shot him a quick glance, as if checking that he meant what he said.

She didn't seem to be playing hard to get, and definitely wasn't flirting. Suddenly he had an idea. Ros looked confident and strong but was it possible . . . could she be shy about relationships with men? Was that why she'd never married?

They'd be living in the same house, so he'd find out if it was shyness. At least, he hoped he would. He very much wanted to get to know her better.

He felt guilty about that, with Susan so recently dead, but in all honesty she had faded into a non-wife role years earlier, starting after Betty's birth, when they had stopped sharing a bed.

Jan went out into the grounds of Esherwood to begin his nightly round, slipping into an area of thick vegetation to stand perfectly still and listen to the sleepy evening bird calls. He loved the grounds of this house, could understand why Mayne was doing everything he could to preserve it.

What a shame his employer had to change the interior, to make it into flats and sell it off in bits and pieces. It seemed inevitable that they'd lose those spacious rooms on the ground floor when they did this. If Jan had any money, he'd be the first in the queue to buy one of the flats.

He was about to move on when he heard something, so once again stood motionless, listening hard with his eyes half-closed for something other than the bird calls. Yes. There it was again. Someone was creeping along under the trees, trying not to be heard.

Whoever it was had better than average skills at moving quietly, but not as good as Jan's own. Fortunately he had good night vision and well-honed skills. Very few of these people's lives had ever depended on learning to move silently through the night, as his had when he was escaping from the Nazis in Europe. There were some advantages to living on an island. He'd always envied the British that protection.

Because his eyes were accustomed to the dark, he managed to make out the silhouette of the intruder, who was quite a tall man. But he made no attempt to follow him yet. He hadn't seen the other man who'd tried to kidnap Betty, only the young fool they'd captured. But from Victor's description, Barham was a tall man.

If it was him, what was he doing back here? Surely he wasn't . . . no, he couldn't be making another attempt to kidnap the child? Could he? Only, why else would he come back and risk being caught?

Jan shook his head in reluctant admiration for the sheer nerve of the man. Clever, because it'd be unexpected, but Jan intended to make sure he didn't succeed. The people at Esherwood had accepted Jan when he was no one, a refugee with no home and little beyond the clothes he stood up in. In turn, he would defend them and those they cared about whenever it was needed.

He pulled the revolver loaded with blanks out of his pocket and set off after the intruder. You're in for a shock, fellow!

Watt Barham found a place from which he could see into the kitchen. He'd followed his employer's instructions and done his best to help poor Peeby. Now he would leave the clumsy idiot to the lawyer and do his best to help himself. Once he'd earned the large bonus the old lady had promised him for this job, he'd be off, and she could find someone else to do her dirty work. People like that never did it themselves.

The occupants of the big house hadn't thought to draw the curtains, so he watched them as they sat round the table eating a meal, looking comfortable with one another. His stomach rumbled, but he ignored that. He'd eat when he'd done what he'd come here for.

He envied them that close friendliness, but they were fools not to draw the curtains, fools who'd get a few shocks tonight . . . unless things went very wrong.

The children were seated at one end of the table, the end furthest from the door, with Betty in the middle of the group.

He'd have to wait until they went to bed then break into the house and drag her out of bed. Not easy. Very risky, in fact; and even more risky if she was sharing a bedroom, because he'd have to deal with her companion first.

But if anyone could do that, he could.

They didn't have a dog here, fortunately. It was much harder to get past a watchdog unless you killed it, and he didn't hold with killing working animals that you couldn't eat. They didn't deserve that.

Should he, shouldn't he risk trying to capture the child? He would be taking a big risk.

Jan continued to watch Barham from the vantage point he used whenever he needed a break, at the top of a staircase in a ruined building. He'd made sure the way to it was brushed clear of debris, so that he could go up and down what was left of the stairs silently. From here, he could still keep an eye on the house and rear yard. Tonight, however, he set his small satchel down without taking out his bottle of water or having a snack.

After a few minutes of watching the shadow Barham cast as he stood observing the house, Jan guessed the man must be waiting until everyone had gone to bed. He took a chance and slipped away, going round to the front of the house, where he let himself in with his key and waited in the hall until someone came out of the kitchen.

It was Ben. Good.

'Shh. It's only me.' Jan stepped out from the shadows at the side of the big entrance hall and put one finger on his lips.

Ben, who had switched on one electric light near the door to the kitchen, stopped at once and waited, his hand still on the door handle.

Smart lad, that.

Jan went close enough to be recognised and murmur, 'Barham's come back and is outside watching the kitchen. We don't want to alarm him, so don't go back in shouting that he's out there. Don't even say it quietly, in case he can lip read. What did you come out for?'

'To find a book I was telling Betty about.'

'Find it. And find me some paper at the same time. I can write a note for Mayne and you can show it to him inside the book.'

Ben nodded eagerly, as excited as any lad worth his salt would be to be involved in an adventure.

When they were ready, Jan said, 'Give me a couple of

minutes to get outside at the back before you give the book to Mayne. We don't want this man to escape, do we?'

Ben returned to the kitchen with two books. He gave one to Betty, then turned to Mayne. 'I found a book you might be interested in, Mr Esher.' He handed it over, open at the page with the note in it.

Mayne stiffened slightly, scanned it and said aloud, 'You're right. It's a good book, that one. Show the illustration to Mr Travers.'

'I want to see it,' Gillian said at once.

Ben dug her in the back as he passed, hissing, 'Shut up. Something's going on.'

Judith overheard him and said quietly, 'Gillian, will you help me clear the table?'

Looking sulky, her daughter got up and started carrying dishes into the scullery.

Mayne put his arm round Judith, giving her a hug and whispering, 'Get the children upstairs as if they're going to bed, but keep them all in your bedroom and tell them not to get undressed. Barham's come back for Betty.'

By now, even Gillian had realised something was going on. She continued to clear the table as Victor passed the book to Ros.

Betty jumped up. 'I'll help you, Gillian.'

'Come and help me, instead,' Ros said at once, handing the book back to Mayne. 'I'm not sure where to put your clothes when I unpack.'

'There's something wrong, isn't there?'

Such stark fear showed on the child's face that Ros put an arm round her, turning her away from the window.

'Let Betty peep out of your bedroom window,' Mayne said. 'If there's someone still watching, we want to tempt him inside.'

One by one they went out, as if going to bed. Judith followed them.

Mayne stayed till last, locking the outside door as loudly as he could, then switching the kitchen light off.

He didn't go upstairs but stayed in the hall, whispering to Victor to join the others in Judith's bedroom. 'Jan and I can deal with one intruder,' he said. 'You make sure the others stay out of the way. I wouldn't put it past Ben to try to sneak down and help us.'

'All right.'

Mayne went into the library and undid the floor bolt of one of the French windows, but left them locked. It was a simple lock with a big key, and would be easy to pick. If they offered the intruder too easy a way in, he'd be suspicious.

He chose a position behind a bookcase near the library door, from where he could keep an eye on the hall, but be ready to pounce if the intruder walked into the trap this way.

Then quietness fell on the house as people waited, upstairs and down.

As everyone left the kitchen, Barham moved back from the window and watched lights come on upstairs. He noted carefully where they were, counting the windows of that wing of the house.

Suddenly two girls appeared at one window, staring out at the garden. One of them was Betty Travers. A woman came up behind them and pulled them back. She looked as if she was scolding them.

He smiled. 'Thanks, ladies. Very helpful.'

As the lights in that room went out, he waited for about half an hour, then began to move slowly round the house, checking doors and windows.

Once he thought he heard someone behind him and swung

round, heart pounding, but a small animal ran across the path. He smiled at it.

When he found the library doors locked but with a very old sort of lock, he grinned. Easy to pick that. But nonetheless he stood still and listened carefully for a while. There was no sound of anyone moving, outside or in.

Upstairs the last light went out at that moment, which reassured him a little. Still, best to be sure, so he waited, counting patiently up to five hundred. That had saved him from getting caught a couple of times in the past.

He came to the end of his counting. Nothing had stirred that sounded like a person, so with great care he picked the lock of the French window and opened it. Even then, he didn't go in but stepped back and counted again.

All right, he told himself when he reached five hundred for a second time. It looked safe to go inside.

Propping the French window open so that he'd have an easy exit available, he moved quietly into the room, wishing the moon were even half full. But it wasn't and the inside of the house seemed very dark after the starlight outside.

It wasn't going to be easy to get hold of the child, but he'd counted the rooms, which gave him a start. There was a lot of money at stake, so he was prepared to take a huge risk tonight. If things worked out, this would be the last crime he ever committed.

He began to creep across the room, annoyed at the mess through which he had to weave his way. Twice he nearly tripped and made a slight sound. You'd think rich folk would keep their houses tidier than this.

He got near the door to the hall, noting that it was slightly open. He'd only have to pull it back another inch or two to get through. As he started to edge cautiously through into the hall, however, someone grabbed him.

It was a trap!

Well, they weren't going to catch him. He punched the person in the face and ran back across the library. He was nearly at the French window when he realised someone had shut it.

Then the world exploded into pain.

When he came to, he was trussed up and a light was on. He kept his eyes closed as he tested the bonds, but whoever had done this knew his business.

'I know you're conscious again,' a voice said, a voice with a slight foreign accent. 'Stop pretending.'

So he opened his eyes and saw two men.

The smaller one yanked him so that he was sitting upright with his back against the wall.

'I'm Mayne Esher and this is my house,' the taller man said. 'We know why you're here. How much is Mrs Galton paying you to kidnap Betty?'

Barham said nothing. He wasn't stupid enough to blab. And he still had one ace in his hand, or at least he hoped he had.

'I can make him talk,' the smaller man said.

'If he doesn't talk willingly, I might just let you do that,' the other one said.

But Barham was watching them and he knew his life and secrets were safe. The big one was too soft-hearted to kill, or even hurt anyone, and the smaller one, though he looked as if life had made him harder, didn't have a killer's eyes.

Damn! He should have managed without that last big payment and left Mrs Galton as soon as the war was over. Thank goodness for the tiny fault in his heart that had prevented him from passing his medical.

But whatever happened now, there was no prison built that he wouldn't find a way to break out of, sooner or later.

The smaller man shook him again. 'Answer the question, you.'

'I won't talk, whatever you do,' he told them. 'And you're not the sort to force me.'

As they studied him, he stared defiantly back.

'We'll call in Sergeant Deemer in the morning,' Esher said. 'Till then we'll lock him in the cellar. There's a large cupboard there which will keep him safe.'

'I'll make sure of that,' the smaller man said.

Barham didn't resist as they marched him down to the cellar.

The storeroom was dark and cramped. He'd expected them to release him from the ropes, but they only adjusted his arms to give him a little more movement. Someone had made a good job of tying him up, sod them.

He made himself as comfortable as he could and managed to get some sleep, but he woke a few times, woke and cursed them both, but that foreign sod most of all.

He wasn't feeling very hopeful now. You could make all the plans on earth, but sometimes they didn't work out.

9

In Brighton, Daniel O'Brien kicked a stray pebble along the promenade and stared down through the rolled barbed wire that barred both the upper and lower promenades. The beach below looked a right old mess, littered with chunks of metal, driftwood, blocks of concrete and who knew what else the Army had planted there to prevent an invading force from landing.

He looked longingly at the sea, which was making a shushing sound as it lapped to and fro on the pebbles. He'd have enjoyed skimming a few of those smooth pebbles along the surface of the water, or even taking off his shoes and socks and plodging along the shallows.

He smiled at his instinctive use of the word 'plodge', which reminded him of his childhood in Lancashire. His parents had taken him for a week to Blackpool each year, staying in the same boarding house.

The beach there had lovely firm sand, not pebbles like this one. He and his father had built magnificent castles, and as he'd grown bigger, he'd insisted on building his own, leaving his parents to sit quietly chatting. Perhaps that had helped turn him into an architect.

His parents loved the sea air and had retired to Blackpool just before the war, selling their shop for a comfortable amount of money. His father had been in the ARP during the past few years and his mother had run a clothing exchange. He really ought to go and see them before he settled down to work on Esherwood.

He'd meant to visit Rivenshaw on one of his leaves, but something had always intervened to prevent that. He hoped it'd prove as friendly a town as Mayne claimed, and hoped most of all that the job would be as interesting as it sounded.

He studied Brighton's pebbly beach, turned into an ugly wasteland behind those barriers, and sighed. When would the beach be liberated?

There were a lot of barriers left over from the war, both physical and mental. He still had nightmares where he re-lived some of the things he'd seen and done. The nightmares were becoming less frequent, thank goodness, but they still jerked him awake in a cold sweat of fear, his heart thudding as if he'd been running; the bedcovers in a tangle from his thrashing around.

The British had won the war; now they had to win their way back to a true peace. And that wasn't going to be quick or easy, anyone with sense could see that. But oh, the joy of knowing you'd never have to kill someone again! Of knowing you could walk safely along a dark street without worrying about bombs raining down on you.

In spite of the ugliness around him, he smiled.

His biggest regret was the loss of years of the work he loved, years he'd never regain. He could have been designing homes, doing constructive, meaningful work, instead of destructive war work.

He also regretted his hasty marriage, even more so now that his wife had run off with a damned Yank. That irked the hell out of him. She was in the middle of obtaining a divorce in some town over there called Las Vegas. Her new man must have money or influence to get her over there so quickly.

It would take six weeks to get a divorce, she'd written, and she'd send him the paperwork as soon as they were both free or contact him if she needed anything else.

Only six weeks to wipe out their marriage, he'd thought, both amazed and saddened. Sometimes that seemed too quick, but at other times he felt it couldn't happen fast enough.

He and Ada had been in trouble long before the end of the war, of course. They hadn't quarrelled, well not much. It was mainly that they were two very different people who'd rushed into a wartime marriage and then found they didn't particularly enjoy living together. He was neat; she was untidy. He liked to read quietly in the evening; she wanted to go out dancing or to the cinema, or to meet friends at the pub. He liked to go out occasionally, of course he did, that was how he'd met Ada, but not every night.

Thank goodness they hadn't had any children! She'd have gone mad if she'd had to stay in during the evenings and look after a child. And he couldn't have let her take a child of his away to America. Never that.

As Ada had requested, he'd written a statement to say he agreed to a divorce, and had it witnessed by the local headmaster and a lawyer. He'd told all his friends that getting divorced was all right with him. He kept it to himself that he didn't feel right about how it had happened. She should have left him *before* being unfaithful.

She said she'd divided their shared goods equally when she packed up his things. She wasn't claiming any money from him, because her new fellow had more than enough. He'd inherited a house from an elderly relative last year, but Ada didn't want any share of that. So really she was being very fair.

He hadn't checked the boxes of possessions she'd left, couldn't bear to open them and, anyway, he trusted her about that at least. He'd asked his cousin Jennifer to find somewhere to store them.

Ah, what was he doing on the promenade, mooning about like this? He'd arranged to meet an old Army friend for a drink and to catch up with what the two of them were doing. John was a close friend, who knew what it had been like during the war. They'd talked a lot in the long hours of waiting between the various bursts of activity, and they'd looked out for one another.

Then Daniel had been transferred to the special unit and met Mayne, Victor and Francis. But he'd still kept in touch with John.

The other reason Daniel had come to Brighton was to look at the Pavilion. He'd always loved that ridiculously extravagant structure. It seemed to say that architects could design what they wanted – well, as long as they found someone with money to pay for the building.

He smiled at the thought that he was an architect again, not a soldier. He'd been demobbed early, on condition that he went into building work in Rivenshaw. He would start work soon . . . only somehow he didn't feel like facing Mayne and Victor quite yet.

They knew him too well, would see the restlessness in him, the uncertainty. He had to sort his inner demons out before he headed north.

Daniel sat in the corner of the pub, toying with his glass, making the half pint of beer last. He had no head for drink and enjoyed the conviviality of pubs and the company of his friends far more than the alcohol. John was a good friend and never tried to push him into drinking round for round.

The group of men round the table, friends of John's, were reminiscing about the war, as people inevitably did when they got together.

'Remember the night the Odeon was bombed?' one of the locals said.

'That was bad. My cousin's wife and daughter were killed, poor things. He joined up afterwards, even though he was in a reserved occupation.'

They looked at Daniel who was listening quietly. It seemed to help people to tell of such incidents, sometimes over and over, so he said nothing to interrupt them, just nodded encouragingly.

'Fifty-five killed in all in that attack,' another man said. 'My friend was working at the hospital as a stretcher bearer. Never seen a dead body before. He was as pale as a corpse himself by the time he'd finished that shift.'

His neighbour nudged him. 'Frank's just come in. Change the subject.' He whispered to Daniel, 'Frank lost his brother in the Odeon bombing.'

One by one the other men went home, leaving Daniel and John.

'Sorry about that,' John said. 'Not a very cheerful evening for you.'

'It helps put things into perspective and I'm beginning to see that people benefit from talking it out. My wife might have left me but she's alive still. And so am I. We're the lucky ones.'

John nodded. 'They talked of "thankful villages" during the 1930s, do you remember? Places where no one who went to fight was killed during World War I. Maybe we should talk about "thankful families" for this war. No one in my family was killed, thank goodness, so we'd qualify.'

He took another sip of beer. 'Ah, let's change the subject. I'm sick of harping on about the damned war. It's over. Have you heard about a chap called Berthold Lubetkin? An architect. Well known before the war.'

'Yes, of course I've heard of him, though I've never visited any of his buildings. That sort of work isn't really relevant to me at the moment. I'm going to be helping turn a historic house into flats. Lubetkin's stuff is very modern, so it's not high on my list of things to see.'

'It's well thought of by those who know. They praise the way he brings in lots of light. There's a block of flats in Highgate called Highpoint. It's supposed to be one of the finest middle class housing developments in the world. I thought it might give you a few ideas for your new project with this Esher chappie. You did say that was for middle class people.'

'I doubt it'd be relevant. My friend Mayne is keen to keep the historic feel of his house, and that in itself will be an interesting challenge.'

'Then you won't want to join me in a trip to London? Aubrey, a friend of mine, has inherited a flat in Highpoint. They say that building is Lubetkin's masterpiece, seven storeys high, built in two cruciform towers. Aubrey has invited me to visit and look round the interior of his flat, and of course the shared spaces like the lobby.'

Daniel paused, glass halfway to his mouth. 'I might be interested in seeing it if we can actually get inside a flat. I'd like to make sure the flats at Esherwood get good light in them. Look, I don't have a fixed date for starting in Rivenshaw and I told Mayne I had a few things to do first so . . . '

'Come with me on Monday. I'm spending a few days in London, staying in a small hotel in Highgate, within walking distance of the flats. You can stay for one day or for the whole week. Aubrey won't mind you joining us. He's a sociable fellow. Do say you'll come.'

'All right, I will, though only for a day or two.' He held out his hand and they shook on it.

The decision felt right, more than right. It was as if fate was guiding him in the correct direction, which wasn't yet

Rivenshaw. Strange, that. He didn't usually believe in such presentiments.

He'd take his sketch pad, though it was nearly used up now. He'd have to try to find some more pads in London, even if he had to buy them on the black market. And pencils. He'd need a lot of pencils. His fingers were suddenly twitching to start drawing.

'Thank you,' he told John.

'What for?'

'Getting me interested in architecture again.'

'I didn't do much, Daniel.'

'It was enough to make me feel like an architect again.'

'Ah well, I'm glad.' After a pause, John added quietly, 'That sodding war upset a lot of people. It'll linger for a while inside us all, I should think.'

'Yes. Do you . . . get nightmares?'

'Hell, yes. What sane person wouldn't after what we've seen and done?'

Daniel gaped at him. That one remark made him feel instantly better about his nightmares, made him feel better than anything else had since the war ended. 'What sane person wouldn't,' he repeated slowly. 'That says it all. You know, you always did have a gift for getting to the crux of a problem.' He raised his glass to his friend, who clinked glasses and winked at him.

Such a sensible chap, John. Pity he wasn't the marrying sort, because he should leave his seed behind, but he was frank about his proclivities. He seemed very fond of this friend Aubrey, was talking of moving in to live with him. That didn't stop him being a good man to have at your back during a war, and a good friend generally.

'I'm looking forward to our trip,' Daniel said in surprise. He suddenly felt as if his former enjoyment in exercising his mind and creating something beautiful was returning in a warm trickle! He had to blink hard not to weep at that first real sign of a renaissance.

Early on Saturday morning, Sergeant Deemer was surprised to see Mayne come into the police station again.

He'd just sent his prisoner off to Manchester with two of their constables. Who knew how long that would take before the poor fellow was dealt with? It wasn't an urgent case by any standards, because the would-be kidnappers had failed in their purpose. Judge Peters had written a brief letter to accompany the young man.

Thank goodness that was done with.

'How can I help you today, Mr Esher?'

'Jan and I caught Peeby's accomplice last night.'

'What? I thought he'd be far away by now.'

'No. Barham came back and tried to take Betty. Not short of cheek, is he? Luckily Jan spotted him in the grounds and we were ready for him when he broke into the house.'

'Broke in?'

'Yes. Picked the lock on the library door.'

'That grandmother of hers must really want her back for Barham to take such a risk.'

'More likely, from what Victor says, the old lady doesn't like being thwarted once she's set her mind to something. He says Mrs Galton is big on appearances. I'd guess she offered Barham a lot of money. Anyway, we have him locked in the cellar.'

'What did he say?'

'Nothing. He refuses point-blank to speak. I didn't like to march him through the streets tied up, so I thought I'd take you and your constable back to fetch him. I have the car.'

Deemer suppressed a sigh and checked the clock. He'd been looking forward to leaving the station in the hands of a relief constable with more seniority than Farrow and more sense in his head, too. Johnson was due to arrive at nine o'clock.

'Can we wait a few minutes till my relief arrives? I don't like to leave the place unattended.'

'Yes, of course. How's Peeby?'

'Gone off to Manchester. I feel sorry for him, but not sorry enough to let him go.'

The phone rang just then and Deemer picked it up.

When he put it down, he was frowning. 'Johnson's sick. I'll have to send for Farrow, which I was hoping not to do.'

'Don't you trust him to keep an eye on Barham?'

'No. And it means I'll have to work part of the weekend shift instead of Johnson doing it. I'm getting a bit old for such long hours, I am that.' He went to the door and stopped a passing lad, offering him sixpence to take a message.

The lad brought back a reply that Farrow hadn't yet got up, so would have to get dressed.

'Lazy devil!' Deemer said scornfully.

It was a full half an hour before the constable arrived, by which time the sergeant was champing at the bit to bring back the second prisoner.

'Barham won't have gone anywhere,' Mayne said, amused.

'He might escape. You never know with some of them. They can be very tricky.'

But Barham was still in the cellar. He'd been released and fed, watched over by Jan and Victor.

'I want to protest at being held for nothing,' he said, as soon as he saw the sergeant.

'You can do your protesting down at the police station,' Deemer said sourly. 'At the very least you broke into this house.'

'It was a mistake. I was told by a man in the pub that they had Peeby locked up here for the night because you don't have proper cells at the police station, and that they'd boasted about giving him a good beating to teach him a lesson.'

'And if you think I believe that, you'll be telling me next there are fairies at the bottom of your garden.'

'Where is the poor boy, then? I haven't seen any sign of him here.'

'Mr Peeby is safe in Manchester. Where you'll be joining him soon.'

But when he rang up his superior, he was asked to charge Barham and hold him until Monday, when a van would be sent to fetch him, because the Manchester lockup was full.

'That means I'll have to take turns keeping watch with Farrow. Someone will have to be there night and day. I don't like leaving him in that young fool's hands at all, but there's no one else, and I can't stay awake for two days and nights.'

10

'I think we could all do with a restful weekend,' Mayne said when he got back from the police station. 'And whether you go to church or not tomorrow is up to you. But I don't attend the parish church because I don't have any respect for the minister there.'

He looked at Judith as he spoke, knowing the minister had been very unhelpful when she was having trouble with her so-called husband.

'I don't attend church at all. The war finished that for me. I'll probably take Betty for a nice long walk.' Victor picked up his dirty plate and took it into the scullery.

Judith turned to Mayne. 'I need to go shopping today, or we'll run out of food. Do you need anything? Always supposing the "anything" is available, that is.'

'No, but I'll come with you,' Mayne said at once.

She lowered her voice. 'That wouldn't look good. We have to be careful.'

'I'm fed up of being careful. Anyway, how will you carry everything?'

'I'll get them to deliver it.' She grinned. 'They love to deal with Esherwood, now that you've paid off your parents' bills. You really ought to do some gardening. There are all sorts of things trying to push through the tangles of weeds in the vegetable garden. Check out whether there's anything edible.'

'I'll help you, Mayne,' Gillian offered. 'I'd like to learn how to garden. We didn't have one at our old house.'

'I'd help too, but I've arranged to go round to my friend Pamela's,' Kitty said. 'Sorry.'

'And I've arranged to play cricket.' Ben hit an imaginary ball across the kitchen, shouted 'Six!' and gave himself a cheer.

'In that case,' Victor said, 'I'll take Ros and Betty out to explore the grounds. If you'd like to, that is, you two?'

They both nodded vigorously.

'Keep an eye open for strangers, Vic,' Mayne said quietly before he went out to work in the garden. 'I don't think there will be any problems now that Barham's locked up, but yell if you need help. I'd probably hear you from just about anywhere in the grounds.'

Victor grinned. He had been famous when training new recruits for his extremely loud voice. 'I reckon we should be all right.'

He soon found that he had no need to tell Betty not to stray too far away from him and Ros. She stayed within two or three yards of them and kept peering around anxiously. He felt furious all over again with his mother-in-law for making the child so nervous.

It was Ros who had the most success in distracting his daughter. She soon found out that although Betty had grown up in a country village, she'd never been allowed to roam freely in the countryside. Ros pointed out birds, named them and explained their feeding habits. A few times she stopped and asked them to stand still to listen to various bird calls. She seemed perfectly at home out of doors.

'You make me realise what an urban creature I am, even though I lived in a village after my marriage,' Victor said. 'I don't know half as much as you do about the countryside. I'm finding this very interesting.'

'I used to go out with my father at weekends. He was an amateur naturalist and loved being out of doors. And then, after he died and Mother married Cliff, I got out of the house as often as I could, rain or shine.'

The sharpness of her tone made Victor stare at her thoughtfully. 'You get an edge to your voice when you speak of your stepfather.'

'I hate him! He's a disgusting man.'

He could see how much talking of Cliff upset her. 'Did he . . . pester you? I mean, in ways he shouldn't have.'

She hesitated, then nodded slowly.

He kept his tone gentle, but felt angry inside as he did every time he heard of a young girl being pestered by an older man. 'I've known it happen, even in the best of homes.'

'How did you guess?'

'I was a lawyer, dealing with poorer people for at least half the time. And I may do that sort of work again one day. It was very satisfying.'

'Life wasn't very happy after my father died, because my mother needed someone to cling to and I was only a child. So she married again quite quickly. But no one would have believed me if I'd said anything about Cliff, least of all my mother, so I mostly avoided him. Luckily, I was tall for my age and someone at school showed me where to kick him to hurt him.'

She saw that Betty was listening and looked at Victor. 'It never hurts to teach a little girl that.'

He frowned, then nodded permission.

Ros explained to Betty how to kick rough men and boys where it hurt, though only if they tried to hurt her. When the child gaped at these instructions, she added, 'It never does any harm to be prepared. Men's bodies are made differently from women's, you see.'

Betty nodded solemnly. 'I know. I saw the garden boy

washing himself with the hose pipe once.' She flushed. 'I shouldn't have looked, but I wondered if he was like the statues I'd seen pictures of in books.'

'And was he?'

Betty wrinkled her nose. 'Sort of. But he was much thinner, and you could see his ribs sticking out. I don't think he got a lot to eat. He used to pinch fallen fruit out of the garden sometimes. I never told on him because he always looked so hungry.'

'I'd not have told on him, either.' Ros took her hand, swinging it as they walked along.

Victor took the child's other hand and winked at Ros over his daughter's head and she looked surprised for a moment, then winked back.

Between the two of them and the other children at Esherwood, his daughter was learning a lot of what he'd have called 'practical sense' and he was glad of that. He didn't want to raise Betty like a hothouse flower, who couldn't help herself. It wasn't a good thing to always need looking after, as her poor mother had. As Ros's mother had, too.

He didn't think their troubles with Mrs Galton were over yet, not by a long chalk, but he'd fight back. And if she got the courts on her side, he'd run away if he had to. He wasn't letting that arrogant woman hurt this delightful child fate had given him.

Farrow decided to leave one light on in the police station. He didn't feel comfortable in the dark, not with a criminal locked up just down the short corridor. Barham was fast asleep every time he peeped into the cell. He wished he was too.

He wasn't used to this sort of night duty, where nothing was happening, and kept dozing off when he sat down. He started walking round the station. In the end he felt so tired, he couldn't stay upright, so sat down. After a moment or two, he laid his head on his crossed arms and sighed tiredly.

Sergeant Deemer had threatened him with blue murder if he let Barham escape, but how could a man get out of a cell with such a heavy iron door? He'd just grab a little nap.

Farrow jerked awake suddenly as someone knocked on the door of the police station. He glanced at the station clock. Two in the morning. Who the hell was that?

'Help! Police! They've broken into my house. They've got my wife and say I have to pay up to get her back.'

The constable hurried to look out of the front window. A man was standing there, an older man, white hair tousled, eyes staring. He was wearing rough clothes and even as Farrow looked, he raised his hand to hammer on the door again.

'Who are you? Where do you live?' Farrow called out.

'Jimmy Seton. I live on Birch Road, down the bottom end. They've locked me out of the house. I'm afeared for my wife.'

That was a rough neighbourhood. Farrow had been called out to fights there a few times. He hesitated. Sergeant Deemer had told him not to leave their prisoner alone under any circumstances. But you couldn't let some poor woman suffer, could you?

'Just a minute.' He went to the rear of the station and peered into the cell again. Barham was still fast asleep. You'd think he had a clear conscience the way he was sleeping. It wasn't fair.

He'd just nip down to Birch Road and have a look. Sometimes even the sight of a uniform stopped the fighting.

He went back to the front desk, took out his truncheon and opened the front door.

Something hit him on the head from the side the minute he stepped out and as he struggled to lift his truncheon, they hit him again.

He could feel himself losing consciousness, felt the ground coming up to meet him.

The man glanced quickly round, then dragged Farrow back inside. He shut the door and leaned against it for a minute, shaking, then pulled himself together and took the handcuffs from the young policeman's belt.

Puffing and cursing, he dragged the unconscious man behind the counter and handcuffed him to the metal foot rail, then searched a box labelled 'Lost Property' till he found a scarf he could use as a gag.

Only then did he yell out, 'Barham? Where the hell are you?'

'Back here.'

As the newcomer walked back along the corridor, Barham asked, 'Have you got the keys to the cell?'

'Dammit, I forgot.'

'They're on a big ring. Three big keys and a smaller one.'

The man went back and found the keyring attached to Farrow's belt. Unhooking it, he ignored the constable, except for noting that he was starting to regain consciousness, and went back to unlock the cell.

Barham moved quickly out of it. 'Let's get going.'

In the station, he stopped for a few seconds to smile down at Farrow, who was groaning. 'Serve you bloody right.' He kicked the constable in the ribs and led the way outside, locking the door carefully behind him and tossing the keys down a nearby drain. 'Where's the car?'

'Outside town, of course. Where we left it. Couldn't have found a better spot to hide. There's been no one near it all the time I've been there.'

'You should have brought it into town this time.'

'We agreed not to do that, so that no one could identify it. Or me.'

'Well, that means we've got a bloody long walk at this hour of the night.'

They set off walking, with Barham peering over his shoulder every minute or two.

'Ah, stop worrying. They won't find that idiot of a policeman till morning.'

'And I want us to be long gone from Lancashire by then.'

'We need to stop at a stream. I have to wash this flour out of my hair and smarten myself up a bit. We don't want anyone noticing a white-haired man driving the car.'

When they got to a stream, Barham waited impatiently, studying his companion, who was shorter than him. He didn't fancy going back to Mrs Galton. She'd be furious at his failure to bring Betty back to her.

As the older man turned away from the water, Barham punched him on the jaw, then punched him again for good measure, knocking him down. He took the car keys out of the driver's pocket, then all the money and ran off down the road, leaving him groaning on the damp ground.

Mrs Galton's second car, the one used to take servants shopping, was indeed where they had left it when he and Peeby first went into town. Pity they hadn't got hold of the child. It'd have been easy to get her away in such a neat little vehicle.

Barham smiled as he got in. It'd be easy for him to get away in it, too. The chauffeur wouldn't dare report him to the police. His smile grew broader when he saw the chauffeur's uniform cap on top of his pile of smarter clothes. Just the thing to hide his face, though the clothes would be too short for him. Pity.

Pulling the cap down hard, he got in, started the engine and set off. He'd change his clothes later, when he was out of reach of those two fools he'd come north with.

He had a friend in London who'd be happy to buy the

stolen car from him, though not at its full value. Luckily he kept his main savings account in London and he'd hidden his bankbook among his spare clothes. He always tried to keep it on him, in case he had to leave quickly.

He'd go and draw his money out from the bank and tell them he was emigrating – which was true.

Good thing the bankbook wasn't in the name he'd been using since he came to work for the Galtons. He laughed out loud. He'd used several names in the past ten years. It'd feel strange to use his own name again.

As he drove he wondered for the umpteenth time whether to go to Canada or Australia? He felt drawn to both countries. A lot of folk were planning to go overseas, eager to get away from war-ravaged Europe.

In the end, as he shivered in the draughty vehicle, he decided on Australia. He fancied a warmer climate.

Whistling cheerfully he drove south, stopping in an isolated spot to change into his smarter clothes.

He reckoned he'd thought of everything. Well, he hoped he had.

Sod the lot of them, especially that nasty old bitch. From now on, he was going to be respectable. The thought of that made him choke with laughter, but he reckoned it'd make life easier. Why, he might even marry again, not a stupid bitch like the last one, but a decent woman. About time he got himself a son.

Whistling cheerfully he watched dawn brighten the eastern horizon as he headed ever south.

Farrow wasn't found until a passing workman heard him yelling for help early the following morning. Out of sheer curiosity the man went to fetch Sergeant Deemer.

Mrs Deemer opened the front door and scowled at him.

'My husband isn't up yet. Can't he even get a proper night's sleep now? The war is over, you know.'

But when Sergeant Deemer heard why the man was there, he got dressed quickly and hurried across town to the police station.

There was quite a crowd gathered there, listening to the yelling coming from inside. Deemer didn't recognise Farrow's voice immediately, it was so hoarse, but when he did, he groaned aloud.

As he pulled his own keys out of his pocket, he wondered how the hell Barham had escaped and decided yet again that Farrow was too stupid to stay in the police force. Much too stupid.

'Stand back there. Let me through.'

He unlocked Farrow's handcuffs and the constable bolted to the lavatory. By the time he came back, Deemer had sent for the doctor and had a bowl of water ready to bathe his constable's head.

Farrow glared at the sergeant as if it were all his fault. 'I'm giving up this job. I didn't join the police to get attacked and locked up.'

'I should sack you for letting a prisoner escape, but if you're resigning, I'll leave it at that in my report. And you'd better write a report about this incident yourself before you go anywhere, not to mention working out your notice. Tell me exactly what happened, every single detail.'

Daniel strolled along the Highgate street with his friend John. 'Nice little hotel, that.'

'Aubrey's aunt recommended it.'

'I thought you were going to live with Aubrey. I'd expected you to be staying with him.'

'I'm thinking about it. Not sure what I'm going to do yet.

It's a big step to take.' He stopped and pointed. 'There you are! That's Lubetkin's building.'

'Nice, neat exterior, but it doesn't look . . . well, all that special.'

'You need to see the whole place. It's the interior that I find exciting.' John led the way inside. 'Promenade architecture, as you can see.'

'Slow down. You've been here before but I want to take it all in.' Daniel moved forward a few paces, then stopped and turned round in a circle. 'Verrry nice! Wonderful light. And look at the amenities: a place to meet friends and there's even a tearoom.'

'Plus swimming pool and tennis courts for residents outside.' John gave Daniel more time, then looked at his watch. 'Let's go up. Aubrey has one of the better three-bedroom flats in the nearest wing of the building, the lucky devil.'

Daniel found the interior of Aubrey's flat as full of light as the public spaces on the ground floor, and immediately made a mental note that if he got the chance to design modern houses for less wealthy people, he'd do them with bigger windows than usual. They would cost very little more than standard windows and light cost nothing, but it cheered people up to have a bright, airy living area.

He hoped he'd been polite to Aubrey, who was, as John had said, a nice man, but who had held his hand for too long when shaking it.

In the end, Daniel felt it necessary to apologise for being somewhat abstracted. 'It's the building. It's made me think about different ways of doing things. I wonder if you'd mind me leaving. I need to sort it all out in my head. And I'm sure you two have plenty to talk about.'

'I don't mind at all,' Aubrey said with a smile. 'The building has affected other people that way, too. Wonderful, isn't it? I'm so thankful Hitler didn't manage to bomb it.'

Daniel went for a long walk, ending up on Hampstead Heath. He sat down on a bench, gazing thoughtfully at the various buildings he could see in the distance. So many ways of creating shelter, so many styles.

It was dusk before he stood up again and began to stroll towards the edge of the parkland area. He felt ready to get to work, needed to find those pads and pencils.

It wasn't the first time John had set his mind on better tracks. His friend had a gift for helping people in that way. He wondered if he'd thanked him. He didn't think so. He'd have to apologise.

But oh, it felt so good to have his mind focusing on building again.

In the morning the two men met for breakfast.

'Enjoy your walk yesterday?' John asked.

'Very much. I needed the exercise, but mostly I needed to think. I was going to leave for Rivenshaw today or tomorrow, but then I heard about the *Daily Herald* Post-war Homes Exhibition, and since I doubt the others can get down to London, I decided to go and visit it. I gather they've set up five full-scale kitchens for people to study. I must see what I can pick up about the latest fitments for kitchens and bathrooms.'

John clapped him on the back. 'That sounds like the old Daniel. I'll come with you, if you like. They're also displaying scale models of homes built by various methods of prefabrication. I'm rather interested in that.'

'Good. I'll look at your prefabs and you can study my kitchens, then we'll compare notes. I heard about the Kitchen Planning Exhibition earlier in the year, but I couldn't get away from the unit to see it.'

As he was finishing eating, he hesitated, then said, 'I don't think I've thanked you properly, John. Talking to you has helped me more than anything else since I got demobbed.'

His friend shrugged, looking slightly embarrassed. 'I find if you let people talk at their own pace, they can usually find their own way to a decision.'

'Then you must be an exceptionally good listener.'

'I hope so.'

'Are you going to move in with Aubrey?'

'No. Too risky. You know what the law says about people like me. But I will buy a small place nearby. He and I will still be able to see one another regularly.'

'You must come up to Lancashire for a visit once I'm settled in.'

'I'd like that.'

The exhibition filled Daniel's head with more specific ideas. Looking at the bright new kitchens brought home to him how hard women had to work to keep a home running, and how much better their kitchens could be designed to fit their purpose.

His mind leapfrogged from there to the empty promise the government had made after the Great War. They had promised 'homes fit for heroes', but they hadn't built them, had they? Instead the country, especially in the north, had slid into an economic depression.

And with another jump of focus, he decided that, since women had done men's jobs during both wars, yes, and given their lives sometimes too, it was only fair that modern homes should be 'fit for heroes and heroines'.

He turned his attention to the details of these kitchens. They were more spacious, with the heavy ceramic sinks giving way to stainless steel. Fitted cupboards to a height suitable for working on linked the appliances. No need to do your chopping on a table, in these bright modern kitchens, or hide away in a dark, narrow scullery.

He overheard women oohing and aahing over the convenience of these designs and asked one or two what they liked best.

'I like it all,' one said, sighing. 'I want one of those refrigerators, and a modern washing machine too, and I'm going to get them one way or another.'

He and John ambled on, studying everything carefully. Though a lot could be done, there were strict regulations about size, cost and materials, even for private homes. You simply weren't allowed to build big houses, not with building materials so scarce and the need for homes so urgent.

The two men grimaced at the limitations.

'The government has got used to dictating how we live, hasn't it? They're not going to let go willingly.'

John shrugged and led the way to have another look at the models of prefabs. He indicated an aluminium prefab designed by the Aircraft Industries Research Organisation on Housing. 'I've seen that one being built. Most of the components can be brought to the site on a five-ton lorry. Just imagine that. And they say it'll last far longer than the prefabs made from other materials.'

Daniel was impressed. 'I heard they were building them as fast as they could to try to replace the homes destroyed by bombing. I wonder what they're like to live in.'

'I got talking to people who'd moved into one of the earliest ones erected, and they invited me inside. The rooms seemed rather small, but the women were thrilled to have indoor lavatories and bathrooms, as well as refrigerators and modern electric washing machines. It did my heart good to see how happy they were, after a lifetime in the slums.'

'These can be exciting times for us all,' Daniel said. 'And architects have a lot to contribute. I'm dying to get to Rivenshaw and make a start, but first I need to go and see my parents. I've neglected them shamefully.'

He not only wanted to make sure they were all right, he had to tell them about getting a quick American divorce from Ada. They'd be upset, but they'd understand. His mother especially had never really taken to his wife.

And they'd be able to bring him up to date on what had happened to the rest of the family.

He'd take the time to see them now because he suspected that once he got to Esherwood he'd be very busy indeed.

He'd been selfish lately, acting as if he was the only one who had been affected by the war. But he was coming through that now. Everyone had been affected in one way or another, of course they had.

And now, like everyone else, he was waiting to see who would govern the country. It was taking so much longer for the armed forces' votes to be counted from all over the world, but that was only fair.

If Churchill got in again, which most people thought he would, progress would be slow, Daniel was sure. The government would be trying to go back to the pre-war ways.

But he had a sneaking suspicion that the days of Conservative dominance were coming to an end, if not at this election, then at the next one.

11

Judith had never been so happy. The rest of July passed quickly as she, Mayne and the others worked steadily at clearing the house.

Had the Eshers never thrown anything away, she wondered, amazed at how many possessions the family had accumulated over the years. It was taking far longer to sort them out than any of them had expected.

Mayne might consider himself poor, but she considered him rich and it still amazed her that he could love someone like her. But he did. She had no doubt of that, any more than she doubted her own feelings for him. They chatted as they worked, getting to know one another in the many small ways that make up a relationship. One of the things she liked most was the way he smiled when he first saw her.

One of the things that slowed down the work was knowing what to do with an item. Sometimes all four adults would pass it from one to the other. Was it valuable or worthless? Which pile should it be put with: antiques, small valuables, bric-a-brac, rubbish? Silver items were easy in one sense because they were hallmarked, but some were so small they couldn't be worth much, surely . . . or could they?

Even Mayne had little clear idea of the values and Judith was beginning to worry that they might throw something away that had value, or sell it for only a fraction of its real worth. She'd been poor too long to want to risk losing even a few shillings.

On the Friday following their first full week of clearing out, she raised the matter with the others after tea. The four children had gone upstairs early, not to sleep but to play boardgames they'd unearthed from the nursery. From the laughter echoing down the servants' stairs, they were enjoying themselves.

The adults continued to sit round the kitchen table chatting. Everyone was tired but, like her, they were pleased with their week's work.

Judith waited for a lull in the conversation to ask, 'How are we going to find out whether these smaller items are valuable or not, let alone how much they're actually worth?'

No one spoke for a moment or two, though they all looked thoughtful. Then Mayne said slowly, 'Well, I know which things are old and treasured family possessions, and I've heard many of the stories behind them, so I have some idea which are the most valuable. But even so, I must admit, I have no idea what they're worth or how to find out for so many other things.

'I shall need to bring in an expert from Manchester. There is one my father has used before to sell things. He's well known for dealing in fine antiques, but I doubt he'll be interested in the smaller items.'

Judith wasn't going to let him throw good money away. She couldn't bear that. 'But there are hundreds of smaller items that may not be antiques but are still worth good money: crockery, silverware, ornaments, books. We don't know even approximately what they're worth but they're not rubbish. Even I can tell that.'

'I suppose not. I wasn't born in the days when the family had plenty of servants and gave lavish dinner parties, so a lot of the pieces haven't been used since my grandfather's time and I've never even seen them before. At least most of the silverware really is silver, not silver plate.' He shrugged. 'As for the ornaments and china, we'll just have to put them up for auction and get the best prices we can.'

She felt annoyed by this. 'It may not seem much of a difference to you whether we get three pounds for a single item or five; to me, there's a big difference, and it mounts up with so many things involved. It's foolish not to find out from someone who knows. If we do that we can insist on a fair price for every single thing we sell. You'll need money to set up your building company as well as the land and this house.'

'She's right,' Victor said. 'I grew up making every penny count, too. We can't possibly be experts at everything. But multiply all those extra pounds we might get if we take care of how we sell them by the number of small items and it could add up to quite a decent sum of money for you to invest, Mayne.'

'Well I suppose I can ask around, see if anyone knows a suitable person,' Mayne allowed. 'Trouble is, the antiques trade hasn't got going yet after the war, like many non-essential services, and I don't think we'll be seeing goods making top pre-war prices for a while. I'll have a think about it.'

'We'd better not sell anything till we're sure, then.' Judith wasn't satisfied with his answer or his attitude, because he didn't sound at all hopeful. But she hadn't the faintest idea how to find the information they needed, so let the matter drop for the moment. But she wasn't going to give up. *Look after the pennies and the pounds will look after themselves.* It was still a good rule and she felt her careful ways with money were something she could bring to their relationship and their business.

She stole a glance at Mayne. He'd been surprised by her stubbornness about this, she could tell. But she wasn't going to be a meek wife, not even with a kind man like him. She wanted much more out of the post-war world. She wanted to marry the man she loved. But she also felt a burning need to be recognised for her own skills and abilities.

She was capable of so much more than what her narrow life had previously allowed her. Sometimes she felt like a flower bursting into bloom. No: a whole flowering bush with buds, young flowers and big open flowers popping out. She smiled at how fanciful she was being, then the smile faded and determination filled her.

She wanted her children to have a fulfilling life, too. And she'd make sure they got every chance she could give them, not just a grammar school education.

The following Monday, Ros went into town to shop for the whole group's food. After queuing for ages to get what they needed, she left the grocer and greengrocer to send the goods up to the big house. Even with the still-tight rationing, there was more than she could carry comfortably.

She passed a second-hand shop and couldn't resist stopping to look through a tray of worn books labelled CHEAP. She liked to have a book on the go and had gone through Mayne's library at the big house, checking the books piled on the floor and in the cellar, because she knew she was welcome to borrow any of them. But his books didn't appeal to her. She read stories for relaxation, to escape the cares and sorrows of her own life, not for information.

A friend in the Wrens had introduced her to romance novels and she loved the way such stories took you out of your everyday world and always had happy endings. She knew these tales weren't true to life – she wasn't going to meet a prince or rich man in disguise – but you could dream of love, at least, couldn't you?

Ah! She spotted some of the familiar brown covers and

pulled out several well-worn books published by Mills & Boon. She checked them carefully, putting one back because she'd already read it. Should she buy all three others? They were only twopence each. Oh, why not? She was earning a good wage every week now, more than she'd ever been paid before now that Judith and Mayne had suggested an amount.

She must get used to the fact that she could spare sixpence now and then to feed her imagination with the happy stories it craved. The police hadn't yet given her any of her money back, but Sergeant Deemer had told her that Cliff had voluntarily handed over what was left, in the hopes of getting a lighter sentence. She wished they'd lock him away forever, so that he couldn't hurt other people.

Unfortunately the woman he'd been living with had vanished and taken some of the money with her, so Ros wouldn't get as much back as she'd hoped. The sergeant said she wouldn't receive the money until after the case came to court. The trouble was, she needed it now. She had such a ragged set of clothes, she was ashamed sometimes to be seen in them and of course Judith and the others saw her washing on the line.

She had clothing coupons to spare, because she'd been able to wear her Wrens uniform most of the time during the past few years, but where did you start when you needed absolutely everything: underwear, daily clothes, a good warm coat for the winter?

An old gentleman stopped beside her and picked up the book she'd just put back, which surprised her. Men didn't usually read romances and were often scornful of them.

He saw her staring at him and grinned. 'It's for my wife. Could I ask why you put it back? Isn't it a good story?'

His voice wasn't that of a gentleman, even though his clothing looked expensive. He spoke rather harshly, with a strong northern accent. And it wasn't the Rivenshaw accent, either, but sounded as if he came from somewhere near Liverpool. She didn't recognise him from before the war, but then she wouldn't. She'd lived in the poorer areas and worked behind the counter in the corner shop till she'd joined the Wrens.

She realised he was still waiting for her to answer his question. 'It's a lovely story, but I've read it before. I hope your wife enjoys it. It's been published for a while, though, so she may have read it too.'

He tapped his forehead. 'No. She definitely hasn't read this one. I've got a good memory for details and I do the buying because she doesn't like to be seen shopping for this type of book.' He chuckled. 'I don't give two hoots whether people approve of romance stories or not. If I want something, I buy it.'

'I'm the same when it comes to books. I don't let other people tell me what to read.'

He studied her openly, head on one side. 'I haven't seen you in town before. Are you new to Rivenshaw?'

'No. I grew up here. We lived in Sycamore Street. I left a few years ago when I joined the Wrens and I haven't been back for ages because I was stationed in Scotland.' She looked down at herself. 'A lot of people don't recognise me these days. I joined up as soon as I could. I was only seventeen. The food was plentiful and I grew six inches in the first eighteen months.'

'You weren't the only one to eat better in the forces. I've heard a few lads say that. Did you enjoy your time in the Wrens?'

'Oh, yes. Very much. I worked with some great women.'

He was turning to go into the shop when his attention was caught by something. 'Ah! See those two little china figures on the right. They're worth several times what Pointer's asking. I shall buy them as well.'

He saw her disapproving look and chuckled. 'It's all right.

I'll pay him half the extra profit when I sell them again. I don't need to penny pinch these days but I still enjoy buying and selling.'

'Doesn't the owner know his trade? He's new since my time. He seems a nice man.'

'A bit soft, but he's learning fast about prices and how to treat customers who want to cheat him.'

She picked up all three books and followed him into the shop, watching the way he dealt with Mr Pointer. He didn't just hand over the money; he seemed to be teaching the new owner what to look for, pointing to the information underneath the figurines and explaining what else you looked for in such items.

Once he'd left, she asked the shopkeeper, 'Who is that man?'

'Mr Woollard. Surely you've heard of him? He's quite a figure in the town these days, made a fortune during the war.'

'I've been away, and though I've heard of him, I haven't seen him in person before.'

'There's some as don't like him or the way he earned his fortune, but I speak as I find. I used to do odd jobs for him before the war, and went to see him when I was invalided out last year to ask his advice. He was very helpful, lent me some of the money to buy this place.'

He looked round with a proud smile on his thin face. 'I'm making a living now, even selling junk, because people's crockery breaks and there's not much in the shops. They have to replace it with something.'

Mr Pointer's pride in what he'd achieved touched her. She could appreciate the effort it took to do that from a poor background. She paid for her books and left, thoughtful now.

When they were eating lunch, the others teased her for being absent-minded, so she told them about her encounter.

'Why did you need to buy books?' Mayne asked in surprise. 'There are plenty here that you can borrow.'

She could feel herself flushing. 'I like to read romances. They always have happy endings and that cheers me up. There aren't any romances in your library, Mayne. I already looked.'

'So who was this man who bought one for his wife?' Judith prompted.

'I asked Mr Pointer. It was Mr Woollard. I've heard you talk about him and you always seem disapproving, but I liked him. I think he understands what it's like to be poor, but he seems to have plenty of money now.'

'You must be the only person in town who does like Woollard,' Mayne said.

'No, I'm not. Mr Pointer likes him too. Mr Woollard not only lent him part of the money to start up the shop, he's teaching him about second-hand goods.'

'Ha! It's a miracle, then. Look, Ros, Woollard's a war profiteer.'

'Well, he's a kind one, then. And what's more, I was wondering if he'd be the person to ask how best to sell the things whose value we're not sure of. He seemed very know-ledgeable about the items in the shop.'

There was dead silence.

'I don't think so,' Mayne said curtly.

She didn't press the point, but she thought he was wrong not even to consider it. Mr Woollard might be getting on, but he still had the air of a cheeky urchin, for all his fine clothes and wealth. As a child, she'd played on the streets with lads like him and understood them.

If he'd made a fortune by war profiteering, well, that was wrong, but not everyone was born with a silver spoon in their mouth. Which was a stupid saying, but it expressed how she felt at the moment.

Perhaps he'd had a poor childhood, been hungry, and that had spurred him on to make money any way he could. She hadn't been hungry till after her father died, but she'd never forget how ravenous she'd been sometimes during those years of living with Cliff.

She wished she had a bit of money behind her, like Mayne and Victor did. It must make you feel secure. They could afford to look down their noses at people. She couldn't. Not that she thought she was likely to lose her job here. She wasn't that insecure now. Both men were very complimentary about her work, she got on well with Judith, and she loved little Betty dearly, even though it was foolish to love someone else's child. But still, life could toss you down at the drop of a hat. She never forgot that and was always a bit on her guard, even in the good times.

She might be able to afford the occasional sixpence for second-hand books, but she'd still save most of her wages and not buy any clothes until she'd seen how much money she got back from Cliff. Well, unless there were some things left in the clothing exchange she'd heard Judith mention. Perhaps she'd go and have a look through their stock later in the week.

In the meantime, she'd forgotten to tell the others her news, such important news. 'I found out where my mother's grave is. Well, approximately.'

'What do you mean by "approximately"?' Victor asked.

'Mum was put in a pauper's grave plot with nine other people. I can't even buy her a headstone, let alone put flowers on her grave!' She couldn't stop her voice wobbling as she said that.

Judith hurried round the table to put her arms round her and Ros clung to her for a minute.

'I'm so sorry. So very sorry. Here. Take my handkerchief.'

'Thanks.' Ros mopped her eyes, muttering, 'I hope Cliff rots in hell when he dies!'

'At the very least they'll lock him away.'

* * *

Two days later Victor said he had a meeting in town and asked Ros to keep an eye on Betty. He didn't say where he was going, which wasn't like him, but she didn't think anything of it.

That afternoon, he asked her if she could spare him a few minutes. 'Kitty will keep an eye on Betty for me. I have some news for you.'

She was puzzled, but hoped it was to do with Cliff and the money he'd stolen from her.

Victor took her out to the remains of the rose garden, a peaceful spot where Jan had put a rough old bench he'd found behind the shrubbery. 'Shall we sit down for a few minutes?'

He sounded so solemn she began to worry. What now?

'There's no easy way to put this,' Victor began.

'Just say it straight out, then.' She couldn't imagine why he was hesitating. She doubted he was going to sack her, but what else could make him look so sad?

'Very well. I've been to see the man in charge of the paupers' graves and—'

Her stomach clenched with fear and she looked at him numbly, waiting.

'I've found out exactly where your mother is lying. She was the last person put into that mass grave, as they start a new one for every ten people who die and whose families can't afford to bury them.'

Shame filled her, because only the very poorest let their relatives be buried on the parish.

'We can, if you like, have her coffin exhumed and put into a proper grave.'

It was the last thing she'd expected to hear. 'Are you sure?'

'Yes. We'll have to pay various expenses, like grave diggers, and a plot of her own, and there should probably be a new burial service. Oh, and you'll want a headstone, I'm sure.'

'Oh. Right. Can I . . . wait and do this once I get my money back?'

'The man said it'd be better to do it as soon as possible, before the coffin disintegrates. They, um, use the cheapest wood for these people.'

Disappointment brought tears to her eyes. 'I don't have enough money.'

He took her hand. 'But I do.'

'That's kind of you, but I don't want to get into debt, and anyway, you're going to need all your spare money to invest in the flats.'

'I can spare enough to help you. Let me do this, Ros. It's important. I can't visit my wife's grave, because her parents buried her in their mausoleum, which is a horrible dark place to which only Mrs Galton and her lawyer have a key. I understand exactly how you feel about not being able to visit your mother's grave, believe me.'

Silence pooled around them for a few moments, then he raised her hand to his lips. 'Let me do it. If things work out between us as I hope, the money won't matter.'

'All right.' And then she was weeping, held close, given a handkerchief. She felt a kiss on her hair as she sobbed against his chest, and his warm, strong hand was there at her back, holding her safe and close.

When she stopped weeping, he said quietly, 'So we'll do it?'

'Yes. Thank you, Victor. What must I do?'

'Go into town, sign some papers, pay some money.' He looked at his wristwatch. 'We could set things in motion now, if you like. Get the whole thing started, anyway. They told me it'd take over a month to complete the job.'

She looked down at herself in her shabby clothes, knowing her eyes must be red with weeping, but couldn't bear to wait another minute to get started. 'Let me just change into my Sunday best.'

'If that's important.'

'It is. And Victor . . . thank you. I can't tell you how much it means to me.'

'As I said, I do understand. And . . . I care about your happiness.'

She nodded, her heart too full to answer him without weeping again.

Thursday July 26th arrived at last and everyone who could do stayed near a wireless to listen as the results of the General Election were announced for the various constituencies.

Even the children were interested. Ben gave his mother a quick, furtive hug. He thought himself too old to cuddle her openly these days. 'This is like what you told us when the war ended, isn't it?' he asked. 'Another time to remember.'

'Yes, darling.'

'Who do you think will win the election, Mr Churchill or Mr Attlee?'

'You heard from Mr Travers what it said in the *Chronicle*: the Gallup Polls are forecasting a Labour victory.'

'Miss Peters says that'll never happen. She thinks people will stay loyal to Mr Churchill.'

Victor joined them in time to hear that remark. 'Well I think Labour will win by a mile. The people of Britain have won their peace. Now let's see what they can do about winning another battle: social justice for everyone.'

Ben winked at his mother and slipped away.

She didn't let herself smile, but Victor had said this several times already.

Mayne was less optimistic about any political party's ability to deliver social justice for everyone, but he believed an attempt at it was long overdue.

Anyone who remembered the thirties and the hard times people had endured then surely wouldn't want the old times to return. Even as a boy, he'd seen men out of work on street corners, seen hungry, listless children sitting at the edge of the kerb instead of playing cricket in the street.

As the commentator continued to report one Labour victory after another, they all stayed near the radio set until, in the six o'clock news, a landslide victory was announced for the Labour Party.

'What surprises me,' Judith said, 'is how Churchill could have lost the election by so much, when he was such an inspiration to everyone during the war.'

It was Victor who answered. 'Because he was a great war leader, but ordinary people don't think he'll look after them in peace. Well, judging from his election speeches, he doesn't understand what life is like for ordinary people.'

'What do you want out of this new government, Ros?' Victor asked.

She didn't hesitate. 'A welfare state, if that's what they call it? So that people like my mother won't die worrying about doctors' bills. So that everyone can get proper treatment when they're ill. I've read parts of the Beveridge Report and it was full of fine ideas. Let's hope this new government means what it said about putting them into operation.'

'I care most about better housing,' Judith said thoughtfully. 'I've read articles in the newspapers about the dreadful housing shortage. We're not too badly off in Rivenshaw, because we didn't lose a lot of houses to bombing, but my heart goes out to those poor people in London and the other big cities, who've lost all the possessions they held dear and haven't got a real home any more. I had to fight to keep my house sometimes when Doug was boozing the money away, so I was very close to having nowhere to live. Well, I didn't have anywhere for a short time, though thanks to you, Mayne, we came here.'

He took her hand. 'I'll make sure you always have a proper roof over your head from now on, Judith.'

Ros watched them enviously. Sometimes the two of them forgot the other people in the room and let their love for one another show. She turned and saw Victor gazing at them too, then he turned to her.

'Are you feeling more secure here now, Ros?'

'A bit. But I'm still only an employee, aren't I? And employees can be sacked at the drop of a hat.'

He looked at her in shock. 'There's no way we'd ever sack you, Ros. You're a really hard worker.' He lowered his voice so that Mayne and Judith couldn't hear. 'And once I've sorted out Betty's future properly, and am sure no one will try to take her from me, I'll start looking at my own future.' He took her hand under cover of the table and gave it a quick squeeze.

But fine words and hand squeezes didn't guarantee anything. She knew that better than anyone. Cliff had been full of fine words when he'd been courting her mother. Even she'd been fooled by them and thought him a kind man. And look what had come of that!

Victor wasn't like her stepfather, though, of course he wasn't. He was a fine man and a very loving father. But he was from a family far better off than hers. He hadn't grown up in a near slum.

She knew he liked her, dreamed one day something might come of it, because she certainly liked him. But it was better not to hope for too much, wiser to keep your innermost thoughts to yourself till it was safe to let them out.

She changed the subject back to the election and Mr Attlee's visit to Buckingham Palace to see the king, wondering what two such different people would find to chat about.

PART TWO
August 1945

12

At long last, on the Wednesday after the General Election, a letter arrived from Daniel. Mayne hurried out to the stables to show it to Victor. 'Look! Daniel's written at last and he's bubbling with enthusiasm. He sounded so unlike himself in his last letter, I was worried.' He thrust the piece of paper into his friend's hand.

Victor scanned the few lines of scrawl and handed the letter back. 'It's good to hear from him. I've missed the old devil. He doesn't say much about what he's been doing, does he?'

'He sounds eager to get going on designing the flats, though. And will be here as soon as his mother has put on a family reunion.'

'It's my guess Daniel was more upset about his divorce than he let on,' Victor said thoughtfully.

'Well, anyone would be. You don't start a marriage expecting it to fail.'

'I know how he feels. You plan to spend your life with someone then they're suddenly taken from you.'

Mayne glanced at him quickly. Was his friend talking about Daniel or himself?

'Some men have found it hard to adjust to peace,' Victor said.

'Are we talking about the same person, Daniel who was

the life and soul of any gathering and seemed able to deal with anything that happened at the unit?'

'I've been reading about it in the newspaper. Big changes can upset anyone. People have more time to brood, apparently, now the war's over. I don't have time to think about anything except keeping Betty away from her grandmother.' He shrugged. 'Perhaps that has helped me change direction more quickly. And although I'm sad about Susan, I knew she was frail. We were more good friends than husband and wife for most of our marriage, but I didn't expect to lose her so quickly. I wasn't at all prepared for the speed of that.'

Mayne couldn't find any words of comfort, so patted his friend's shoulder a couple of times.

'I'm all right,' Victor said gruffly.

'You may find someone more compatible this time round.'

'What do you mean by "this time round"?'

'Am I mistaken? Aren't you interested in Ros?'

Victor sighed. 'Yes, I am. But there's Betty to think about. Till all that's settled, it'd be selfish of me to indulge myself. And so soon after Susan's death, too.'

'Rubbish. If you like Ros enough to want a relationship with her, well, that gives Betty another person to look after her. Judith says Ros loves Betty already.'

'Betty seems fond of her, too.' Victor stared into space for a moment or two, then changed the subject. 'What about Francis? Have you heard from anyone about what's happened to him?'

'Not a word. It's beginning to worry me. It's not so much his money we need for the project as his expertise with modern machinery.'

'What if he backs out?'

'We'll manage somehow, I suppose. But I think we'd do better with his help. He has a real sense of what's likely to come in the future. I don't understand why he hasn't written, though, even if it was just a few words on a postcard to reassure us. Maybe I should go and visit him, check that he's all right.'

'Wait a little longer. Wars aren't easy for men in the forces.'

'This war was hard on civilians too. Very hard. And then those damned Yanks came along, flashing money, making promises. And don't forget that Francis married hastily, to a woman whose family were comfortably off.'

'Well, his parents had done quite well at making money, it sounded like.'

'Ah, but *her* parents and grandparents were solicitors and had always had money. I met her a couple of times. Spoiled brat, if you ask me.' Victor shook his head sadly.

They were both quiet for a few moments. Some of the men returning to civilian life were having a really hard time of it.

It wasn't just the hasty marriages that needed sorting out, or ending; there was one man in Rivenshaw who'd been a prisoner of war. Even after a month at home, he was skeletally thin and looked so ill that Mayne felt upset whenever he saw his former schoolmate. The poor fellow walked round town most days but never stopped to chat, just seemed to need to walk about freely.

Yesterday he'd nodded in response to Mayne's greeting, and that had seemed like a step forward.

Daniel sat on the train, glad to be on his way to Rivenshaw at last. His parents were settling down to a peacetime life again and he'd caught up with most of his relatives at the family reunion, heard how they'd got through the war.

He was looking forward to seeing Mayne and Victor. And Francis, of course, though he didn't know Francis as well as the other two.

To his annoyance, his train was delayed and he missed

his connection with the local train from Manchester to Rivenshaw. He went looking for a cup of tea. For once, the refreshment room was open, though there was very little on offer and the buns looked rather tired.

'Cup of tea and one of those buns, please,' he said.

'The lady was here first.' The woman behind the counter jerked her head to the left.

He turned in surprise. He hadn't noticed the woman in a nondescript beige coat because she was squeezed into a corner. There were no buns set out there, but she was pretending to study the empty display case at the end of the counter.

He looked back at the attendant, who rolled her eyes in the direction of the window that looked on to the station concourse. When he followed her gaze he saw a tall, well-built man who seemed to be searching the crowd for someone.

He noticed the fear on the other customer's face as she glanced quickly round and realised the man was moving towards the refreshment room. He moved instinctively to shield the woman from sight.

'I think you're trying to hide from that man,' he said in a low voice. 'Shall I stand next to you as if we're together or do you want me to leave you alone?'

'I am trying to hide. Please stay there. Thank you.'

'He's coming inside. It'll be easier to hide you if I put my arm round you.'

Her eyes searched his face and she gave a little nod as if he'd passed some test. 'All right.'

She stood in his arms, surely the stiffest woman he'd ever embraced. He didn't dare move a muscle in case he frightened her. He could feel her trembling slightly, and that upset him. Why was she so afraid? They were in a public place, after all.

The door opened and cooler air blew in, bringing the smells of steam and engine oil.

'Can I help you, sir?' the attendant asked.

There was no answer, but Daniel heard the door bang shut.

'He's gone, miss. He walked towards the exit.'

'Thank you, both of you,' the woman said.

Daniel stepped away from her.

'Do we need to fetch a policeman?' the attendant asked. 'There's always one on duty. I could run and get him.'

'No. Keith would just pretend we're engaged and had a quarrel. He's done it before. He can be very convincing. We used to be engaged, but I wrote to him two years ago to break it off. Two years! Only he won't accept that. He keeps writing to me as if we're still engaged.'

'Why did you break it off, if you don't mind me asking? Did you meet someone else?'

'Yes. I saw Anthony a couple of times at dances and he was so different, so kind, such fun, I knew I couldn't stay with Keith any longer. I'd been going to wait till the end of the war to break up with him, but the war went on and on. I didn't feel I could go out with the other fellow till I broke it off with Keith, so I sent him a letter. Only I didn't have much time with Anthony. He was killed a month after we got together.'

'Aw. That's hard luck.'

She shrugged but her eyes were sad. 'Yes, well, when Keith came back, he acted as if we'd never broken up, refused even to discuss it. He started following me about, standing outside our house for hours. It gave me the shivers. I didn't even dare go out on my own after dark. And my dad's too old to defend me if Keith . . . lost control. He has a fearful temper, you see. So I left.'

'Have you got someone to go to?'

'Yes. Well, I think so. An uncle. Keith won't expect me to go to him, because my father hasn't spoken to his brother for years, can't even say his name without cursing him. I don't know what happened between them, Dad won't say, but I'm hoping my uncle will help me. If not . . .' she shrugged. 'I'll manage. I'm not the shy little thing I was before the war.'

The attendant brought a cup and plate. 'Here you are, miss. Do you still want the tea and bun, sir? Only there's a train due in and we'll be crowded out soon.'

'Yes, please.' When Daniel's plate and cup were dumped in front of him, he hesitated then asked, 'Shall I join you? If this Keith fellow comes back, he won't look at a couple as quickly.'

She gave him a wary look, then gestured to the hard wooden chair opposite her. 'All right. Thanks.'

'I'm Daniel O'Brien.'

'Stephanie. But people usually call me Steph.'

She didn't volunteer her surname, so he didn't ask. After all, he'd probably never see her again after today. She wasn't his type anyway. A plain Jane of a woman, scrawny, with a determined expression, wearing dowdy clothes. He preferred women who took a pride in their appearance.

Just as they were finishing their snack, the attendant said suddenly, 'That fellow's coming back, miss.'

'Oh, no!'

Daniel glanced out of the window. 'Look, Steph, I've got to catch my train. Why don't you walk out of here cuddled up to me, then go and hide in the ladies' rest room? I promise not to take advantage of the situation.'

She looked up at the clock on the wall. 'I have a train to catch too, at three o'clock. I'm going to a place called Rivenshaw.'

'Good heavens, so am I!'

'Thank you for your offer, then. It may get me on the train.' She took a headscarf out of her shabby leather handbag and tied it round her so that it partly shaded her face.

Daniel stood up, picked up his suitcase.

She picked one up too. 'I have a trunk to collect as well.'

'Snap.' He pulled her towards him. She was small enough to nestle against him.

As they walked out, he bent his head as if talking to her and when the man pursuing her got closer, Daniel muttered, 'I can kiss you to hide your face.'

'Oh. Well, go ahead, but no tongues.'

He kissed her lips, finding to his surprise that he liked their softness. Then he moved to kiss her cheek as they passed the man.

The fellow didn't give them a second glance.

They summoned a porter and had both trunks put in the luggage van, then, still with his arm round her, they moved along the train.

'Do you have a first-class ticket?' he asked.

'Yes. I thought it'd be easier to avoid Keith. He won't expect that.'

'Good. That makes things easier.'

As soon as they were in the compartment, she pulled away from him and sat in the far corner next to the corridor, pulling the headscarf over her face and leaning her head against the window as if she'd fallen asleep.

Daniel sat near the outer door, ready to stop the fellow if he tried to get into their compartment. But no one came near them and, though the minutes seemed to tick by very slowly, at last the guard blew his whistle and the train began to move.

'I'd better check that this Keith fellow is still in the station. We might be in trouble if he's got onto the train.' Daniel lowered the window and looked out. 'Ah. He's still standing by the ticket collector.' He pretended to wave to someone, then closed the window and sat down.

As the train gathered speed, Steph sat up and began to

tidy her hair, dragging it back into a most unflattering bun.

Did she always wear it like that, Daniel wondered, or was she doing it to put him off? She had no need to worry. She might have soft, kissable lips, but the rest of her was very utilitarian. He liked women with more style. Give Ada her due, she'd dressed beautifully. He'd always been proud to be seen with her.

'Will you be all right once we get to Rivenshaw?' he asked after a while.

'Oh, yes. I'll take a taxi to my uncle's.'

'That's all right then.'

They didn't chat. He was tired and she seemed lost in thought. Which wasn't surprising.

As they parted company outside the station, he said, 'Good luck with your uncle.'

'Thank you.'

But she was already turning away.

Strange little incident, that, he thought. Then another taxi arrived and he hailed it. He was looking forward to seeing Mayne and Victor again. Looking forward to all sorts of things now.

Steph leaned back in the taxi, so tired she felt as if she was filled with lead. It had been hard getting away from Keith. How he'd managed to follow her into Manchester, she didn't know. She'd thought she'd given him the slip, but of course, anyone who saw her luggage as she left home would guess she was making for the railway station. How else would you escape?

The taxi drew up in front of a comfortable house. When the driver opened the door, she asked him to wait to unload her luggage. 'I'm, um, not sure they'll be expecting me.'

He looked at the house. 'Well, they've got plenty of room, haven't they? I'll have to leave the meter ticking. It'll cost me money to wait around.'

'That's all right. I can pay.' She tried to straighten her clothes as she walked up the front steps and rang the door-bell.

'I'll get it, Nora,' a man's voice yelled.

The door was flung open and she found herself staring at a man so like her father in appearance that for a moment she couldn't speak.

He frowned at her. 'We don't buy things at the door.'

'I'd hardly come in a taxi if I was selling door-to-door, would I?'

He looked beyond her. 'Why have you come, then?'

'I'm your niece, Martin's daughter.'

He didn't say anything, just waited for her to go on.

'I know you and my dad don't get on, but I need to get away from Salford. There's a man come back from the war, and he's . . . following me around. I'm afraid he's going to harm me. And Dad's not been well.'

One more minute ticked slowly past as her uncle studied her, then he held the door open. 'You'd better come in then. I'll see to the taxi.'

She was left standing in the hall, feeling awkward.

She looked round. Her dad was right. His brother Ray had done well for himself. Very well indeed, to judge by the size of this house and the way it was furnished.

Her dad said Ray had made money through black market profiteering – and worse – which was why the two of them had fallen out. She didn't care about that. She only cared about finding somewhere safe from Keith till she could work out what to do.

'Mind out, lass.' She stepped hastily back as her uncle and the taxi driver lugged her trunk into the hall, and then the driver went back for her suitcase.

And all the time she could only stand there like a frozen fool, because she'd thought of how to get here, how to introduce herself, but she hadn't worked out what might happen next.

'I . . . I don't want to be any trouble,' she faltered.

Her uncle's expression was kind. 'Eh, you're my niece and I'm glad to help you. Whoever he is, the fellow ought to be shot at dawn for frightening you so much.'

She could feel tears of relief start to trickle down her face, tried in vain to hold them back.

'Come here, lass.' He gave her a big hug, rocking to and fro, dwarfing her but not frightening her like Keith did, instead making her feel safe. 'Did you think I'd turn you away?'

'I wasn't sure. Even Dad didn't think you would. But it was the first good thing he'd said about you in years, so I wasn't sure.'

'He always was a Holy Joe, our Martin. I bet he's still living in a terraced house and working for someone else.'

'No, he isn't. He has a second-hand shop, good-quality stuff not rubbish, and he sells some antiques as well. He's good at finding things that are valuable. He's quite comfortably off, actually, but he's not a well man and he couldn't protect me against Keith.'

'What about the police?'

'I went to them and they said it was just a lovers' tiff and none of their business. But I was really frightened of Keith. He's changed, came back from the war bigger and . . . and more violent.'

'Will he find out where you are?'

'Probably. I thought I could stay here for a few days, if you didn't mind, then I'd see if I could find a job somewhere no one knows me and change my name.'

'Do you want to do that?' He sounded surprised.

'No. But I think it's the only way I'll escape Keith. He followed me to the station in Manchester, so he'll come here eventually, I'm sure. He's clever, methodical and ruthless. He's got his mind set on marrying me and it doesn't seem to matter to him whether I want to or not. He says . . . if he can't have me no one else can.'

She shivered as she said the words. They'd haunted her dreams for the past week, ever since Keith had cornered her and made his intentions plain.

She found herself being hugged and rocked again.

'I'll look after you, lass. No need for you to go to Australia.'

Closing her eyes, Steph leaned against her uncle and let out a long sigh of relief. Perhaps she'd be able to sleep properly tonight.

But could Uncle Ray really protect her?

13

Daniel helped the taxi driver heave his trunk on to a rack at the rear of the vehicle, then shoved his suitcase on the back seat. While the driver was strapping the trunk in place, he stared round, enjoying his first sight of the town centre. This big open square would be quite pretty once the bomb damage was made good and the shabby buildings brought up to scratch again. A few trees would improve it, too.

Shivering in the cool, damp air, he got in beside the driver, who was a taciturn fellow. Giving up the attempt to chat, Daniel looked out of the window. The taxi slowed down to turn right onto a street that had houses along one side only: large Edwardian villas overlooking a park.

The park was now, like many others in Britain, divided into allotments with hardly any grass undug. They'd left a few fine trees in place, thank goodness. What had Mayne said the park was called? Oh yes, Parson's Mead. Quaint name.

The taxi slowed again to turn into a drive next to an old house, which was the only dwelling at the narrow upper end of the almost triangular park. This would probably be the Dower House, where his friend's parents lived. It wasn't small, by anyone's standards. How big was the main house, then?

The grounds the drive twisted through were in a mess.

Someone had recently removed a barrier near the entrance and the heavy chain lay on the ground, several yards long, still attached to one of a pair of concrete bollards. Trees in full leaf blocked a clear view of the big house but he could see the end of a Nissen hut to the right of the building, and a large wooden shed beyond it.

Then the house came into view and Daniel leaned forward involuntarily. What a pretty manor house! Or it would have been once. Like most other buildings in the country, it looked shabby now, with minor weather damage here and there. He'd bet the rooms inside were large with that gracious air old houses sometimes got. It would be such a pity to divide them up, which they might have to do, to make flats.

The exterior was a symmetrical structure, in spite of the fact that it looked to have been built piecemeal, a mixture of different ages and styles of architecture. Somehow the shapes of the various parts formed a harmonious whole, with creeper covering the changes from one era's design to the next.

Architecturally, he shouldn't have liked it, but he did. It happened that way sometimes, a building having an unexpected synergy, where the whole became of more value than its individual parts. The house was large, though small by comparison with the bigger stately homes like Chatsworth. There was one wing that turned backwards and would give the house an L shape from the rear.

To Daniel's surprise, it looked like a home not a showplace. He hadn't expected that. He'd have to try to work out how the effect had been achieved and see if he could keep that feeling.

Sadly, when you looked more closely, you could see the need for quite a lot of maintenance work. One or two upstairs windows were boarded up, the glass in others was cracked and the woodwork needed attention. It was hard enough to obtain glass. How did you get hold of glass that would suit these old windows? Older glass had imperfections, which were part of its charm.

He'd have to check that Esherwood was structurally sound before he even began to work on designs for flats.

Again, he thought what a shame it would be to pull the old house apart, cut into the elegant plasterwork of the Georgian ceilings he'd heard about. If only Mayne could have afforded to live there. He jumped in shock as someone touched his shoulder: the taxi driver.

'Sorry, sir! I need to get on. If you could pay me and help me to unload your things, I'll leave you to it.'

'Of course. I was just—'

'Daniel!'

He turned as Mayne came hurrying out of the house. They shook hands vigorously, but that wasn't enough so they pounded each other on the back a few times for good measure.

The driver sighed loudly.

'Just let me pay this chap.' Daniel added a reasonable tip to make up for keeping the man waiting, which brought a brief smile to the dour face. Then, as he and Mayne started to lug the trunk towards the stairs leading to the front door, Victor came out. Daniel dropped his end to shake hands with another good friend.

By that time, two women and four children were standing at the top of the three shallow steps that led into the house, smiling at him. They looked as if they lived there, so Daniel turned to look questioningly at Mayne. 'May I be introduced?'

'Of course, but let's get your things inside first. It's spitting with rain already.' He gestured to the group. 'We're thinking of starting our own platoon. Go back inside everyone, and I'll introduce you properly. It's going to pour down any minute.'

Daniel smiled as he helped carry his trunk inside. He'd not even noticed the incipient rain, he'd been so fascinated by the old house.

Once they'd been introduced, the rest of them went back to work, leaving the three men to catch up with each other's news.

'He's good looking, isn't he?' Ros said, once the children had resumed their efforts to clear out another of the store cupboards in the old nursery and schoolroom. Judging by their previous efforts this would entail trying out a lot of the toys and arguing about whether they would be worth anything. 'He seems rather quiet, though, not at all what I expected from their descriptions.'

Judith considered this, head on one side. 'He's quite attractive, yes, but he looks strained at the moment, rather than quiet by nature, if you ask me.'

'Mmm. I think you're right. A lot of men are having difficulty adjusting to civilian life, aren't they? Oh well, come on. Let's go and chivvy those children to stop testing all the toys. We need to finish clearing out the nursery floor, so that we can move everyone up there.'

While they were working, Ros asked hesitantly, 'Have you and Mayne thought any more about asking Mr Woollard's help with valuing the smaller goods?'

'Mayne's against it. He doesn't approve of war profiteers.'

'Mr Woollard was never prosecuted for black market dealing.'

'Everyone in town knew what he was doing, though. There was even talk of him receiving stolen goods.'

'Oh, no. Surely not! He doesn't seem the sort to do that. And we desperately need help with the valuations.'

'Woollard asked a while ago if he could buy into the building company, but Mayne doesn't really want that, either.

He admits the man has helpful connections, though, so perhaps we can work on him, change his mind and persuade him to give Woollard a chance.'

'Yes. Ideals are all very well, but you need to be practical when it comes to money.' Ros would never again be careless, or even generous, with her own.

'Come into the sitting room and meet my wife, your Auntie Edna.' Uncle Ray didn't wait for Steph to reply, but led the way into a large, comfortable room, where a woman was sitting with a blanket over her knees. She looked unwell, her face pale and weary.

'Edna, love, this is my brother Martin's girl. Steph's come to take refuge with us.'

His wife listened intently to his explanation, and held out her hands to her niece, clasping them for a moment and studying her face. 'We're really glad to have you here, love. Stay as long as you like. We've been too quiet for our own good lately and we'll enjoy a bit of company. I've had a bad bout of 'flu but I'm getting over it now.'

'I don't want to bring trouble on you. If Keith follows me . . . '

Edna smiled at her husband, a warm loving smile that he returned with one equally loving, Steph noted.

'You couldn't find anyone better to help you if you're in trouble than your uncle. He and your father had a rough upbringing and my Ray knows how to look after himself and those he cares about. This Keith fellow had better watch out if he goes after one of our family.'

'Oh. Well, thank you. We'll see how things go. I'm really grateful to be here.'

'I'll have to leave Muriel to show you up to your room. I find those stairs a bit trying yet.' She picked up a little silver handbell from a small table next to her and rang it. Within a minute, someone knocked on the door and a woman of a similar age to her mistress poked her head round it.

'Muriel dear, come and meet my niece. Steph will be staying with us for a while.'

The maid nodded to Steph, her eyes shrewd and no hint of subservience in her bearing.

'The other front bedroom, do you think, Muriel?'

'Yes. You get Thomas to help you with that trunk, sir. This way, miss.'

'Come down when you've unpacked and we'll have some tea,' Edna called after her niece.

'Thank you.'

Steph picked up her suitcase, refusing to let the elderly maid carry it upstairs for her, and was shown to her bedroom. It had every comfort, including a plumbed-in handbasin, and a view towards the moors, where rain was sweeping across the horizon like a curtain of grey muslin.

'It'll do the missus a world of good to have you staying,' Muriel said. 'She's been very low since she was ill. It drags you down, the influenza does. Let me show you the bathroom.'

She led the way into a lovely modern bathroom at the rear of the landing. 'You'll have this to yourself, miss. The master and mistress have the other one on this floor, and there's one for the servants upstairs. He looks after us, the master does.'

Three bathrooms! Her family home was comfortable, but not as luxurious as this one, Steph thought. Her father would have been scornful about how the money for it had been obtained, but she liked what she'd seen so far of her uncle and his wife. Already they'd made her feel as if they were all family, even though she'd never met them before.

They hadn't mentioned any sons or daughters. Did they have any children or grandchildren? Her father hadn't kept in touch with his brother after they fell out, so hadn't known much about Uncle Ray's family. Though he'd known their address. Strange, that. Her father hadn't kept in touch with his youngest brother, either. Will lived in Devon and was scornfully dismissed as having a 'bit of land' and being content to stay there with his sheep.

She wondered how her own younger brother was getting on. Dick hadn't come back from the Orient yet, and wouldn't till they won the war with Japan, she supposed. If he'd been home for good, she might have felt safer facing Keith. But then again, she didn't want to put her family at risk, because sadly, her father was starting to show his age.

It wasn't fair! Why should Keith be able to drive her away from the people she loved most in the world?

Left alone in the bedroom she unpacked the two dresses she'd put in the top of the suitcase, shaking one to try to get some of the creases out. But it stayed obstinately crumpled, so she abandoned the attempt and put it on anyway.

Afterwards she took down the tight little bun and did her hair in her usual style. She ran lightly down the stairs and followed the sound of voices, deliberately coughing so that they'd know she was coming to join them.

'Is that you, Steph?' Her uncle turned and gaped at her, mouth open. 'Good heavens! I can't believe my own eyes. What have you done to yourself?'

Daniel was tired after his travelling and opted to go to bed early, so Mayne and Judith decided to go for a stroll round the grounds before they went to bed. It was one of the ways they could spend time together without anyone from the town seeing them and thinking the worst of their relationship.

They saw Jan near the Nissen hut and stopped to chat to him.

'Do you think we need both you and Al keeping watch at night now?' Mayne asked.

'Yes, I do. I chased someone away only half an hour ago. I think they see the big house as fair game. They think you live in luxury.'

'We haven't lost much since I employed you and Al, so you must be doing a good job.'

Jan scowled. 'I don't like to lose anything, even firewood. This lot were after the bricks you've piled up to use again. Building materials are hard to come by. Maybe you should get a watchdog. They can sense people coming before we can.'

'The place is in too much chaos at the moment, indoors and out.' He gave Judith a wry smile. 'I'm afraid your Ben will have to wait for his dog.'

Judith shrugged. 'As long as we get him one eventually. I think it's good for children to have the responsibility of looking after a pet.' She turned back to Jan. 'How's Helen? Wasn't she seeing the doctor about that wound of hers around now?'

Jan's face changed instantly to a beaming smile at the mention of his wife's name. 'She's well. Her arm is much better these days. It's still weaker than the other, but she's so pleased not to need the bandage any longer and the doctor says it'll gradually regain most of its strength.'

'That's good to hear. My friend Daniel arrived today,' Mayne said.

'The architect?'

'Yes. He's already muttering to himself as he walks round the house. You'll have to pop in and meet him before you go off duty in the morning.'

'Miss Peters told us Mr Woollard's niece arrived this afternoon as well, to stay with him for a while.'

'Daniel met her on the train. He said she was a plain little dab of a creature. I didn't know Woollard had any nieces, though I've heard him mention a nephew or two. Didn't one drop in for a visit? Yes, I'm sure he did. I forget his name. I hope the niece isn't like her uncle.'

'Mr Woollard is always very pleasant to me.' Jan didn't wait for an answer but carried on with his rounds.

'You see, Mayne. That's another person speaking well of Woollard. You're too severe about him,' Judith scolded as the two of them walked on. 'Ros is still saying we should ask him to value the smaller items for us and you haven't found anyone else to do it.'

'We can wait till we've cleared everything out.'

'I don't agree. We have to start selling things soon or you won't be able to get ready for the building work. I can't believe how much we've brought down, just from the attics, and most of it has some value. And that doesn't include the more valuable things in the secret room up there. I sometimes wonder how everything fitted in.'

She waited a minute and added, 'Why don't you let me ask Mr Woollard?'

'Because it sticks in my gullet to work with a war profiteer, however pleasant he is to talk to.'

'There are big companies who've made huge profits during the war. What are they but war profiteers?'

He stopped walking, setting both hands on her shoulders and holding her so that he could see her face. 'Do you really think we should ask Woollard to help us?'

'I think we should ask him if he's interested and what he could do to help, then decide.'

'He wants to invest in our building company. What if he makes that a condition of helping us?'

'We'll cross that bridge when we come to it.'

Mayne started walking again. 'I'll discuss it with the other chaps and—'

As they went round the final bend in the drive, the front

door of the Dower House opened and a woman came out, turning on the step to say a final goodbye to her hostess.

'Oh, no!' he muttered. 'It's Caroline. Acting as if my mother is her best friend.'

Judith's heart sank, but she wasn't going to show her nervousness to these two women who had shown her nothing but hostility. 'Just say hello and walk on.'

'It's impossible to do that. My mother will try to keep us talking so that both she and Caroline can aim their poisonous remarks at you.'

'I know what they say about me. But I also know it isn't true. And so do my friends.'

His former fiancée called, 'Hello, Mayne!'

His mother swung round and looked across at them. As she saw Judith arm in arm with her son, her smile vanished and a scornful look took its place.

'Good evening, Caroline; Mother.' He would have walked past.

'I hadn't thought to see you walking out openly with *her*,' his mother said. 'What are people going to say?'

And just like that, something snapped in Mayne. 'Why would I not be walking out with Judith? We're courting. It's what courting couples usually do.'

'I can't believe that my son would—'

Someone's hand grabbed her by the shoulder and she was pulled into the house. Her cry of shock cut off abruptly.

Mayne's father stepped outside and held the door closed against his wife's tugging from inside. 'How nice to see you, Mayne. And Judith too. How are you, my dear?'

He let go of the door, waited a moment to make sure his wife wouldn't come out again, then walked across and held out his hand to Judith. 'And how are your delightful children? Still doing as well at school?'

She was so taken aback by his cordial greeting after his

wife's sharp words, that she stammered as she shook his hand. 'Y-yes. They're doing really well. Um, thank you for asking, Mr Esher.'

Caroline glared at them and made a disgusted sound in her throat.

Reginald looked at her as if she were an insect crawling up the wall. 'If you intend to continue visiting my house, Mrs McNulty, I'd appreciate it if you were more polite to my son and my daughter-in-law to be.'

Caroline pressed her lips together and, without a word of farewell, marched off down the drive. Her dramatic departure was spoiled by her turning her ankle on an uneven piece of ground and stumbling clumsily.

Mayne let out a long slow breath of relief. 'Thank you for your support, Father.'

'My pleasure. I hope you two have children as intelligent as Judith's other three. I've heard nothing but praise from the trustees for Kitty, my dear. That girl has a fine brain and you must definitely send her to university.'

Judith beamed at him. She was very proud of Kitty, who had won the Esherwood Bequest at the beginning of the war. It paid all the fees and costs of a girl attending the Rivenshaw Girls' Grammar School, or she couldn't have afforded to let Kitty go.

Since then, her son Ben had won a scholarship from the town council to the boys' grammar school and they were now waiting for Gillian's results. Like many other things, these had been delayed by the end of the war. Surely Gillian would win a scholarship to grammar school? She was just as clever as the other two.

Reginald nodded and went back towards the house. But as he opened the door, the sound of loud sobbing echoed out into the evening, wiping out Judith's feelings of pride and pleasure.

'Your mother will never accept me,' she whispered to Mayne.

'No. She has trouble with everything these days, including me taking on a job like building, which she thinks is too lowly for her son. And she's still complaining that my father handed Esherwood over to me, instead of selling it to Mr Woollard. She keeps repeating herself over and over, acting very strangely.'

'I wish you didn't dislike Woollard. He really is the best one to consult.'

Mayne was silent for a few paces, then said, 'Actually, I don't dislike the man. He has his good points. It's the way he earned his fortune that upsets me. But I'll think about it.'

They walked on and she sought for a way of changing the subject, but Mayne stopped and said, 'I meant what I said to my mother. I intend to court you openly from now on. I love you and I'm very proud of how you've coped with a difficult life and it's not your fault that your so-called husband turned out to be a bigamist.'

'It's too soon. Miss Peters said we should wait a few months, give the scandal time to die down.'

'I'm not waiting any longer. You and Doug were apart for years during the war. It's not as if you were still living together, even.' He pulled Judith into his arms and stopped her protests with a kiss.

Over her shoulder Mayne saw Al Needham, the other security guard, walking towards them, but the younger man turned away with a grin.

Eventually Mayne pulled away from her to catch his breath and Judith sighed with contentment, nestling against him. 'When I'm with you, my darling, anything seems possible.'

'Then let's get married soon.'

'People will talk.'

'They'll talk anyway, whenever we marry.' He waited a moment, then added, 'You know they will.'

She hesitated. 'Ask me again once the war is truly over.'

'And you'll say yes?'

'Of course I will, you fool. Do you think you're the only one with feelings . . . or longings? You're not getting a virginal bride, you know.'

'I don't long for anyone but you these days, though. We'll make a good life together, I'm sure.' He took hold of her hand and they turned back towards the big house, their joined hands swinging to and fro, in time to their steps.

Victor found Daniel in the library, searching for a book to read. 'Fancy a drink?'

'Not if it means tramping into town.'

'I was able to buy a half bottle of rum last week, so we can have our drink here. I was saving it for a celebration. Rum isn't my favourite tipple, but I got a lemon as well, so we can add hot water and make a toddy. One thing I miss about the Army is the mess and the booze we could get there. What do you miss?'

Daniel's voice was suddenly harsh. 'I don't miss the Army at all.'

'Come into the kitchen while I get my ingredients together.'

Victor didn't comment on his friend's bitter tone, but led the way to the rear of the house. To his relief, they found no one there. 'The children are in the old nursery, playing games and chatting. They get on really well, and my Betty loves having them around. We even found a wireless for them to listen to.'

'Kitty's not really a child; she's almost grown up.'

'In some ways. But she usually has her head in a book, so she's still a bit naïve at times. How about you? I can't help noticing that you seem rather quiet.' He handed Daniel a steaming glass and sat down at the table, taking an appreciative sip of his own drink.

His friend hesitated then sat down at the other side of the table. 'I felt a bit lost for a time after the war ended. And . . . I was upset about Ada.'

'Even though you hadn't been getting on all that well with your wife?'

'You noticed?'

'Of course we did. But you didn't talk about it, so we kept our mouths shut.'

'It felt as if I'd failed. I'd really wanted a good marriage like my parents have. And I was angry with the way she broke up with me. She not only left me for a bloody Yank, she was with him even before we separated.'

'Know anything about him?'

'I had an anonymous letter from a neighbour saying he was rich and good looking, and I'd better watch my wife.'

'All rich men are good looking,' Victor said sarcastically. He waited and when Daniel only stared down at his drink, running his fingertip round and round the rim of the glass and saying nothing, he asked, 'So what have you done about how you felt?'

'I went to see my friend John in Brighton. He always seems to see the world with a sane eye. And talking to him did make me feel better. Then he took me up to London to see Lubetkin's masterpiece block of flats, which was wonderful. By the time I left him, I'd realised I was as near normal as I could be after a war and should stop blaming myself. What about you? How are you coping? I'm so sorry about Susan.'

'I'm sorry she died, of course I am, but I haven't had time to brood about that.' He shared some of the details of his escape from his mother-in-law. 'I still think that woman will come after Betty.'

'We'll all keep an eye on her. I like your Ros, by the way.'

'My Ros?'

'Isn't she? Your feelings show in your eyes, even though neither of you act as if you're together in that way.'

It was Victor's turn to stare down at his glass. 'I don't know what to do. It doesn't seem fair to drag Ros into my troubles. She has her own. And Betty has to come first until I've sorted that side of things out.'

'Ros looks at you fondly when she thinks no one is watching.'

'Judith said that, too.'

'Don't wait, Victor. If I learned one thing from that damned war, it was to seize the moment. Some day I'll tell you about other moments I had, and didn't seize. Oh well, maybe I'll meet someone else and learn to forget my failures.'

Mayne and Judith came in just then.

'Want a glass of toddy?' Victor offered.

She shook her head. 'I'd better go up and suggest my children go to bed. And then I'll follow suit.'

'Just a minute.' Mayne grabbed her hand. 'I want you fellows to know that we're going to court one another openly, and Judith has agreed to marry me as soon as the war in the Far East ends.'

'Judging by what I heard from a fellow John knows in London, that won't be long,' Daniel said. 'There's something hush-hush going on.'

'It can't end too quickly for me.' Mayne gave Judith a quick hug.

His two friends raised their glasses. 'Congratulations, Judith. You've got a good man there.'

She flushed slightly then inclined her head in acknowledgement of their good wishes.

Mayne walked her into the hall. 'Shall we tell your children tonight or tomorrow?'

'Tomorrow. It hasn't really sunk in yet. Goodness, I'll have to start planning what to wear. Not easy with rationing.'

'Maybe there'll be something you can alter in one of the trunks from the attic.'

'I ought to provide my own wedding dress.'

'We're still fighting a war. Fancy clothes don't matter to me. It's you I'm marrying. Anyway, those clothes up there are only rotting away. I wonder if Ros would like some?'

'I'll ask her. She's desperately short. About our getting engaged . . . Let's tell the children in the library before breakfast. I can't rely on my friends to keep it to themselves.'

'Yes. About eight o'clock suit you?'

'I'll get them there by then.'

She stood on tiptoe to kiss his cheek and the gentle touch of her lips seemed to linger as he watched her go upstairs.

When she turned at the top to look back at him, he waved and her smile was glorious. He realised he was smiling, too.

The following morning Judith asked her daughters to come to the library before breakfast. 'I've got something to tell you.'

'Why can't you tell us now?'

'I want to tell you all three together. Could you ask Ben to join us, Gillian?'

When her younger daughter went to the little bedroom next door to tell her brother, Kitty gave her mother a thoughtful look. 'Good news?'

'I think so.'

'I bet Mayne's asked you to marry him.'

Judith could feel herself flushing.

Kitty gave her a cracking big hug. 'I'm so glad for you, Mum. You deserve a good man after Dad.'

'And for yourself? Is it all right with you to have him as a stepfather?'

'Of course it is. I really like him.'

Gillian came back just then. 'Like who?'

'Mayne.'

'Is it—'

'Let's go down,' Judith said hurriedly. 'I'm getting hungry if you aren't.'

Ben came clattering along the landing after them. 'What's the matter? We don't have to leave Esherwood, do we?'

His mother stopped to stare at him in surprise. 'No, of course not.'

'Good. Because I like it here.' He overtook them by sliding down the banisters then rushed into the library ahead of them.

'That boy has more energy than a cageful of monkeys,' Judith said.

'He's a boy,' Kitty said indulgently. 'They don't grow up till much later than us girls.'

Inside the library Mayne was waiting for them and Ben was sitting on a nearby reading table, swinging his legs.

Mayne held out his hand and Judith took it, turning to face her children. 'You knew that Mayne and I were . . . thinking of getting married.'

'Of course we did,' Ben said. 'Everyone in town knows. You look at each other with soppy expressions on your faces all the time.'

'We do?'

'Yeah. I bet Kitty you'd be married before the end of August.'

'Oh, well. We have decided not to wait any longer to . . . to make our intentions known. We're going to get engaged officially, and we'll marry as soon as the war in the East ends.'

'I'd marry your mother tomorrow, if I could,' Mayne said with a fond smile.

Gillian beamed at him and nudged her sister, saying loudly, 'Aww, they're looking soppy again. Isn't it lovely?'

Judith smiled at her daughter's teasing, but had to ask. 'So, you're happy about it?'

'Of course we are,' Ben said. 'Mayne won't hit you and I like living here. There's so much to look at and do. I haven't been bored for a minute since we moved in.'

'Good. As soon as the war in Japan ends, we'll arrange it. A quick ceremony in the registry office and then we'll have a nice meal and—'

'No. We're doing it properly. In church,' Mayne said. 'The Methodist chapel, if you don't mind. I like the minister there. We'll decorate the chapel with flowers and find you a pretty dress . . . In fact, we'll have a proper, old-fashioned wedding.'

'Can I be a bridesmaid?' Gillian demanded at once. 'Can we find me a pretty dress to wear, too, Mayne? I've seen some in those big trunks in the attic.'

'You and Kitty can help yourselves and find something for your mother, too.' He pretended to frown at Judith but it wasn't very convincing. 'Do as your daughters tell you, woman. We're not skimping on this wedding.'

Both girls giggled and hugged him. Ben shook his hand. Seeing the easy way Mayne accepted their attentions, Judith felt tears of happiness trickle down her cheeks.

Her son came and put his arm round her. 'Don't cry, you daft thing. I never know why females cry when they're happy.'

'I don't know either, Ben. I just . . . can't help it.' She fumbled for her handkerchief and gave her nose a hearty toot, then more tears flowed. 'I'm so very happy,' she said apologetically.

They all laughed gently at her, and she joined in.

14

The following Monday, August 6th, was the August Public Holiday and now that school had closed for the summer, there was an excursion train running to Blackpool. Some of the younger children had never seen the sea because of the war, so quite a few of the citizens of Rivenshaw were treating themselves and their families to a day out.

No one at Esherwood felt like making the trip, but they did agree to have an easier day.

Ros took Victor and Betty for a walk to the moors – not the 'real moors', she told them, but the lower edges of the beautiful rolling landscape.

Ben went out to play football with some friends from school, while Gillian and Kitty amused themselves by acting out scenes from a book they'd found called 'Plays for Children'.

Mayne insisted Judith take time to sit in the garden and simply chat to him. 'You work too hard,' he told her when she said she'd planned to clear out a cupboard in the scullery. 'Sit and talk to me instead.'

And she couldn't resist that.

Everyone gathered in the kitchen just before six o'clock for their evening meal, looking relaxed and happy. Mayne helped Judith serve the food while Gillian finished setting out the cutlery.

Ros set two dishes of potatoes down in the middle of the

table and glanced at the clock. 'Shall I switch on the BBC news?'

'Good idea.' Victor watched her stride across the room to turn on the switch that warmed up the wireless, his thoughts on anything but the latest news bulletin. He loved her bright, healthy look, her strong body. And when she came back to sit next to him, courting her seemed the right thing to do.

But the announcer's first few words were enough to make everyone forget what they were doing and turn their full attention to the wireless.

President Truman has announced a tremendous achievement by Allied scientists. They have produced the atomic bomb. One has already been dropped on a Japanese army base.

Mayne and Victor exchanged horrified glances, because they'd heard hints about the capacity of the new weapon and had thought it'd only be used as a threat.

It alone contained as much explosive power as 2,000 of our great ten-tonners. The President has also foreshadowed the enormous peacetime value of this harnessing of atomic energy.

Daniel buried his face in his hands. 'They did use it,' he muttered. 'Oh god, how many did they kill with a bomb that big?'

'Surely Japan will surrender now?' Judith asked.

It was Victor who answered. 'Who knows? We can only hope and pray that no one ever has to drop a bomb that big on a group of innocent people again. That side of warfare makes me feel physically sick, even though I agreed that we had to defend ourselves against Hitler.'

Betty edged round to stand by her father, looking frightened at the sudden tension in the room. He pulled her to him as if she were a lifeline, and though she clung to him, she reached out to hold Ros's hand as well.

The happy mood that had lingered after the announcement of Mayne and Judith's wedding plans a few days previously now vanished as abruptly as a soap bubble.

Judith's children exchanged glances, understanding the implications of a bomb so big and aware from the reactions of the adults that this one was terrible.

Ros broke the silence. 'It must have been far worse for them than the London Blitz. I still can't get the scenes of destruction after the Blitz bombings out of my mind, even though I only saw them on the newsreels at the cinema. I don't think I ever will be able to forget them. I hope they don't show pictures of this – what did he call it? – this atomic bomb.'

'We can only pray the war in the Far East will end quickly now,' Victor said.

No one spoke for a few moments. How could you tell what would happen? Japan seemed so far away, its people so exotic and different as to be beyond anyone's comprehension.

They kept the wireless on, listening in vain for an announcement that the war was finally over.

After lunch the next day, Ros offered to do the grocery shopping, needing to get out of the house. She decided to buy a couple more books to take her mind off the atomic bomb.

It seemed as if fate was on her side when she met Mr Woollard at the second-hand bookshop. 'Did your wife like the book?'

'Very much.' He indicated the young woman standing

next to him. 'This is my niece, Steph, come to stay with us for a while.'

'Nice to meet you.' The two young women shook hands.

'I wonder . . . if you're going into town, could you spare the time to show Steph round a bit, Miss Dawson? She doesn't know anyone yet and what do I know about young women's interests?'

His companion looked embarrassed. 'There's no need to trouble Miss Dawson, Uncle Ray. I'm sure she has plenty to keep her occupied.'

'I can spare an hour,' Ros said. 'Anyway, I'll probably be standing in a queue for ages, so we can chat and get acquainted. I'd welcome some company.' She held up the basket. 'It's my turn to shop for everyone.'

Mr Woollard beamed at her. 'There. I knew you'd be a good person to ask. I wonder . . . is it true that Mayne's openly courting Mrs Maskell?'

'Yes and we're all very happy for them.'

'I didn't agree with Miss Peters about keeping their relationship quiet. Everyone in town knows how badly Mrs Maskell's so-called husband treated her, and even a blind man could tell how much she and Mayne love one another. I'd send my good wishes, but I'm probably the last person he wants congratulations from.'

He sighed as if he regretted that and, to Ros, he looked sincere. She hesitated, then asked, 'I wonder if you could spare me a moment before you leave? There's something I want to ask you about.'

He pulled out his silver watch and closed one eye to squint at it, as if having trouble seeing the details. She'd seen other older men do that. 'Let's go and have a cup of tea then, Miss Dawson. The Daffodil Cafe will be open by now.' He gestured down the narrow street that led towards the town square.

'Don't you want to find a book for Auntie Edna?' Steph reminded him.

'I'd forgotten. Could you ladies choose a couple for me? Ones you really like.'

Between them, Ros and Steph sorted out two books he was sure his wife hadn't read, finding that they both enjoyed the same authors.

While he was paying, Steph said in a low voice, 'You really don't have to look after me. I can perfectly well wander round the town centre on my own.'

Ros shrugged. 'I'm new to town myself and most people have been lovely to me. I'm happy to help you in my turn.'

'Thanks, then.'

In the cafe, Mr Woollard somehow cajoled the owner into fetching them slices of cake from her secret store. They were thin slices, but the sweetness was such a treat.

He turned to Ros. 'Now, lass. What were you wanting to talk to me about?'

She explained about the myriad small items at Esherwood and the difficulty of valuing them.

'I could definitely help there. I did a lot of buying and selling even before the war, and I have a fair idea of prices and values. If I say so myself and I'm not being vain, I really do have an instinct for what's going to rise or fall. It helped me get my start, that did. But are you sure Mayne Esher will want to deal with me.'

'May I be frank?'

'Please do.'

'He thinks you handled stolen goods during the war, and that's the main reason he's hesitating. I can't believe that of you, though.'

Mr Woollard stared at her in shock for a moment then slammed his hand down on the table, making the crockery jump and tinkle. 'Damnation! I knew that would come back to haunt me.'

She felt bitterly disappointed that he was admitting it, was usually a better judge of people. 'It's true, then?'

'No, it damned well isn't. A fellow who was working for me set that up, and I sacked him when I found out. I kept it quiet because I didn't want to be responsible for him being sent to jail when he had a wife and four children to support. But I made sure he and his family left this town.'

'There. I didn't think you were a thief,' Ros said.

'I'm not.' He grinned. 'Well, not exactly a thief. I did accept some goods during the war that hadn't been handed in to the government, extra farm produce for instance. And I didn't ask where some things came from that had been manufactured on the sly. But I always drew the line at encouraging the theft of people's personal possessions.'

He chuckled suddenly. 'Why, if I hadn't been able to get hold of black market elastic, half the ladies in the town would have had their knickers falling down. It was one of my best sellers all through the war, elastic was.'

They all laughed and Ros felt a sense of relief.

'I'll wait to hear from you about those goods you need valuing,' he told her as they parted company.

She watched him go. She believed him absolutely, because he looked you straight in the eyes.

Surely Mayne wouldn't refuse to deal with Mr Woollard when he heard that it was someone else who had been fencing stolen goods in his name?

After her uncle had gone home, Steph kept Ros company in the various queues and the two of them chatted, finding they had a lot of other things in common, besides the books they read.

The queues seemed particularly long and slow today. As

they left one shop and joined yet another queue at the butcher's, Ros said wearily, 'One day, we'll be able to shop without all this queuing. I can't wait for that day to come.'

'And we'll have shops full of all sorts of goods. Just imagine that. I'd sell my soul for a bar of proper chocolate. Or a box of Cadbury's Roses. I got one for my birthday in 1939 and I've never forgotten how delicious they were. I know they had to stop making proper chocolate because of the war, but ration chocolate isn't nearly as good, even if you can get it.'

Someone came out of the shop and everyone moved up a step or two, after which the ladies in the queue settled down again to wait.

Ros looked round at the other women, many of whom were chatting quietly. 'If we all nipped in and out of shops without needing to queue, we wouldn't meet and chat to as many people, though, would we?'

'I suppose not. But I don't exactly meet friends at the shops, just chat to whoever is next to me to pass the time. And I haven't got any friends in Rivenshaw.'

'Except for me,' Ros said with a smile.

'Thank you. Except for you, now,' Steph agreed.

Just as they were coming out of the butcher's, Daniel passed by on the other side of the street. 'That's one of the men who's going to turn Esherwood into flats,' Ros said.

'I met him on the train coming here.'

He saw Ros and came over to join them, immediately taking the basket from her. 'Let me carry that for you.'

'I can manage.'

'I know you can, but it wouldn't look good if we walked back together with you carrying it. That'd brand me an ill-mannered lout. And anyway, it's heavy.' He hefted the basket to get it more comfortable.

'It's heavier than usual because I managed to get some bones for making soup stock.'

'That'll be nice. Aren't you going to introduce me to your friend?'

Both young women looked at him in surprise, then Steph said, 'We've met already, Daniel.'

'We can't have done. I'd definitely remember someone as pretty as you. Though come to think of it, your voice does sound familiar.'

'You saved me from Keith. On the train.'

He gaped at her. 'Steph? Oh, my goodness! You're Steph? You can't be!'

'Well, I am. Which shows how good my disguise was.' She turned to Ros. 'Daniel helped me out of a difficult situation when we were travelling to Rivenshaw. I was very grateful.'

He shrugged. 'I didn't do much.'

The town hall clock began to chime the hour and Steph checked her wristwatch automatically. 'Is it that late already? I must get back to my aunt. She's not been well and needs cheering up.' With a nod, she walked away.

Ros had to give Daniel a poke in the side to make him start walking. 'You still look shocked.'

'I am. I didn't recognise her, not at all. She was dressed so dowdily and she had her hair in a tight bun. As for the hat she was wearing, ugh! My grandmother wore hats like that. And then she pulled the hat off and tied a scarf on, and you could hardly see her face.'

Ros was intrigued. 'Why did she dress like that? She's wearing very nice clothes today. I love the material of her skirt. I can't imagine her looking dowdy.'

'Well, she looked dreadful. Clever of her. Some fellow was pursuing her. They used to be engaged and she broke it off two years ago when he was overseas. But he's back now and says he's still going to marry her. He follows her everywhere, apparently. I think he must have lost his marbles.'

'Sounds like it.'

'Um, who is she, exactly? I mean, what's she doing in Rivenshaw?' Daniel asked.

'She's Mr Woollard's niece. She's staying with them.'

'The fellow who got rich during the war? The one Mayne doesn't want to deal with?' He let out a low whistle of surprise.

'Well, I think Mayne should see what Mr Woollard can do to help before he makes up his mind about anything. Those piles of things we're sorting out won't vanish without some help, you know. And I'm like Judith. I've been poor enough not to want to give anything away for even a penny less than its value.' She laughed. 'Even when they're not my things and I won't be getting the money.'

She set off walking again. 'Let's move briskly. I need to stretch my legs. Dawdling round the town and standing in queues makes me want to run and shout. Don't look so worried. I won't do that. But we can at least move quickly now.'

When they got back to Esherwood, Ros put away the shopping and went to find Mayne. Only the children were in the house and they said Mayne had taken the other grown-ups outside.

She returned to the kitchen, where Daniel was about to brew a pot of tea.

'Are they coming down? Shall I use the big teapot and make enough for everyone?' he asked.

'They're outside, apparently. Let's go and find them before you brew up and check whether they're ready for a break.' She added mockingly '*Waste the food and help the Hun,*' echoing one of the many wartime posters and sayings.

They stood outside the kitchen door listening.

'Over there!' Daniel pointed.

He and Ros followed the faint sound of voices to the Nissen hut. It had been decided not to deal with its contents till they'd cleared the house, but though they hadn't finished doing that, the double doors at the nearest end of the semi-circular structure now stood open and voices were coming from inside it.

Daniel patted the corrugated iron roof as they passed. 'Simple but effective structure, and strong too. I don't know what we'd have done without these during the war. I slept in a Nissen hut for several months at one camp. Once I stopped banging my head against the lower part of the ceiling, I found it perfectly comfortable.'

Inside, Mayne and the others seemed to be arguing about the things they'd found. He looked up with a smile as Daniel's shadow fell across the floor. 'There you are! Look how they crammed stuff in here. You'd have to move some of it out to get to the back. We can't even see what's there.'

'What brought you out here?' Ros asked. 'I thought the plan was to finish clearing the nursery floor before we tackled this.'

'We got fed up of pulling out small items and trying to sort out which were valuable, so we decided to give ourselves a change. Blame the sun. It kept shining in and inviting us out to play.'

'Then I suggested the Nissen hut and that was it,' Judith said. 'We've all been dying to explore the rest of the inside.'

'I'd only looked at the inside once,' Mayne admitted. 'But I remembered there were tools in here. You said last night it'd be hard to get hold of tools and minor equipment like nails, Daniel, so I thought I'd check that I remembered correctly.' He grinned. 'Well, that's my excuse, anyway.'

Judith brandished a notepad and pencil at them. 'This time I'm making a rough list of what there is at the front of the hut.'

Daniel couldn't get further in than a couple of yards, because the way was blocked by piles of wooden planks, used but not badly battered, reaching almost to the ceiling. He pulled a couple down and looked across the gap he'd made. 'Aha! I can see pre-war boxes of screws and nails, and . . . some bigger boxes which may contain tools. Steady me, will you?'

With Mayne's help, he clung to the top of the pile of planks, stretched his arm out and managed to scrabble his fingers across the side of a box and dislodge it on to the planks. 'OK. Let go.' He jumped down and opened the box.

'Look at that! A plane. Just as it says on the label. These tools are going to be worth their weight in gold. How could the Army have left them here?'

'I doubt anyone knew exactly what there was by the time personnel had changed a few times at the convalescent home,' Victor said. 'This was probably some project that was planned but never carried out. I found one like that once when I was transferred, but not on this scale. You don't think . . . someone was hoping to come back and retrieve the tools, do you?'

Everyone was silent for a moment or two.

'Well, if they do come back, they're not getting anything. These are ours now. The Army sent my father a letter when they left saying we could have anything left behind, as long as we cleared the place up ourselves and didn't try to charge them for our trouble. They said it'd cost them too much to sort such things out, not to mention transporting and storing them.'

Victor whistled. 'Looks like you've got a windfall here. That wood alone is worth a lot. They're first grade planks, not full of knot-holes. I wonder what's behind all of it.'

Mayne looked thoughtful. 'Who can tell? I have a vague memory of my father writing to tell me the Army was intending to put up other Nissen huts in the grounds, so that they could house men there for short training courses.' He gestured to what looked like the tops of pieces of corrugated iron, stacked behind the planks and further blocking the way to the rear. 'Do you recognise any of those components, Daniel?'

'They look like some of the interior parts of a Nissen hut. I wonder if they're complete kits? If so, we may be able to sell them. I gather people have taken over some of the abandoned Nissen huts because they're desperate for somewhere to live.'

'We could even erect them ourselves if we needed workshops.' Victor stepped back. 'Well, we can't do anything about the stuff further inside without taking all these planks out of the front part, and then the first layer of things behind. And where would we put them to keep them safe? Leaving the stuff piled up like this behind a locked door is a good way to protect it.'

'I agree,' Mayne said. 'The rest of it can wait for our convenience. Let's go and have tea now. I'm ravenous. Did you get anything wonderful at the shops, Ros?'

'Potatoes, carrots and some slices of so-called brawn. Has the baker delivered today's loaves?'

'Yes, they came a while ago.'

'We can maybe find some lettuces in the kitchen garden. Those Jan planted for us aren't ready yet, but he found some self sets half-hidden at the back. They're growing quickly now the light's getting to them.'

'I think we ought to use Jan's skills for more than keeping watch at night,' Judith said. 'He's a very clever man.'

'We will,' Mayne assured her. 'I've already offered him a better job in our company.'

'Well, make sure you lock this place up carefully,' Daniel said. 'And don't tell anyone about what's inside. There are people who'd literally kill for stuff like that.'

'A bit dramatic, don't you think?'

'No. You've got a real treasure trove in there.'

As they stood outside the Nissen hut, they passed the ruins of the stables, which had been used for target practice.

Daniel stopped to gesture at them. 'We need to knock that lot down. What's left of the walls is dangerous in places. You know how children love playing among war ruins. If a wall fell on them, they could get injured. Besides, we can re-use the bricks and some of the beams look OK, too, if you don't mind a few stray bullet holes.' He turned to Mayne. 'Actually, you've got far more stuff here than I'd expected. It'll save the company a lot of money and a lot of trouble getting hold of building materials.'

'And a lot of time, too,' Victor said. 'You know how long it takes to get goods. Some of them take months after ordering. Getting a car can take over a year. I doubt that'll change for a while. If I hadn't had to leave my old home in such a hurry, I'd have resurrected my car.'

'Can't you go back and get it? We could do with some vehicles.'

'I'm not leaving Betty and I'm definitely not taking her anywhere near Mrs Galton.'

'Get a legal injunction and send someone else to fetch it for you.'

'Who?'

'If Al can drive, he'd be a good person to send. He's not in awe of anyone.'

'You know, that might be a good idea. I'll think about it.'

As they went into the kitchen, Mayne said, 'I'll have to charge the company for these goods, I'm afraid. I don't want to sound mercenary, but—'

'It's not mercenary,' Victor said at once. 'If you own something valuable, you don't give it away. We're just glad you're letting us take a share in the company and providing so many useful items, not to mention the land itself.'

He hesitated, then added, 'It's not that I don't trust you, Mayne, but we ought to sort our partnership out legally. I saw a brass plate outside a lawyer's rooms in town. Now, what was he called?'

'Melford's our lawyer and he's a good chap. Of course, you can use anyone you like, but I'd advise against Gilliot.'

'No. I trust you absolutely, so if you don't like this Gilliot, then we'll use Melford. I need to see someone about Betty, as well.'

Mayne nodded, but he sighed as he cradled his cup of tea in his hands, wishing, as he had so many times before, that he didn't have to sell his home. He kept thinking he'd resigned himself to the necessity, but then the thought of the changes and the loss of the spacious rooms he'd played in as a child would hit him all over again.

Once Esherwood was turned into flats, it would never again belong to his family. That hurt, dammit. It hurt so very much.

Judith slipped her hand into his and gave it a quick squeeze.

He tried to smile at her but couldn't manage it, so kept hold of her hand for a moment or two. She was a comfort, as well as a joy.

Ros waited till the adults were alone that evening before she spoke. The children had done the dishes from the evening meal, then gone off to play tiddlywinks, for which they had a major contest going.

She cleared her throat to get the others' attention. 'I learned something this morning about Mr Woollard and I'm now absolutely sure he'd be the man to help us sell our bits and pieces.'

Victor shot her a warning glance but she was determined to speak her mind.

'I thought I'd made it plain that I don't want to work with

him,' Mayne said, his smile vanishing and his expression chill.

'I know. But that was because you thought he'd been dealing in stolen goods.'

'Woollard was never convicted, I must admit, and no one could understand why.'

'He wasn't convicted because he didn't do it,' Ros said, her eyes challenging his.

'I can assure you that there was definitely fencing of stolen goods going on in Rivenshaw during the war and connected with his business.'

'You were away a lot of the time, so how can you be sure exactly who was involved, though?'

'My mother told me about it.'

'She can't be sure of the details either.'

'And you are?'

'I met Mr Woollard in town again today and I asked him about it.'

'Goodness! He must have been furious with you for being so blunt,' Judith said.

'He was angry, but not at me. It was one of his men who did it, and when Mr Woollard found out, he sacked the man and forced him to move away from Rivenshaw. He didn't call in the police out of pity for the man's wife and children.'

'Or because the police might have looked more closely at what he was doing.'

She jumped to her feet, hands on hips. 'You're determined to think the worst of him, aren't you? Well, you're wrong, Mayne Esher, absolutely wrong. Mr Woollard is a bit of a softie underneath all that bluster and I don't believe he's a thief. You're cutting off your nose to spite your face by not asking his help, and your partners' noses too. What has he ever done to you for you to be so mistrustful of him?'

Mayne flushed and stared at Ros. 'Are you quite sure of your facts?'

'I'm sure of what he said and that I believed him.'

Judith looked at Mayne as the silence lengthened. 'Why don't we ask his opinion about selling things without committing ourselves to letting him into the business? You said he helped you when Caroline was being a nuisance and you found him more pleasant to deal with than you'd expected. You could at least give him a chance. You could even ask him outright about the stolen property, see if you believe him.'

There was dead silence again, then Mayne sighed. 'I suppose so. I just . . . want everything we do to be honest and above board.' He gestured round them. 'I feel it's the last thing I can do for my family home.'

'You don't really want to turn this place into a block of flats, do you?' Victor said gently. 'Even the clearing out is being done more slowly than I'd expected, knowing how efficient you are when you want to be.'

Mayne sighed and stared down at the table for a few seconds before looking up at his friends. 'You're right. I hate to think of giving up Esherwood. Even starting off the project feels worse than I'd expected. Sorry if I've been a bit sharp at times. I know it's the sensible thing to do, but I don't feel sensible about my home.'

Judith linked her arm in his. 'Perhaps, if there are some really valuable things, you might sell them for enough and then you wouldn't have to turn it into flats.'

'And perhaps enough money will drop from heaven to do the maintenance and restoration work the house needs year after year if it's not to fall down,' he said bitterly. 'Not to mention the gamble we've already taken that my father will live for another seven years, so that we won't be hit by death duties.'

After a moment's silence, he shrugged. 'But you're right, Ros. I should give Woollard a chance. Since you get on so well with him, perhaps you'd ask him to have a look at what we've sorted out so far? And we'll all stay with him as he does it, then compare notes. More than that I can't promise yet. As for Esherwood— Oh, hell!'

He let out a little growling noise of mingled anger and frustration, then shoved his chair back and walked hastily out of the kitchen.

'Even I hadn't realised how upset he was, how much he loved Esherwood,' Judith said. 'Too much for his own good, given the circumstances.'

'I'm sure he'll be able to afford to keep one of the flats for himself, at least,' Daniel said.

Judith shook her head. 'That won't be the same. It won't be enough. When you speak to Mr Woollard, Ros, tell him to tread carefully. Explain how Mayne feels about his home. You can be our liaison, since you get on well with him and his niece. Now, let's put the news on the radio. Maybe Japan will have surrendered by now.

But there was no more news from the Far East, only hints of the likely reduction of some food rations, so that the people starving in Europe could be fed.

'I know we can't leave people to starve,' Judith said to Ros later. 'But try feeding a growing boy on what we're allowed. My Ben's always hungry these days. He'll look like a potato if I feed him any more of them.'

Ros put an arm round her. 'We'll manage.'

'Yes. I know we will. But it's hard sometimes.'

'And you shouldn't give him part of your meat ration. You need good food, too.'

'You noticed.'

'So did Kitty. I don't think anyone else did. Look . . . I wonder if there are any rabbits in the grounds. If we could catch an occasional one, we could make some good hearty broth with it.'

'I don't think I could kill one, or skin it.' Judith shuddered.

'I'll do that, but I wouldn't know how to catch one. I'll ask Jan's help about the trap. Will it be all right if I offer him a rabbit too, in payment for his trouble?'

'Of course it will.'

Ros looked out of the door. 'In fact, I might as well do it now. He's just arriving to keep watch for the night.'

15

The following morning, Ros combined a shopping trip with a visit to Mr Woollard. She felt rather nervous knocking on the door of the large villa set in a walled garden, then told herself not to be silly. She was here on business, and she was as good as anyone else.

An elderly maid opened the door.

'Could I please speak to Mr Woollard?' When the maid gave her a puzzled look, she added hastily, 'He does know me, and so does Steph. I've met him a couple of times at the second-hand bookshop.'

'Oh, you're the lass who helped him choose some new authors for Mrs Woollard. She was very pleased with the first book. She isn't up yet, or I'd take you in to meet her. She loves to talk about the stories she reads, good as a radio show, she is. Come inside, miss. I'll only be a minute.'

She left the door open and went to the rear of the hall, returning a minute later, smiling. 'I'm to fetch another cup and plate. Miss Steph's gone out for a walk, and the master's just finishing his breakfast and reading the morning paper. He wants you to join him.'

Ros was shown into a pleasant room where Mr Woollard stood up and gestured to her to sit down at a small circular table near the window.

'I'm here on business,' she began, feeling nervous, in spite of the talking-to she'd given herself.

'Oh?'

'On behalf of Esher and Company.' The three men hadn't given their company a name, which she thought strange, but she thought it sounded better to have one, so she'd invented one on the way here.

The maid came in with another cup and gestured to the remaining toast. 'You might as well finish that, miss, or he'll eat too much. Miss Steph eats like a bird and we don't want to waste anything. There's a new jar of marmalade been opened today.'

Ros couldn't resist. It was ages since she'd had real marmalade. Mostly, since the war, you got the choice of only yellowish or reddish jam, made from plums and any other fruit that happened to be ripe at the time. She buttered a slice of toast and spread the marmalade thinly.

'Put some more on,' Mr Woollard ordered. 'It's good.'

So she did, taking a bite and closing her eyes in sheer delight at the tanginess of the peel. You forgot how good food could taste.

It was a few moments before she was ready to explain the situation to Mr Woollard, but he only smiled benignly, sipped his tea and waited for her to finish eating.

'Now, lass. Tell me why you're here.'

He listened, nodding from time to time. 'That sounds interesting and I'd be more than happy to help. Life gets a bit dull now I'm behaving myself, as I think I told you.'

'Perhaps you'd like to come round to Esherwood this afternoon, then, and take a quick look at what we've found so far?'

'I'd love to. All right if I bring Steph? It's dull for her here and you can only read so many books. She's not used to being idle, either. I might train her to help me when I get a new business going. She's at a loose end and wants to stay away from that crazy sod. If Keith chases her here, I'll know how to deal with him. No one hurts my family!' He stared at her. 'And no one hurts my friends, either. I'm a good friend once I trust someone.'

'I believe you.' And she did.

'Now, just eat that last slice.' He patted his stomach. 'My wife tells me I'm putting on too much weight, so I'd better not eat any more.'

Ros walked back to Esherwood, beaming at the world. She'd done what she set out to do, bearded the lion in his den. She loved her job here. It was really interesting to do so many different things, and lovely to work with people who trusted her. She was beginning to feel part of a team.

It was amazing to her that Mayne, who had so much, who had been born into the upper classes, could be so casual about life and people. Why, he even insisted on them using first names, and joked that they'd all fought in the war, so were allies.

And as for Victor . . . Oh, he was such a lovely man. She sighed happily as she walked, hoping, dreaming . . . Surely she wasn't mistaken about the way he looked at her sometimes?

When she got back, she told the others Mr Woollard and his niece were coming that afternoon, then helped Judith make an early lunch so that they could be ready for their visitors. She smiled as she realised she automatically called the midday meal lunch now, not dinner. How posh could you get?

Afterwards, Victor helped her clear the table then asked her to come outside as he had something to tell her. His face was so solemn, her happy dreams faded. He couldn't be intending to talk about how he felt, then. Not this time. One day, perhaps. What could he want?

There was a chilly wind and rain was threatening, but she always preferred to be outside to indoors, and she knew Victor was the same. She waited for him to speak, hoping the news wouldn't be too bad.

'It's about your mother's grave.'

'Oh.' She always wanted to cry when she thought about her mother, so dug her fingernails into the palms of her hands. A little discomfort could help you control your emotions.

'I've made arrangements for a new plot and for her coffin to be moved there.'

'Oh, Victor, that's so kind of you. I can't thank you enough. I'm—' Her emotions threatened to overwhelm her.

He waited a moment then asked, 'I wondered if you'd like me to order a headstone for the new grave?'

Ros blinked her eyes furiously but couldn't hold back the tears. 'Yes, I would. I'll pay you back one day, every penny, I promise. But if you don't mind paying for a headstone, just till I can save some money, I'd be really grateful. It'll make me feel I'm really with her.'

As the tears escaped her control completely, he muttered something and pulled her into his arms, letting her sob against him.

'I can't go on like this,' he said, sounding almost fierce.

She drew back, staring at him in dismay. Had she been wrong about how he felt? 'I'm sorry. I didn't mean to—'

'Ah, come here, my poor darling. I phrased that so badly. I meant I couldn't go on pretending I don't love you. And I think, I hope, you care for me, too.'

She sagged against him, happiness flowering in her. 'Of course I do. I did understand that you were worried about Betty and . . . and that other things would have to wait.'

'I was worried about her. I still am. But I'm not worried about us becoming a family. Betty loves you too, so why should we wait? Look how happy Judith and Mayne are now. When I see them, I want us to be happy in the same way. I want the world to understand that we love one another and . . . that one day quite soon we'll marry.'

She drew in her breath sharply. 'You mean—'

'I mean I'm making a poor job of proposing, but that's what I'm trying to do. Will you marry me, Ros darling?'

She flung herself back into his arms. 'Yes, of course I will.'

When they pulled apart, he glanced at his wristwatch and said ruefully, 'Look at the time. We'd better help the others get ready for Woollard's visit. We'll plan the details of our future later.'

'Let's find Betty first. We need to tell her before we say anything to the others.'

They went up to the nursery floor, where the children had found a concealed cupboard full of some long dead child's treasures and were pulling them out carefully, exclaiming over the old-fashioned dolls and battered toy soldiers. Kitty was watching them indulgently, seeming more and more like an adult these days.

'Could you come with us for a minute, Betty?' Victor held out one hand. 'We have something to tell you.'

She was across the room in a minute, clinging to him.

'You stay here,' Kitty said. ' We're just going downstairs to show these to Mum, then we're going outside for some fresh air while the rain holds off. We won't be far away. Come and join us when you're ready, Betty love.'

'All right.' She went towards Ros, who was waiting for them at the door of one of the cleared bedrooms on this floor.

Victor gestured to the two narrow beds and they all sat down, Betty next to her father, Ros on the other bed, facing them.

He kept hold of his daughter's hand. 'We have something

to tell you, Betty. Ros and I love one another and we're going to get married.'

She stared from one to the other then got up and did a little jig. 'Oh, goody. Gillian said you were sweet on one another, so I watched you and you do smile a lot when you're together. Not big smiles but little ones, like this.' She demonstrated with the slightest of smiles and an exaggerated fond expression, making them both chuckle.

'You can't hide anything from my clever daughter,' Victor joked.

'Will you have me as a stepmother, Betty?' Ros asked. 'I'd really like that.'

The child plumped down beside Ros, who opened her arms and hugged her closely. But she was frowning. 'There's something I don't want—' She broke off hesitating.

Ros's heart felt as if it had skipped a beat. If Betty wasn't happy with her joining the family, she wouldn't be able to marry Victor. She'd never force the child to accept a new relationship if that upset her. She knew only too well what it was like to live with a new person you didn't like. 'What is it?' she asked softly.

'I don't want to call you "stepmother". It's a horrid word.'

Relief coursed through Ros. 'Is that the only problem?'

'Yes. I'd like you to marry Daddy.'

'It's easily solved. What did you call your mother?'

'Just "Mother". Grandmother didn't like the word Mummy.'

'Then how about we keep Mother for Susan, and use Mummy or Mum for me?'

'Yes, yes, yes!' Betty grabbed a hand of each of them and pulled them up, dancing them round in a happy circle. Letting go suddenly, she ran off down the stairs.

'What now?' Victor asked as they followed.

They heard her shouting, 'Guess what?' as she disappeared into the kitchen.

He chuckled as he took Ros's hand. 'Remind me never to tell Betty a secret unless I want the whole world to know it.'

'She's had to keep things to herself for so long. It's lovely to see her joining in with the others, saying what she wants. I was even pleased when she was naughty yesterday. Come on! Let's go and face the music, Mr Travers.'

'They'll be glad for us.'

Mr Woollard and Steph arrived punctually at two o'clock in his luxurious car. Judith and Mayne were in the drawing room. The sight of the big gleaming vehicle made Mayne breathe deeply and mutter something about 'ill-gotten gains'.

Judith jabbed her elbow in his ribs. 'You are not a judge and jury, Mayne Esher.'

'You don't understand. When you've put your life on the line while people like him stay at home and get rich, you can't easily forgive.'

'Mr Woollard would have been too old to fight, anyway, but he'd still have faced danger from the bombing, and he did his share of fire watching, I know. Nearly everyone did something, Mayne, not just the soldiers. And actually, his black market goods weren't all bad. It cheered people up sometimes to get a little extra something to eat.'

'There were other ways of getting treats.'

'Rich people could go out for meals in restaurants and not have to give ration points, but poorer people didn't have the money. Lots of poorer people saved up for the odd black market treat. I would have done if I'd had money to spare. As it was, I relied on Mr Woollard for my knicker elastic. You try managing without that.'

He hadn't really thought about it that way. He admired her enthusiasm and put his arm round her shoulders as they went into the big front sitting room to watch Mr Woollard get out of the car, then help his niece out.

Judith continued speaking and Mayne wasn't sure whether she was talking to herself or to him now.

'I stayed home, but I worked in that horrible factory producing materials for the war. It was hard, filthy work and I was paid a pittance, but it was for the war effort, so I didn't complain. It wasn't only the men and women in the forces who fought, you know. We did our bit on the home front.'

He opened his mouth to say something, but she carried on.

'We civilians had a hard time of it, Mayne. Rationing, everything in short supply, our jobs changing to war work, plus fire watching. I read in the newspaper about one woman who had an incendiary bomb fall into her garden and set the fence alight. She tipped a heavy plant pot over it to put it out, because they said not to pour water on them in case they exploded. If that's not facing danger, I don't know what is.'

'I'm sorry. I wasn't thinking.'

'I did a lot of thinking while I scrubbed floors and packed war supplies. A lot. The war's all but over now, Mayne. It is over in Europe and surely the Japanese will surrender soon? Don't keep it alive in your heart.' She clapped her hands to her mouth. 'Oh dear, sorry to harangue you like that but you do need to give Mr Woollard a chance. Everyone deserves a chance.'

He pulled her closer for a quick kiss on the cheek.

As the door knocker sounded, she gave him an equally quick kiss back, then tugged him into the hall. 'Come on. Open the front door and let your guests in.'

She kept surprising him, was changing almost daily, growing in confidence, and that was good. Well, he thought so. She was a very intelligent woman and he guessed this was the first time she'd dared let it show. Doug Crossley would just have thumped her for answering him back or for showing that she knew more than him.

'You're good for me.' He opened the front door. 'Do come in, Mr Woollard, Steph.'

The others joined them in the hall: Ros coming from the kitchen, Victor and Daniel, still arguing amiably about some point of architecture, from upstairs.

After introducing Mr Woollard to Daniel, Mayne led the way to the unused but damaged rooms at the rear of the ground floor, where they'd put the various types of item they'd found, keeping the piles separate.

Mr Woollard stopped to look at the missing banisters and then stopped again in the doorway. 'Goodness, I'd heard that the Army treated this place badly, but you'd not believe it if you hadn't seen it for yourself. Look at that panelling. What were they thinking of? That's early eighteenth century, if I'm not mistaken.'

'It is.' Mayne was surprised and pleased by his visitor's knowledge. 'I was shocked when I saw what they'd done to the house.'

The older man was studying the piles of things and the rows of ornaments. 'You've got a heck of a lot of stuff here, Esher. Worth a packet.'

'And there are plenty of other things elsewhere,' Mayne said ruefully. 'This is only the ornaments and the Army beds. I can't believe how many ornaments there are.'

'Your ancestors must have loved pretty things. Don't move!' He lunged forward and picked up an ornament that had been knocked over and was lying on the very edge of the table in danger of being knocked off.

After dusting it with his pocket handkerchief, he studied the rim for chips. 'Good thing this didn't get broken. It's quite valuable, you know. About thirty pounds' worth at the moment but it'll go up in value once the country settles down to peace.'

They all gaped at him.

'Thirty pounds for that!' Judith exclaimed. 'It's ugly and crude.'

'But very old: seventeenth century, I should think.'

'Are you sure?' Mayne asked.

'Aye, lad. I'm certain. I enjoy old things. I swore when I was a lad with patches on my breeches that one day I'd live in a big house with beautiful ornaments and paintings. I don't collect any old thing, mind.' He made a sweeping gesture with one hand. 'Most of this lot isn't to my taste. What I love most is crystal and silver – and certain paintings.'

He walked on, picking up and putting down some more ornaments. 'But I know my china too. I used to sell things for people short of money during the war and when I took them to experts, I learned from them. No one was ever cheated on the price I got for them, but I did take a percentage for my trouble.'

Judith could see that Mayne still looked shocked, so asked when Mr Woollard stopped moving, 'What about the other ornaments?'

'Well, even from here I can see quite a few that I'd call plain solid pieces, worth five or ten pounds each, and a few more valuable ones. I'd need to spend quite a bit of time here to do a proper valuation, though. Maybe you'd like to be my secretary for that, Steph love, and write all the prices and descriptions down?'

'I'd enjoy it.'

He turned to Mayne. 'These aren't the really valuable things, are they?'

'No. There's a lot of silver and some paintings that even I know are valuable.'

'Good. I'm looking forward to seeing them.' He studied the room. 'Mind you, these will still add up to a tidy sum if you sell them to the right people. Do you want to show me the others?'

Mayne hesitated, caught Judith's pointed glance and nodded.

'Should we leave you two men to deal with that?' she asked.

'We'll let the others get on with their work, but I'd like you to stay with us, Judith. And Steph, of course. And bring that notebook of yours. We'll never remember all the details.' He turned back to Mr Woollard and said stiffly, 'Thank you for doing this.'

'Aye, well. It's self-interest partly, Esher.' He gave his urchin's grin. 'And curiosity, of course.'

Once the others had left, he said, 'Let's put it on a proper business footing before we do anything else, eh?' At Mayne's nod, he went on, 'If I do this valuing job for you, I shall want ten per cent of what the articles make.'

'Mmm. I see.'

'However, if you let me buy into the company, as I mentioned before, just in a small way, say a five per cent share, I'll not only put money in, but do the valuations and sales for free as part of my contribution.'

'You don't mince your words.'

'No, I don't. Not when I want something. You'll find I can help in several ways. Supply of building materials, for one.'

'Why are you so keen to join us? You've never been friends with the Eshers. It seems . . . strange.'

Woollard gave his niece a wry look. 'Steph will tell you I'm fretting for something to do. My wife insists that I stop most of my other . . . um, dealings, now the war's ended, but I like to keep busy.'

Mayne had to ask. 'If we're being frank, I need to know something: did you ever fence stolen goods?'

Woollard looked him straight in the eyes. 'No, never. It was one of my employees who did that, and I put a stop to it as soon as I found out.'

After a moment's silence, Mayne nodded acceptance of this statement. 'All right then. I'll think about what you're offering, talk to my partners and get back to you.'

'Fair enough. You should never rush into a business deal.' He looked round. 'Now, what about the real valuables? I give you my word that I'll keep what you show me to myself.'

He held out his hand to seal the bargain and Mayne shook it, then gestured. 'This way. There are some of the real valuables in the cellar and others in the attic.'

From behind Woollard, Judith was beaming at him. Mayne's heart lifted at her obvious approval. She was going to be good for him, he could tell. So the sooner they were married, the better, as far as he was concerned.

He'd have a word with her about that later. He didn't want to wait a day longer.

16

That same afternoon, a man arrived in Rivenshaw by train. Ted watched him get out of a first-class compartment and put his briefcase and small suitcase down for a moment, then brush his dark, well-tailored suit with a grimace.

Fussy devil, Ted thought. Even if there were smuts, who'd see them on that suit?

Might be a chance for a fare, though, he decided and hurried out of the station to start his taxi. He sat in it grinning as he watched the same man stop at the entrance to the station and stare round as if the town square smelled bad. After a few moments, he spotted the waiting taxi and hailed it.

Ted eased his vehicle forward. 'Yes, sir?'

'Can you take me to a good hotel?'

He got out and picked up the small overnight case, putting it in the boot. 'Best place for a gentleman like you would be The Golden Fleece. Trouble is, it's outside the town, so them as stay there usually have their own cars.'

'Is there somewhere in or near the town centre?' The man added, with the long-suffering sigh of someone prepared to make a great sacrifice, 'I'm only here for one night, so as long as I find somewhere clean, I'll manage.'

'There was the Red Lion, but it got bombed early in the war.' Ted gestured towards the gap in the buildings that surrounded the main square, where the pub had once stood. The space had been cleared of rubble, but the ground was still covered with bits of broken brick, which showed through the weeds and thistles now flourishing there. He missed the place, had drunk many a pint there in the old days. Good ale, they'd served.

His passenger sighed loudly. 'There must be somewhere else, surely?'

'You could try Mrs Hope's. She takes in travelling salesmen, the better sort, and everyone speaks well of her for cleanliness and comfort. She'll do you a nice, plain meal as well.'

Looking as if he'd bitten into a lemon, the man nodded. 'Very well. Take me there.'

When the taxi stopped outside a three-storey terraced house with basement, the newcomer said curtly, 'Wait for me here.'

He knocked on the door and spoke to Mrs Hope, gesturing to the taxi by way of an introduction.

After studying him carefully, she nodded.

He came back to pay his fare.

Ted got his passenger's suitcase out of the boot, but didn't carry it up to the door because he didn't like the man's snobbish attitude. When he stared at the coins in his hand, he was glad he hadn't done anything extra. Most people who dressed well tipped well. This one had only added twopence to the fare.

'Mean bugger,' he muttered, then frowned and moved his taxi further along the street. 'What's he doing in Rivenshaw, anyway?' On this thought, he switched off the motor and went round the back of Mrs Hope's lodging house to speak to his pal George Hope.

'Just brought you a guest. Arrogant sod, he is. Respectable enough, but turned up his nose at the sight of the town centre.'

He paused, then added in a low voice, 'The thing is, what's a fellow like that doing here, eh? He's not happy to be in Rivenshaw, that's for sure. And . . . he reminds me of that lawyer chap, whatsisname, Gilliot. Same sneering look to his damned face. Makes you wonder . . . '

As he let the words trail away, the two friends exchanged thoughtful glances.

'I'll keep an eye on him while he's staying with us,' George said. 'Especially after what Sergeant Deemer said.'

'Aye. Can't be too careful,' Ted agreed. 'If someone tried to kidnap that little lass who's staying at the big house, they might try again. The sergeant asked me to spread the word to watch out for suspicious strangers and I'm going to tell folk to watch this one.'

'Betty was in the same class as my granddaughter at school, and though she was only there for a few days before the holidays began, Lily liked her. Only they can't play together because her father doesn't let her go out on her own, just in case it happens again. Not nice, treating a little lass like that. I'll keep my eyes open.' George tapped the side of his nose and the two old men parted company.

When fate brought Ted near the police station an hour later, he went inside to see Sergeant Deemer and mention the stranger who had looked at Rivenshaw so scornfully.

The sergeant sighed. 'There's always something to disturb the peace, isn't there? As if I haven't enough on my plate with the new Area Inspector. I was sorry Upham had a seizure. At least I knew what to expect with him in charge. You're probably worrying about nothing this time, my old lad. You can't accuse every stranger of bad intentions, you know.'

'I didn't like this one's face,' Ted repeated stubbornly. 'Or the way he sneered at Rivenshaw. Good little town, this is. And if he was visiting someone here, he wouldn't have had to ask me about a hotel. They'd have told him where to stay.'

'Hmm. Well, you keep your eyes open and get back to me if you see anything fishy going on.'

'I won't let you down.'

As Ted went inside, the sergeant muttered, 'I bet he checks under the bed every night for burglars as well, just to be sure!'

Ted heard this and scowled. He'd never seen Deemer in such a bad mood. What was causing that? Was the new Area Inspector so bad?

Mayne hesitated at the top of the attic stairs, glancing back down at Judith, who was poised two steps behind him. Woollard was standing behind her at the turn in the stairs and Steph was still on the landing. They were all waiting for him to open the door, but he felt uncertain about revealing family secrets.

He looked at Judith, saw her mouth the words, 'Go on. It's all right.'

With another sigh, he pushed back the heavy wooden door and switched on the attic light. He couldn't just leave the valuables hidden here; he had to do something with them. But he didn't need to reveal how the secret door opened. 'Could you wait there a minute, please?'

He hurried across the dusty wooden floor and opened the secret door before calling out to the others to join him. Then he began to pull out the paintings one by one, pausing occasionally to study a favourite.

The others helped him prop the paintings carefully against trunks, boxes or the more solid pieces of furniture, so that they would be both safe and visible.

He watched Woollard start to prop a delicate oil painting of a young woman against a dusty chest of drawers, then stop. He set the painting to one side and took out his pocket handkerchief to dust the chest. What was he doing?

'Eighteenth century, if I'm not mistaken,' the older man said. 'Look at the patina on it and the inlay work. Done by a master, that was. I'm not an expert on furniture, though I've picked up a fair bit, but you should get someone who knows to look at this. Could be worth a packet. There's a fellow in Leeds who knows his stuff and is honest. You won't catch him telling you it's a load of rubbish, then offering to give you a fiver to take it off your hands.'

Mayne stared at him in shock.

'Been told that before, have you?' Woollard asked.

'A dealer told my father that during the war, used those exact words about a pair of bookcases with lovely bevelled glass in the doors. I had to buy them off my father myself because my mother was nagging for more money, twenty pounds it cost me to keep them. I'll show them to you when we go down.'

Some other pieces of furniture had vanished from the Dower House, where they'd been taken for safety, even after he'd asked his parents not to sell anything without consulting him. When he taxed his father with that, Reginald had denied selling anything and refused to discuss it further. But he'd avoided his son's eyes, and Mayne could only guess it had been his mother's doing. She had been so very angry about the limitations of the war and his father's mismanagement of the family money.

She was still angry with Mayne for not letting his father sell Esherwood, so that she could end her life in luxury. She hardly spoke to him these days. He didn't know whether she was growing forgetful, as old people sometimes did, or was punishing him by not answering his questions. And as these and other pieces of furniture probably couldn't be traced, he didn't see the point in making a fuss now, but he would take care that she got no chance to sell any others, though maybe he should tell her he knew what she'd done, as a warning.

He'd have to ask his father to keep an eye on her. He'd mention how many books could have been bought with the money they should have got for the missing pieces. That ought to get his bookworm of a father on side.

Mayne realised the other three were waiting patiently for him to continue. He gestured towards the secret room. 'Sorry. I was remembering something. Look, I've got some silver here, the bigger pieces. The smaller ones are in the cellar, together with some other valuables. I'll just get some out.'

'Before you do that we should talk about those paintings. Some of them are very good and the artists are ones I've heard of. I can't even begin to guess their value, except that it'll be high,' Woollard said. 'You'd do better with them if I dealt with an expert for you.'

He held up one hand to stop any protest. 'It goes against the grain with me to give things away for a fraction of their value. You should take it slowly. Only sell when you need the money. Prices will start to go up again once the country recovers from the war. It may take a few years – well, it will take years – but it'll be worth the wait.'

Mayne thought that over, but had to admit Woollard had a point. He was well known in the town for driving a shrewd bargain over anything, small or large. 'All right. Shall we look at the silver now?'

'Let's have a look at a few pieces, just to get some idea.'

Mayne brought out a tray he'd always loved and a smallish wall mirror with a beautiful silver frame.

Woollard stroked them with the fingers of a lover and Mayne's resentment about needing his help died down still further.

A few minutes later, after examining the hallmarks, the older man stepped back. 'You're sitting on a fortune, lad, if you sell this lot carefully.'

'I didn't think it'd be all that valuable. We've never been a rich family.'

'But you've had some ancestors with excellent taste. They might have bought quite cheaply, but they bought well.'

'You think so?'

'I'm certain of it.'

'Well, let's cut to the chase. How much do you think what you've seen so far is worth, roughly?'

Woollard shrugged. 'Let me have a quick look at the rest of the silver, before I hazard a guess – and it will only be a rough guess. No, there isn't any need to pull any more out. I can see enough from the doorway.'

He studied the other big pieces, stared into space for a moment or two, then gave an approving nod. 'Now, can we go and look at the other small stuff?'

'I'll have to put these away first.'

They looked at him in such surprise, he blurted it out before he could stop himself. 'My mother has sold things before for a fraction of their value. I don't want to give her the opportunity to take any of the better stuff from up here. I don't think she has a key. There was no sign of anyone getting into the room when I first came back to Rivenshaw.'

Into the stunned silence he added, 'Please keep that to yourselves.'

Woollard was the first to speak. 'We all have relatives who cause problems for us.'

When things were locked away, Mayne led the way down to the cellars. 'There's a hidden storeroom, not intended as a secret place, but as a strong room, I think. It was fairly easy to hide the entrance, so I put more stuff in it.'

As he began to move aside the broken furniture he'd placed across the entrance, he found Judith beside him, ready to help. Without a word, Steph and her uncle began moving the smaller items. Mayne was so used to dealing with this on his own, it felt strange to have help, but in a nice way. Something inside him felt warmed by it.

When he gestured to Woollard to go inside and handed him the torch he kept on a shelf there, it was a gesture of trust, he realised. He was actually starting to trust the man. He hoped he wasn't mistaken.

Woollard spent only about ten minutes looking at things, then put the torch back. 'As I said, your ancestors had very good taste. We should lock this place up carefully.'

Mayne nodded and was about to close the door when he realised something was missing: one or two objects, in fact. He shone the torch slowly across the shelves. He hadn't moved those objects, he knew he hadn't, but they were no longer there.

'Is something wrong?' Judith asked.

'Yes. There are a few items missing.' He knew Woollard hadn't taken them because he'd been in view the whole time.

'I didn't think anyone else knew of this storeroom.'

'Only my parents. Um . . . has my mother been up to the house at all?'

'I don't think so. Not that I've seen, anyway. But we're not here all the time so, if she has keys, we'd not know whether she'd been here, would we?'

'My parents could still have a set of keys. She said they'd mislaid them.' He stepped back and looked at the pieces of furniture he used to hide the entrance, some of them quite heavy.

It was Steph who asked quietly, 'Would your mother be strong enough to move these things on her own?'

'No.' He had a leaden feeling in his stomach.

'There must be two people involved, then, and they've put everything back carefully because you didn't notice.'

'Yes.' Mayne felt sick with disgust. His mother couldn't have . . . could she? And who would have helped her? Not his father, he was sure. Then he remembered how friendly she and Caroline had become. If she'd done this, she'd have found a willing helper in his former fiancée, who seemed desperate for money.

They must have kept watch for times when everyone was out. No one would have challenged his mother for walking round the grounds, anyway. He'd seen her do that himself.

He realised someone had spoken to him. 'Sorry. What was that?'

'You'll need to change the lock,' Woollard said. 'And quickly. I know a fellow who'd do it and keep quiet about it, too.'

'Could you call him in, please.'

'As soon as I get home. In the meantime, you'd better make sure the house isn't left unoccupied.' His voice changed, became more bracing. 'Now, let's take another quick glance at the cheaper ornaments, then I'll give you a rough estimate to think about.'

'Yes. Thank you. That'd be . . . helpful.' Mayne locked the door of the storeroom and let the others help him put back the furniture, then scuff the dust around about to hide their footprints.

As he was obliterating what was clearly a woman's footprint near the edge of the area, Judith pointed to the right of his shoe. 'Stand still a minute. What's that?'

He saw something glittering in a crack at the bottom of the wall.

She picked it up. 'An earring. Do you recognise it?'

For a moment he thought of pretending he didn't, but knew he couldn't fool her, even if he fooled the others. 'Yes. It belongs to my mother. It's not all that valuable but it was her mother's and she's very fond of these earrings. Don't say anything to her yet. I'll keep it in case . . .'

He let the words trail away. In case of what, he wondered. There could be no doubting now who had stolen the pieces of silver. The only doubt was what to do about it. 'Let's go into the library again. There's a table there we can sit round.'

Woollard sat opposite him, waiting till they were all ready for him to speak. 'I can only give you a broad guess at this stage, Esher, but I think the very least you could make would be . . . ' He leaned forward to whisper the amount in case anyone was eavesdropping.

'Don't say that aloud or even write it down,' he cautioned. 'Remember how they used to tell us "Careless Talk Costs Lives". Well, it's the same in business. In this case, if someone hears about how valuable some of your stuff is, they'd be queueing up to break in and rob you.'

Everyone nodded.

Woollard leaned forward again, his voice still low. 'Actually I think you could get more than double that, Esher, if you sell carefully and don't rush it. Perhaps three times as much, if you're lucky. Once they start having big art sales in London like they used to, who knows what'll happen to prices. I worked in one of those auction houses for a few months, years ago, learned a lot.'

Mayne stared at him. 'Three times as much! You can't be serious!'

'Never more serious, lad. I mean, Esher.'

The younger man looked across the table. 'I don't mind you calling me lad.'

Woollard gave a little nod, smiling benignly, knowing this acceptance of being called 'lad' was a peace offering.

'That's . . . unbelievable,' Judith said. She looked stunned, and no wonder, Mayne thought. She had spent most of her life juggling halfpennies. Even he hadn't expected to raise more than a tenth of the lowest amount Woollard had suggested.

Steph waited patiently, her eyes going from one to the other, quiet as a shadow.

Mayne let out a long, calming breath, then pulled himself together. 'I'll discuss your proposals with the others and get back to you tomorrow, Woollard. But I'm beginning to think . . . well, I'm pretty sure now that we may be able to work together.'

'I'd like that. It won't be my fault if we can't.' Woollard pushed his chair back and stood up. 'Me and Steph will get off home now. You've a lot to think about. There's no need to show us out.'

At the door leading into the hall, he stopped and turned round. 'I'll have that locksmith chap up here by tomorrow afternoon at the latest. And I'll tell him to come the back way, not go past the Dower House. People in town recognise him. He's been dealing with their locks for forty years or more. He can be discreet about his customers' business, though.'

'Thank you.'

Once they'd heard the front door shut behind him, Mayne let out another long breath and reached for Judith's hand. He tried to speak but didn't dare say it aloud.

She said it for him, very quietly, for his ears alone. 'Maybe, if he's right, you'll be able to keep Esherwood.'

'I daren't hope for that.' Mayne pulled her close and buried his face in her hair, saying in a muffled voice, 'I just . . . daren't . . . hope. Not after resigning myself to the loss.'

She hugged him tightly. 'I know, my darling. I know.'

After a while he pulled back to look at her earnestly. 'You're the joy of my life, Judith. I am so very glad I met you.'

'Oh, Mayne, what a lovely thing to say.'

But he fell silent again, so she asked quietly, 'What else is upsetting you? Talk about it.' As if she couldn't guess!

'My mother. I shall have to deal with her, somehow, put a stop to her stealing things. I can't think how best to do it, though. It's not only about that; it's about you too. If she feels aggrieved, she'll lash out, say things about you that aren't true. I don't want her to hurt you. She has a lot of friends in this town.'

Judith could understand how betrayed he felt, but had to let him sort this out with his mother himself. She took pride in being able to stand up for herself. 'Don't hold back because of me. My happiness doesn't depend on her approval. And as I don't move in her social circles, what does it matter if her friends snub me?'

'It might not only be her friends who do that, but the people they speak to. Rumours spread horribly quickly.'

'She won't be the only person in town to say nasty things about me. I ignore them, though it's not fair on the children. But life is never easy, Mayne. Never. Now, let's think about what to do next about the money side of things. If I can help in any way, you have only to ask.'

'I know that. I just have to work out what to do about it all,' he said slowly. 'If there's even half a chance . . . '

17

George Fitkin looked round his bedroom at the lodging house in disgust. It was clean enough, though tiny – a working man's room. He wasn't used to staying in such shabby places, hadn't done that even during the war. He felt it demeaned a lawyer of his birth and breeding, just as it had demeaned him to be judged unfit to serve his country. The fact that his heart fluttered occasionally had never stopped him doing anything.

No, best not to think of that. He'd think of his main client instead. She had become very dependent on him, as he'd planned, and now he had her where he wanted her.

She wasn't a pleasant woman to deal with, but he could manage her. Oh, yes. It had surprised him that she would pursue this matter, because it wasn't really worth it, but she was so insistent he'd thought it best to go along with her for the time being.

Setting his suitcase on the bed and adjusting it so that it was lined up neatly with the slats of the wooden foot of the bed, he took out tomorrow's shirt and shook it. Good. Not too badly creased and most of it would be hidden under his waistcoat. He opened the door of the wardrobe and hung it up carefully, put his pyjamas under the pillow and his slippers near the bed. After setting out his shaving materials on the wash stand, he closed the case and stood it in the corner.

Only then did he leave the room with his briefcase, satisfied all was in order.

As he reached the bottom of the stairs, the landlady popped her head out of a doorway at the rear of the hall. 'Going out again, are you, Mr Fitkin? Don't forget, the evening meal will be served at six-thirty precisely.'

'I won't forget, Mrs Hope. Now, I wonder if you could help me. I need to consult a lawyer.'

'We've got two lawyers in Rivenshaw, both newcomers.'

'Could you give me directions to their places of business and tell me something about them? I need to consult someone about . . . an inheritance.'

She was happy to oblige and started with a Mr Gilliot, who always looked down his nose at you. She went on to a Mr Melford, who had fought in the war and come back earlier in the year. A lovely man, he was, always had a kind word for everyone.

George listened to her patiently, getting away at last without offending her. He shuddered as he walked down the street. The woman could certainly talk! And she had such a common, northern accent, too. How horrible that sounded.

It was a pity there were only two lawyers to choose from. He didn't like the sound of this Melford fellow at all. If you had a kind word for everyone, it probably meant you had a lower-class clientele.

He'd definitely try Gilliot first.

If neither of them was suitable, he'd have to find someone in Manchester the following day. He hoped that wouldn't be necessary. He didn't want to spend another day away from home, disliked having his daily routine upset.

And since trains still weren't running to time, who knew how long it'd take to get back. He'd been held up twice on the way here. A shocking state of affairs.

* * *

That evening at Esherwood, people gathered to prepare and serve their meal, a task they all shared, under Judith's supervision. The conversation inevitably turned to Japan and when it would surrender.

'They'll surely admit defeat soon,' Judith said. 'That horrible atomic bomb must have shown them that our side has weapons they can't win against.'

'Who knows what they'll decide?' Daniel frowned. 'I've met chaps who've been out there and they say the Japanese won't give in easily.'

Kitty paused as she laid out the cutlery. 'There'll be another public holiday when they do surrender, won't there? Like we had for VE Day. I loved the bonfires and fireworks, but most of all you could feel people's happiness.'

'And there might be dancing in the town square again.' Gillian jigged to and fro in time to some rhythm in her head. 'I love dancing. Daniel says he'll teach me to jitterbug.'

'Only if I can find a partner to practise with,' he cautioned. 'I'm a bit rusty.'

She grabbed his hand and twisted to and fro, as if dancing with him. 'Can't you practise with me?'

'Not as well. Such a pity you didn't go to the cinema very often. You'd have seen it there in the newsreels.'

'We didn't have enough money before,' she said. 'We did go a few times, though.'

Judith shook her head. Whatever Gillian thought, she blurted out, no matter who she was with. Still, everyone here knew how poor they'd been when they were living with Doug.

'I didn't know you were a dancer, Daniel,' Ros said. 'I'm terrible. My mother used to say I'd got two left feet.'

He shrugged and twirled Gillian round twice, making her laugh. 'Oh, I have my moments.'

That child seemed able to cheer his friend up more than

anyone, Victor thought. How infectious her happiness was!

'This time it'll be called VJ Day.' Ben turned to Betty. 'Which stands for Victory in Japan, my young friend. We'll have to think what to do to celebrate.'

She beamed at him. 'There are nine of us, enough for a real party.'

The way she talked about parties, it was clear Betty hadn't been to any proper ones, just read about them. He exchanged glances with his sisters. However poor they'd been, their mother had made little celebrations for them. 'We'll definitely have a party, won't we, Mum? And you can help us get things ready, Betty.'

'Ooh, yes!' She jigged about in excitement.

'That boy of yours has a kind heart,' Mayne whispered to Judith as he carried the dish of boiled potatoes to the table. That brought a proud expression to her face.

When Victor put the radio on for the six o'clock news, however, there was again no mention of a Japanese surrender, only that the Russians had declared war on Japan.

'What does that mean?' Ros wondered. 'It's a bit late for the Russians to join in the war in the Far East, if you ask me. They should have been there earlier on. It's more or less sorted out now and they don't deserve any of the credit.'

'I bet . . . ' Daniel paused, looked at the children, then said it anyway, because you couldn't prevent intelligent children like these from understanding the war and its consequences, not after all they'd lived through during the past few years. Poor Betty could remember nothing but war.

'What do you bet?' Victor prompted.

'I bet the Americans are going to drop another bomb. That'll be why the Russians have declared war. They can't become involved in the final stages if they've still got a non-aggression pact, or whatever they call it, with Japan.'

Mayne was horrified. 'Surely the Americans won't do that? One atomic bomb was enough to make the point.'

'Who knows? We can only wait and see. I know we're all eager for the war to end, but nothing we say or do here in Rivenshaw will affect how it happens. We're civilians now, thank goodness.'

The silence that followed this exchange was heavy with apprehension.

Victor looked at his daughter's worried face and wished Daniel had kept his thoughts to himself. He changed the subject to something more cheerful as they began to serve the food.

To his relief, George Fitkin found Mr Gilliot a very suitable person to deal with. Even better, Gilliot seemed to dislike the group of people living at Esherwood and was eager to help make them 'toe the line' legally.

The two men had a very fruitful chat and laid their plans carefully.

'We can't go through the local police sergeant,' Gilliot said at one stage. 'He's a real sycophant where the Eshers are concerned, as are many of the people who were born and bred in Rivenshaw.'

'Which you weren't?'

'No. I came here because I was able to purchase a legal practice on advantageous terms when one former partner died and the other grew too old.'

'Do you have relatives nearby?'

'No. I'll bring my own family here once the war's over. I have a wife and two young sons. They're staying with relatives in the country until then. I'm keeping my eyes open for a suitable house to buy.'

George nodded, but immediately forgot this. He didn't care about the family life of insignificant country lawyers but people always liked to talk about themselves, so you had to humour them if you wanted their full cooperation. 'So how exactly do you advise me to approach this?'

'Through the new Area Inspector. I'll look into that for you. I know him quite well. The police sergeant will warn the people at Esherwood if you let him know anything.'

'That sounds like a good plan. My client is, of course, prepared to pay well, and I'm authorised to give you a generous retainer immediately to compensate for your efforts.' He took a cheque out of his briefcase and wrote Gilliot's name as the payee.

After a further exchange of particulars and details of how best to contact one another, the two men parted company.

Smiling, Gilliot walked to the bank and deposited the cheque. When he got back, he took out the remains of a bottle of brandy he'd been keeping to celebrate the end of the war. Now he had something of his own to celebrate. Not only would this be a lucrative job, but he'd make sure that Esher and all his friends got their come-uppance. Arrogant sods, the lot of them.

He raised his glass to their downfall.

The following day, they kept the radio on in the kitchen at the big house, once again expecting to hear an announcement of Japan's surrender. But the day passed and there was nothing on any news bulletin. Daniel found the suspense wearing and couldn't settle to anything.

They were all sure they'd hear something on the six o'clock or nine o'clock news, which was when major announcements were usually made. They ate in near silence, listening carefully. But once again, there was nothing about Japan.

Late that night, however, just as the adults were talking of going to bed, the telephone rang. Mayne went to answer it and came back almost immediately. 'It's for you, Daniel. Your friend John calling from London.'

'Ah. Perhaps we'll find out what's going on.'

Daniel came back five minutes later and announced baldly, 'I was right. John thought I should know that a second atomic bomb has been dropped on Japan, on a place called Nagasaki. He was worried whether it'd upset me.'

He looked round the table and added in a tight voice, 'It has upset me, of course it has. More than I can put into words.'

'Perhaps a drink would help?' Mayne offered. 'I've got some wine hidden in the cellar and we could—'

'Thank you, but no. Save it for a celebration. I'm sorry, but I can't bear to discuss this second bombing. To my mind, it was utterly unnecessary and tomorrow the government will be trumpeting about how magnificent this action was. There's nothing magnificent about killing hundreds of people. Nothing.'

He stood there as if he didn't know what to do, then strode to the outer door, calling over his shoulder, 'I'll go out for a walk round the grounds, if you don't mind. I need some fresh air and the moon's bright enough to see my way.'

He left without waiting for an answer, letting the door bang shut behind him.

'Surely Japan will surrender now?' Ros said into the heavy silence. 'And the use of another atomic bomb will mean a quicker end to the war, with fewer casualties on our side – at least, I suppose that's how the government justifies such massive bloodshed. If so, I hope they're right.'

Victor looked at her sadly. 'Who can tell? But don't forget the Japanese attack on Pearl Harbor, or the London Blitz. Or even the way our side bombed Germany. No one can remain blameless during a war, not if they want to win.'

Her voice was full of emotion. 'But the war's nearly over

and we're British. We should be above further gratuitous slaughter of innocent people.'

'I agree.' Victor looked towards the door. 'Poor Daniel. He's had a surfeit of killing. I've seen men get to that stage before. If the war hadn't ended, he'd have had a breakdown. I'm not sure that he isn't working his way through one anyway. Thank goodness for his friend John. He sounds to be a very great comfort to Daniel.'

No one said anything for a few moments, then Victor looked across at Mayne and Judith. 'What a time for us to get engaged! Should we even be discussing marriage till there really is peace? Till life settles down.'

It was Judith who answered him. 'Yes, of course we should. Life goes on through tragedies and triumphs. Even when you think you can't cope with another thing, when the world is going mad around you, you somehow manage to survive.'

Mayne put his arm round her shoulders. He knew she was thinking of her own previous circumstances.

She patted his arm with one hand, then reached for his hand and kept hold of it as she went on, 'If we can survive six years of war, we can survive a rather nasty ending to it all.'

'Let's do more than survive,' he said suddenly. 'Let's get married as soon as we can. A quick civil ceremony and to hell with churches and inviting distant relatives you never see. Let's get married then throw a big party for the people we really care about.'

Judith stared at him in shock. 'I thought we'd agreed to wait till the war was over before we married.'

'I thought we were beginning to change our minds about that. The war is over, in all but name. There won't be a third bomb, I'm sure, won't be any more battles either. There will be peace negotiations – real peace – a final announcement and the clearing up of the mess war leaves. That clearing up will probably drag on and on, so why wait? It'll cheer everyone up to have a wedding, don't you think?'

Victor thumped the table, beaming at Mayne. 'I agree absolutely. It's an excellent idea. Ros, darling, what about following their example? Do you want to wait for a fancy ceremony?'

'No, of course I don't. I just want to become your wife – and Betty's mother. I don't even care about having a wedding party.'

He grinned. 'Betty will. You can't disappoint her.'

'Let's make it a double wedding, then,' Judith suggested. 'If we get special licences, we can do it quite soon.'

'I can't get married till I buy some new clothes,' Ros protested. 'I don't have anything even half-decent to wear after years in uniform. Everything I own is shabby or else they're working clothes. No one gets married in dungarees!'

'We'll find you something to wear in one of the trunks in the attic,' Judith promised. 'I'll help you alter an outfit if necessary. Mayne's already suggested it.'

He nodded. 'Ben will need clothes as well. There must be some of my cast-offs up there. I grew so fast when I was his age that I rarely had time to wear out my clothes. And I notice he's shooting up, too.' He grinned. 'I did manage to tear or damage some of them, so they'll be perfect for Ben.'

She smiled, but it soon faded. Ben was always damaging his clothes and it was so hard to replace them, a constant worry. 'Who shall we invite to the party?'

'We'll have to invite a few duty people,' Mayne said. 'Unfortunately, that includes my mother and father. Well, Dad will be all right, but she will cast a shadow over the proceedings.'

'Surely she's getting used to the idea now,' Victor protested.

Mayne looked at Judith. 'Has she started speaking to you?'

'No. She still looks down her nose when we meet in town and walks straight past me.' And people noticed that.

'What about Dad? How does he treat you?'

'Oh, he usually stops for a chat. Mostly he asks how Kitty and Ben are going at school, and whether we've heard about Gillian's scholarship yet.'

'My father has a two-track mind: books and history, and the education of intelligent children. Mother gets away with murder, because he doesn't care deeply about her.'

Judith saw that Mayne was still looking worried. 'Don't let your mother upset you, darling. We have so much love, we can afford to be generous to an unhappy woman.'

'It's not that. She probably thinks something will happen to prevent us marrying. Or even that she can find some way to stop us.'

'What? Surely she won't go so far?'

He took hold of Judith's hand. 'I'm not sure how far she'll go. She's changed so much in the past few years, I feel I don't know her any more. She's getting a bit strange and forgetful, actually.'

'The war was hard on older people.'

'She didn't have a hard war, believe me. But I won't allow anything or anyone to prevent our marriage. Can you make a list tomorrow of who you want to attend the party? Don't skimp. Mrs Needham must come, for one.'

'You don't mind me inviting her?'

'Why? Because she cleans for us? I think very highly of her, because I know what a good neighbour she was to you during the years you were with Doug. Besides, I enjoy her frankness.' He grinned suddenly. 'I'll pit her to win against my mother any day. That's why she's lasted as a cleaner at the Dower House. My mother daren't upset her too much.'

'How many guests can I invite?'

'As many as you wish. I intend it to be a big party. Not

a sit-down meal, just bits and pieces to eat. But we still have some wine in the cellar, so everyone can drink the health of the bride and groom. We'll hire help to serve the food and drink. You, my love, are not working on your wedding day. Oh hell! I just realised . . .'

'What?'

'I'm going to have to ask Woollard's help with the catering. I don't usually approve of buying black market stuff, but a wedding is something special. And anyway, the war is just about over now. But . . . '

'That means you'll have to invite him.'

'Precisely.'

'I like him. Admit it, you're starting to like him too. And his wife will be thrilled to come, I'm sure. Don't forget to ask his niece. We can't leave her out.'

Mayne glanced across the room and nudged Judith to look at their two companions. Ros and Victor had their heads together, whispering, and were both looking blissfully happy.

'Some things are going wonderfully well,' he said softly and puller Judith closer.

On Friday the 10th of August, it was announced that Japan had surrendered. But this wasn't the official end of the war, they were told. That wouldn't happen till terms had been agreed and firm arrangements made. It didn't stop small boys from collecting packing cases and bits of wood for celebratory bonfires. But it wasn't until the evening of Monday the 14th of August at 11 p.m. that the BBC warned listeners to stand by for a special announcement at midnight.

Of course none of the adults at Esherwood went to bed, and the children were woken up, to their great delight. If this announcement was what people expected, it would be something to remember and they could sleep later the next morning.

Just before midnight, the radio announcer told listeners to stand by and everyone fell silent.

The Prime Minister spoke in his usual quiet way. Judith took Mayne's hand as Clement Attlee gave the British people the happy tidings that Japan had accepted the Allies' terms.

Japan has surrendered. The last of our enemies is laid low. . . . Peace has once again come to the world . . . Long live the King!

Everyone exchanged hugs, then the women wiped their eyes and the men pretended that they weren't feeling emotional, while the children yelled and danced around. For once Kitty didn't join the adults, but danced Betty round the room, then swapped partners to let Betty dance with Ben, and the more skilful Gillian dance her round.

Outside, church bells rang, the hooter sounded at the mill again and again, people yelled and cars sounded their horns.

'They'll be dancing in the town square,' Judith said wistfully.

'Can we go and see it, Mum?' Ben pleaded.

'I don't like to leave the house,' Mayne worried.

'Ros and I will stay here,' Victor offered.

Daniel spoke in such a low voice, they had to listen carefully to hear what he said. 'I'll stay too. I'm glad it's over but I don't want to dance in the streets. I just want . . . I don't know, to sit quietly, to feel happy that no one else will be needlessly killed.'

'Can Betty come with us, Mr Travers?' Ben pleaded. 'I'll hold her hand all the time. It'd be a shame to leave her out.'

'We'd love to have her join us,' Mayne said. 'We'll watch her carefully, Victor.'

'You can trust my Ben,' Judith added. 'If he promises to do something, he won't let you down.'

Her son beamed at her and grabbed Betty's hand.

When they'd left, Victor said thoughtfully, 'Churchill would have made the announcement more memorable. He had such a knack for words.'

'But not a knack for peace,' Daniel said. 'Anyway, who cares how it was announced? The main thing is that we're clear of war and killing now. We lost some good men to gain that peace.'

He quickly brushed tears from his eyes and went to stand outside in the back yard for a few minutes on his own, staring up at the stars and passing clouds. He wondered what Ada was doing now. Had she got the divorce? Was he a free man? What would 'free' mean in post-war Britain?

Oh, who knew anything?

Gradually the peace of the evening seeped into him. Ignoring the distant sounds of revelry, he sat on a bench and enjoyed the star-filled sky, with only a few faint drifts of cloud to hide the beauty above him.

Victor and Ros went to the front door to listen to the distant noises coming from the town. They chatted to Al Needham as he passed, because he was still keeping watch.

'Don't you want to join in the celebrations?' Al asked.

Victor shook his head. 'No. I'm glad it's over. But I want to enjoy the thought of peace quietly.'

'I agree. Six years is a long time to be at war. I lost three relatives, including a brother. Young men, all of them. I've been thinking about them tonight, I don't know why. I was only a young lad when it started, couldn't wait to be old enough to join up.'

'You're not all that old now.'

'I feel old sometimes. Fighting and danger make you grow up quickly. And yet, other times I feel young and want to shout and run like young Ben does. I was glad to get demobbed early to work for your building company, I can tell you.'

When Al moved on, Ros linked her arm in Victor's. 'I'm glad you let Betty go with the others. She needs to have a more normal life.'

'She won't be able to do that until Mrs Galton gives up, and something tells me the woman won't do that easily.'

'She must love her granddaughter very much underneath.'

'She doesn't love Betty at all, only the idea of the child having Galton blood in her. She also sees my daughter as a way of making further useful connections by marrying her to a suitable rich man as soon as she's old enough, something her own daughter failed to do. She never forgave Susan for marrying me but, since there was a child and she couldn't have the marriage declared void, she hid her feelings in public. When I had to go away to war, she set about gaining control over my poor wife. Thank goodness she didn't persuade Susan to leave her the guardianship of Betty.'

'Can you do that?'

'You can do just about anything if you pay a good lawyer to put it in fancy words.'

'Well, you're back now and Betty's place is obviously with her father. Even the law will agree about that.'

'Yes. I'm sure you're right.'

'And there will be two of us to look after Betty.'

'You're like a mother to her already. I see her turn to you when she's upset.'

'I love her,' Ros said simply.

So why did he still feel worried? Victor wondered. Because he did. He couldn't shake off a sense of foreboding.

18

Over breakfast, Victor and Mayne announced that they wanted to work on clearing the cellars. They looked sideways at Daniel, but he didn't offer to help them and seemed still to be in a dour mood.

Mayne flourished a mock bow at Judith. 'We'll leave what everyone wears to you ladies. I'm sure you'll be better at going through the trunks than we would be.'

She dipped a quick curtsey, wishing she could walk into his arms. 'I'm sure we'll do it better, too. I wouldn't mind a walk in the fresh air before we go up to that dusty attic, though, so I thought we ladies could nip down to ask Helen to help us. She's such a good needlewoman, and has a real eye for style.'

She gave the men a stern look. 'We agreed to share the work of running the house, so if we ladies are sorting out everyone's wedding clothes, perhaps one of you gentlemen could nip down to the shops? They must be opening for an hour or so this morning because people still have to eat, whether it's VJ Day or not.'

She turned to Victor. 'Betty will be quite safe with us during the day.'

'And if whoever goes to the shops can find something special to eat, we'll have our own party here tonight.'

She knew Victor wouldn't want to risk taking his daughter

into the town's evening celebrations and losing her in the crowds. He was perhaps a trifle overprotective, but that was a good fault, given the circumstances.

'I'll do the shopping,' Daniel offered. 'But you'd do better giving me a list of what you want.'

'It's more a question of what they've got for sale and how that fits with our food points. Mrs Wallis will be able to tell you how many points we have left for each type of food. Buy anything fresh that's not rationed. You know how Ben can eat.'

Her son grinned. 'I'm a growing boy, Mum.'

'Well, don't grow too quickly, or we'll have nothing for you to wear. And Daniel, you do realise you'll have to queue?'

'I had noticed people queuing once or twice. I think I know how to do it.'

They all gave hollow laughs. Queuing drove everyone mad, but it was the only way to get things, so if there was the slightest whisper that a shop had a certain item available, women told their friends and rushed out to line up for it.

Judith watched Daniel walk away with the shopping bags, worried at how tense he was most of the time. Then she shrugged. She couldn't look after everyone, had enough with her own lively brood. She hurried out to check the vegetable garden, picking only the outer leaves of two lettuces, so that they'd continue growing and last longer.

After that, she insisted on all three girls joining her and Ros in the walk. Left to herself, Kitty would sit around all day with her head in a book.

As they strolled down the main drive, she saw the curtains at the Dower House twitch. She was more worried about what Mrs Esher would do about her son's marriage than she had admitted to anyone, but was determined not to let the woman's spite get her down. She didn't even talk about that to Kitty, who was as much a friend as a daughter these days.

The worry was always there, though, at the back of her mind, because every now and then she overheard spiteful remarks in town and had to remind herself that 'what can't be cured must be endured'. Damn Doug Crossley.

Compared to her former life, she didn't have much to complain about, though. She pushed the worries to the back of her mind and concentrated on enjoying the fresh air. It had a damp feeling to it, as if rain were brewing.

Daniel was glad of something mindless to occupy himself with. He walked into town, hardly noticing the people he passed. He had joined the queue at the grocer's before he realised that the young woman standing in front of him was Steph.

'Oh, sorry to ignore you. I was thinking about something.'

She gave him one of her solemn stares. 'About the war and whether it's been worth it?'

He looked at her in surprise. 'How did you guess?'

'You're not the only person in England to be thinking that today, Daniel. My uncle and I were talking about it over breakfast.'

'You're right. Of course I'm not the only one.'

She laid one hand on his arm. 'I had a friend who was at the same stage of recovery as you. Sadly, he had to go back and fight, still feeling troubled about what he was doing. He didn't return. You're one of the lucky ones, Daniel. You've survived the war and it's really, truly over. I'm sure you'll gradually get better, come to terms with what you saw and did.'

When he didn't answer, she asked in a lighter tone, 'You don't mind if I call you Daniel?'

'No, of course not.' She was so easy to talk to, he admitted, 'I can't help feeling guilty about surviving, when so many haven't.'

'Of course you do. But fate has given you the chance to rebuild your life. We're all facing a time of renewal in many ways. And if we don't do that wholeheartedly, the others will have given their lives in vain. I must say your project sounds very worthwhile. Don't you find that comforting? There is such an urgent need for houses, and who better than an architect to work on supplying comfortable modern dwellings?'

The queue edged forward, so they shuffled another few steps with it.

'How do you do it?' he asked suddenly.

'Do what?'

'Make me feel better. You did it before as well.'

She flushed slightly. 'Do I?'

'Yes. And you're right. I am a bit . . . lost. But I can build a new life gradually.'

Again she touched him, so briefly it might have been a butterfly landing on the back of his hand. 'If I can help, in any way, don't hesitate to come to me. I'm a good listener. And after all, you helped me when I was in trouble.'

'I was glad to. You haven't heard from that Keith fellow?'

'No. But my uncle will help me if Keith comes after me again, I'm sure. Uncle Raymond can be very fierce when it comes to protecting those he cares about. He'll make a good partner in your project, you know. Once you let him into the group, he'll prove his worth.'

It was her turn to hesitate before sharing some information. 'Uncle Raymond really needs something worthwhile to do. I think he feels guilty about how much money he made during the war. I'm sure you'll all benefit from an association.'

'Well, let's hope so. We've talked about it with Mayne and I think he's happy now to let your uncle join us. Um . . . will *you* be staying in Rivenshaw?'

'Yes. I've been offered a job here.'

'Really? What as?'

'My uncle's assistant – helping him run his businesses, not acting as a secretary, mind, but being trained as a junior partner.' She smiled at the surprise on his face. 'Not usually a woman's job, but he says it's whether you're capable that matters, not whether you're able to have a baby or not. And he doesn't think my cousin Irwin has got what it takes. Irwin rang up yesterday talking about emigrating to Canada.'

After another shuffle forward she added, 'It'll be nice to work for a man who doesn't think women are inferior. I won't put up with a patronising attitude from anyone. Women are just as good as men and have proved it during the war.'

The woman next to them stared in disapproval, obviously listening to what they were saying.

Steph lowered her voice. 'Oops. I forgot we were queuing. I'm enjoying living with Uncle Raymond. He seems to have mellowed, from what my father said about him.' She chuckled. 'You should hear the family tales about his wild youth.'

'What changed him?'

She tilted her head to one side as if it helped her think, reminding Daniel of a small bird searching for something to peck. He liked watching her, he decided. She was so neat and pretty, when she dressed normally. And yet he wasn't attracted to her as a woman, nor did she seem to be attracted to him. They were more like friends, or cousins.

'I think it was meeting my aunt that helped my uncle most,' she said. 'They love one another very much, you know. My parents merely tolerate one another. If I ever marry, and I'm not sure I want to after Keith, I shan't settle for anything less than that sort of love.'

'Mayne and Judith are the same. So close you can almost see the link between them. When they get married, they're going to have a big party. I'm not sure I can face that. As for marriage, I don't feel like trying it again. I'm obviously no good at making a woman happy.'

'The break-up with your wife was quite recent, I think you said.'

'It happened during the past year. I'm not sure exactly when she met the Yank. Come to think of it, I may be divorced by now. He wangled her a flight to America and she's getting one of those quick divorces they have in some states. She assures me it'll be legal here in Britain. She's going to send me a cablegram when it comes through.'

'I think divorce should be easier here in Britain too. A lot of people made hasty marriages during the war and why force them to stay together when they're never going to be happy? I'm so glad I didn't marry Keith.'

The shuffling progress of the queue had brought them to the shop window now. He looked at their faces reflected together in the big sheet of glass, which had had its wartime strapping removed and was shining brightly in the sun. Steph was several inches shorter than him, barely coming to his shoulder. 'Look, Mayne and Judith are going to invite your family to the party after their wedding. Will you come with me? Help me face it?'

'If you like. But just as a friend. No hugging and kissing.'

'No. I realise that.'

She nodded, as if endorsing their arrangement.

The woman in front of them must still have been eaves-dropping, because she turned round again, with a hissing intake of breath as she frowned at them in disapproval.

Daniel saw Steph lower her head to hide a smile under the brim of a rather more attractive hat than the one she'd been wearing when he met her, and suddenly he was having trouble hiding his own smile as well.

Another shuffle forward took the disapproving woman

right up to the counter, where a youth wearing a long white apron leaned forward to serve her.

Daniel and Steph waited patiently for their turn.

'You should look at what's on sale today while we wait,' she said quietly.

'Judith said to buy anything that's not rationed. I was going to ask the shopkeeper's advice. Perhaps you could help me sort out whatever's suitable, though?'

'Yes, of course. Ah, here we are.' She smiled at the woman who had moved forward to serve them. 'Good morning, Mrs Wallis. How kind of you to open the shop today. What do you recommend?'

Daniel watched Mrs Wallis bend over backwards to help them. He thought Steph would make a good assistant to her uncle, would be an asset to any employer. She was such an intelligent, sensible sort of person and got on well with people.

He walked home part of the way with Steph, not speaking, feeling comforted by her presence. It suddenly dawned on him that she made him feel the same way his friend John did, as if there was sanity spreading from her into what had been an insane mess of a world.

Even, as if there were hope of him finding his own peace one day.

When it came time to go their separate ways, his smile wasn't forced. 'I shall look forward to seeing you again, my friend.'

She paused at that, then nodded. 'I shall too. I enjoy your company, Daniel.' She held out her hand. 'Friends, eh?'

'Yes.'

Nothing more needed to be said. They'd established the rules of their acquaintance. He didn't have anything more to offer any woman at the moment. It was Steph who was offering him so much, and would make someone a fine wife one day. If she ever decided to marry. He'd be happy to dance at her wedding.

What an unusual woman she was!

Judith, Ros and the three girls strolled along the edge of Parson's Meadow, admiring the ripening fruit and vegetables in the various allotments.

Helen's house was partway down, overlooking the park. When they explained the reason for their visit, she was delighted at the thought of helping them choose wedding clothes and left everything to come up to the big house with them straight away. 'I was just feeling like some company. Jan's asleep after his night's work.'

Outside, they met Helen's neighbour and their kind friend, Miss Peters. When that redoubtable old lady found out what they were doing, she invited herself along as well.

So it was four women who escorted the girls, taking the back route to Esherwood, because it was beautifully sunny and everyone agreed they'd enjoy a longer stroll before they tackled the dusty trunks in the attic.

'We'd better put away the firewood Jan and Al have collected first,' Mayne said to Victor once the women had left. 'If we don't, someone may manage to snitch a few pieces. It won't take long with two of us.'

'Three of us,' Ben said. 'I'm nearly as tall as you now, Mayne.'

'You are indeed. Come on then, Mr Muscles. Afterwards we'll start on the cellar, and yes, Ben, you can help us there, too. It's more than time it was cleared out. I think the Army dumped anything broken down there and forgot about it.'

'Well, we may find things we can repair, so we'll take our time, eh?' Victor said. 'Make Do and Mend is still a good motto and will be for years, I should think. We'll never forget that phrase, will we? Anyway, the shortages won't vanish overnight and it'll take time to turn factory production from war materials to civilian items.'

It didn't take long for the three of them to stack the wood and lock the door of the stable they were using to store it. Al and Jan had already taken their share home, because like many other people, they found the coal allowance barely enough to keep them warm in winter.

As they went into the kitchen, Mayne thought he heard something, so paused to listen carefully. Yes. Someone was knocking at the front door. 'I'll just go and see who it is,' he said to Ben.

But as he reached the door leading from the kitchen corridor to the big entrance hall, he heard the front door open. His mother's loud voice rang out clearly, 'See. No one at home.'

He paused instinctively, turning to the others and putting one finger on his lips. What was his mother doing coming in without being invited? And who was with her?

'The men might stop working in the stables at any time, though,' the other woman said.

That was Caroline's voice! What the hell were these two up to? Mayne wondered.

He looked sideways at Victor and Ben and shook his head, again putting one finger to his lips. To his relief both of them nodded and didn't even try to whisper.

'Maynard stacked a lot of things in the cellar storeroom,' Caroline said. 'We'll grab a few more bits and pieces quickly and be out of the house again within five minutes.'

'Yes. We'll do that.'

The two women began walking across the hall towards the cellar door, which was near where he was standing. Mayne moved backwards, pushing the kitchen door almost closed to hide from them.

Only when his mother and Caroline had gone down the cellar steps did he open the door again.

'I knew she'd been stealing things,' he said in a low voice. 'Now I'm about to catch her in the act. Damn it, a man should be able to rely on his mother!'

'I'm sorry,' Victor said.

'Yes. So am I.'

Ben kept quiet, staring from one to the other, looking slightly puzzled.

'Stay here,' Mayne said to him. 'Don't let either of those women go out through the kitchen.'

The lad nodded. 'I'll bolt the back door, shall I?'

'Good idea.' Mayne went to stand in the shadows at the top of the cellar steps, with Victor behind him. For once he was glad of the dim lighting below him.

'I wish Maynard didn't put such heavy stuff in front of the storeroom door,' his mother complained.

'We don't need to move it all. Just these few pieces, then I can slide inside and pass things out to you.'

'Yes.'

'I'll be careful not to leave any gaps on the shelves.'

'Yes.'

'They haven't noticed the other things we took, have they, Dorothy?'

Sick to the stomach at what his mother was doing, or letting Caroline do, Mayne moved quietly down the stone steps, glad he was out of sight of the two women at the far end of the cellar.

When he and Victor reached the bottom, they paused and listened to the two women grunting and puffing as they moved the furniture back from across the entrance to the store.

Only when the two women had finished whatever they were doing inside the storeroom and pushed the furniture back, did Mayne step out of the shadows. 'I'm afraid we did notice what you two were doing today.'

He saw Caroline glance quickly round, then step to one side.

'You keep an eye on the other one,' Mayne murmured to his friend, then turned back to his mother. 'Before you start lying to me, I should tell you that three of us overheard what you were saying when you came into the house, and then Victor and I heard you plotting to steal from me.'

Caroline made a sudden dash for the stairs but Victor grabbed her.

'Ow!' he cried as she bit his hand and started up the stairs.

But quick as she was, he managed to grab her foot and this time he took care how he held her.

In the meantime Mayne had been watching his mother. 'You can start by giving me back the things you stole today, and then we'll go to the Dower House and get the other pieces.'

'I shan't do it. I have a right to my things. This was my home.'

'Empty your pockets, mother.'

'Don't you dare lay hands on your own mother.' She folded her arms across her chest.

He looked at her. Even in the dim light of the cellar, she looked strange, her eyes too bright and feverish, her expression more that of a defiant child than a mature woman.

'Well you get them out, then. If I have to I'll unload your pockets myself.'

He didn't like doing it, but when she didn't move, he pulled one of her arms gently behind her back, ignoring the way she screamed and tried to kick him.

When she sank to the floor in an effort to escape his grasp, he found it easier to manage her, treating her as he'd been taught to treat prisoners of war, a skill he hadn't really used before.

'Stop it! Stop! You're hurting me, you brute!' she yelled. 'I'm your mother. Let me go.'

He knew he wasn't hurting her, so said only, 'I'm not hurting you, but you have hurt me greatly by trying to steal from me.' Grimly he patted her down, unloading three small silver items from her pockets.

Once he was sure he'd cleared her pockets, he grabbed her handbag and upended that on the ground. Jewellery. Minor stuff, but would bring in a few pounds here and there. And it was part of the family collection, not anything she'd brought to the marriage. He recognised every item.

'I'm taking your keys to this house, as well.' He picked them out of the jumble and shoved everything that was left into her handbag, before allowing her to scramble to her feet.

'Your father will have something to say about this,' she threatened.

'To me or to you?' he asked wearily, shoving the handbag into her grasp.

She didn't reply to that, but pouted, again looking like a sulky child. What had got into her?

'Want me to turn this one's pockets out?' Victor asked from the foot of the stairs.

'Yes, please.' Mayne barred the way. 'No, stay where you are till we've finished, Mother, or I'll tie you to a chair.'

She began to weep, but he ignored her.

There were quite a few small silver items in Caroline's pockets and handbag.

Even Mrs Esher stopped crying to stare at them. 'You said you'd only taken a couple of things, Caroline.'

The younger woman shrugged. 'I've got debts.'

'You lied to me, cheated me.' Mrs Esher began to cry again, scrubbing her cheeks. 'Everyone lies to me. I can't trust anyone these days, not even my own husband.'

Mayne ought to have felt sorry for her, but he knew how she could use tears to get her way, and he remembered that she had hardly ever comforted him when he had wept as a small child. She'd hardly ever held him either and he'd soon learned not to go to her for sympathy.

Mayne moved to the cellar stairs. 'Let me show you out, Mother. Victor, will you see Mrs McNulty out?'

'Yes, of course.'

At the top of the stairs he stopped in dismay. Judith and the other women, including Miss Peters, were walking towards the main stairs. They fell silent at the sight of him holding his mother.

He couldn't stop his voice coming out harshly. 'We had intruders. These two were after the silver. We took back the pieces they'd stolen and we're just showing them out.'

When she saw who the intruders were, Judith gaped for a moment, then looked at him in sympathy, before saying briskly, 'Let's get out of the way, then.'

But Mrs Esher stopped and dragged back against her son's grasp, yelling, 'She's a whore! A whore in my house. Shame on you, Maynard! Shame!'

'Mother, stop this.'

'I won't stop speaking the truth. And I'll find a way to stop you marrying her, see if I don't.' She looked across at Judith. 'Those bastards of yours are never going to live in my house, if I have to burn it down.'

Mayne grabbed his mother's arm and hustled her towards the front door, shocked at her vehemence and cruelty.

Victor followed with Caroline and waited for Mayne to give the word to release the women.

He spoke to them first. 'If you ever come here again, either of you, I'll call in the police and report today's burglary.'

'They won't believe you,' his mother said shrilly. 'And I'm an Esher. This is my house. I had a right to my things.'

'They're the family jewels, not yours. I have two witnesses to back me up as to what you were doing, and now you've admitted stealing in front of some other people.'

'What?' His mother laughed hysterically. 'Who would believe that whore of yours?' Head held high, Dorothy Esher stalked out.

Caroline paused, also looking across at Judith. 'No one will take you seriously as mistress of Esherwood. And Mayne will soon lose interest in you. You're just a novelty to him.'

Judith smiled. 'I don't take much notice of what thieves say.'

Mayne turned to her. 'Nothing my mother or Caroline say can make me stop loving you, Judith.'

The look Caroline gave him as she followed his mother outside would have curdled milk.

'You'd better keep an eye on that one,' Victor said. He sucked the bite on his hand. 'She talks posh but fights like a gutter child.'

'I need to speak to Judith for a moment.'

'Of course you do.'

But Judith smiled at him bravely and said only, 'I'm all right, Mayne. No need to make a fuss.'

Miss Peters stepped forward. 'I'm glad I witnessed that. I shall be able to help squash any rumours they try to start, and believe me, people trust my word more than they trust your mother's.'

But he knew that not even Miss Peters' support could stop all the rumours his mother and Caroline would set flying.

He watched his brave darling lead the way up the stairs, admiring Judith's courage yet again. What a wonderful woman she was.

'You and I are both lucky in our brides-to-be,' Victor said quietly.

'Yes. But Judith won't find it easy.'

'Life is never easy. She'll cope, though. She's got the courage of a lion, that lady of yours. And from what you've told me, things were even worse for her with that bigamist fellow. I gather he used to beat her.'

Mayne realised he'd forgotten Ben and when he saw the hurt look on the lad's face, he gave him a hug, repeating his promise. 'Nothing they say or do will stop me loving your mother, Ben.'

But Ben was still worrying. 'Your mother shouldn't say things like that about Mum. It's not fair because it's not true.'

'I know. But I can hardly sew her mouth shut. It hurts me as well as Judith. But you'll have learned by now that life is never straightforward. Once Judith and I are married, I'll try to be a father to you and your sisters, if you'll let me.'

'Thanks.' But Ben's eyes showed their pain. Mayne knew how much those children loved Judith, how hard their life had been till their father was put behind bars.

'Here's a tip for you. Don't ever try to answer my mother back,' he warned. 'If there's one thing that infuriates her, it's when someone refuses to react to what she's saying or doing. She absolutely hates to be ignored.'

'Who was the other lady? I've seen her in town, going into the posh shops.'

'Caroline McNulty. She and I were engaged once, then she left me for a richer man.' He laughed suddenly. 'Which was one of the luckiest things that ever happened to me.'

Ben gave him a quick, furtive hug. 'I think you're one of the luckiest things that ever happened to Mum.' He stepped back, his face a little pink. 'I'll go and see what they're doing in the attic, if you don't mind. I want to make sure Mum's all right.'

'Good idea. Come down and join us in the cellar later if you want. Or stay with your mother if she needs you.'

19

Daniel walked along with the heavily laden basket. Mrs Wallis was being very generous with her customers today. He'd heard her say several times, 'It's not every day we celebrate the end of a war, is it? We'll worry about new supplies later.'

Because the basket was awkward as well as heavy, he decided to use the shorter route up the front drive. They all usually took the longer way round to the back of the house to avoid Mrs Esher's spying on everyone's comings and goings. She didn't even try to hide what she was doing these days.

But to his annoyance, he met her and the woman Mayne had once been engaged to storming along the drive from the big house, both of them looking furiously angry.

'There's another of them,' the older woman screeched, pointing to Daniel.

Startled, he stopped to gape at her, whereupon she picked up a stone and hurled it at him. 'Get off my property. And tell that whore my son's sleeping with to do the same.'

She missed him by a mile, but the younger woman followed her example and she didn't miss, hitting him a stinger on the temple.

Mindful of his booty from the shops, which included some eggs, he didn't stop to argue or protest but hurried past them towards the big house. To his utter amazement they picked up more stones and followed him, hurling them as well.

When he heard Mayne's father yelling, he risked turning to see what was happening. Mr Esher ran out of the house and went up to his wife. Their words rang out clearly, so loudly were they both shouting.

'What the hell do you think you're doing, Dorothy?'

'Showing our son's fellow conspirators what I think of them. Maynard has been manhandling me. He threw me out of my own house.'

Mr Esher looked puzzled. 'You weren't in the Dower House.'

'Of course I wasn't. Esherwood is my home. Where else would I mean?'

'But it isn't our house now. It belongs to Mayne.'

'It'll always be my home and I won't give it up. I won't.' She threw her last stone at her husband, close enough to hit him in his face and knock off the spectacles that were perched on the end of his nose, as usual. Then she ran past him into the Dower House, wailing at the top of her voice, 'You don't love me any more.'

Reginald Esher gaped after her, then bent and picked up his spectacles. 'Oh, no! She's broken one of the lenses, damn her! It takes ages to get a replacement, too. How shall I manage?'

Daniel had been keeping an eye on Caroline, who had been edging sideways. To his relief, she suddenly ran off down the drive. He wondered what on earth had been going on at Esherwood while he was out to upset the two women.

'I'm sorry!' Reginald called to Daniel. 'I don't know what got into my wife. Your cheek's bleeding. I hope they didn't hurt you too badly.'

Daniel patted his cheek with his handkerchief, feeling sorry for the old fellow. 'It's just a graze, I think.' Bad enough to make him wince when he touched it, though.

Reginald glanced towards the Dower House, then came closer to Daniel, saying in a low voice, 'I wonder if you'd tell Maynard that I need to see him? It's rather urgent.'

'Of course I will.' Daniel looked towards the Dower House. 'But I think you'd better come up to the big house and speak to him there. Mrs Esher seems very upset about something and I don't think she'd welcome a visit from her son, from what she was yelling. Do you have any idea what set her off?'

'Not the faintest. I didn't even know she'd gone out.'

Pieces of paper suddenly cascaded out of an upstairs window. Mr Esher let out a yelp of dismay and started running towards the house. 'That's the manuscript for my book. She's run totally mad this time.'

Daniel set down the basket and went to pick up the papers, leaving Mr Esher to deal with his wife. The woman's behaviour today was bizarre. He didn't like to think it about Mayne's mother, but, well, she was acting like a madwoman.

As he was putting a stone on top of the papers to hold them down, he heard more yelling coming from the house, and would have left them to their quarrel, except that Mr Esher suddenly started yelling for help, sounding frantic. This was accompanied by the sounds of crockery smashing and Mrs Esher screaming abuse.

Dear heaven, what was going on?

He couldn't refuse to help.

'Daniel's been a long time at the shops,' Judith said, as the women stood surveying the attic, deciding where to start. 'There must have been a long queue at the grocer's.'

'Or perhaps he met Steph in town,' Ros said. 'Those two seem to get on like a house on fire.'

'They're just friends,' Kitty said.

The four women looked at her in surprise.

'How do you know that?' Judith asked.

Kitty shrugged. 'I've watched you and Mayne. Anyone can tell that you two are in love. You go all soppy when you smile at one another.'

'Oh, do we, miss.' Judith pretended to punch her daughter's arm.

'Yes, and Ros is the same with Victor.'

'I know what you mean,' Betty said. 'My dad does look soppy sometimes when he's talking to Ros.' She looked at Ros warily. 'I wasn't trying to be rude.'

'You weren't being rude, darling. I'm not ashamed of loving your father or of him loving me.'

Betty looked at her solemnly. 'Mother didn't let her feelings show when Grandmother was around. Her face went all stiff. But she did look soppy sometimes when she and Daddy were together at home.'

'You can't fool children. I love their honesty,' Miss Peters said in tones of great satisfaction. 'Now, ladies, how about these clothes?'

There was a clattering on the bare wooden stairs leading up to the attic and Ben appeared in the doorway. He looked across at his mother. 'Are you all right?'

'Yes, darling. Of course I am.'

'If that woman calls you terrible names in public again, I'll . . . I'll . . . ' His voice trailed away. 'It's not fair. You didn't do anything wrong.'

'What woman?'

'Mrs Esher.'

'Best to ignore people like her, young man,' Miss Peters said briskly. 'They enjoy it when you get upset.'

'Mayne said that too. It's all very well, but she—'

'We'll ignore that,' his mother said firmly. 'Now, we're here to sort out clothes. Are you staying, Ben? If you like, we can find you something first, then you can go back to join the men. There are some boy's clothes in the trunks apparently.'

He scowled. 'They'll be old-fashioned and they won't fit me.'

Helen put an arm round his shoulders. 'I'll alter them, if necessary. I've done that for Jan.'

'Oh. Well, thank you.' If her husband wore clothes she'd altered, Ben decided she must be good at it, because Jan's clothes fitted him well. He liked Jan. Well, he liked Helen too. Everyone in the family did.

They separated to open trunks, finding two containing clothes suitable for younger men. After much discussion they decided on a dark suit that Judith assured her son would be perfect for best.

He stared at it, fingering the beautiful material. 'It's . . . not bad.' He'd never owned a suit before, just oddments of clothing bought second-hand.

Gillian came across to touch the material too. 'It's very fine wool. It feels so soft. I hope we can find me something nice to wear, too.'

'Just let me see if I can find a shirt and tie for your brother . . . What about these, Ben?' She held the shirts against him in turn. 'We'll take them both. Which tie do you like best?'

He chose a pale blue one with stripes of darker blue and black, then wrinkled his nose. 'The clothes smell a bit musty.'

'They've been shut in old trunks. Go and hang the suit on the line to air. I'll wash the shirts tomorrow. Don't forget, we're having a party tonight. It is VJ Day, after all.' She smiled as she saw Betty do a little dance on the spot at the mention of their party.

'I've found some clothing in this trunk which might suit Kitty,' Helen said. 'Look. This blue would be wonderful with your dark hair.'

Kitty picked up the dress. 'It's the same colour as bluebells. Will it fit me?'

'Try it on. You can go into that small room to do it.'

They continued to sort out clothes for everyone and even Ben lingered to see what each trunk would reveal.

A couple of times, Judith went to look out of one of the dormer windows. 'I still can't see any sign of Daniel. Ben, would you mind going to look for him and asking him to hurry up? I need to know what he's bought if I'm to plan this party.'

'All right. Are you making anything to eat soon? It's half past eleven and I'm famished.'

'Just let me look at these dresses and I'll get you some food.' The trunk Ros had just opened contained some beautiful silk evening gowns and she couldn't resist.

'I wonder if any of them will fit me?' Ros held one up to herself, laughing at how short it was. 'I'm too tall for most of these. Oh, look at this beautiful eau de nil silk.' She pounced on a gown whose delicate greenish-blue colour suited her.

'It'll be long enough, I think. Turn round.' Helen took it out of her hands and held it against Ros's back. 'It's long enough but it must have been made for a rather plump lady. I could easily alter it for you. Go and try it on.'

Ros returned wearing the gown, and Helen began gathering the folds of material together and muttering to herself. She let go to pull a paper of pins out of her handbag and then pinned the material carefully till the dress fitted perfectly. 'I love this colour on you, Ros.'

'I've never had a silk dress before.'

'Then you've got one now, and we've found you a wedding dress. Judith, we need to sort something out for you and your daughters. Oh, and for Betty too.'

'I already have a party dress,' Betty offered, not sounding enthusiastic.

'I bet it's old-fashioned with lots of frills.'

'It is. I don't like it.'

'We'll find something for you to look beautiful in,' Helen said at once. 'I'll help you once we've sorted out Judith's wedding gown.'

'Really?' Betty whispered, as if she couldn't believe her ears.

'Really and truly.'

A dark rose silk caught Judith's eye and she was sent off to try it on.

'Goodness!' Helen exclaimed. 'It doesn't even need altering. It could have been made for you. Now there are only the girls to fit out.'

Since neither Kitty nor Gillian had ever had a party dress, they were easy to satisfy, which left only Betty. But nothing seemed suitable.

They sent her to fetch her party dress.

Ros looked at it and said thoughtfully, 'If we took all those frills off it, it'd look much nicer. I saw it when I was helping you unpack. It's lovely material and the soft pink does suit you.'

'Do you think so?'

She sounded so doubtful, Helen gave her a hug. 'I'll make sure it looks nice. We'll have to start the alterations quickly, though. There's a lot to do.'

'I'm not bad at plain sewing,' Ros offered. 'And I'm sure I've seen a sewing machine here somewhere, in one of the bedrooms, I think. Quite a modern one, too.'

'I know where it is,' Kitty said.

Helen's expression brightened. 'Can I borrow it, do you think, Judith? I could get things done much more quickly if I had a sewing machine.'

'I'm sure Mayne doesn't even know it exists. It's an old fashioned one, though.'

'Doesn't matter. It'll still be quicker than hand sewing. I

used to borrow the farmer's wife's sewing machine and whiz things up for her too. When I came here and discovered that my aunt didn't have one, I was so disappointed. I love sewing. I looked in the second hand shop, but there aren't any for sale, so I was going to put in an order for a new one. It'll take months for one to come through, though.'

Judith picked up her dress and the others followed suit. 'Let's go down and make something to eat. Ben will be ravenous by the time he gets back. In fact, I'd expected him back before now. Kitty, will you go and find him, see what he's doing. I can't think what's keeping everyone. I hope nothing's wrong.'

Helen glanced at the kitchen clock. 'I must get going. Jan will be waking up soon and he'll be hungry too. He's still making up for his years on the run from the Nazis, I think. He's always ready to eat. Have you thought of a date for the wedding yet? How long do I have for the alterations?'

'We can't do anything about getting a special licence till after the two days of public holiday. So we should have time to alter the clothes and hang them somewhere till the day comes.'

Ros looked at the pile of dresses. 'We don't want the bridegrooms seeing these. Shall I wrap everything up in sheets and help take them down to Helen's?'

'Good idea. By the time you get back, I'll have some food ready,' Judith said. 'But we're running low, so I'm hoping Daniel will be bringing other groceries from town for the party.'

Ros helped Helen carry the bundles, taking the short cut via the rear of the house and along the track that led to the back gardens of the elegant villas near the park. This track had been used by delivery men bringing coal and other major items before the war, but with only coal being delivered, and that irregularly, it was rather overgrown now.

★   ★   ★

When Daniel burst into the Dower House, he followed the sound of Mr Esher yelling and Mrs Esher screaming. Upstairs he found the poor man trying to get a big wooden ruler with brass corners away from his wife, who was hitting out at any part of him she could reach. As he was scrawny and she was a plump woman, he was having difficulty.

Daniel crept up behind her and snatched the weapon. She screeched even more loudly and turned on him instead, kicking and scratching, for lack of another weapon.

He stepped back, holding up one arm to protect his face and she took both of them by surprise, pushing past him and running out of the room. She slowed down on the stairs, making for the front door.

'Get her back!' yelled Mr Esher. 'She's a danger to everyone in this mood.'

Being younger and fitter, Daniel soon caught up with her, sorry to see Ben and Kitty nearby, gaping at the commotion.

'Mrs Esher is – um, upset,' he panted, trying to keep hold of her.

Mr Esher came to his aid, grabbing his wife's other arm. 'Could you fetch Mayne, Ben? And Kitty, would you run to Doctor Carberry's and ask him to come here as a matter of urgency? No one's answering the phone at the surgery.'

'Shall I tell him Mrs Esher is . . . not herself.'

'No, tell him the truth. She's gone mad,' Mr Esher said grimly. 'She's been "not herself" several times, and he knows about that, but she's never been this bad before. Tell him I said that.'

As Mrs Esher chose that moment to yell loudly for help and try to get free, both Kitty and Ben set off running in opposite directions, while Daniel and Mr Esher dragged the struggling woman back into the house and tied her to a chair.

★ ★ ★

At the doctor's surgery, Kitty rang the bell and waited impatiently for someone to answer.

Mrs Carberry came to the door, frowning.

'Mr Esher says can the doctor come to his wife. It's urgent.'

'It's a public holiday. Can't it wait? My husband needs to rest sometimes, like other people.'

'I don't think it can wait. Mr Esher says to tell the doctor his wife's run mad. She's kicking and screaming, acting really strangely.'

'Mrs Esher is?'

'Yes. I saw her myself.'

'You'd better come in.'

Kitty explained to the elderly doctor what she'd seen and he shook his head, making a tutting sound. 'I'd better come. Just let me get my bag. We'll take my car, just in case.'

She didn't ask in case of what, was already worried about what she'd seen.

He got the car started. 'Hop in.' As he drove along, he said quietly, 'Tell me exactly what you saw.'

So she told about Mrs Esher screaming and kicking, about the bruise on Daniel's face and Mr Esher's spectacles with one lens cracked.

'You're a very observant young woman,' he remarked.

'I like watching people and helping them. It must be wonderful to be a doctor like you and help people all the time.'

'We doctors help as many as we can but, sadly, we can't help everyone. Aren't you the girl who won the Esherwood Bequest?'

'Yes.'

'Well, if you're that clever, you're intelligent enough to become a doctor yourself one day.'

She gaped at him. 'Doesn't it cost a lot of money?'

'Your mother is marrying an Esher. There will be enough money for university, if you want to study medicine, though it's hard work and not all the tutors approve of women becoming doctors, even in this modern age.' He drew up in front of the Dower House.

When he heard the shrill noises from inside, he muttered something, grabbed his bag from the back seat and ran into the house.

Kitty didn't move for a moment or two, still marvelling at what he'd said. It would never have occurred to her to think of becoming a doctor. But he'd said it as if it were perfectly possible. And he should know.

Was it possible? Could she really go to university? What was it like there? How did you get a place to become a doctor?

She realised she'd been sitting in a half-dream and got out of the car quickly when Ben yelled at her to hurry up.

'What's the matter with you, Kitty? I had to speak to you twice.'

'Never you mind. What do you want?'

'Mayne said we should go back to the big house and let Mum know he'll be busy for a while. He wants us to take the basket of shopping back because he needs Daniel's help.' He lowered his voice. 'I think Mrs Esher really has gone mad, don't you?'

'Mmm.'

'Are you sure you're all right, Kitty?'

'I'm fine. Just thinking about something.' She didn't share her dream with her brother. It was too new and too precious, and he might mock it. But she held it close to her heart, to take out and study in quieter moments.

Was Dr Carberry right? Could she really become a doctor? Dare she even try? What if people laughed at someone like her aiming so high?

But what if she succeeded?

20

Mayne went down to the Dower House in his car, in case he needed to take his mother . . . somewhere. He didn't let his thoughts linger on where that might be, but hurried into the house, where he found Daniel helping his father keep watch over Mrs Esher. Mayne was shocked to see that they'd had to tie her to a chair.

Another car drew up just then and the doctor came inside and examined Mrs Esher, who fought and cursed him in a manner very unlike her. He gave her a sedative, but it was a while before this took effect and he waved to them to be quiet when they tried to ask him questions. He observed her carefully the whole time until she was calmer.

When she was slumped quietly in the chair, looking half asleep, he took Mr Esher and Mayne into the sitting room, leaving Daniel to keep watch. 'Your wife will have to be admitted to hospital, Mr Esher. St Paul's would be the best place for someone in her condition.'

'The asylum!' Mayne's father gasped, his face white and shocked.

'I'm afraid so. You have a telephone? Why didn't you phone me?'

'We did, but no one answered.'

Dr Carberry sighed. 'Ah. My wife thinks I need a rest and she doesn't always answer the telephone. We're none of us getting any younger, are we, Mr Esher? Now, may I use your phone?'

He was on the phone only for a short time, speaking in a low voice. When he came back into the sitting room, he said, 'They'll send the ambulance. It'll be easier to get her in and out of it. I'll wait with you till they come.'

Mr Esher watched the men carry his wife out to the ambulance, then swayed and clutched the wall. 'I feel dizzy.'

The doctor took him back into the sitting room. 'Let your son go with me to the hospital. You need food and a rest. At your age, these unhappy events take a greater toll than when you were young.'

When Mayne came out, Daniel offered to go to the hospital with him and he gratefully accepted.

'You'd better come in my car,' the doctor said. 'I can get more petrol as needed. I doubt you can.'

Mayne nodded. It was a constant problem to obtain petrol, because the ration wasn't generous. He hoped it would become easier once they started work on converting Esherwood.

It was mid-afternoon before the two men got back. They walked up to the big house from the doctor's surgery, stopping at the Dower House to tell Reginald what was happening.

'Will you be all right?' Mayne asked his father.

'Yes. I dozed off and I feel a little better now.'

'Have you had anything to eat?'

Reginald frowned. 'No. I don't think so. No, definitely not. But I had two cups of tea.'

'Let's sort out some food for you, then. Or you could come up and eat with us tonight.'

'I think I'd be better on my own.'

They made sure he had something to eat, then walked to the big house in silence.

★   ★   ★

Judith, Ros and Victor were in the kitchen, chatting quietly.

'Ros, could you get me some food?' Daniel asked quietly. 'Anything will do. Just a piece of bread and a scrape of jam or something.'

Mayne put an arm round Judith. 'I need to talk to you privately. We'll go into the office.'

When they were alone, he found it hard to tell her, could only cling to her for a few seconds, gathering strength to put the horrors of the day into words, finding comfort in the warmth and softness of her embrace.

'What is it, love?' she prompted at last.

'They've admitted my mother to St Paul's. She . . . she's gone mad, I suppose you'd have to say. They don't know what's causing her to act so strangely, but it's possibly senile dementia. It happens like this sometimes; people are bewildered and they become violent because they don't understand what's happening to them.'

As Judith put her arms round him and cuddled him close, he went on talking in a low voice. 'They've had to lock her in the secure part of the hospital because she was so violent. Mother has been a little strange lately. But I didn't realise . . . How could I?'

'I doubt anyone would have thought of that.'

'She wasn't like this when I was a lad. She's never been loving – nothing like you are with your children – but she's grown steadily worse since the war began: irritable, changing her mind, unreasonable at times. I thought it was just about losing her comfortable life. I never expected this.'

'It's no one's fault, Mayne, least of all, hers. Things . . . happen to people.'

He knew she was thinking of her own bigamous marriage. 'The thing is, how can I marry you with this taint hanging over my family, on top of what you've been facing? And if we do marry, how can you and I bring children into the world with their very sanity at risk?'

'That sort of thing happens to old people sometimes, Mayne. They change, become forgetful. You said the doctors mentioned senile dementia. I've seen it happen in families I grew up with. I don't think that's something inherited in the sense you mean. Has anyone else in your family ever gone mad?'

'I don't know. I'll have to ask Dad. I don't know much about Mother's family. They moved away and she didn't keep in touch with them because her brother married someone she considered unsuitable. She always was a snob.'

'The war could have made the senile problem worse, you know, Mayne.'

He looked at her in surprise. 'I don't know what you mean.'

'Because you didn't grow up in the poor part of town.' Judith sighed. 'People can become ill in many ways when they don't eat properly. Sometimes, though this is usually the men, they make their own booze and that's dangerous. All the grownups in one family died because of that a few streets away from us when I was a child. I never forgot it. My best friend was sent away to an orphanage.'

He waved one hand dismissively. 'Mother won't have been drinking illicit booze. I've never seen her the worse for drink, though she does enjoy a glass of wine with her meals sometimes. They took a supply with them to the Dower House from the cellars. But it can't be that.'

'I'm not saying it is, just that it might be due to something other than an inherited problem.'

'Let's hope so, because if it is inherited, there's no way I'd bring children into the world to face what I saw today.' He shuddered and dashed a hand across his eyes. 'I had to deal with a lot of dreadful things during the war, but I've never seen anything that upset me as much as my mother screaming and kicking like a wild woman.'

'What is your father doing now? Should we invite him to stay here, do you think? He's not the sort to cook or look after himself.'

'He wouldn't come. He's going to write to my mother's brother to ask him about the family, whether the illness has appeared before. And he's going to look into senile dementia, buy a book on it if necessary. He always thinks he'll find the answers in a book, but sometimes there are no answers. Dr Carberry said they don't understand why this happens to some people.'

'I could look it up at the town library as well, if you like. I doubt you'll have books about that at Esherwood.'

'Let's wait till we know more. I don't want everyone in Rivenshaw gossiping about it. I have to go to St Paul's tomorrow afternoon with Dad to talk to the doctor, and they'll probably tell us more then. I know I shouldn't burden you, but will you come with me, darling? You're so practical.'

'Of course I will. In fact, if you tried to stop me, I'd summon a taxi and follow you.'

He buried his face in her hair. 'How did I ever get lucky enough to meet you and win your love?'

'I'm lucky too. And since we're together now, this is one of the times we'll be able to support one another. I wish we were married already. It'd make it all easier. Let's go and get a special licence as soon as the VJ holiday is over.'

'Good idea. The Methodist Minister will marry us straight away. He's a delightful man.'

They stood in each other's arms for several minutes before they moved again.

Even then, she watched him carefully, giving him time to pull himself together before she spoke.

She wasn't going to let him be all noble about this, she decided. His mother's problem might be something that could prevent them from having children, but nothing – nothing at all – was going to prevent her from marrying Mayne. She had never felt so comfortable and 'right' with anyone in her whole life.

'Come on,' she said at last. 'We have to get ready to celebrate VJ Day.'

'I don't feel much like celebrating.'

'Well, I do. And so do all the others. You can't spoil their day.'

'No. Of course not.'

'And it'll cheer you up.'

His only answer to that was a sigh.

The party at Esherwood that evening was augmented by Helen and Miss Peters, and even Mayne's father was persuaded to join them for a while. He looked a bit lost at first, but cheered up somewhat as people chatted to him.

Jan and Al took it in turns to join the party for a few minutes but kept a close eye on the grounds. They'd had to chase a couple of tipsy revellers away and had deterred others simply by standing at the front or back gates and glaring at them.

The adults drank wine that Mayne had unearthed from the cellar. He'd piled things in front of the wine store when the house was requisitioned, leaving a few bottles out in another area. Those had all vanished, as he'd expected, but no one seemed to have bothered to check behind the various piles of old furniture, let alone move them or throw them out. The cellars were large enough to provide space for all that the house's occupiers had needed to store.

The children drank a concoction based on the orange juice given to young children by the government, with a little extra sugar added to it and a couple of bottles of fizzy lemonade, provided by Mr Woollard. His chauffeur had brought a few bits and pieces across to Esherwood with his compliments, and that had included a can of petrol.

Judith hadn't the heart to refuse the gifts. She knew Mayne would need extra petrol to get to and from St Paul's, and it was thoughtful of Mr Woollard to think of that. And she stared in delight at the box of chocolates, longing to open it. She couldn't remember the last time she'd had a chocolate, let alone one from a fancy box like this.

'Getting rid of his ill-gained loot,' Mayne muttered. 'Or trying to bribe us.'

Judith dug her elbow hard into his ribs. 'Don't be such a grump! My mouth's watering already and you know you're going to need the extra petrol. He's done this out of kindness.'

'Am I a grump?'

'Just a little bit. But it's been a hard day, so I'll forgive you.'

'Very hard.'

They all ate a meal together, laughing and joking, then found some music on the radio. Soon Helen got everyone dancing, even Miss Peters and Mayne's father, who moved sedately round the edge of the hall together.

Then the music grew more lively and Ros whispered in Betty's ear, giving her instructions, after which she announced that Betty was going to lead a chain to dance the conga round the house.

The little girl pulled the other children into the chain one by one, tapping each person on the shoulder as an invitation to join in. Each person held on to the shoulders of the one in front. She led them round the room, moving in time to the music and beaming so happily no one could refuse to join her.

Gradually she got everyone up.

Mayne was the last one sitting and he didn't really feel like joining in. But he hadn't the heart to refuse when Betty stopped in front of him and tapped his shoulder, her face alight with joy. He went to join the end of the chain, where he found himself holding Miss Peters' bony shoulders.

Betty then led the chain out to the entrance hall and they danced round it, moving in and out of the other rooms till they were breathless. When the music finished and a voice began speaking on the radio, Mayne slipped away to turn off the wireless and they carried on dancing, singing cheerfully to provide music.

In the end, Miss Peters had to fall out, fanning her face. Victor let his daughter continue for another circuit of the ground floor, then picked her up to stop her, swinging her round a couple of times, calling, 'Bravo! Well done, darling.'

They returned to the kitchen and Judith opened the box of chocolates, telling the children to make each one last.

Since they were getting tired, they played a few quieter games, silly games where you had to say a word connected to the last one called out, and do it within a count of ten. Even 'I spy' was fun that night.

Then Miss Peters brought out a parcel. 'There are quite a few layers,' she said, 'but I only had newspaper to wrap it in. There's a small present inside and small coins in between some of the layers. We'll put the radio on again and I'll turn the sound down whenever you have to stop passing the parcel, then whoever is holding it can unwrap another layer.'

She beamed at them as they played, managing it so that each child won a coin and Betty won the big prize. Everyone guessed this was deliberate, but no one complained.

'What were they doing to celebrate in the town?' Daniel asked during the lull that followed.

'Street parties for the children, I suppose,' Ros said. 'It's what people usually do. Those who don't have a lot to spare give the treats to the children. And there will be bonfires, of course. Boys do love bonfires.'

'The grownups will probably be dancing in the town square by now,' Judith said. 'I heard someone talking about how to celebrate last week. I must be getting old. I don't even want to go out.'

Eventually they started talking about going to bed and, as usual, Betty was sent up first.

Victor walked up the stairs with his daughter. 'Did you enjoy yourself, princess?'

'Oh yes, Daddy. It was my first real party.'

'Surely you went to children's birthday parties when you were living with your mother?'

'They weren't fun like this one, so they didn't feel like parties. We had spelling games and riddles,' she explained with awful scorn. 'Who wants to spell words at a party? That's not fun. Then we sang nursery rhymes and songs the governesses chose. Nursery rhymes are for babies. We never danced round the house in a line singing Bing Crosby songs. Judith knows all the words to them, doesn't she?' She leaned closer to whisper, 'But Ros has a terrible voice.'

'I know.' He waited at the door of the bedroom Betty shared with the other girls until she was ready for bed, then tucked her in and kissed her soft cheek.

'One day, we'll have our own home,' he promised.

'I don't want to leave Esherwood. I like living here.'

He liked it too, and not for the first time wondered if Mayne might be persuaded to sell him a small piece of land to build a house on, near his friends but with space for his own life with his new wife.

Even if Mayne did agree to it, would the town council allow Esherwood's grounds to be subdivided and built on? Town councils could have the stupidest rules about where you were allowed to build houses, and their powers seemed to have increased during the war. And the government had made rules about how big new houses could be – which wasn't very big at all.

He walked slowly down the stairs, smiling and pausing for a moment on the landing as a burst of laughter erupted from the kitchen.

In the silence that followed, he heard what sounded like a gun shot outside and jerked instantly to attention. Jan only had blanks but he'd not fire even them without a reason.

As the people in the kitchen began speaking again, the front door opened and a figure slipped inside the house. Victor moved into a darker patch of shadow behind a very ugly marble statue on the landing and watched. What the hell was going on?

The intruder moved across the hall towards the stairs, running up them confidently, as if he knew exactly where to go.

Victor guessed then what this was about and his heart sank. Not again!

He waited till the man had reached the landing, then stepped out of the shadow of the statue, punched the stranger in the face and sent him spinning across the floor. At the same time, he yelled, 'To me! To me!'

Another figure was running up the stairs before the echoes of his calls had died away. Victor would have trouble dealing with two of them on his own, so he made sure his back was against the wall as the intruder scrambled to his feet.

'It's me,' a voice he recognised said.

'Thank goodness.' Al must have been following the intruder. Victor grabbed the fellow again before he could get away and Al grabbed his legs, bringing him to the ground.

The stranger bucked and struggled, but by that time Mayne and Daniel had run up the stairs. Faced with four angry men, the intruder gave in, standing quietly, his eyes going from one to the other.

'Are we never to have any peace?' Victor felt awash with anger at having their lovely evening spoiled.

'Let's see who we've got.' Mayne ripped off the man's knitted balaclava. 'He's a stranger to me.'

Al scowled at him. 'Nobody I've ever seen in Rivenshaw.'

'I don't recognise him from the village I used to live in, either,' Victor said. 'Did Mrs Galton send you?'

The man twitched at the sound of her name, as if he recognised it, but still said nothing.

'It must be her. But why did she hire a stranger? And how did he know his way inside the house? He was definitely making for the bedrooms.'

Anger boiled over and Victor shook the man suddenly. 'Who – are you – working for?'

But though their captive didn't fight back, he didn't speak.

Daniel put one hand on his friend's shoulder to stop him continuing. 'You'll get nowhere with him.'

'Well,' Al said. 'It's late so I vote we lock him up till tomorrow morning. He can talk to the police then.'

Ros watched from the hall and as the men brought their captive down the stairs, she started up them. 'I'll go to Betty.'

'Thanks,' Victor said. 'I kept expecting her to come out of the bedroom but she didn't.'

'She must have been too scared.' Ros went into the bedroom the three girls shared, but the child wasn't in her bed. She stopped in the doorway, her heart pounding with anxiety. 'Betty! It's all right. We've caught the intruder.'

There was a sound and the child crawled out from under a pile of boxes. She had tear streaks down her cheeks and flung herself into Ros's arms.

'What were you doing?'

'Ben made me a hidey hole in case anyone tried to kidnap me again.'

'How clever of him.'

She snuggled closer. 'It's Grandmother, isn't it? She's sent someone else after me. She's still trying to make me go and live with her.'

'It's probably her, but she didn't succeed, did she? And even I wouldn't have guessed where you were hiding, because those boxes look to be full of books. But from now on, you're not coming up to bed on your own. If none of the others are going to bed, I'll come and stay with you till they do. I won't let anyone take you from me and your father, I promise.'

She sat down on the bed, with Betty on her knees and held her close until the child had calmed down, by which time Victor had come back up to join them.

'They've locked the intruder up in the old butler's pantry. It only has a tiny window.'

He gave his daughter a hug and pulled Ros into the embrace as well. 'The three of us will make a lovely family, won't we?'

Betty sniffed and managed a wobbly smile. Then she brightened. 'But I hope you have more children, because I've always wanted brothers and sisters. Gillian said I might get some after you marry. I wouldn't be on my own if I had brothers and sisters, would I?'

'You're not on your own now, darling,' he said. 'You have us.'

'We'll do our best to oblige about brothers and sisters, though,' Ros added. 'I'd like a bigger family. Now, how about going to bed? I'll stay with you till Gillian comes up.'

The other girls both came to bed shortly afterwards, knowing how anxious Betty would be.

'You can get into bed with me, Betty, if you like,' Gillian said. 'Just for tonight.' She held up the edge of the covers as Betty scrambled across to the other bed.

That girl had a kind heart, Ros thought as she put the light out and left the room.

'It can't go on like this,' Victor said, when he and Ros rejoined the others. 'I'm going to hire a lawyer. Mrs Galton's not getting hold of my daughter. I think she's mad, going to this extent.'

He realised this wasn't a tactful thing to say. 'Sorry, Mayne. I don't actually think she's mad, not in that sense. She's an arrogant old woman, soured by grief, who's had her own way all her life, because half the village is dependent on her family for employment. It's bloody stupid that she's making such a fuss. Sorry for the language, ladies, but it is stupid. She'd never want to look after a child herself.'

'They used worse language than that when things went wrong on the farm,' Ros said lightly. 'And I'm sure Judith will have heard worse when she worked in the mill. So go ahead and swear if it helps. There are no hothouse flowers here.' But she too glanced sideways at Mayne, as if uncertain whether Victor's words had upset him.

'It's all right,' he said. 'What happened today with my mother . . . Well, frankly, it was awful, but I'm not close to her in the way Judith's children love her. It's worrying that she's become irrational, but not devastating, so you don't have to tread on egg shells when you speak about her.'

'Mayne and I are going with Mr Esher to St Paul's tomorrow to talk to the doctor there,' Judith said. 'So if you can keep an eye on my three, Ros, I'd appreciate it.'

'Of course. They're no trouble.'

'Did you find out who the intruder was? Did he tell you whether it was Mrs Galton who sent him?'

'He refuses to speak, but he seemed to react when I mentioned her name. None of us have seen him before. We've got him locked in the butler's pantry for the night.

The window's too small for an adult to get through. We'll call in Sergeant Deemer tomorrow.'

Victor sighed. 'This can only be Mrs Galton's doing. Where does she find people like that to do her dirty work? I'd expected it to be Barham again. I hope he isn't waiting outside.'

'Al said there was no one else in the grounds, and if anyone could tell, it'd be him, surely?' Daniel said.

'How could the fellow hope to take a child from a house full of people?' Mayne wondered.

'If enough money is offered, some people will try anything. Perhaps he was going to wait till everyone was asleep. Or maybe he thought you'd be celebrating till the small hours and he'd be able to kidnap her before you went up to bed,' Jan said. 'He must have been watching through the windows and seen her say goodnight and go upstairs. Good thing I spotted him, eh?'

'You did well.'

He moved towards the outer door. 'Better get back on duty, eh?'

'And we need to get to bed,' Judith said. 'Come on, everyone. We'll have a quick clear up and then get our sleep.'

'I'll keep watch down here for a while,' Daniel offered. 'I don't sleep very well these days.'

'There's no need to keep watch with Al and Jan in the grounds,' Mayne said.

'Well, I'm not ready for bed anyway.'

'Try a cup of warm milk,' Ros suggested as they left him to it.

Daniel sighed as he went to find a book and, since the kitchen chair wasn't comfortable, took it up to his bedroom. Maybe he could read himself to sleep. At least if he was out of sight, the others wouldn't fuss over him.

21

In the morning Victor got up early, went outside to find Jan to back him up, then unlocked the door of the butler's pantry.

It was empty. When they investigated, they found that the window glass had been removed from its frame. Damn! They should have checked the state of the window frame more carefully last night. Their prisoner had managed to pry out the crumbling old putty holding the glass in place, and had wriggled out. In the darkness Al and Jan wouldn't have seen that there was no glass in the window.

Victor was furious at himself. He should have sat up and kept watch over their prisoner. He'd drunk two or three glasses of wine during the course of the evening, and mustn't have been thinking as clearly as usual. There was no excuse for his stupidity, none at all.

There were a couple of smears of blood on the edge of the frame where nails were sticking out. It must have been a tight fit for the man to squeeze through.

Beside him, Jan was cursing in Polish, something he only did when extremely annoyed. 'This fellow must have been skilful and quick, because I came this way several times during the early hours of the morning. I should have checked the window more carefully, gone closer. I knew where you were keeping him.' He thumped one clenched fist into the other in annoyance at himself.

'I doubt you could have seen that the pane of glass was missing unless you climbed up a ladder. The window is above head height from the outside, because of the slope of the land. He'd have had to jump down from there, so I hope he hurt himself.' Victor looked at his watch. 'There won't be anyone at the police station yet; we'll have to wait until nine o'clock to tell Sergeant Deemer what happened. The intruder will be far away already, I'd guess, so there's no desperate hurry.'

'I can try to follow his trail across the grounds and see which way he went. I'm good at reading the signs.'

'All right. It won't do any harm. At least it's light now.'

Jan did find a trail, but once it led off the grounds of Esherwood into the paved streets, there was no way of continuing. The man could have had a car waiting or taken the early milk train. Who knew?

'I wonder what he was going to do with Betty?' Jan said.

'Take her to her grandmother. There's no other reason for him coming here. That woman won't get another chance to capture my daughter, though.'

'How will you stop her. You say she's used to getting her own way and has plenty of money. What will she do next, do you think?'

'Go to the law. Though how she'll persuade them she is a better person to look after my child than I am, I can't imagine. Perhaps she'll find a judge who believes money is the most important thing in a child's upbringing.'

'Then you should have an escape plan ready in case the law decides on her side.' Jan gave him one of those clear-eyed looks. 'You cannot rely on justice, or on this grandmother woman telling the truth. I escaped during my years fleeing across Europe because I always, always had other things I could do if my first plan didn't work.'

He hesitated, then added, 'You can send her to us, if you have to hide her quickly. I could make a place in the garden that they wouldn't easily find.'

'I can't ask you to put your own right to stay in England in jeopardy.'

Jan laughed softly. 'You didn't ask. You and your friends helped me when I was in trouble. If I can ever pay you back in any way, I will. And I know Helen will agree with me. My wife considers you and everyone at Esherwood like a family, and I hope I'll be allowed to do the same.'

'Thank you.' He offered his hand and the two of them shook, as if sealing a bargain. 'I'm going to see a lawyer as the first step.'

'Ask Miss Peters for her advice as well. Her brother the judge may know what to do for the best. I've met him. He is a wise and clear-thinking man, kind as well.'

'Good idea.'

But Victor sighed as he walked away. He hated the thought of trouble coming to his daughter, of having always to watch out for it, absolutely loathed it. Just when they were teaching Betty to make friends and enjoy life.

His wife had been weak, had let her mother take over her life once Victor had been called up to fight for his country. You couldn't put a child's life above your country's needs however much you wanted to.

But now the war was over, his child's safety and happiness would come before everything else, and he knew Ros would be with him on that.

Veronica Peters rose early, as she always did. The older she got, the less sleep she seemed to need. She was just pouring her first cup of tea when the telephone rang.

'Is that you, Ronnie?'

Her youngest and only surviving brother called her that. No one else in her generation of the family was alive to do so. 'Who else would be picking up my telephone?'

'You're on your own?'

'Yes.'

'Listen carefully and name no names. One of the men in my profession got a little tipsy last night during our celebrations and let something slip. I doubt he'll remember this morning what he said, but it upset me. I lay awake for a good while thinking what I should do about it.'

'Go on.'

'I can't really do anything . . . yet. But you can. Listen, you need to go and see that young man who's staying with your friend in the big house. Tell him they'll be coming to take his daughter away from him tomorrow morning.'

'Who will be coming?'

'I'm not naming names on the phone.'

'Sorry. I wasn't thinking.' She knew the operators sometimes listened into calls. 'But how can anyone do that? The man is the child's father, and a good one, too.'

'Money can still buy lawyers who would swear that black is white to suit a client's needs.'

His voice sounded bitter and she knew why. Dennison hated any act of so-called justice that was based on a manipulation of facts by a lawyer who was good with words. In fact, her brother had gained a reputation for defending the underdog and she was proud of him for doing that.

'It's a pity the person in question isn't married.'

'He's about to get married.'

'Ah. When?'

'Soon.'

'The sooner the better, Ronnie. In fact, it might be best if he isn't there when they come for the child.'

'I'll make sure of it.'

'Good. In the meantime, I'll go and speak to a couple of friends about an idea I have, then I'll come over to Rivenshaw. All right if I spend a night or two with you? I'm staying with those friends who live only ten minutes away from the town if you need to contact me before I leave them to come to you tomorrow afternoon.'

'I always enjoy your company. I'll be glad to see you. And I'm sure I'll manage to arrange the other thing.'

When she put the phone down, she left the teapot where it was and hurried next door. For this, she needed help. When you were past eighty, you weren't as spry as you used to be. It surprised her sometimes when she stared at her wrinkled face in the mirror how old she was. She didn't feel old in her head, though her stiff old knees reminded her of her age every now and then.

Jan hurried round to the back door of the big house, going in without knocking. 'Is Victor here?'

Mayne looked at him in surprise.

'Something's happened. Miss Peters sent me to speak to him. And she particularly warned me not to tell you what it's about. You'll understand why later.'

'I'll go and fetch him. Pour yourself a cup of tea.'

When Victor came down in his dressing gown, Jan drained his cup and stood up. 'We need to talk privately.'

'You can say anything in front of Mayne.'

'Not this time.' Jan gave them both a wry smile. 'Miss Peters' orders.'

Daniel came in, looking bleary-eyed, as if he hadn't slept. 'Is something wrong?'

'Victor has a problem,' Mayne told him. 'Why don't you two go into the library?'

Victor led the way. 'What's wrong, Jan?'

'Miss Peters received a phone call this morning from a person she won't name but we can guess who it is. Trouble's coming and she needs to see you. She has some suggestions about what you should do.'

Victor got dressed quickly before walking back with Jan. He went into his friend's house then crossed the back gardens to visit their next-door neighbour, Miss Peters, without anyone seeing him.

'I got your message. I gather there's something wrong.'

'Yes. Or there will be. I was speaking to my brother on the telephone this morning and . . . let us say he accidentally let some information drop.' She fixed Victor with a piercing gaze. 'This must stay between the two of us and if you ever tell anyone else, apart from Ros, who I got the information from, I'll deny it. My brother is acting rather on the edge of the law in even raising the matter with me.'

His heart sank. 'I won't say a word about it to anyone else. I give you my word.'

She explained what her brother had told him. 'He didn't name names, but it seems fairly obvious what's being planned.'

He felt sick to the soul to think of Betty being taken from him. 'I can't understand why Mrs Galton thinks she'll win if it comes to a legal case.'

'Nor can I. One has to wonder what she's got up her sleeve. In the meantime, if you want my opinion, you should arrange to get married as soon as this holiday is over. I'm certain a married man will stand more chance of keeping his daughter than a widower who doesn't have a woman to mother the child. And Ros having been in the Wrens will stand you in good stead, too.'

'Good advice, Miss Peters.'

'See that you follow it as quickly as you can. In fact, you might like to leave immediately and spend the night in

Manchester, so that you can get to the registry office early tomorrow morning.'

'You think so?'

'I'm sure so. You don't want the police coming to Esherwood and stopping you leaving.'

'Definitely not. I'll take your advice.'

'If I were you, I'd not leave from Rivenshaw station, either.'

'No? How do I get anywhere else? I don't have a car and you don't want me to involve Mayne in what I'm doing.'

'There's a taxi driver called Ted Willis. Anyone can tell you where to find him. He'll take you where you want to go. Tell him I sent you, but make sure no one else hears that. But it'd be good if people heard you asking for him. That eliminates anyone else at Esherwood from being accused of involvement in this affair.'

'I'm much obliged for your help, Miss Peters. And for your brother's help.'

'I haven't done anything, nor has he. And you haven't seen me today. Knock on my front door on your way back and I won't answer it. Someone will be bound to see you.'

He went out via the back gardens and Jan and Helen's front door, then walked into the town centre.

Deciding to do this as publicly as possible, he went into the grocer's shop and asked the owner where he could find a taxi driver called Ted Willis. She was able to supply the information.

'Not trouble, I hope, Mr Travers? You don't need your ration cards back?'

'Family business I need to attend to,' Victor said. 'But it should only take a couple of days. I'd not disturb Mr Willis on a public holiday if it wasn't an emergency.'

'Oh, Ted won't mind. Always ready to earn a bit extra, he is.'

Victor found the street and knocked on the door of Number

Fifteen. When an older man answered the door, he asked if he could speak to him in private. Only then did he reveal that Miss Peters had sent him and what he wanted Ted to do.

'She was sure I could trust you not to tell anyone that she was involved.'

'Always glad to oblige a friend of that lady. And how can she be involved?' Ted winked at him. 'I haven't set eyes on her for days, have I? Where exactly do you want to go, Mr Travers?'

Sergeant Deemer strolled along to the police station, having had an enjoyable evening of celebrations on what people were calling VJ Day, even though some people were saying the official VJ Day would come later, once the peace was signed, sealed and delivered. No one minded the thought of another public holiday and more celebrations.

There had been no major interruptions to the sergeant's own enjoyment, no trouble in Rivenshaw beyond noise, music and rowdy singing.

Of course, he'd walked round the town centre a couple of times to keep an eye on things, once with his wife, later on his own. But he hadn't really been needed.

It felt good that the war was over everywhere now, in Europe and in the Far East. People were happy about that, even though they knew that the food and other restrictions wouldn't end overnight. But maybe they'd be happier if ships could get to Britain with cargoes of food. He hadn't had a banana for years. They were his favourite fruit.

Deemer could now start planning his retirement proper. He'd come out of retirement to work as a policeman when the war began, doing his bit like many other older men, so that younger, fitter men could engage in the actual fighting. But he was well over seventy now and wanted a more peaceful life during his remaining years.

His heart sank when he saw Victor Travers pacing up and down outside the police station, radiating impatience and anxiety. Not a man to worry you for no reason, Mr Travers, but today was supposed to be another holiday so what could have upset him?

There was no sign of Constable Farrow, who was supposed to have opened up the station by now. That young man was not reliable. Deemer should have got him thrown out of the police force immediately, not let him work his notice.

Sergeant Deemer got out his keys, ready to unlock the main door. 'How can I help you today, Mr Travers?'

'We caught an intruder at Esherwood last night.'

He unlocked the door. 'Ah. Better come inside and tell me the details. A burglar, eh?'

'No. He was trying to kidnap my daughter.'

'Another attempt?'

'I'm afraid so. It'll be her grandmother's doing, because there's no one else who would arrange such a thing. It's well known in the village she lives in that Mrs Galton doesn't give up easily when she wants something and she wants control of my daughter, who is her only grandchild.'

'I'm afraid I can't do anything about the lady, not even report her to my superiors, unless you have proof that she's behind the kidnapping attempts. But I will send Farrow with you to bring in the intruder. I'll be happy to charge him with attempted burglary.'

'Unfortunately, the man escaped. He managed to remove the putty round the window pane of the room we'd locked him in then take out the glass and wriggle through the hole. We'd thought it too small, but unfortunately, he managed to get through it. Left a little blood behind where a couple of nails were sticking up, but I dare say he counted it worthwhile.'

'Ah. Pity he got away. But at least the little lass is safe.'

'For the moment. I know you can't help us without proof, but I thought you should be informed, just in case they try anything else. I'm going to ask Miss Peters' advice on my way home.'

Mr Travers didn't meet the sergeant's eyes as he said that and Deemer wondered what he was holding back. Something, that was sure. All those decades in the police force had made Deemer good at reading the truth behind someone's face and words. But he trusted Travers, so he didn't challenge him.

'Miss Peters is a very wise old lady. You couldn't do better than consult her, sir, and perhaps her brother too.'

'I doubt I'll encounter her brother. He doesn't live in Rivenshaw, does he?'

Another avoidance of eye contact. The man didn't lie easily. So it was probably something to do with the judge as well, Deemer decided. Well, Judge Dennison Peters could manage his own affairs without any interference from a lowly police sergeant. And if the judge was involved, it'd not be anything unlawful, which was another reason for leaving them to sort things out themselves.

He frowned as he remembered something. 'I did hear that Judge Peters was intending to resign now that the war is over. Can't remember who told me. Of course, he won't do anything till the legal system in Britain is set to rights and emergency measures rescinded, but he's in his seventies now. Us old chaps will have to step aside eventually and let the younger folk run things.'

Who was it who had told him about the judge retiring? He wouldn't feel right now until he remembered. 'Sorry. You were saying, Mr Travers?'

'I can't imagine the police station in this town without you to manage it, Sergeant. People think very highly of you.'

Sergeant Deemer could feel his cheeks heating up. 'Very

kind of you to say so, sir, I'm sure. Ah, here's that dratted constable of mine. What time do you call this, Farrow?'

He shooed his subordinate into the police station but stayed by the door for a few moments longer, watching Mr Travers walk away and wondering what he could do to help the man keep his daughter.

Then he suddenly remembered where the rumour had come from. Mr Gilliot had mentioned Judge Peters retiring to Farrow a couple of days ago, though why an arrogant sod like him should bother to tell this to a lowly police constable, Deemer couldn't work out. Unless it was to get the information to the sergeant, as a kind of warning. Hmm. He'd have to think about that. There was a lot to think about today.

Wiser heads than his would be thinking, too, putting plans together for the whole country. It would be a mammoth task for the government to set things up for peace again. Just think of all the factories and mills that had been changed to produce war materials. Deemer could remember the long years of depression and unemployment that had followed the Great War. He did hope it wouldn't happen this time.

No, those in power would have learned better what to do, surely? And reorganising for peace would be a task gladly undertaken. Mr Attlee had said in his radio broadcast, 'The last of our enemies is laid low.' Deemer wished the last of his own enemies had been defeated, but as soon as you caught one criminal, another seemed to pop up, even in a quiet little town like Rivenshaw. Like this latest incident . . .

A cold wind whistled round him. He looked up at the grey sky and shivered. Rain was brewing. As he went inside the police station, he admitted to himself that trouble was brewing too. He could feel it in his bones.

Things were in a sorry state when a nasty old woman tried to take a child from her father's care. Deemer might not have met the old lady in person, but he was sure she was nasty because Mr Travers was as decent a chap as you could hope to find, and one who'd served his country.

Maybe he'd better spread the word about the intruder and the child being in danger. Not officially, as the sergeant, but as a private citizen. Yes, why not? He had a few old and trusted friends in Rivenshaw who would keep their eyes open for strangers turning up, he was sure. You couldn't be too careful.

The law sometimes let people down but he would never do that willingly, not till they nailed him in his coffin.

And he rather thought Judge Peters felt the same.

Caroline had her bags all packed. Her brother came upstairs to carry them down for her.

'Who is this friend that you're visiting?' Michael asked.

'Someone I met at a party.'

He stared at her in surprise. 'I don't call that a friend.'

She shrugged. 'We got on rather well. I'm only staying with her for a couple of days, then I suppose I'll have to go back to Scotland.'

'You made your bed . . . '

She glared at him. He always had been a sanctimonious prig who thought he knew better than anyone else. But she didn't say that. She might need his help in the future. In the meantime, she had some pieces of silver to sell, and serve Mayne right for not realising she already had some stashed away. The money from those would tide her over for a while.

Pity Mayne had discovered her and his mother before she could find anything really valuable. Good thing she'd hidden some of the pieces in her clothing every time. Dorothy had been so dopey, it had been easy to fool her. As for Mayne, Caroline hoped that Judith female would make him miserable.

Michael was looking at her with a worried expression. 'You'll be all right?'

'I'm a bit short of money. You couldn't spare the odd quid, could you?'

He sighed and fumbled in his pocket, pulling out a five-pound note. 'There. And good luck.'

'Thanks. Something will turn up, you'll see. It always does. I'll find a way to escape from that dull village in Scotland.'

'Good luck with that. I must admit, I wouldn't fancy living there myself.' He opened the front door. 'I'll just put your cases in the car while you're saying goodbye to Joanna.'

She went into the kitchen and dredged up a smile for her sister-in-law. 'Thank you so much for having me.'

Joanna merely nodded.

'I'll . . . um, see you soon.'

'Not too soon, I hope.'

Caroline turned and left the kitchen, going straight out to the car. If she never saw her sister-in-law again, she'd be glad of it.

22

Once the arrangements had been made with Mr Willis for the taxi, and the sergeant informed about the intruder, Victor set off back to Esherwood through streets still decorated with limp and often ragged bunting, brought out of attics for the occasion. The ashes of one large bonfire were still sending up little curls of smoke, and quite a few of the people he passed looked tired and heavy eyed, though cheerful.

As instructed, he knocked openly on Miss Peters' front door. He knocked again, but there was still no answer.

The neighbour on the other side from Jan's house popped her head over the garden wall. 'She mustn't be at home. Can I take a message?'

He looked at his wristwatch. 'I'll come back another time. It's not urgent.'

'If I see her, who shall I say called?'

'Victor Travers.'

She repeated his name and went back to pulling up the weeds in a front garden full of vegetables.

It couldn't have been more convenient that the neighbour had seen him and taken his name. Miss Peters would be pleased at how well her little plan had worked.

He walked briskly towards Esherwood, deciding what to do next.

★　★　★

When Victor got back, Mayne came out of the kitchen to meet him. 'Am I allowed to know what's going on yet? And what about Daniel?'

'No. Better if neither of you know, so that, if necessary, you can swear in a court of law that you had no idea what I was going to do. Do you think you could keep Judith and the children away from the kitchen and back garden for half an hour or so? You too, Daniel; perhaps you could sit in the library to read instead of in the kitchen?'

To his relief, Daniel got up from the kitchen table with a quick nod.

Mayne smiled at him. 'I'll take Judith and the children down to the cellar to check a few things out. I won't let anyone come up again for half an hour. Will that give you enough time, Victor?'

'Yes, thank you. Now, I need to speak to Ros.'

'She was doing some weeding. She and Judith decided that everyone needed a quiet day, her included. What shall I do about Betty?'

'Ask her to wait for me in her bedroom. I'll find Ros and speak to her first. We can sit on the landing window seat to talk.'

Ros listened intently as Victor went over what he'd found out that morning and what he thought they should do about it.

'Would you be willing to marry me as soon as it can be arranged?'

'I'd marry you this minute if I could, Victor.'

'Good. We should be able to get a special licence tomorrow, but I think you have to wait 24 hours after that to marry. I don't think it'd be wise to do our waiting here, though.'

'We can find somewhere to stay in Manchester.'

'That's what I was thinking. We can pretend we're visiting family there and go sightseeing. I'm sorry you won't have time to alter that dress you found.'

She looked at him ruefully. 'I shall be a very shabby bride, I'm afraid.'

'I don't care two hoots about that, as long as it's you that I'm marrying.' He kissed her, then pushed her away again. 'We need to hurry. If you can pack what you and Betty need for a couple of days away, I'll tell her what's going on.'

His daughter listened intently to what he had to say. By the time he'd finished, she was looking extremely anxious again. He hated to see that expression back on her face, when she had been so happy during the party.

'I won't let your grandmother take you,' he promised.

'If her lawyer tells the police you have to, how can you stop her?' she asked. 'I've heard Grandmother say she can get anything she wants with Mr Fitkin's help.'

'Oh, can she? Well, her lawyer won't take you away from me, whatever he does. If we have to run away to Australia to escape her, we will, all three of us.'

But Betty didn't look convinced. 'Even then, Grandmother would find us.'

As she went to help Ros pack, he heard her say, 'I need to take Mummy's photo and the rag doll she made me. I take them everywhere with me.'

Ros immediately found room for them. He smiled. Was there anything his beloved didn't take in her stride? What a wonderful woman she was! He hoped she would give him more children. He felt hopeful that all sorts of good things were possible when he was with her. She had a similar effect on Betty.

As he sorted out what he would need, he continued to wonder what it was that had made Mrs Galton believe the law would be on her side. There had to be something specific or she'd not be sending a lawyer to take Betty away from him.

What the hell could it be?

When they were ready, the trio slipped down by the back stairs, waiting to make sure the kitchen was unoccupied before they hurried out into the garden. Ros had her own and Betty's things in a knapsack, while he was carrying a small suitcase with a change of clothing in it.

He noticed that his daughter kept glancing over her shoulder, as if afraid of pursuit and was both relieved and glad when he saw the taxi waiting for them in the back lane, as agreed.

'Thank you, Ted.' Victor opened the rear door of the taxi for Ros and Betty, then slid into the back with them.

'My pleasure, Mr Travers. Now, I hope you don't think I'm interfering, but my wife has sent a hat for your young lady to wear and, if you don't mind it, this is an old hat of mine for you. They'll help hide who you are. If you can slide down to kneel on the floor, Miss Betty, just till we leave the town, your father can cover you with my old overcoat.'

'What an excellent idea!' Ros exclaimed, cramming the hat on her head and helping Betty hide.

Ted waited till they were settled, then switched on the engine, put the car into gear and drove away. He took a circuitous route along the back laneways between rows of houses, then stuck to the narrow country lanes once they'd left Rivenshaw.

'Betty can sit up between you now,' he said, once they were well out of the town.

She did that, sliding one hand into her father's and the other into Ros's.

As they drove along, Victor prayed as he had never prayed before that this would work, that as a married couple they would be able to convince a judge to leave Betty with him.

First things first. He had to get married. And that made him glance sideways at Ros who was looking thoughtful.

'All right?' he asked. 'No second thoughts?'

She gave him a sudden blinding smile. 'I'm very happy indeed about what we're doing.' She bent forward to say in a low voice, 'Betty, we haven't asked you before, but will you be our bridesmaid? We won't have time to get proper dresses, but we can buy some flowers, I'm sure, and carry those. That'll make us all feel very special when your Daddy and I marry, won't it?'

'Yes, please. I'd like to be your bridesmaid. Then I can press one of the flowers to remember it all by, can't I?'

'Good idea. I'll press one of mine, too, if you'll show me how.'

'I love pressing flowers. I have an album of them in the village house. Daddy says we'll get our things back one day so I'll show it to you.'

Victor felt his daughter relax slightly as she sat between them. He loved to watch the loving, yet practical way Ros dealt with her.

There was no way he was letting that child endure a strict and soulless upbringing like the one that had been inflicted on his poor wife.

In the afternoon, even though it was another public holiday, Mayne and Judith went to St Jude's hospital with his father to see the doctor in charge about Mrs Esher.

The doctor was quite young for such a responsible position. He walked with a pronounced limp and gestured to his foot. 'Legacy of Mr Hitler. I hear you too fought against him, Mr Esher. The injury got me back here, at least. The former doctor in charge had died of old age, so they decided I could be released to do the job. Don't worry. Before the

war, I had finished my training as a psychiatrist, so I do
have a fair amount of knowledge in this area.'

Mayne looked at his father, expecting a response, but
Reginald was sitting stiffly, mouth firmly closed, looking so
harrowed, Mayne answered for him. 'Thank you for reas-
suring us about your skills, doctor.'

'You're welcome. Now . . . I don't have any good news,
I'm afraid. One can never be quite certain with such, um,
illnesses. I'm fairly certain, however, that your wife is suffering
from senile dementia, Mr Esher. There is sometimes a rather
aggressive stage and I think that's what's happening with
her at the moment.'

He paused to let that sink in, then added, 'She won't get
any better, however carefully we look after her, I'm afraid.'

Reginald Esher gave one quick nod as if to show he understood, then stared down at his clasped hands, again without
speaking.

'The thing we have to decide today is whether you want
to keep her at home or put her into the care of someone
used to dealing with such cases.'

Once again, Mayne waited for his father to speak and
when he didn't, said it for him. 'Lock her away, do you
mean?'

'I'm afraid so. If you take her home, someone strong will
have to watch her every minute of the day and night.'

'I hadn't realised this sort of thing could happen, that my
mother could go downhill so quickly. Though she hasn't
seemed herself since I got back.'

Reginald cleared his throat, looking embarrassed. 'She's
been acting strangely for a while. I thought she was angry
about the war and losing the big house, but I can see now
that she was quite irrational at times. And the woman I
married wasn't . . . well, Dorothy was never spiteful, whatever other faults she had. She's changed greatly.'

The doctor nodded, waited, then asked again, 'And her future care?'

'There is no one but me and I couldn't look after her.' Reginald sighed. 'She's a strong woman. I needed help to subdue her and bring her here. Who knows what harm she might do to herself or to others, if she escaped?'

There was silence, then he added, 'I don't have a lot of money. How much will it cost to have her cared for?'

'Don't worry about that, Dad. I'll make sure there's enough money to place her somewhere comfortable.' Mayne was glad when Judith gave him a slight nod, as if in approval. 'Not in a luxurious place, but somewhere comfortable at least. Perhaps you could recommend a suitable nursing home, doctor?'

'I'll give you a list and you can contact them. I'd advise you to snap up a vacancy if you find a place you like the looks of. However, I'd recommend keeping her here for a week or two first. We'll need to settle her down and work out what drug dosage she'll need in order to keep her calm.'

He hesitated again, then added, 'I'd not advise you to visit her till we've got her settled. She was very difficult this morning. And . . . I'm afraid I also have to warn you that most patients with her problem die within a year or two. Once they refuse to eat, which they do as they grow more . . . detached from the world, there's little we can do. I see no point in force-feeding them.'

Mayne was sure it would be his responsibility to make arrangements for his mother's care, given his father's impractical nature. And they'd also have to arrange for someone to look after his father's domestic needs.

When Judith took his hand and gave it a little squeeze, he returned the gesture. Just to have her with him today was a huge comfort. 'Thank you, Doctor. When should we come back to see her?'

'Perhaps you could telephone at the beginning of next week?'

'Very well.'

As Mayne drove home, he decided to give his father something else to think about. 'Judith and I intend to get a special licence and marry quite quickly, Dad. We're going into Manchester this week or next to get the licence.'

'Good idea. And see that you treat her better than I treated your mother. I was lying awake for much of the night thinking about it and I can see that I've been very selfish.'

A short time later, he muttered, 'You don't expect people to change so drastically let alone so suddenly, do you? Well, it seems sudden to me.' His voice tailed away.

Mayne could see his father in the rear view mirror, an elderly man with untidy grey hair, rather thin on top, badly in need of a haircut. He was hunched up, looking utterly miserable. In fact, Reginald Esher appeared years older than he had even a couple of days ago.

But what comfort could you offer?

'We'll find a part-time housekeeper to look after the house for you, Mr Esher,' Judith said.

'Yes, I can see that I'll need one. I don't know anything about housekeeping. But won't that be rather expensive?'

'We'll help you work something out.' Her voice was gentle. 'Perhaps you should let Mayne deal with your finances completely from now on?'

'Yes. I'm not good with money. If you just tell me how much there is to spend on books every month, Mayne, I'll leave the rest to you. And I'll give you the whole advance for the books I'm getting published to put into the family pot, eh?'

'Good idea, Father. But how about you keep it for buying books? The family pot will be all right if I'm handling your money and you keep to the guidelines I give you.'

'Yes. I'll do that. Thank you.'

Mayne took his left hand off the steering wheel and gave Judith's hand another quick squeeze to say thank you for guiding them to this solution, then concentrated on his driving.

It seemed to take a very long time to drive back to Esherwood, and once there, Judith insisted on going into the Dower House with Mayne's father to sort out his food for the day.

'I'll walk back,' she said.

'All right. Thanks for doing this.' Mayne drove slowly up the drive, trying to avoid the potholes. As he got out of the car it started to rain. He knew Judith could borrow an umbrella from the Dower House, but the rain wasn't heavy and it might stop before she returned, so he didn't go back for her.

He couldn't get the sight of his mother in that dreadful state out of his mind, and prayed neither he nor Judith would decline in health and understanding when they grew older. It was a truly dreadful state to see anyone in and painful to know you were helpless to do anything about it.

Manchester seemed like another world after Rivenshaw. Victor grimaced. 'I'd forgotten how grey and busy a city centre can be on a dull day.'

The streets were crowded, full of people shopping after their two days of holiday celebrations. It was overcast and there had been a couple of showers already, but many faces were bright with happiness.

He overheard one woman telling another, 'I can't wait for my Henry to come home.' Which summed it up, somehow.

They had to queue to purchase their special licences, but none of them minded that. Victor sat patiently between Ros and his daughter. For the moment, it was enough simply to be together.

When they received their precious piece of paper, Betty asked, 'When will you be getting married, Daddy?'

'We have to wait 24 hours, though the man next to me whispered that no one was checking things like that at the moment, so we could get married first thing tomorrow morning.' He looked at Ros and Betty. 'Can you stand another queue, so that we can book to be married tomorrow?'

Betty jumped up and down in excitement. 'Yes, yes, yes!'

'As long as we're married,' Ros said softly.

Oh, we'll do that properly. We don't want anyone saying our marriage isn't legal. And anyway, I want us to be together for a very long time.'

Her smile was glorious.

When they came out into the street they found a taxi and asked for a recommendation for somewhere to stay for the night. 'Two rooms,' Victor said. 'You ladies won't mind sharing one, will you?'

After they'd found a decent boarding house, Victor chatted to the landlady, then came running up the stairs. 'Mrs Horrocks says there's a second-hand clothes shop not far away, which sells better quality garments. How about we go and look round it, see if we can find you two ladies something pretty to wear?'

That distracted Betty, who had started to look anxious again. It distracted Ros, too, when they got to the shop.

'This is far too expensive for me,' she whispered.

'But not for me, my love. Betty, let's take Ros inside and force her to try on clothes.'

'But—' Ros wasn't allowed to finish her sentence but was dragged inside by two laughing people.

She had never seen so many pretty clothes, or considered buying such expensive garments. But Victor enlisted the shop's owner to help them and, between them, they found

Ros a pretty dress in hyacinth blue, with a darker blue coat and a simple hat that suited her.

He refused to listen to her protests and bought them, then turned to choosing an outfit for Betty. Again, the owner was helpful and Betty was provided with a summer dress and cardigan, which she confided in a whisper were the prettiest things she'd ever owned.

'Grandmother always buys old-fashioned things.'

Her expression was so blissful, Ros had to hug her. 'You'll be the prettiest bridesmaid ever. Now, let's go and explore the centre of Manchester. I've never had the chance to do that before.'

In the evening Victor took them out for a meal, to save fuss about food coupons, since they hadn't been able to bring their ration books with them. Well, it would have given them away to even try, wouldn't it?

They were in bed by nine o'clock.

Ros kept the bedside lamp on and watched Betty quickly fall asleep. Tomorrow she'd be Betty's stepmother and just let anyone try to take her daughter away from her. She loved the child almost as much as she loved the father.

Whatever they had to face, they'd do it together; if necessary, they'd flee overseas together.

Who would have thought one of the saddest days of her life, when she'd discovered that her mother was dead, would lead to such happiness?

23

On the Friday morning following the two public holidays, it seemed strange not to have Victor, Ros and Betty at Esherwood.

Ben kept staring out of the window and sighing. More than once he said, 'I wonder where Betty is now?'

Gillian seemed equally lost. 'They won't take her away from us, will they, Mayne?'

'We hope not,' was all he could offer in comfort.

When the phone rang, he headed for the door. 'I'll answer it.'

He came running back almost immediately. 'It's for you, Daniel, a transatlantic call.'

Daniel stood up at once, calling over his shoulder, 'It'll be Ada.'

Slow footsteps announced the return of Daniel.

'Bad news?' Mayne asked at the sight of his scowl.

He shrugged. 'Sort of. Ada is furious with me because I haven't checked my share of the goods and chattels, and written to accept how they've been divided up. It's holding up the divorce apparently, and she wants a written quittance from me within the week, sent airmail. I don't think I can get it to her so quickly, but I'd better try.'

'Can't you just send her a piece of paper?' Judith asked. 'After all, you said you trusted her.'

'She's got it into her head that everything must be done properly and is insisting that I go back to check the things she left for me and that I get a reputable pair of witnesses to sign that I've done it.'

He made an angry sound in his throat. 'The last thing I want to do is travel anywhere. The trains are going to be crowded and slow after the holiday. And I was going to do some sketching of ideas today. Insomnia is very good for one's creativity and I had a few ideas during the night about how to convert this house.'

He seemed about to say something else, then stopped.

Mayne waited.

'Oh hell, I'd better go and do it. I dare say my cousin will let me sleep on her sofa. Is there somewhere I can store my stuff at Esherwood if I have it sent here? Perhaps I could put it at the back of the cellar till I decide where I want to live.'

He snapped his fingers as an idea came to him. 'If we find the components for building another Nissen hut or two in the one that's tightly packed with stuff, maybe I could buy one off you, Mayne, and make myself a home plus office on site? I'm not good company at the moment and I'm not sleeping well.'

After a pause, he added, 'I need more time to settle down in civvy street, I think. I am getting better, but not as quickly as I'd hoped.'

'Of course you can store your things in the cellar,' Mayne said. 'And if we can put a Nissen hut together for your home and office, it'll be very convenient for us all. I'm sure you'll find somewhere to erect it.'

'Thanks. I'll leave today and get it done, then arrange for my things to be brought here. Do you think we'd get permission to erect another Nissen hut, Mayne?'

'We'll persuade the town council that it's needed for an

office if we're to provide housing. And that is a high government priority, after all.'

'So they say. Words are easy. It's deeds that count.'

'I'm hoping us being builders will be the Open Sesame for all sorts of things we need. We can't convert Esherwood to flats, if we have to hang around waiting for permission to do each stage.'

Daniel looked at him thoughtfully. 'That's where Woollard would come in useful, I should think. We are going to let him in on the company, aren't we?'

His words seemed to hang in the air for a moment or two, then Mayne nodded. 'Yes.'

'Good. Sorry to leave you at such an interesting time. When Victor comes back, tell him I wish him well when he confronts the dragon.'

He turned at the door to say with one of his rather sad half-smiles, 'You two are not to get married till I come back. I want to be there. And Betty will insist on us holding another party, I'm sure.'

When Daniel had gone upstairs to pack, Mayne turned to Judith. 'It might be good for us to get away from here for the rest of the day. It looks as if the rain is blowing over, even though it won't be a sunny day. Then if the police do come for Betty, they'll not find anyone to question.'

'We can't leave the place untended,' Judith protested.

'How about I nip down and ask Helen and Miss Peters to come up here for a few hours.' He grinned. 'I'd bet on Miss Peters any time for routing arrogant visitors.'

'We should get Al and a friend to come back as well, just in case this Mrs Galton tries to use force again. Al can doze somewhere and they can wake him if he's needed.'

'Why not? I like the idea of giving the dragon a run for her money. It'll do her good not to find anyone here to bully.'

He looked at the three children. 'Go and get ready for a long tramp over the moors.'

All three had been listening and nodded, though Kitty sighed.

'We'll do anything to help Betty,' Ben said gruffly, in a voice that occasionally jerked into a deeper register or broke in the middle of a word. 'She's like a little sister to us now.'

The two girls nodded vigorous agreement.

It was good to see how well the young people got on, Mayne thought as he got ready. That made for another type of peace. He very much wanted a peaceful home life from now on.

His main regret, and it was a big one, remained the coming loss of Esherwood. He felt like weeping about that at times, but of course grown men didn't cry. There was simply nothing he could do about saving Esherwood as a home, which would need a large amount of money now for restoration and after that for maintenance. Even if he could sell the antiques well enough to restore it, he couldn't support its ongoing expenses. The most he could do was preserve the fabric of the lovely old house by turning it into flats.

That would probably take every penny he possessed, so he could only hope the flats would sell quickly.

When she found out the reason why, Miss Peters was delighted to oblige Mayne by keeping watch at the big house. Helen was happy to come too and keep her company. Since there was a lot of hand sewing needed with such delicate fabrics, she could do her pinning and shaping of the wedding clothes as well there as at her own house.

She woke Jan, who'd come home from his night of keeping watch at Esherwood and gone straight to bed. 'Could you continue your sleep in the library at the big house, love? I'll feel safer with you nearby.'

'Of course I can.'

He was the most adaptable person she'd ever met about sleeping and living arrangements: a legacy of his years of wandering round war-torn Europe. The miracle was that he'd survived, made his way to England and they'd found one another.

Mayne and his family went off for their walk, calling in at Al's house to ask his help keeping watch. Like Jan, he was sleeping, but his mother got him up as soon as she heard why he was needed and sent him off to find a strong friend to help him as well.

They all had a bad feeling about coming trouble.

That done Mayne decided to try to set his worries aside and enjoy the day. He'd done his best for Victor by arranging to take his family away. He was sure his friends would guard Esherwood and confound Mrs Galton and whomever she brought with her.

He smiled at the thought of anyone trying to browbeat Miss Peters, then turned to listen to what Gillian was saying.

But it wasn't easy to relax. He kept wondering what was happening back at Esherwood.

That same morning Ted Willis parked outside the station, as there was a train due and he might be lucky enough to pick up a taxi fare. Of course there was also the chance that he might be wasting his time, because trains still got delayed without warning.

He watched a big car arrive in town, coming along the road that led from the south. It parked just round the corner from the town square, out of sight of most people, but Ted could see it quite clearly. Why hadn't its driver parked it in the square, as most newcomers did? And how did a stranger know where to go, anyway? Ted was sure it was a stranger, as he would have remembered a car like that if he'd ever seen it in Rivenshaw before.

An old lady was sitting bolt upright in the back of the large vehicle, with a policeman he didn't recognise sitting beside her. He screwed up his eyes and could see from the uniform that the fellow was a police sergeant. He didn't know who the old lady was, but from what his friend Sergeant Deemer had told him, he could guess. Oh, yes.

Who was the strange policeman, though, and what was he doing here, when they already had their own Rivenshaw police sergeant?

He saw Gilliot's car nose out of the side street outside his rooms and stop next to the other vehicle. There were a couple of young men in the back: fellows Ted knew by sight, fellows who were always getting into fights.

Gilliot got out and began to talk to the strangers. Oh, how Ted wished he could hear what they were saying!

On that thought he turned and saw a couple of young lads he knew standing on the corner, looking as if they were dying to get into mischief. He beckoned them across to his taxi, rubbing his forefinger and thumb together to indicate a chance of earning some money. They raced across to join him at once.

'Come round the other side where no one can see you,' he said. 'Lads, I want to find out what those people near the big cars are talking about and where they're going. I'll give you sixpence each if you can find out anything useful. If they mention any names, try hard to remember them. How about it? Can you do that without them realising you're eavesdropping.'

'Yes, Mr Willis.'

Young Jimmy tossed his ball to his friend and they began running round, throwing it to one another, moving gradually across the square to the two cars. Jimmy let the ball drop and roll near the group. He chased after it, pretending to knock it into the gutter by accident.

That lad should become an actor, Ted thought, in admiration of how innocent their playing looked.

It took Jimmy a moment or two to retrieve the ball and start throwing it to his friend. The other lad then dropped it further up the slope from the cars and let it roll down towards them before he managed to pick it up.

Ted grinned. You'd swear that ball had rolled near the group twice by accident.

The other lad began tossing the ball from one hand to the other, as if taunting his friend. He didn't move away till the driver of one of the cars yelled at him.

When the people started getting back into the cars, Jimmy and his friend came haring across the square again. 'They're going to Esherwood, Mr Willis. Sounded like they wanted to find a little girl. I couldn't hear her name. The old lady is called Mrs Gatton or something like it. That's all we could hear.'

'Well done!' Ted tossed two sixpences at them and drove across to the police station on the other side of the square, running inside to find his friend.

'Sergeant Deemer's not here,' young Farrow told him.

'What? Where is he, then?'

'Had to go and deliver a summons for Mr Gilliot.'

'Oh, did he? Where to?'

Farrow laughed. 'Old Barney, of course. They're always after him for something, but he makes himself scarce. I don't know why Mr Gilliot bothers.'

But he was talking to himself. Ted was already running back to his car. He knew where Barney lived and he was worried about what those posh people were up to.

His mother had always said you got just as many villains wearing fur coats and top hats as wearing rags, and she'd been a wise old bird.

He had to find Deemer quickly.

Jan went to take a nap in the library, while Helen and Miss Peters opted for the big sitting room at the front of the house, where they settled down to chat and sew. From there they could keep watch on the drive and have warning of anyone coming.

About an hour later Miss Peters said suddenly, 'I can hear something.'

'So can I.' Helen put her needle into the material to keep it safe and laid the dress on a chair in the corner.

Not one but two large black cars appeared at the far end of the drive, bumping majestically in and out of the potholes as they slowly approached the house.

'Who are all these people, do you think?' Miss Peters asked. 'I don't like the looks of it. In times of austerity, they've brought two big cars to deal with one small girl. And one car at least must have come from the south. Where did they get their petrol to drive so far?'

'I think I've seen the first car in the distance in town, but I don't know who it belongs to.' Helen studied it carefully.

'They're trying to intimidate Victor with a display of strength, I should think,' Miss Peters said scornfully. 'If so, they don't know him very well. And they won't intimidate me.'

'I think I'd better go and fetch Jan in case they try to push their way inside. Al and his friend said they'd wait out of sight at the back in case they were needed. He's probably snoozing somewhere while he waits.'

Miss Peters clamped her fingers on Helen's arm to stop her leaving. 'Just a minute! That policeman in the leading car isn't Sergeant Deemer. They must have brought this man in from somewhere else. And there are two large young men in the back of the second car. Why would they need all those people?'

'Because they're prepared to use force.'

'I don't like this. Let me answer the front door. They'll be more likely to treat a judge's sister with respect and courtesy.'

Then she shook her head. 'No, we can't rely on that. I'm

only one old woman, even at my fiercest. We won't take any risks.' She broke off and pulled a business card out of her handbag, scribbling a phone number on it and passing it to Helen. 'Wake Jan and then telephone Sergeant Deemer. Ask his help. After that, telephone my brother at this number and tell him I need him to come here urgently now. Right this minute. I'll delay these people for as long as I can, and try to keep them out of the house.'

'Shouldn't we wait and see whether they go away when they find neither Victor nor Mayne at home?'

'No. That might give them the opportunity to stop us seeking help. My brother was coming across to join me later today anyway. He's not far away. He knows I wouldn't ask for urgent help without a good reason. He'll come immediately.'

Helen took the card and ran into the library to wake Jan but he was awake already.

'I heard a car. Who is it?'

'There are two cars and we don't know who's in them yet but there are a lot of people. Miss Peters feels uneasy. I have to telephone Sergeant Deemer and then her brother. Could you stay near her?'

'I'll do that, though I'll keep to the background, ready to help if I'm needed.'

But she was already on her way to the telephone, so he went to keep watch.

Miss Peters let the knocker sound twice before she went to open the front door, calling out and pretending to struggle with the bolts. Actually she was slipping them into place even as she shouted, 'Just a minute! This door is very stiff.'

Someone tried the door handle, which outraged her.

'Hurry up! We're here with a court order,' a voice she recognised called from outside.

Gilliot. What was the lawyer she detested doing mixed up in this?

Her instincts hadn't let her down. They meant to cause trouble. Nothing good had ever come of Gilliot being involved with the people from Esherwood, because he hated Mayne and anyone connected with him. He hated Miss Peters too, come to that.

She smiled grimly and called, 'Hang on a minute. I think the bolt's moving.' Only after counting to twenty, bumping her hip against the door and rattling the bolt did she slide the latter right back and open the door. She didn't move away from the opening to let the woman standing there inside, though.

'How may I help you?'

'I'm Betty's grandmother, here to see her and her father.' The plump elderly lady seemed about to walk in, as if by right, but Miss Peters didn't move out of the way.

Mrs Galton let out an angry puff of air and looked to another gentleman with a briefcase as if for help.

Miss Peters didn't like the way the two muscular young men from the car had placed themselves on either side of the group. These people were definitely ready to use force.

The lawyer brandished a piece of paper right in front of her face. 'We're here on official business to speak to Mr Travers. Kindly let us in.'

Miss Peters batted the paper away with some force and he had to scrabble with both hands to keep it from blowing away.

'Oh?' she said. 'And why does it take so many of you to speak to him?'

He waved the paper at her again, this time not so close to her face. 'This is an official warrant to take his daughter into her grandmother's care, so that the child can be properly looked after.'

Anger rose in Miss Peters' narrow breast, making her heart

flutter, but she held the anger back. 'Let me see the warrant.'

'This is no business of yours. Kindly step back and let us inside, then fetch Mr Travers.'

Two other young men came round from the side of the house, just as muscular as the ones flanking the group of visitors.

'Trouble, Miss Peters?'

'I'm afraid so, Al. These people seem to want to push their way in. This is Mayne Esher's house and they claim they're here to see Victor, who is only a guest. However, Victor isn't here, so why should I let them in?'

Gilliot moved forward and said in his harsh voice, 'Get out of our way, woman. We don't believe you. You're trying to keep the child hidden.'

Al stepped forward with a growl of anger at his rudeness.

When she saw that his presence had distracted the group, Miss Peters stepped quickly back inside and slammed the door in their faces.

Someone yelled and a man laughed. Al, it sounded like.

As she slid the bolt back into place, Miss Peters called, 'Let me reiterate: neither Mr Travers nor his daughter are here, and the owner of this house is away as well, so I don't intend to let you in. Kindly come back another time.'

Feeling a bit dizzy, she sagged against the heavy door, one hand to her pounding heart. 'I'm getting too old to have adventures,' she muttered, ignoring the shouting from outside.

Helen came running from the back of the house to join her. 'I was listening to what they said. The cheek of it! Trying to push their way into Mayne's house.'

Miss Peters clutched her companion's arm, still feeling lightheaded.

'Are you all right? You look pale?'

'Did you lock the back door, Helen? If not, go and do it now.'

'Jan has trained me to be careful. Yes, I locked the back door.'

'Did you get through to my brother?'

'I'm afraid not. But I—'

'Sorry, but I don't feel—' Miss Peters crumpled suddenly to the floor.

Horrified, Helen bent to check the old lady's pulse. It was beating tumultuously.

Jan ran across to join them, bending down to pick Miss Peters up. 'She weighs nothing.' He carried her into the front sitting room and laid her down gently on a sofa. 'I think we need to send for the doctor.'

'Go and phone him. His number is next to the phone in Mayne's office.'

'What happened to make her faint?'

'I don't know exactly. I was just coming back when she darted back inside the house and locked the front door on them. She turned to me and started to speak, then fainted. Look how white her face is. She's wonderful for her age, but I want the doctor to see her. I'll stay with her and you be ready to let him in. I'm sure he'll come quickly. Everyone thinks a great deal of Miss Peters.'

The thumping on the front door made her furious. She went to the sitting room window and hammered on it to attract the unwelcome visitors' attention.

Gilliot came storming over to peer at her through the window. 'Open that door immediately.'

'I'll do no such thing. The people you want are not here and your bullying has caused Miss Peters to faint. We're getting the doctor to see her.' She saw the cynical look on his face and yelled, 'This isn't a pretence.'

He smiled and shrugged. 'That's no business of mine. It serves her right. She shouldn't have interfered in things that are none of her business, then she wouldn't have got upset.'

Anna Jacobs

He came right up to the window, framed his face with his hands, trying to see through it.

Miss Peters was lying on the sofa, looking more dead than alive.

Helen wiped away the tears and yelled at him, 'If she dies, I'll make sure you regret it! You'll lose a lot of business, because she is much loved in this town. Now go away and leave us in peace.'

'I'm here with my client to search for Mr Travers and we're not leaving until we've done that. Don't you understand what a court order is?'

'I don't care about your court order. Victor has left Rivenshaw. He's not a fool. Do you think he'd wait here for you to take his daughter away from him?'

'I don't believe you. He couldn't have known we were coming; no one in Rivenshaw did. We brought in our help from outside the town. We are not leaving until the sergeant accompanying us has searched the house. And what's more, if you don't open that door, we have the right to force an entry. Where is the owner? Why isn't Esher answering his own door? Or is he too afraid?'

'Mayne afraid of you?' she asked scornfully. 'He most certainly isn't. I already told you: he isn't here. He and his family have gone out for the day.'

She heard a faint sighing sound and went back to kneel beside the sofa, chafing Miss Peters' thin old hands as the old lady began to recover consciousness. She prayed the doctor would come quickly and would be able to help her old friend, who was more like an aunt than a mere neighbour.

She couldn't imagine the town of Rivenshaw without Miss Peters, who had helped so many people during her long lifetime.

24

Judith looked at Mayne, then exchanged exasperated glances with her elder daughter. He had fallen behind the others, was frowning, not looking where he was going. He tripped even as she watched.

She went to stand in front of him, hands on hips, putting out one hand to stop him bumping into her. 'Mayne Esher, stand still and talk to me.'

He blinked and stared at her. 'What? Oh, sorry. I was lost in thought.'

'Thinking about what's going on at Esherwood?'

'I'm afraid so.'

'You're not the sort to avoid a confrontation, that's why. And it's upsetting you. Listen, everyone! Do any of you really feel like a walk? No, I thought not. We're all too worried about Betty. Let's go back and face them.'

'Do you mind?' Mayne asked.

'I keep wondering if Betty's come back,' Ben admitted.

'And if her grandmother tries to bully us, she'll not find us jumping to obey orders,' Kitty added. 'As for being afraid of her. Poof!' She waved one hand dismissively then smiled mischievously. 'Come on, Father-to-be. Let's go back.'

He smiled at them warmly. 'I like my new title very much, Kitty. All right, folk. Let's go back and face whoever comes. It's my house, after all. I've been worrying that they might force their way in and damage things in a search for Victor. Just think of all our piles being scattered and mixed up, after the hard work of sorting things out.'

Judith shuddered.

'We'd better hurry!' Ben led the way, not waiting for permission.

Mayne took Judith's hand and raised it to his lips. 'Thank you for being so understanding. Sometimes you seem to know me better than I know myself.'

'I love you, that's why.'

'I love you, too.'

They set off at a cracking pace, taking short cuts through side streets and back alleys. But Mayne stopped them from approaching the big house by the rear drive.

'We're going in the front way. I'm not skulking around on my own property.'

As they passed the Dower House, his father came rushing out. 'Do you know who the people in the big car are?' he demanded. 'They stopped here and spoke to me very rudely, demanding to be told whether this was Esherwood.' With awful scorn he added, 'Mistaking the Dower House for the big house! Can't they see it's not large enough to be a manor house?'

'What did you say to them?'

'I stayed in my office and shouted down to them to mind their manners, and I refused point-blank to let them inside. Good thing I'd locked the front door. They actually tried to get it open.'

Mayne stared in shock. 'They tried to break into your house?'

'Yes. And if Gilliot hadn't driven up just then and set them straight about it being the Dower House, I think they'd have done it too. You were right about him. He's a poor sort of fellow and I'm glad you took your business to Melford instead, so—'

'I have to go. I'll explain later, Dad. Come on, everyone. We'd better get up to the big house quickly. No, wait a minute. Ben, go and fetch Mr Melford. Tell him to hurry. Tell him we have officials overstepping their powers here and trying to break into my house to find his other client, Mr Travers. Don't let him tell you no. This is extremely urgent.'

Ben nodded and set off the way they'd come, running along the side of the park.

Mayne and the others continued up the drive, not stopping till they'd reached the group gathered at his front door.

One man was shaking the door till Al dragged him away from it. The two were about to come to blows when Mayne arrived.

'What the hell do you think you're doing?' he roared as he pushed through the group to plant himself in front of his own front door.

Al stepped to one side, grinning. 'About time you arrived, Mr Esher. I've had a job to stop them breaking into your house.'

Mayne glared at them. 'Who are you and why are you here?'

A narrow-faced elderly man in a dark suit and a shirt with an old-fashioned, stand-up collar stepped forward. 'I'm Mr Fitkin, Mrs Galton's lawyer, and we have a magistrate's order giving us the right to enter your premises without permission, if necessary, to get that poor child to safety.'

'By "that poor child" I suppose you mean Betty Travers?'

'Naturally. The court has awarded temporary guardianship to her grandmother.' He gestured to the old lady in outmoded clothing. 'Pending a hearing about permanent guardianship, of course. A little girl needs a woman's guidance.'

'Well, let's get one thing straight before we even discuss this ridiculous idea of taking a child away from the father she loves. Even if you did break into my house, you'd not find Victor Travers or his daughter here. They've left.'

'Where did they go? When did they leave?'

'They didn't tell me where they were going and I didn't ask. I'm not Victor's keeper. If he chooses to move somewhere else, that's up to him.'

Gilliot moved to stand beside the older lawyer. 'You're lying, Esher, trying to protect your friend. But even an Esher can't go against the law. We demand that you comply with the order and allow us to search the premises.'

'I refuse to admit *you* to my house under any circumstances, Gilliot.' He turned back to the other man. 'My own lawyer will be here soon. You can argue with him.'

A police sergeant standing to one side, a stranger to Mayne, stepped forward. 'I'm afraid the warrant gives us the right to search these premises, sir, whether you give permission or not. It'd be easier if you let us in.'

'I'm not doing anything till my lawyer arrives. I've told you the truth: Victor and his family have left and I don't know where they've gone. And where, may I ask, is Sergeant Deemer? What are you doing undertaking police work in Rivenshaw?'

'It was felt that Sergeant Deemer was biased and an outsider could act impartially.'

'Who told you that?'

The officer didn't reply, but his eyes went to Gilliot.

'Gilliot said that, I suppose, since he's the local lawyer. What's impartial about you supporting a man who bears a grudge towards me and who's accusing me of being a liar? That sounds as if you've pre-judged the situation based on what he's told you, without consulting me.'

His voice grew suddenly louder. 'I did not, sir, serve my King and country for over five years, to be treated like this.'

The man looked upset, then, as Gilliot cleared his throat, he said, 'I'm sorry, sir, I really am. But we still need to search these premises.'

'After my lawyer arrives.'

'Do your duty this minute, Sergeant!' Fitkin said.

The sergeant shook his head. 'I think it's reasonable to wait until his lawyer gets here.'

Just then Helen tapped on the sitting room window to attract their attention and they all turned towards the right. She opened the small top pane a little and called, 'Their bullying has made Miss Peters collapse and I've sent for the doctor. But I'm afraid they'll come in and upset her again if I let him in.'

'Bullying a lady of nearly eighty,' Judith said scornfully. 'How very brave you are!'

The sergeant flushed but Mrs Galton said in the over-loud voice of someone going deaf, 'She should have done as ordered and let us in.'

Gillian moved to stand in front of her. 'I thought you'd be a nasty person, from the way you treated Betty. And you are. You don't care about anyone but yourself. I'm glad Mr Travers took Betty away, even though we'll miss her.'

Mrs Galton's face went nearly purple. 'How dare you speak to me like that, girl? Go away at once.'

'Why should I go away? This is my home. And besides, I'm only speaking to you in the way you speak to other people. If it's wrong for me to speak like that, it's wrong for you, too.'

'How dare you—' She broke off as they heard a car approaching.

Dr Carberry's battered old Austin drove up and stopped.

'Take him round the back,' Mayne whispered to Judith.

She nodded and ran towards the car, slipping into the passenger seat and speaking urgently to the doctor. As the car started moving, she gestured to Helen, who was still standing at the window, to open the back door.

'Stop them!' Mr Fitkin called.

But by that time Al and his friend had blocked the way round to the back. They heard the engine stop and there was the sound of car doors slamming.

Shortly afterwards, Judith proved she'd got inside the house by appearing at the window of the sitting room and waving triumphantly.

'This is becoming quite interesting,' Mayne whispered to Kitty, who was standing next to him.

'That old lady is like a villain in a Charlie Chaplin film,' she replied.

'If it were a film, more cars ought to start arriving and people should be running round,' Ben said.

The police sergeant approached Mayne. 'I will ask you one final time to open that front door, Mr Esher.'

'Not till my lawyer has arrived and—'

Another car turned into the drive and Ben gave a shout of laughter. 'Here comes another one.'

'Why is that boy laughing?' demanded Mrs Galton, looking affronted. 'Send the impudent creature away this minute.'

Mr Fitkin went to stand next to her and say rather irritably, 'He lives here, Amelia. We can't send him away.'

'I don't know what the world is coming to when hobbledehoy lads are rude to their betters.'

But no one was listening to her. They were waiting to see who was driving up to the house this time.

The car stopped and a thin elderly man got out, stopping for a moment to study the people gathered there. Then he went up to Mayne and offered his hand. 'Esher.'

'Judge Peters.'

'Where is my sister?'

'Inside the house. She fainted under the stress so we called the doctor, who has just gone in to see her.'

'Could you explain what's happening, then? I got an urgent message from my sister to join her here.'

'These people are threatening to break my door down to get inside. They're looking for Victor Travers and his daughter, and won't accept my word that he's left. I don't know where he's gone.'

'Oh, won't they?' He turned to study the group. 'Sergeant Leggat. Don't you work out of Manchester? What are you doing here?'

'If I may have a private word, sir?'

'No, you may not. In fact, we shall consider everything people say from now on to be part of a preliminary hearing, because I've been sent here to sort this situation out. So I'll ask you again: why are you here and not Sergeant Deemer?'

Mr Fitkin cleared his throat as if about to speak and Judge Peters turned a basilisk stare on him. 'I did not ask you, sir, so kindly wait your turn.'

Easing his collar with one finger, Sergeant Leggat said, 'Your honour, my inspector was told that the local sergeant would be prejudiced and wouldn't do his duty.' His eyes turned towards Fitkin and Mrs Galton, making it plain who had told the inspector. 'He therefore sent me to see that Mr Fitkin and his client get justice, sir.'

'Well, I'm here now and officially taking charge. I have orders from above to stop this turning into an embarrassing witch hunt. This is 1945 not 1745.'

Mrs Galton said in her loud voice, 'And who exactly are you?'

The sergeant said hastily, 'This is Judge Dennison Peters, ma'am.'

She turned to the judge. 'Then I think you should—'

His voice was chill. 'You will have your turn to speak, madam. Kindly allow me to get on with my task.'

'There's another car coming along the drive, sir.' Al pointed out, raising his voice above the shouting.

Mayne turned round. 'Ah, good. That looks like—yes, it is Sergeant Deemer.'

The judge said curtly, 'You can leave it to the local man now, Sergeant Leggat, unless he asks you for your assistance.'

A few heavy raindrops splattered loudly against the window panes and everyone looked up at the sky.

'I'm sorry to impose, but is there anywhere we can continue this under shelter, Mr Esher? An outhouse, perhaps?'

'Now that you're here, your honour, I'll be happy to offer you my entrance hall – for those who need to be involved, which doesn't include those two strong-arm fellows. But I'm not allowing access to the rest of the house. We've been sorting out the contents and I don't want them disturbed.'

'Very understandable.' Judge Peters turned to look at the two young men who had come with Mrs Galton. 'What are they doing here, Fitkin?'

'We brought them along in case of trouble, sir.'

The judge stared at him in surprise. 'What on earth do you think Esher's going to do, attack you?'

'We . . . were told he and Mr Travers might be . . . angry.'

'So would I be if you tried to force your way into my house. Anyway, those two fellows can wait in the car. And are the other young men yours, Esher?'

'Yes, sir. But they can go round to the kitchen. No need for them to be involved now.'

'Happy to make myself scarce, Mr Esher.' Al went off with his two friends, whistling loudly.

Mayne gestured to Helen to open the front door for them.

Mrs Galton would have pushed her way in first, but Ben got in her way and Mayne went first. The rule might be ladies go first, but he wasn't letting that woman queen it in his house.

Judge Peters followed him. 'Where is my sister?'

Helen was standing in the doorway of the sitting room. 'Miss Peters is in here, and she's recovered enough to scold us for sending for the doctor. He's with her now, so could you please wait a few moments to see her?'

'Yes, of course. Give her my love. I'd better deal with this lot first anyway.'

But Helen lingered in the doorway to say, 'You're not going to take that child away from her father, are you? She adores him.'

'I'll need to see young Betty first. Do you know where her father took her?'

'To Manchester first, I think, but I have no idea what their plans were after that. I'd guess they'll come back once they've completed their business there. Victor doesn't seem like the sort to run away. Ros was with them, too.'

She hesitated, than added, 'He's going to marry her and she's marvellous with Betty. She's just been demobbed from the Wrens and— Uh-oh, here comes trouble.'

Mr Fitkin, having escorted his client to a chair, came across to the judge. 'This is most irregular.'

'You're Mrs Galton's lawyer, I gather?'

'Yes, I am. As well as a long-time family friend. Fitkin is the name. My poor client has been distraught with worry about her granddaughter.'

Judge Peters looked across the room. Far from looking distraught, the elderly lady in question was scowling at everyone and when Ben went to stand near her and scowl back, she shouted at him to keep his distance and brandished her walking cane.

He took one step backwards to stay out of her reach and would have remained there, but his mother called him away.

His voice floated clearly across the hall. 'Well, I didn't like the way she was looking at you, Mum. She's a very rude woman.'

The judge hid a smile as he looked back at Fitkin. This was rapidly turning into a farce. 'I am deeply concerned that this whole affair has been managed in an unprofessional, not to say hole-in-the-corner way. I'm not impressed by your methods, Fitkin. You do no credit to our profession. What concerns me is the child's welfare and happiness.'

'That is what concerns my client, why she wishes to look after her granddaughter.'

'Whether that would be best for the girl has yet to be proved. I shall make no decision until Mr Travers returns, which I gather he's expected to do in a day or two. And as I shall be staying with my sister just down the road, I shall be available to continue this informal hearing at that point.'

'But surely—'

'I do not advise you to press for a formal hearing now, Fitkin. The local authorities are not happy to see a good man hounded, especially one who is going to invest money in building new houses and flats. You are aware that this is a high government priority, I presume?'

'Yes, but—'

The judge lowered his voice. 'Certain authorities in London do not wish this to become a public scandal, because Esher and Travers have an impeccable war record, and this country owes a lot more to them than can be revealed.'

Fitkin said nothing, but his expression went sour at the words 'war record'.

Judge Peters looked round. 'Could I please have everyone's attention? I shall sit over there and call you across in turn to tell me about your part in this affair. Mr Esher? Could I start with you, since this is your house and you've kindly allowed us to use it? Sergeant Deemer, can you please make sure we're not interrupted.'

'Yes, your worship.'

'Afterwards I shall need to speak to you as well, Sergeant.'

The judge questioned Mayne, Judith and Helen one by one. Then he took a short break to check on his sister.

She had recovered enough to be sitting in a chair, enjoying a cup of tea and a scone. 'How's it going, Den?'

'Oh, as you'd expect. That old harridan is insisting on getting custody of the child, but I'd pity any child given into her charge. However, we must get to the bottom of the whys and wherefores of her claim. She and her lawyer seem unduly confident about the outcome. Have you seen the child with her father, Ronnie?'

'Yes. Several times.'

'How do they get on? Is she afraid of him, nervous in his presence?'

His sister chuckled. 'Betty adores Victor. It would be a terrible thing to take her away from her father. She's a delightful child but too quiet, so he and Ros are teaching her to enjoy life again. Apparently, as her mother grew weaker, the grandmother took charge and imposed what sounds to have been a very strict and joyless way of life upon that poor girl.'

'I can't make a decision until I've seen Betty and her father for myself.'

'Of course not. But you'll find I'm right.'

'I could never doubt your assessment of a situation. You should have been a lawyer.'

'Women weren't encouraged even to go to university when we were young. But I've always managed to keep myself busy and do a bit of good in the world.' She sighed, then shook her head as if to banish unhappy thoughts. 'I may be slowing down a little, Den, but I'm not done yet.'

324

Anna Jacobs

'Of course not.'

He kissed his sister's cheek and went back to continue his questioning, leaving the grandmother until last, to her barely suppressed fury.

Mrs Galton came across the hall when the judge called her, with Mr Fitkin by her side. They both looked so smug, he became mentally alert.

'Before you question my client, sir, we would like to submit a piece of evidence that shows incontrovertibly that she is the proper person to look after the child.'

'The child has a name,' Judge Peters told him irritably.

'Betty, then.' It was said wearily as if the name of the child didn't matter.

Fitkin opened his briefcase and handed over a piece of paper. 'This sets out the last wishes of the child's mother. If you'll read it, you'll see that there's only one possible verdict in this case.'

'Do you always tell the judge what to do?'

Fitkin opened his mouth, then shut it tightly again.

Peters took the piece of paper, looked at what it said and studied the shaky signature at the bottom. His heart sank. It was certainly a compelling piece of evidence. 'I see.'

'Well?' Mrs Galton asked.

'I still wish to meet the child and her father before I come to any decision.'

'But you cannot go against the mother's dying wishes.'

'Do not try to tell me my job, Mrs Galton.' He stood up. 'Now, perhaps you'd find somewhere to stay in Rivenshaw and we'll wait for Mr Travers to return.'

'I must make it plain that if you don't do the right thing, I shall take this matter to the highest court in the land,' she declaimed in her booming voice.

Everyone turned to stare at her.

'I have not announced any decision, so you can't take it anywhere yet. Mr Fitkin, kindly keep your client in order. Now, we must leave Mr Esher to the peace of his own roof and assuming that Mr Travers returns to Rivenshaw, I shall see you all again tomorrow. Or the day after.'

He stood up and moved towards the door, gesturing towards it. 'If you please, Mrs Galton.'

She didn't move. 'Are you not going to search the house?'

'Why would I do that?'

'To look for Betty's father. He's hiding somewhere here, I know he is.'

'I have Mr Esher's word that his friend is not on the premises. As an officer and a gentleman, Mr Esher is, I feel, honest and trustworthy.'

It took a tug from Mr Fitkin, and a hurried, whispered consultation, to make her move on.

Peters followed them to the door and watched her drive away, followed by Gilliot, then went back inside, shaking his head.

He doubted whether the woman would accept his decision, unless it was the one she wanted. He still wasn't sure about that.

He also had to guard against this situation blowing up into a full-scale scandal, which would risk revealing what Travers and Esher had been doing for the latter part of the war, something the authorities would not be at all happy about.

Mayne went across the hall to join the judge. 'Everyone's gone into the sitting room. Will you join us for a cup of tea?'

'I'd be pleased to.'

'Could I ask what's wrong?'

The judge hesitated, then said quietly, 'They have a piece

of paper purporting to be signed by the mother, asking the grandmother to look after Betty. They insist the child is afraid of her father.'

'That's an absolute lie. Betty loves her father and runs to hug him when they've been apart even for an hour.'

'Whether she does or does not love him isn't as important as the mother's wishes, given the fact that the father had spent very little time at home with his child during the war. Mrs Galton is, apparently, prepared to take this to the highest court if I don't rule in their favour.'

'Oh, hell.'

'And that could result in a long and messy court case, during which it's more than likely the child will be sent to stay with her grandmother anyway. They prefer to leave a girl in a woman's care.'

'Damn that old harridan.'

'What's more, if it became a scandal, what you and Travers were doing during the war might also be revealed. Certain people don't want it even hinting at.'

Mayne suddenly realised why a famous judge had been brought into what was, after all, a trivial matter. 'So the authorities will do whatever it takes to quieten the Galton woman, even if that means giving Betty into their care, because they don't want word to get out about the place where we worked.'

'I'm afraid so. I gather the government is planning to keep it for future use . . . just in case.'

25

The next morning passed very slowly. There was no sign of Victor, Ros and Betty, nor did they telephone Mayne to say they were all right, let alone tell him where they were and when they were coming back.

After their midday meal, Ben and his sisters went to sit on the stone steps outside the front door, making no attempt to play or read.

'You won't make her come back more quickly by sitting here,' Judith told them two hours later.

'Waiting here feels better.' Ben had that stubborn look on his face.

'Well, it's a fine day, so you'll come to no harm.' She went to join Mayne in the office, where he didn't seem to be getting much work done. 'My three are upset.'

'I'm rather worried myself. That piece of paper might be genuine.'

'A mother would have never signed away care of her child to that woman.'

'Darling, Victor's wife was dying. She may not even have realised what she was signing. But the courts will still take her alleged wishes into account.' He took her hand and pulled her to sit on his lap. 'Apart from anything else, this is preventing us from going into Manchester and getting a special licence. I wanted to marry you early next week.'

Their kiss was sweet but cut short by Ben yelling from the entrance hall, 'They're here! Come quickly, everyone!'

The station taxi, driven by a beaming Ted Willis, pulled up at the front door and Victor, Ros and Betty got out of it.

While her father was paying Ted, Betty ran to her friends, shouting, 'Guess what? We got married, and I was the brides-maid.'

Her words were greeted with smiles, but these soon faded.

'What's happened?' Victor demanded. 'I can see something has.'

Mayne gestured towards the house. 'We'll go inside and I'll tell you.'

'Not the sitting room, the kitchen,' Ros said. 'It always feels like the heart of the house to me. And if this is going to be bad news, that's where I want to be.'

When they were gathered round the kitchen table, Judith said, 'First things first: congratulations, you two. When did you get married?'

Victor took Ros's hand. 'Late this morning. They're keeping the registry office open for longer hours at the moment, there's such a rush to wed. I'm very happy they are, and happy with my new wife.'

'Ros is my stepmother now,' Betty said. 'Only I'm going to call her Mummy, not Step-Mummy.'

'That's lovely,' Judith told her, then looked at Mayne.

He took a deep breath and described what had happened the day before.

'Oh, damn the woman to hell and back!' Victor exclaimed. 'How did she get Susan to sign such a thing?'

Betty lost her sparkling happiness. 'I'm not going back to Grandmother. I'm not.'

'It might be good tactics to phone Miss Peters' house and

let the judge know you're back before anyone else tells him,' Mayne said. 'He wants to speak to you as soon as you get back.'

Victor looked grim. 'All right. I'd rather get it over with. But if they do the unthinkable and say Betty has to go back to that old witch, we'll have to make a run for it.'

'They might be prepared for that and stop you.'

'Jan said one should always have a second plan ready, and in this case I'm going to follow his advice and have Ted waiting outside and Al nearby with your car, if you agree.'

'Yes, but I hope it won't be needed,' Mayne said.

'Thanks. You're a good friend.'

'I don't know what to suggest to help you with this,' Mayne admitted. 'Anyway, come and phone the judge from my office.'

Victor held out his hand to Ros. 'Come with me. Do you mind staying with Ben and the girls, Betty?'

Ben immediately put his arm round her shoulders. 'We won't let the dragon eat you, little one.'

Betty was very quiet, frowning, cuddling the battered rag doll her mother had made her, as she always did when she was upset.

No one knew what to say to her.

When Victor and Ros came back, they were grim-faced.

'He's holding a hearing today at four-thirty. He wanted to hold it at the police station, but I managed to persuade him to hold it here.' Victor looked at them bleakly. 'Frankly, it'll be easier to run away from Esherwood, if we look like losing. I think we should get Ted and his taxi in position ready to make a run for it, so we'll have to put our cases into the boot ready.'

Judith looked at him in shock. 'Are you that worried about losing?'

Anna Jacobs

'Fitkin is known to have played some very sneaky tricks on his clients' behalf, and I've no doubt he's got some sort of evidence that'll be hard to refute. And Mrs Galton is a very rich woman. She can pay people to lie. For all we know, she may have some so-called witnesses nearby, ready to give evidence.'

'I'll go and ask Mr Willis not to come to the back door,' Ben said. 'There's a place he can park behind the stables, where no one will see him.'

'Good idea. We'll put you in charge of that.'

Judith looked at Mayne, wondering whether this would get her son in trouble.

'If things go wrong, Ben,' Mayne said, 'You're to play stupid and tell them you thought Victor and Ros were arranging to go off on their honeymoon after the hearing. Can you do that?'

'Yes.'

'Don't come back in the taxi. Walk back. Come in the front way, whistle and try to look cheerful.'

'All right.'

'We'll need to take as much as we can with us, so I'll need bigger suitcases. Could you let me have some of those old ones, Judith?'

'Of course.'

'Where will you go?' Mayne asked his friend. 'Broadly speaking, no details.'

'I haven't the faintest idea,' Victor said. 'I'll work it out if the worst happens. Far away from here, that's for sure. Tell them I used to talk a lot about emigrating to Canada, if they ask.'

'I'll send for Al and his friends,' Mayne said. 'Just in case they bring in the heavies today. Kitty and Gillian, will you take a note to Mrs Needham's, and go there the back way? If anyone asks, you're just visiting an old neighbour.'

When they'd done all they could think of, it was nearly time for the hearing, and the only thing left to do was wait for the other people to arrive.

Judge Peters and his sister were the first to drive up to the house, accompanied by Sergeant Deemer and his clerk. Before he got out of the car, the judge asked to be taken to the hearing room straightaway and said he didn't want to speak to anyone until the proceedings began.

Mayne was surprised, but did as he'd been asked, showing them into the dining room.

'Shall I bring Victor and Betty in?'

'Not till the others are here. I want to make it plain that I've had no communication with Mr Travers, as the good sergeant and his clerk will bear witness.'

When Mrs Galton and her lawyer arrived, they were again accompanied by the two burly young men. Mayne refused to let the latter into the house and got into an argument with Mr Fitkin about it.

The judge himself came out to say, 'They have no part to play in the hearing, Mrs Galton. I don't know why you insist on bringing them.'

'I want to make sure no one can spirit that poor child away after you bring down your decision,' she said.

'They are to wait outside at the front, then, where I can see them from the window. Please come this way.'

They went to sit at one side of the big dining table and the judge nodded to Sergeant Deemer. 'You can ask Mr Travers and his daughter to join us now.' He looked at Mr Fitkin as he added, 'I wish to make it plain that I've not seen or spoken to Mr Travers yet.'

Mrs Galton snorted in a way that showed her disbelief.

Judge Peters leaned forward. 'If the sound you just made, madam, indicates your disbelief, in other words, if you're accusing me of lying, then I shall be charging you with contempt of court.'

She gaped at him, then looked to her lawyer for advice.

'Amelia, I've told you to be patient and let me guide you.'

The use of her first name surprised the judge.

Victor arrived, holding Betty's hand, with Ros walking behind them.

'Who is this female?' demanded Mrs Galton. 'I see no reason for her to be here.'

'Mr Fitkin, if your client cannot keep quiet, she must wait in the car.'

The look she gave Judge Peters would have curdled milk.

'Come and sit by me, Betty,' the judge said.

'I want to stay with my daddy.' She was clinging to Victor's hand, not even looking in her grandmother's direction.

'Sit near the judge, dear,' her father told her.

'Come and give me a kiss first, Betty,' Mrs Galton said.

The child stared at her in surprise. 'Why? You never wanted me to kiss you before?' She backed hastily away from her grandmother.

'You don't have to kiss anyone you don't want to.' Judge Peters patted the chair next to his and waited till she'd sat down. 'Do you understand why we're here today?'

'Yes. Grandmother wants me to go back to live with her. But I don't want to.'

'Why not?'

'I had to keep quiet all the time and stay up in the school-room with my governess.'

'You came and took tea with me,' Mrs Galton said.

'Not after my mother fell ill.'

'I protest,' Mr Fitkin said. 'This child is too young to speak in a court. She doesn't understand the implications of what is happening.'

'She seems to understand my questions perfectly well,'

the judge said mildly. 'Mr Travers, will you please tell me why you want to look after your daughter?'

'Because I love her. Because I'm her father.'

'You never showed any signs of love!' Mrs Galton shouted. 'You were away most of the time.'

He turned to her. 'I was serving my country in a time of war. Like many other men in the armed forces, I had no choice about where I went.'

'You didn't even come when we told you Susan was dying.' Mrs Galton dabbed her eyes.

'You didn't tell me she was dying, only that she was ill.'

Ros put her hand on his arm and he patted it as if drawing comfort from her closeness.

Mrs Galton thumped the table. 'Just look at him! Fondling his whore at a time like this. Send that female out of the room! It's not decent to have her here.'

Victor stood up, glaring across the table at the red-faced old woman for a moment, then putting his arm round Ros and saying, 'I'd like to introduce you to my wife, Judge Peters. Ros and I were married this morning. If you'd like to see our marriage certificate, I have it with me.'

'I was the bridesmaid,' Betty said. 'And I love Ros.'

Mr Fitkin stood up. 'This is all beside the point, your worship, as you well know. The guardianship of this child was left to Mrs Galton by her mother as she was dying.' He pulled out the letter and brandished it.

There was silence in the room, then Betty astonished them by saying, 'Mother told me about the letter you made her sign.'

'Are you sure?' the judge asked.

'Yes. She didn't like signing it, so she gave me another letter. I've got it here.'

'Show me,' he said.

Mr Fitkin stood up as if he intended to look as well.

'Keep your place, sir. You will get your turn later to view the evidence.' Judge Peters turned to the child, who was struggling with the rag doll.

'Mother sewed the letter into the doll, where no one could find it. I need some scissors. I can't get it open.' She looked to be on the verge of tears.

The judge pulled out a penknife. 'Show me what you want doing and I'll help you.' He paused to look at Victor. 'Have you seen this?'

'No, your worship. I didn't know there was anything inside the doll. I just knew that Betty took it with her everywhere and loved it, because it was her mother's last gift to her.'

The judge looked down. 'The stitches are very uneven. They don't look as if they've been tampered with. Please come and look at this, Sergeant Deemer, and I suppose you'd better see it too, Mr Fitkin, but do not touch it, any of you.'

They stood in a semi-circle and he began to cut the stitches one by one. What had seemed to be a patch of a different type of material was revealed to be a flap. As they pulled it open something crackled inside the doll.

'Shall I pull the paper out for you, Betty?' he asked.

'Yes please. I don't want to tear it.'

Judge Peters tugged gently, taking his time and pulling out a folded piece of thin paper. 'May I read it?'

'Yes. It made me cry when Mother showed it to me.'

He began to read aloud:

To whom it may concern
  If you're reading this, it means that I'm dead. I'm worried about what will happen to Betty afterwards. My mother made me sign a piece of paper making her my daughter's guardian, but I didn't use my normal signature and I left a letter out of my name. Betty can tell you the difference in signatures.

*I want my child to be looked after by her father. My
mother is a strict and selfish person, who has no patience
with children.*

*I've been too tired lately to stop her imposing her
'Children should be seen and not heard' views on my
daughter.*

*Victor will be able to bring joy back into our child's
life, as he brought joy into mine.*

*Victor, I'm sorry I've been so cowardly with my
mother, but when you're in pain, it's hard to know what
you're doing sometimes. I can only say I did my best.*

Please don't give my child into my mother's care.

Susan Mary Galton

Mr Fitkin snatched the piece of paper from the judge's
hand and screwed it up, but when he threw it across the
room towards the fire burning low in the hearth, Mayne
snatched it from the ashes before the flames could take
hold.

'Sergeant Deemer, make sure Mr Fitkin doesn't leave the
house,' the judge said loudly. 'After this is over, he is to be
charged with attempting to destroy evidence. In addition, I
shall myself report him to the Law Society for improper
behaviour.'

He smoothed out the piece of paper, laid it down next to
the one Fitkin had produced, and turned to Betty. 'Show
me why your mother's signature on this paper isn't her real
one, please.'

Betty went to him confidently and pointed to the deliberate
omission of a letter from the signature on the document
asking Mrs Galton to be Betty's guardian, not to mention,
the extra squiggle at the end of the name. Then she showed
him the real signature.

'I've got letters from my mother at home,' she said. 'In Helstead. They have her real signature on them, too.'

'I have letters from Susan as well,' Victor said.

'In that case, I have no hesitation in saying the child should stay with her father,' the judge said quietly.

'You promised me you could make them give me the child, George Fitkin,' Mrs Galton suddenly shrieked. 'You've cheated me.' Her face crumpled and she began to sob loudly. 'What will people say? I've told everyone I'll be looking after her. What will they say?'

'Quiet, woman!' roared the judge. 'I'll write up my decision. Mr Fitkin, I will also ensure that you will not practise law again in this country.'

The other man shrugged. 'I wasn't going to anyway. Travers isn't the only one to have got married, though I think I've made the better bargain. My wife has enough money for me not to need to work again.' He turned to gesture towards Mrs Galton, who was looking her full seventy years and almost ready to collapse.

'You've married Susan's mother?' Victor exclaimed in amazement.

'Yes. Amelia needs someone to look after her.'

'But you must be twenty years younger than her.'

Fitkin shrugged and walked across to his wife. 'What does that matter? It means I can look after her better.' He tugged his wife to her feet. 'Come along, Amelia. You've lost and it's probably a good thing. You know you don't like children.'

He turned to the judge. 'Have we your permission to leave? Or are you going to prosecute me?'

'As long as you keep quiet about this, this fiasco, we'll forget it ever happened. But you will be hearing from the legal authorities. I care very much that the law is respected and justice given to people.'

Fitkin shrugged and led his wife from the room. They could hear him calling for their chauffeur.

No one spoke until the car had driven the Fitkins away.

'The air feels cleaner without them,' Mayné said. 'Congratulations, Victor, on your two beautiful women.'

Ros grinned at him. 'I'm not beautiful and you know it, Mayne. But Betty might be one day.' She picked the child up and smacked a kiss on her cheek. 'We are going to have such fun together, my little love!'

Victor put his arms round the pair of them and smiled at the other people in the room, his eyes bright with unshed tears.

The door opened and Ben came in. 'Did we win?'

'We certainly did,' Mayne told him.

Ben let out a shout of joy, grabbed Betty and danced her round the room. And suddenly the children began singing and tugging other people up to join them in a conga line.

Betty was shoved to the front of it and led the way round the ground floor of the house, which echoed now to the sounds of joy.

The following day Gillian came running into the room at Esherwood which Judith was using as an office. She stopped, checked over her shoulder as if not wanting to be overheard, then held out a letter addressed to her mother.

When Judith took it, her daughter stood, looking apprehensive.

'It's from Rivenshaw Town Council. It's got a stamp on the back saying "Education Department". I remember that from when Ben got his news. Do you think it's about the scholarships? Do you think I've passed?'

'Only one way to find out.' Judith tore open the envelope and read the letter quickly, then gathered her daughter to her for a big hug. 'You've not only passed, you've won a fee-paying scholarship like your brother did, you clever girl. Oh, I'm so proud of you. Here. Read it.'

Gillian hugged her convulsively, took the letter her mother was holding out and read it quickly, then sucked in a long shuddering breath and read it again. 'I did it,' she whispered. 'I got a scholarship to the girls' grammar school. Oh, Mum. I did it.'

Then she burst into tears.

Ben was passing the door of the room and stopped. 'What's wrong with her?'

'Nothing,' Judith said. 'Do you want to tell him, love, or shall I?'

'I will.' Gillian beamed at her brother. 'I passed and I got a scholarship.'

He let out a yell and gave her a hug, a gesture of affection he usually reserved only for his mother or Betty. Then he grabbed Gillian's hand and pulled her from the room. 'Let's go and tell Kitty.'

As they ran off to find their elder sister, Judith went to find Mayne and share the news with him.

Happiness flooded through her. Everything was starting to settle down. She could now begin to plan her wedding.

EPILOGUE

It was a glorious early September day, so Judith and Mayne decided to walk into town to get married.

The postman arrived as the wedding party was getting ready to leave Esherwood.

'Best wishes to you and your lady!' he cried as he handed Mayne several letters, then pedalled off down the drive.

'Just a minute! It's from the town council.' Mayne tore the letter open and let out a yell, dancing Judith round in a circle.

'What does it say?' Victor demanded.

'They're giving us permission in principle to turn Esherwood into flats and if we have the materials for Nissen huts, to erect them too, as long as they're used for housing people and the council approves the sites. We're to work with their planners on this.'

'So you needn't have worried that they might not be co-operative. May I?' Victor took the letter and read it, with Ros looking over his arm at it. 'That's excellent news. Really excellent. Daniel will be thrilled when he hears this.'

'Such a pity he had to stay for his uncle's funeral,' Mayne said. 'When he rang to wish us well, he said he'd be back soon and was dying to start planning in detail how to convert the house into flats.'

'I've had several enquiries already,' Judith said. 'I don't think we'll have any trouble selling them.'

They all smiled at one another in satisfaction.

'The whole country will be rebuilding, people are so desperate for places to live,' Mayne said. 'I can't wait to get started.'

Victor grinned at his friend. 'Yes, but first, we're going to get you married to this brave lady here.' He offered his arm to his wife of a few days. 'Come along, my love. As best man, I need to nudge these people along or they'll be late for their own wedding.' He gestured to Mayne and Judith to lead the way.

They strolled down to the Methodist chapel in a large group.

The two women were dressed in clothes from the attics of the big house: beautiful fabrics, skilfully altered by Helen. Even their hats had come from the same place.

The bride looked over her shoulder and smiled as her children followed them down the drive. 'I've never seen you looking so smart, Ben.'

'I've never had to give anyone away before,' he muttered to Kitty. 'What if I make a mess of it? Why can't Mum ask Victor to do it?'

'You won't make a mess. We've had a little practice. And you're proud to be doing this, you know you are.'

'And I'm a bridesmaid again,' Betty said, skipping for a few yards out of sheer joy. 'Three bridesmaids for this wedding. Isn't that grand?'

Their friends were waiting for them at the little chapel, and the minister greeted them with, 'How delightful to see so many happy people.'

A hush fell as he began the ceremony.

Ben played his part, blinking his eyes furiously as he gave his mother away, then stepped back to stand next to Betty. He fumbled for a handkerchief and didn't find it.

She shoved one into his hand and he blew his nose.

Kitty and Gillian weren't attempting to hide their happy tears.

As they came out of the chapel, they found the reporter from the newspaper waiting with a photographer supplied by Mr Woollard, who was now officially recognised as a partner in their future building business, even if he hadn't yet signed the paperwork.

Then it was back to Esherwood, where a party was held with more of the wine from the cellar.

'It's been a long time since this house has hosted a big party,' Mayne said. 'It feels good.'

They stood for a moment, looking round, then were swept from one person to another to be congratulated and asked about their future plans.

It seemed a long time before the happy couple could escape to their bedroom, but even the best of parties have to come to an end.

'At last!' Mayne framed Judith's face with his hands the minute they'd closed the door behind them. He kissed her gently, letting passion rise slowly. 'My love, my wife, my joy.'

'I think this has been the happiest day of my whole life,' she said softly.

'The best is yet to come.' He scooped her up and carried her to the bed . . .

She wept afterwards and he stared at her in consternation. 'What's wrong? What did I do?'

'I didn't know it could be like that, so gentle, so wonderful.'

'It was never like that for me before, either. So joyful. We're going to have a wonderful life together, my darling.'

ABOUT THE AUTHOR

Anna Jacobs grew up in Lancashire and emigrated to Australia, but she returns each year to the UK to see her family and do research, something she loves. She is addicted to writing and she figures she'll have to live to be 120 at least to tell all the stories that keep popping up in her imagination and nagging her to write them down. She's also addicted to her own hero, to whom she's been happily married for many years.

ASK ANNA

Is there any one era or place which you particularly love writing about?

I love writing stories set in Lancashire, where I was born and grew up. All my family surnames are Lancashire names, so the area and its people are part of me. I like writing from 1730 to just after World War II (so far) because there were some fascinating things happening there – and not just cotton mills! And I like to take my characters up on the moors, which was my big treat as a child. My Auntie Con used to take me walking there because my parents preferred driving. I have been driven through (without stopping) nearly every major town in England!

When you embark on a new book, do you know from the start it is to be the first in a series? If yes, do you know all the plots of each subsequent book, or does inspiration strike while you are writing the first?

I'm totally incapable of plotting the details of a whole book in advance, let alone a whole series. But as I love spending more time with my characters, I mainly write groups of stories nowadays. I have a fairly solid foundation of knowledge about my period, but I like to find 'gaps in history', i.e. backgrounds that haven't been done to death in novels. I do any specific extra research before I start writing.

Where do you get your inspiration from?

People. The world is full of them, and history books and autobiographies are full of the words of people who have gone before. Even historical paintings can tell you so much. I'm eternally fascinated by what people do and why, how they cope, what makes one person crumble and another deal with the most extraordinary situations. Burglars would be so disappointed in my house, because I don't collect jewellery or objet d'art, I collect people's stories and books.

In my daily life I sometimes stop and think 'What if my heroine was in this situation?'. That can happen anytime, anywhere. I always write the possibility down in my ideas file. I have dozens of plot ideas waiting to be used. I wish I didn't need eight hours sleep every night! Such a waste of writing time . . .

Are you ever tempted to revisit past series and to write more about the characters?

Yes. And readers ask for that, too. For instance, there's *Freedom's Land*. My first agent said it was one of the best books I'd ever written and I love it to pieces. It's a single story but I have ideas for follow-ups, and new characters regularly walk through my dreams. One day I'm going back to 1926 to continue writing about the group settlement movement in Western Australia. But I don't want to continue my first series (*Gibson Family Saga*) because I might have to kill Annie, the central character, and I couldn't bear to do that.

Do you have any particular favourites amongst all the characters you've written about over the years?

There's Annie in the *Gibson Family Saga*. I wrote five books about her and her family. She was a wonderful 'person'. And there's Bram in the *Traders* series. He's of middle height, scrawny, not particularly good looking and yet he's the best and most romantic hero I've ever created: a wonderful warm, loving man whose love for his wife and family sometimes brought tears to my eyes when I was writing about it.

While writing do you have any rituals, routines or particular schedules that you like to follow?

I'm a morning person, always have been. I can't write after the sun goes down. I get up about 5.30am and have a little routine. I go through my emails, have my breakfast and shower, play card games on the computer. After a while it feels as if something goes click in my head and my imagination fires up. I follow any major break during the day with a few more games of cards to get me going again. Habits are good things for that. It doesn't matter what the habit is, as long as your mind recognises it as the precursor to writing.

What is your favourite part of your writing process?

Polishing the 'dirty draft', a term I invented for the first full version of the story. I find I get better stories if I write as fast as I can. I can polish much more quickly than when I first started writing – well, you would after writing around eighty novels! I set aside a week without interruptions and go through the story, trying to make every detail, every action more telling. And if a story needs a second polish, which has happened a couple of times when life has hit me on the head while I was writing it, I polish the whole thing again.

Do you have any favourite writing spots, somewhere that really gets your creativity flowing?

My office. I have a huge one, with gorgeous crimson curtains and lots of books. I've only to walk into it to feel good about getting on with my latest story. I can't write nearly as easily anywhere else. I have four desks, which are permanently untidy, but with really comfortable office chairs and a beautiful glow of silence and peace.

Don't miss the next book in
Anna Jacobs' heart-warming
Rivenshaw
saga:

ANNA
JACOBS

A Time to Rejoice

But can they ever put the past behind them?

Out in hardcover in May 2016